T

2

WHILE THE
MUSIC LASTS

Also by Suzanne Goodwin

THE RISING STORM
CHANGE OF SEASON
TO LOVE A HERO
LOVERS
DAUGHTERS
FLOODTIDE
COUSINS
SISTERS

WHILE THE MUSIC LASTS

SUZANNE GOODWIN

LITTLE, BROWN AND COMPANY

A *Little, Brown* Book

First published in Great Britain in 1992
by Little, Brown and Company

Copyright © 1992 Suzanne Goodwin

The moral right of the author has been asserted.

A CIP Catalogue record for this book is available
from the British Library.

ISBN 0 316 90388 4

Typeset in Bodoni by Leaper & Gard Ltd, Bristol.
Printed and bound in Great Britain by
BPCC Hazells Ltd
Member of BPCC Ltd

Little, Brown and Company (UK) Limited
165 Great Dover Street
London SE1 4YA

Part One

CHAPTER ONE

There was a beach in Brighton beyond the West Pier which had worn and sea-battered breakwaters, high enough to shelter behind when the wind had a bite in it. All the beaches were very slightly different from each other; Isobel had noticed that from the time she was a small child. Some shelved steeply so that you could slither and slide down the shingle, others were more gentle; some were scattered with lumps of chalk pitted with holes; and some, like the beach which Isobel's family had made their own, were a combination. It was steep but not vertiginous, and at low tide, at the end of both its breakwaters, were deep pools where crabs hid among the seaweed.

Isobel liked certain things to remain the same, it was the other side of a character lured by the unfamiliar. You could rush forward, she felt, as long as there were people and places on which you could rely to stay exactly where they were. When explorers advanced, they kept a line of bases – the food and shelter for the return. The beach at Brighton was such a base. Whenever Isobel visited Brighton she liked to make a pilgrimage to the sea front. Whether in a heatwave or the most cutting December wind, she would check that the shingle still shelved and the breakwaters still sheltered. 'Good old beach,' Isobel would say.

In 1928 a great deal of Brighton, Sussex and the world had altered since the time Grace and Frank Bryant originally brought first one small daughter to a boarding house on the Brighton front for a holiday, then a second and finally, when there were four

3

daughters and Frank was earning more money, to a rented house near the West Pier. It was from the house, Innisfree, that the girls frolicked down to the chosen beach.

Every summer was spent there. Grace carried her deck chair down on the shingle and sat, not bothering to read, contentedly staring at the sea. The girls played and swam in the often icy water. Their father travelled to London and back during the week on the Brighton Belle, and used to arrive on the beach in the evenings, carrying paper bags full of William pears.

Isobel remembered all this as she walked down the broad expanses of Brighton front, turned when she reached the special beach, and slid down towards the sea, pebbles rising round her in a clatter, as if she were nine and not nineteen years old.

It was a weekday. She was a fugitive from her shorthand and typing class, having lied to the teacher and said she had a splitting headache. The teacher, stout, cross, with dyed red hair, said all she needed was 'a couple of aspirins', but Isobel managed to look agonized, imitating her mother's genuine pain when she had a migraine. Isobel knew that what *she* needed was solitude.

She was pale, dark and thin. Her flat chest suited the present late twenties fashion. Her three sisters envied her boyish figure and told her she did not appreciate her good luck. When wearing the fashionable silk jersey dresses, Claire flattened her bosom with a kind of bandage, and Julie stuck stamp paper on her nipples.

Isobel came to a slithering stop in the middle of the pebbles. It was May, and the beach was empty. For nearly a month the weather had been bitterly cold and often dark with rain. When this morning the sun had come out and the lilac in the gardens began to smell as it should do, she knew she couldn't face another day of Miss Blackstone's grating voice, and the awful sight of shorthand outlines.

She sighed. It was not only work she was escaping, but a boy in the class who was learning shorthand as he hoped to become a reporter. He had what Isobel called a pash on her. She leaned her bony elbows on the shingle, thinking about the two of her sisters known in the family as 'the twins'. They were not twins, there was

4

over a year between them, but they looked very alike, pretty and blonde. Listening to them talking and laughing, Isobel knew *they* found dodging unattractive men easy. When they were not attracted to a man, they dodged or joked their way out of his invitations. It was a knack soon learned, they said. Isobel did not find it so. She had been attractive to men for a mere three years – at fifteen she had been as ugly as a young bird, all eyes and bones, and it was only from sixteen until now that men who met her had begun to send out the rays of sex. Isobel disliked admirers, they embarrassed her. They interrupted her thoughts which were on painting or on herself. She wanted to be left alone, free of shorthand and free of men. Above all she wished to be left alone by her mother. She dearly loved her but wished Grace would shut up.

Lying in the sun, listening to small waves and now and again the crash of a large one, for the sea had a swell, she rejoiced in doing nothing. I can paint when I get home, she thought. She decided to continue the charade of the headache with Grace, who could scarcely be unsympathetic since she would believe the martyrdom was inherited from herself.

Behind Isobel, stretching for long distances, Brighton basked in the welcome sunshine, its Prince Regent terraces and balconies unchanged since they were first built, its piers – which would have disgusted him – deserted. The girl stared at the sea. She had secretly put on her bathing costume this morning at home under her dress, and smuggled a towel into her school bag. She wondered if she was brave enough to swim. It'll be freezing, thought Isobel. Good. She went in search of an attendant who was sitting by a line of empty bathing huts.

Inside the hut, with its familiar stuffy smell of wood and canvas and dried seaweed, she stripped off her clothing and hobbled down the sloping shingle into the sea.

The shock made her grasp, it was like being flayed. She could scarcely breathe when the icy water enclosed her, but struck out, breasting a large unbroken wave. Soon the scalding cold wore off and she swam in heaving green boulders of water, as free as a fish. But at last the cold reminded her that she could not stay any longer and, teeth beginning to chatter, she staggered back across the stones to dry and change. Why, she thought, coming out of the hut, hadn't she had the sense to bring an extra sweater?

'Bit nippy?' remarked the old woman sitting on the wooden platform by the huts. 'You're my first for weeks, not counting them lunatics.'

'L-l-lunatics?'

'The ones what come down rain or shine right from Christmas to Christmas. Barmy. You need hot Oxo, miss, and no mistake. There's a kiosk by the pier.'

Isobel dragged her coat round her, and was turning to go when a voice cried, '*You.*'

She spun round to see a figure in fashionable clothes and cloche hat staring at her open-mouthed. It was her eldest sister.

'What are you doing in England?'

'What are you doing on the beach?'

They spoke in unison, gaping at each other. They made a curious contrast, one overdressed and burdened with a large suitcase, the other wet-haired, in a skimpy coat and blue with cold.

'But Viv, I don't understand, you're in Spain!'

Viv's smile was a grimace.

'So I am. In Barcelona. And you are not here either, but at college learning to type. Come on, Belle. You can scarcely speak. What an idiot, swimming today! We'd better go to the Albion and get you something hot to drink.'

Isobel was now seriously chilled and felt she would never be warm again. She walked beside her sister, helping with the enormous suitcase which they carried between them. Teeth still chattering, she repeated her question as to what Viv was doing in England.

'I'll explain when we get to the hotel. Come on, Belle. You'll catch pneumonia if we don't hurry. I wish you could see the colour of your face. Surely you can walk faster than that?'

At the Albion, all was polite welcome, open fires, bustling waiters and a sun pouring through enormous windows overlooking the vulgar Palace Pier. Vivien ordered coffee 'hot, hot, please', and

6

buttered toast. She settled her sister on a sofa in the direct sun and watched Isobel turning slowly from blue to pink.

Swallowing the coffee, heartened by Viv's presence – Isobel had always preferred to be mothered by her sister rather than by Grace, she burst out – 'Explain! Where's Carlos? Why didn't you tell us you were coming?'

Viv looked at her gravely. Viv was unlike the youngest of the Bryant girls except for a short straight nose. She was smallish, and had inherited Grace's way of wearing clothes which never appeared to have a crease. She looked sensible and a little shy and her manner was all quiet practicality compared to Isobel's fits and starts. She was the ideal eldest sister. Her mother had been in the habit of declaring – not to Viv who heard it later cruelly repeated – that her eldest girl was destined to be an old maid.

'She just isn't the type to attract men,' said Grace, who was.

Grace's plan for her quartet was simple. They must be married happily and soon. Viv had been a great source of anxiety. She was still not married when she reached the – to Grace – elderly birthday of twenty-eight. In fact the family had long since given up the idea that Viv would fall in love.

'She keeps men at arm's length,' Claire said.

'She's afraid of sex,' said Julie.

'Poor Viv, what a shame,' said Isobel.

Grace, on the same subject to a friend of her own age, sighed, 'She's an out and out spinster.'

But Viv did marry.

She fell hook line and sinker for a foreigner.

The Bryants knew no foreigners. None of the girls had been sent abroad to learn French or German, none of their friends had produced European visitors to add a touch of colour to unexceptional tennis parties. Carlos Santander was Spanish: a fleshy, worldly, self-possessed and moneyed man, who came into Viv's life and knocked her for six. He was as unfamiliar in her quiet Sussex life as a tropical bird which had escaped from a zoo and was attempting to exist in an English wood. Surely it would die of starvation or get pecked to death by native birds? Not Carlos. He

7

appeared to be a man who made whatever place he settled in suit him by simply changing it. He had an air of authority.

Julie declared he had the sexiest eyes she'd ever seen, and early in his acquaintance with the Bryants tried to capture him. But it was Viv whom Carlos wanted. He married her in three months.

That had been a year ago, and none of the family had been to Spain to stay with Viv.

She wrote them regular and quite long letters. Julie was the one who discussed her the most. It was Julie who exclaimed, 'Viv's house sounds pretty appalling. So hot and huge,' and 'Imagine the food. Fried eggs with rice and bananas, and vast prawns. Viv says they look like dragons.'

Claire was rather jealous that Viv's letters to Julie were more interesting than those she received, and did not ask many questions. Isobel thought it must be blissful for her eldest sister, living in such a romantic country. To Isobel Spain would be one endless opportunity to sketch and paint. As for Grace, she read nothing into Viv's letters but the facts. The idea that her eldest child might not be truly happy was something Grace would not consider.

Sitting in the Albion, Isobel came out of a pleasant reverie of warmth after her chill; she suddenly noticed the expression on her eldest sister's face.

'Viv. Where *is* Carlos?'

'At home, of course.'

'And you've come over for a short –'

'I have left him.'

Isobel's large eyes became enormous.

'But you can't!'

Viv opened her crocodile handbag, a wedding present from her mother, with a good many fixtures and fittings, took out a lace handkerchief and spread it on her knee. She straightened it, ironing out the creases with her forefinger. She said without looking up, 'I shall never go back.'

'But – but –'

'But nothing.' There was a note of sharpness. 'I've come home.'

She was silent for quite a time and then said calmly, 'Awful, isn't it?'

'But don't you love him any more?'

'Not sure. Probably.'

'What are you talking about!'

'Darling,' said Viv, 'I'm tired. I can't tell you the story, and then repeat it all over again to Ma. And later – I suppose the twins are in London? – to them as well. If I have to keep talking about it I really shall be sick. You can hear when I explain to Ma. And by the way, what were you doing on your beach?'

'Thinking. What about you?'

'I meant to do the same. But, since I found you I didn't get the chance.'

'I told them at college that my head was splitting.'

'I'm sure you did.'

'I still don't understand about *you*,' said Isobel. 'I mean, why didn't you go straight home?'

'Now there's a silly question.'

Isobel had finished the toast. Food and drink and the sun on her back, the luxury of the Albion and the company of her favourite sister, gave her a flood of strength. She felt fond and excited. She forgot to be sorry for Viv.

'I'm on your side,' she said.

'Must there be sides?'

'Knowing Grace,' said Isobel, who liked to call their mother by her first name to annoy, 'There will be.'

The girls fell silent. Their mother was divorced; or, as their friend Father Freeman pointed out when the decree was made absolute, she had divorced her husband, father of her daughters. That had been ten years ago, and Grace had been beautiful, admired and vain.

She came from Quaker parents with a good deal of money, and Frank, burly, clever and from the North, with a touch of Irish and a Roman Catholic background, was beneath her. At the time of their marriage, everybody remarked upon that. But Frank made his way and made money.

He had been a soldier for the last two years of the Great War – he'd been in manufacturing and was exempt before that. Safely back at home in peacetime, rising in his business, the father of four handsome daughters, he was hearty, uxurious, cheerful and well-off. He was liked by his friends and Grace had just the husband to suit her.

Suddenly, at forty-five, when all the girls, except Viv, were still very young, he announced that he was leaving her.

'The trouble is, I'm in love,' he said. Grace thought it disgusting. Nobody over the age of thirty fell in love, even twenty-five was stretching it a bit. The woman, of course, was a secretary in his London office. She, like Grace, was a blonde, but Grace had seen her two or three times and declared the hair was bleached. Too outraged to argue, too dignified to throw things and swear, which Frank would have admired, Grace retreated into frozen silence. The divorce was a martyrdom to her. It was *déclassé*, except among the raffish upper classes, and Grace was a middle-class snob. It was shameful and she was proud. It made her look unattractive and she was beautiful.

She had only agreed to divorce Frank because he had said that if she did not, he and Connie would live in sin. Converted to Catholicism at the time of her marriage, Grace had become pious. With burning cheeks, she consulted the family's close friend, Father Freeman. He went to the trouble of getting her a dispensation 'due to special circumstances', and explained, over a stiff whisky in Grace's drawing room one winter night, that she could never remarry or she would be excommunicated.

'If you marry again, Grace, the Church won't recognise it.'

'Of course. I understand, Father. In any case I never shall.'

The priest had a moment of doubt. In her late thirties, she still looked sexy. She had wonderful legs. But for Grace the physical side of marriage had never been of much interest. Frank's passion for her had been flattering and, in a way, she had patronized him in the marriage bed. After the misery of the divorce, she devoted herself to rearing four high-spirited daughters.

Their father rarely asked to see them, and as the years went by

10

he relinquished – Grace said he forgot – a parent's love and interest in his children. Grace lived for them. She chose their school, bought their clothes, nursed them devotedly when they were ill, and helped them with their homework. She coped with disasters, such as Julie being thrown from a horse, and Claire saying she was engaged at fifteen years old. She shouted at them when they climbed dangerously high trees, and dressed in her best clothes for their prize-givings. She scolded Claire for demanding too many dresses, and Isobel for a passion for painting which Grace considered a waste of time. The only daughter who no longer caused any worry was Viv, the future spinster, who had married last year and vanished to Spain.

Now, thought Isobel, unwilling to leave the warmth of the Albion, here's Viv mysteriously back again.

'I wish you'd tell me *something*,' she complained, as Viv paid the bill and asked the porter to order them a taxi for the station.

'I keep on imagining horrors,' added Isobel.

'No horrors. No jollities either.'

'I thought you and Carlos were crazy about –'

'Belle, do shut up. For now, anyway.'

Isobel was offended and told herself she refused to be interested in anybody who snapped at her to mind her own business.

On the train she said suddenly, 'Hey. What am I doing coming home when I should still be at college?'

'I fetched you. I felt I needed your company.'

'Viv. You are a sport.'

'Ma can scarcely object to that,' said Viv, implying a good deal more.

Silence fell between the girls. The train fussed through the May countryside. Isobel leaned forward and spoke again. 'I *must* know what you were doing on our beach.'

'I got back on the night boat from Calais. When I arrived at Victoria, I caught sight of the Brighton Belle. And I knew what I wanted most was just to go to our beach and look at the sea.'

'Because you dread going home.'

'What do you think?'

11

The tone had changed from kindly to sharp again. This time it successfully shut up Isobel. They took another taxi from the station, and were driven through the quiet town up a rough untarmacked track, not yet adopted by the council, to the family's home.

Woodlands, situated in a small Sussex town, was a commodious suburban-looking house built just after the war and not very well built either. A businessman had bought a stretch of woods and fields, hoping to build a group of houses, and even some shops. Two houses had been erected which nobody seemed to want until Frank Bryant came along to purchase the first, and a quiet elderly lady moved into the other. There were no further houses. 'Woodlands', well named, remained among untouched acres of green fields, hawthorn hedges, ditches full of coltsfoot or celandines in spring and spreading woods starred with primroses. Rocky paths wound through forests of bracken, and foxgloves grew tall. There were sandy warrens in the woods where Julie had spotted a badger.

The house was inclined to be damp, and the water which came out of the taps was cloudy, taking some time to settle and become clear. On a summer evening Isobel had found a perfectly transparent worm swimming in her glass of water: she had been delighted.

Frank Bryant had chosen the house for his growing family when they moved from Streatham. He declared that here was a real country life. He used to travel every morning by a fast train to London, returning punctually every evening to be met by Grace at the station. She drove very badly.

Since their father had left, the Bryant girls had grown to adulthood and were no longer in love with the country, but Woodlands was always there and so was Grace. The water still clouded when you filled a glass. The foxgloves still grew, in summer, taller than the girls.

The taxi drew up at the gate, and Viv got out first, paid the driver, and helped Isobel to haul out the suitcase. The last time she had seen Woodlands, she had been looking through the back window of a Daimler, waving her hand at her friends, while her lap, and Carlos's, had been covered with rose petals.

Looking at the familiar white house which she had known almost all her life, she said in a whisper, 'Oh God.'

'Viv, don't be scared.'

'Why not?'

Her sister's sudden collapse shocked Isobel when she saw that Viv was trembling. Not as she had done, from chattering teeth, but with a kind of irregular spasm which was terrible to see. Isobel's heart turned over and she gave Viv what she meant to be a friendly squeeze which was actually a pinch. Viv did not notice. Her eyes and fears were directed towards the house.

In fine weather, the front door was always open and as the girls walked up the path, still holding the arm-aching suitcase between them, a voice called, 'Isobel? Why are you home early?'

Grace appeared in the doorway.

Her whole face, classic and even severe, beamed.

'Why Viv, what on earth, why didn't you send us a telegram, how lovely to see you!'

She hurried towards her daughter, smiling in delight and looking, for a moment, the beauty she used to be.

Viv dropped the case, ran up and hugged her mother. Grace, embarrassed, released herself and set her blouse collar to rights. Isobel, rarely tactful, actually grabbed the suitcase, intending to disappear with it up the stairs but Viv said hurriedly, 'Please stay. I didn't explain to you.'

Her face was agonized and Isobel, still filled with pity, blurted out, 'She's left Carlos.'

Grace's expression changed. She looked angry and old and gave a sort of laugh.

'Indeed? I think we'd better talk. Come into the drawing room.'

Like every other room in Grace's house, it was cleaned, polished and swept before half past nine in the morning. It was large, had many windows, was bitterly cold in winter, but now with the French windows wide open, was full of sunlight and smelled of the flowers on every table. Grace sat down.

'What is this rubbish Isobel is talking?'

'It isn't, Ma. I have left Carlos. I'm not going back.'

13

'I see,' said Grace, seeing nothing.

Isobel sat down on the floor and hugged her knees, breathless with interest.

It was Grace who opened the conversation.

'Has Carlos been unfaithful to you, Vivien?'

'No. I don't think so. Though he would have been eventually.'

'Don't talk nonsense.'

Viv looked at her mother steadily, her alarm was gone.

'Husbands in Spain are all unfaithful, it is part of life. The wives know and don't know. I mean they ignore what happens. The men do as they wish. The women only do what is expected of them. You can't even look at a man if you pass him in the street. Respectable women must look at the ground.'

'*Autres pays, autres moeurs*,' said Grace.

'Oh *Ma*. I knew when I married Carlos that it was going to be difficult, I'm not a fool. What did any of us know about Spain? He tried to explain things to me, and I tried in my turn to understand what he meant. I really tried. But he did not tell me that his mother would be living with us. No –' holding up her hand as Grace was about to interrupt again – 'not as a member of the family in a large house where she and I would meet every day, but as the person in charge. It didn't make a bit of difference to her that Carlos was married. She went on running things exactly as she'd done before. I was simply a foreigner expected to keep in her place.'

'Golly,' said Isobel.

Viv began to talk earnestly. Her mother listened with an expressionless face. The story was bald. It had no fire of passion, no broken hearts. There was in it none of the strangeness of the country which Viv had adopted nor the dark nature of the people from whom she had fled.

She finally said, 'I don't think I'm explaining properly. I'll tell you more later, at present I'm too muddled even to think straight. But Ma, you must believe me. I won't go back.'

She leaned forward and took her mother's hand. She might have been holding the hand of a wax dummy in a shop window for all the response she was given.

'What you've told me does not make sense. When a woman marries she must endure.'

The outrageous statement from Grace, who had divorced her husband with bitterness and never said a good word about him or her successor, struck both her daughters. Isobel glanced at Viv and raised her eyebrows. Viv, refusing complicity, looked away.

'We must pray,' said Grace, standing up. 'I will remember you in my prayers tonight, Vivien, and so will all the family. For the present we will try and make the best of your temporary return. Isobel, go up and make Vivien's bed, please.'

The dramatic news was telephoned to the twins by Isobel. The two sisters were staying the night in Barnes with one of their mother's friends. Both had been out dancing the night before, and it had been too late to return home by train.

Gladys Buffett was useful. She was kind, hospitable and as North Country as their father. During breakfast, hearing what had happened, she remarked with a loud sigh, 'Never does any good marrying a foreigner.'

She had a red face, blue eyes and crimped white hair, and Julie often said she was a human version of the Union Jack.

'Stick to your own kind,' added Mrs Buffett, tucking into bacon and eggs.

The girls, eating her magnificent cooked breakfast, said little. They knew if they gossiped she would keep them for hours, and they were catching the 12.15. The Bryants' life was fixed by timetables. Woodlands had no nearby bus service, and Grace's shabby Austin Seven was constantly racing through the town to catch or meet trains. Following the news of death the family would say, 'We must get the 2.35.' and during the divorce it had been, 'We can just make the 8.15.'

Claire and Julie spent an hour before leaving Barnes telephoning young men to cancel appointments. The girls were much pursued, much admired, often proposed to. Their diaries were crammed every night of the week, and only blank when Grace insisted on their staying home 'because you both look washed out'.

In terms of their appearance, the sobriquet 'twins', descriptive when they were at school, only just held. Both girls had inherited their mother's pale blonde hair and short straight nose. They were tall compared to little Viv. But their differing natures had begun to show. Claire was stylish and snobbish, Julie was wild.

Wisely concealing her feelings from Mrs Buffett, Claire was as horrified as their mother about Viv. Julie was fascinated.

When they arrived at Victoria Station, Claire insisted that they should travel first class, 'So we can talk without being overheard.'

'Who'd be interested?' said Julie. 'Okay, okay, if that's what you want. But you'll have to pay.'

Looking down her nose, Claire did so, while Julie blithely went to the newspaper kiosk and spent the same amount on magazines.

The compartment was empty but Claire waited until the train slipped quietly out of the station before turning a calm face to her sister.

'I've been thinking. It's obvious what will have to be done.'

'Doesn't seem obvious to me.'

'Julie, don't be obtuse. One will have to persuade her to go back to him.'

'By one, I suppose you mean you. Claire, that's a terrible idea.'

'They are married.'

'And I imagine she found he's been straying, sexy old Spaniard. Poor Viv. I always thought she was taking on a bomb with the pin out.'

Claire made a face.

Julie sprawled against the red plush cushions. 'Of course he's been sleeping with the *señoritas*. Serenading them at windows and getting them to creep out of great iron doors. Don Juan in person, bad luck to him. I think she'd better get a divorce and make a clean start. What about Harold? He'd rather suit Viv.'

Claire did not reply. Her sister loved to shock, she was like a child. How many times she used to scramble up high walls, balance at the top and wait for somebody to yell 'Get down, you'll break your neck.' What Julie wanted was attention, preferably horrified. It surprised Claire that people were still taken in, Julie was so

16

obvious. As for the suggestion that Julie's own admirer, Harold, would do for Viv – she was always offering her sisters the men who admired her – it was vulgar.

Julie flicked through her magazines, now and again remarking on shoes or furs. Fashion interested her. Claire looked out of the window at the country burgeoning in the sweet May weather, at cottages, their trees smothered with apple blossom, and sheets pegged out in the garden. There was lilac too. She decided she'd wasted her money on the first class tickets since the discussion had ground to a halt. Then Julie, pushing away the magazines, remarked, 'We'd best tell Pa.'

'We will do no such thing,' was the sharp reply.

Julie groaned. 'He only happens to be our father. He used to be partial to Viv. He said she was so clever and sensible.'

'Sensible!'

'Perhaps it's very sensible to leave a man if you can't stick him, or maybe he's in bed with all and sundry or beats you, even.'

'Stop showing off.'

'Am I? Any of that could be true. Pa must be told.'

Claire bit her lip. My God, thought Julie, Claire looks like Ma sometimes.

'Very well,' Claire agreed. 'But you must tell him. I most certainly won't. I prefer not to see him. I know very well that *you* do, and you see that awful woman too.'

'Yes, I pop along occasionally. How did you guess?' Julie asked.

'I know you,' was Claire's reply.

Julie laughed. 'I didn't tell you because you love to lecture, but I like our Pa. He's cosy. The only grit in the cold cream is our stepmother. She loathes my guts.'

'Indeed.'

'Yes, Claire. Connie hates us because we hate her. Well, Ma does, and you lot do. I don't, but she would never believe that. Poor old Con. She is so jealous. I try. Well ... I sort of bare my teeth at her in what's supposed to be a smile. I never get one back. Then I ask her how she is – I don't give a damn, and I suppose it must show. Later, off she goes to the medicine cupboard in the bathroom for

17

indigestion tablets. She comes back nibbling them between her front teeth – do you remember that rabbit Isobel used to have? Pa looks concerned – could be faking. He asks her how she is and she requests, in moaning tones, a hot water bottle, and then, as a penance, he makes her some tea and *then*, with her safely upstairs with the hottie and the tablets, he looks really relieved and comes back to me. We settle down for a good gossip. The trouble with Con is obvious. She can't have a baby. Don't you think she looks like that? Kind of scrawny.'

Claire had listened to the long speech, looking down her nose, and when it ended, all she said was, 'I don't care what she looks like. I don't forgive her for what she did to our mother.'

'*She* didn't do it, you poor chump. It was Dad. And sex rearing its ugly thingummy.'

'If you're going to start on that subject –'

'Okay, okay. I do love teasing you. Sorry.'

Unlike Grace, Claire melted at a word of apology.

It was Grace, not the other sisters, who met the girls at the station. She allowed herself to be kissed. There was never anybody who looked more awkward and stood so uncomfortably as Grace when being embraced. But she smelled deliciously of French scent.

She told Julie to sit in the back of the cramped car and Claire to sit beside her.

Grace kept the girls in a stern precedence. If the five Bryants crowded into a taxi they literally had to line up and climb inside in order of age. Now Julie was banished to the back, being younger, and Claire was in the front of the car.

Grace set off, driving as badly as usual, constantly slamming on her brakes – she never apologized – so that Julie was pitched forward.

'We are going to have a quiet lunch and talk things over,' she remarked as they bumped up the uncared-for track to the house.

Poor old Viv, thought Julie. Her marriage is going to be chewed over and spat out and where will it get Ma? It's Viv's business, not ours.

The prospect of an entirely female gathering, four sisters and their mother, appalled Julie, for all her kind heart. She had become accustomed to masculine company. She was at present considering a new love affair, her third, with a man over forty and she had planned an evening with him. He had invited her to a first night at the theatre and dinner at the Savoy. Julie had been all set for flirtation, sexy kisses, perhaps bed. The prospect had been exciting. Now she found herself wondering how, with all decency, could she manage to get away and return to London? She could lie about her work, at present irregular, and say Michou wanted her for a show on Monday.

All the way home, thrown forward by Grace's awful driving, laughing and getting back on to her seat, Julie thought about George. But she was glad to be back. Grace's daughters shared, together with an exasperated affection for their mother, a true pleasure in the home she had made.

It was 1928 and a time for breaking out and breaking loose. There were drunken parties, wild dances, the shimmy, the black bottom, there was open talk about sex and even the sniffing of cocaine. Scandals broke out in the newspapers. Nothing was what it used to be, declared the middle aged. But Grace's respectable, regal and rather stupid authority, her appearance, corseted and stately, were what made her daughters comfortable. She was always the same. And the moment they went into the polished hall, with its coat rack and umbrella stand, Grace's plants which flourished under her care, the smell of flowers and food, the Bryant girls felt easy.

In the drawing room, decorated with black, green and gold Chinese wallpaper and chair covers to match, Viv was playing Mendelssohn's *Spring Song*. She stopped in mid-bar as her sisters came into the room, and stood up.

Claire thought she looked awful, white in the face and with black shadows under her eyes. Julie, hugging her, did not notice.

'Where's Isobel?' asked Claire, as Viv shut the piano.

'Ma sent her out on her bike to shop.'

'She'll forget everything and come home with a box of crayons,' said Julie.

'She's not fifteen any more,' reproved Claire.

Conversation for a moment or two had a falseness about it. Everybody was avoiding the great 'Why?' which surrounded Viv like a miasma. Viv was aware of it and joined in the game of pretending her presence was nothing unexpected and that lunch was not looming like a murder trial.

Claire, adept at filling in pauses, like a bricklayer with cement, chatted on. Julie joined in the charade and Viv pretended to listen. She was wondering how, in the name of everything sensible in her own nature, she was going to explain.

Which of them would understand? Her mother had divorced *her* husband. But Grace had never wanted to leave him. The fact that he no longer loved her had come out of the blue and she still repeated, ten years afterwards, that it had ruined her life. It wasn't true, but she had a relish in droning on about it to her listening friends. Nowadays Grace, in her dignified don't-look-unmentionable-facts-in-the-face pose, was content. She had a certain position in the town. She liked going to church. She was an ardent Catholic. Viv knew there was no hope that her mother would understand her.

Following the Bryant order of precedence, Claire was next in her thoughts, and the moment her sister had come into the room Viv saw how things were. Viv had said to Isobel, are we playing Oranges and Lemons? Of course they were.

Wild Julie was scarcely a supporter of weight, since she simply liked outrageous causes. In a battle, Julie was an uncertain ally. This only left Isobel whom Viv felt might just understand. But what kind of fighter in such things was anybody who was only nineteen?

Grace appeared while the false conversation was still in progress. She looked about with a pleasant smile.

'So. Everybody here but Isobel. Isn't she back from shopping?'

'I expect she's fallen off her bike again,' said Julie, with her usual burst of laughter. Grace frowned.

'If I have told her once –'

'Ma. A joke. It's years since Isobel turned up covered with gravel and blood and frightened you into fits. Anyway, there she is.'

A flash of blue and white, and the four Bryants turned to see

20

Isobel skidding by on her way to the garage.

She went into the house through the back door, dumped her shopping on the kitchen table, came loping into the drawing room to greet her two other sisters and threw herself, fanning her face with her hand, on to the sofa.

'That's basket was bl– I mean – heavy.'

'I don't ask you to do much for me,' said her mother, thinning her lips. 'When I do I prefer no complaints. Shall we go into lunch?'

Grace had no living-in domestic help, she said she could not afford it. But a rather too matey charwoman came in every morning, untroubled by Grace's freezing politeness and so indomitably cheerful that Grace finally accepted and even consulted her. Mrs Denton, today, had cooked fish, potatoes, a white sauce, and an apple tart. It was the kind of food Grace had given her children since they were weaned. She did not economize on quality and everything on the table was good. For five people she had ordered an entire hake which lay with its freckled silver skin on a long curved dish. But the boiled fish tasted dull and the white sauce had lumps; Mrs Denton had been in a hurry. The parsley had not been chopped finely either, there were spiny stalks in it.

Julie thought their mother was treating today as if it were Friday, the Catholic day of fish and self-sacrifice and that the choice of meal was symbolic.

It was not until the apple pie had been eaten and Grace surveyed the empty plates that she said, 'Well, Viv?'

'Have a heart, Ma,' said Julie, 'She isn't in the dock.'

But she might as well have been.

CHAPTER TWO

Vivien Bryant had never done a rash thing in her life until she
met Carlos Santander. Her common sense was as much a part of
her as her brownish–blonde hair, unremarkable taste and affectionate unsentimental heart. She resembled her North Country
father in her practicality, and her mother in a kind of embarrassment about anything to do with love. She was a little shy.

Of the four daughters she was the one who took her mother's
divorce the hardest. She had been nineteen when it happened, and
Claire, next in age, scarcely fifteen. It had been up to Viv to comfort
and support Grace and cope with a good deal of the miserable
business, while Grace wallowed in self-indulgent suffering. Viv had
grown up too quickly at that time.

She was motherly by nature and for a while found herself landed
with the curious task of mothering Grace, who turned to Viv as if to
a replacement husband. Then the family's friend, Father Francis
Freeman, blessedly stepped in and took over the floundering girl's
task.

He was the only priest the family knew well. Handsome as a
famous actor, he had private money, rich friends, and ran a rough
parish in the poorest part of Brighton. Grace had met him in
Brighton one Sunday by chance. She had been visiting Kemp Town,
on the east side of Brighton, where some friends of hers lived in a
luxurious flat facing the sea, and St Gregory's had been the only
Catholic church within walking distance. As she approached the
gloomy building she was dubious. She had muttered to Viv that the

22

place looked poor and she was sure some of the parishioners would smell.

They did. Grace looked very unsuitable in smart silk clothes, piously kneeling in a front bench accompanied by the girls in their Sunday best.

The priest delivered a racy sermon. His theme was the choice of names chosen by his parishioners for their children.

'Nelly!' he had proclaimed. 'Is that the name of a saint? And when I suggested to the young mother that the child should be baptized Elizabeth, after St Elizabeth of Hungary, she objected. Peggy – for a Catholic child? Margaret, Margaret, after St Margaret Mary, please.

'As for your sons, we've recently had a spate of Wilfreds. I'm told the children are named after the popular rabbit in the daily papers. Wilfred! Why not Pip or Squeak. Your children, when they grow up, are not going to thank you.'

After Mass, instead of disappearing into the presbytery next door, the priest strode down the aisle, satin vestments flapping and stood in the porch shaking hands and making jokes. Taking Grace's suede-gloved hand he gave her a look of interest.

'I haven't seen you before in my church, Mrs –?'

'Bryant.'

'And these are your daughters?'

They were clustered round Grace, wearing straw hats and looking bright.

'The wheeze in my business,' he said, 'is to get at the young. Well, Mrs Bryant, may I offer you a cup of tea? And can I tempt you to bring these hopeful beauties along too?'

It was the beginning of Grace's only friendship with a priest, or for that matter with a man. Married at eighteen, the only men she knew and entertained were business friends of her husband. She had made no life of her own. But here was a handsome man, interested in her and her daughters, amusing, amused, yet unmistakeably a priest. There seemed a sardonic goodness in him.

The house next door to the church was extraordinary. It was untidy, dusty, filled with dirty silver cups. Francis Freeman had been a star tennis player at school and a rugby half back. Among group photographs of officers in 1914 uniform, flyblown paintings of ships at sea, one or two religious prints which had seen better days, were photographs of some exceedingly pretty women. Every frame containing one of these had a rosary draped round it.

'I do that to keep them in order,' said the priest. 'They are friends, daughters of friends, and they will insist on giving me their pictures. That one is Ailsa Flower, she left for Hollywood recently. I'm told she's making a film of The Dubarry, I'm sorry to say.'

The girls took to the priest as much as Grace did. Later, when Frank Bryant met him, he too liked him exceedingly. As the years passed, Freeman became a kind of godfather to the family or perhaps a rich uncle, although no one knew where his money came from. He was a constant guest at the house and at the time of the divorce a staunch support and tactful negotiator between Frank and his wife. When the painful break was over he was the only person in whom Grace confided and whose good advice she listened to and forgot to take.

The girls continued to like Francis Freeman very much. As they grew up and began to enjoy dancing and evenings out with admirers, Grace suggested the priest might be willing to let them stay at the presbytery if they were out late in Brighton.

'I would much prefer that, Father, to young men driving them at reckless speeds across the countryside, probably being the worse for drink. And besides,' added Grace, 'You will know what time they come home.'

'Can't promise to wait up for them,' said Freeman, 'but they're welcome, and Mrs Duffy will be chaperone. It's all quite respectable.'

So the girls, free to dance their shoes off at the Grand or the Metropole, stayed at the presbytery. The elderly Irish housekeeper looked after them more or less, and Francis Freeman gave them a warm welcome. He treated Claire and Julie as if he were about to hang rosaries round their pretty necks. He insisted on meeting their escorts, who usually liked him, and he made the young men bring the girls home at midnight. He teased and spoiled both of them and they made him laugh. Later, when the twins began to

24

work in London and their invitations were in town, it was Isobel's turn to stay at the shabby old house, sleep on a hard bed, and be given Mrs Duffy's breakfast of rubbery scrambled eggs and strong red tea. The priest took Isobel shopping – he bought her expensive books on painting. And as he had done with Claire and Julie, he took her greyhound racing. They often dined at the Albion Hotel.

The daughter who did not go to stay at the presbytery, who was always pleased to see him at Woodlands but was never forthcoming, was Viv. She was not aware of how often he looked thoughtfully in her direction.

'That eldest girl of yours bothers me,' he remarked to Grace. It was a wet spring evening in 1927. He had telephoned on the off chance to invite himself to supper. Viv happened to be away staying with an old schoolfriend, and Grace was forced to send Isobel on her bicycle for some Johnnie Walker. Together, mother and daughter produced a passable meal and later Grace sent Isobel to bed early. The girl was dropping with sleep, and besides, Grace liked the priest to herself.

'You have said that before, Father,' she said, pouring coffee. She was looking her best in a clinging woollen dress of dull rose pink. The priest had a moment of marvelling that she was content with a celibate life. Nobody, thought Francis, who had reason to know, could say celibacy was easy.

'You don't sound as if you are bothered, my dear Grace. Perhaps you should be.'

He leaned back in his chair, holding the tumblerful of whisky. He was relaxed in the company of a woman he liked and often pitied; he was in the mood to do a little good.

'Perhaps Viv is one of nature's spinsters,' she said.

'That's not exactly charitable.'

Grace blushed slightly. She did not like to be criticized.

'It's something I have often thought. One does *know* one's children.'

He murmured something soothing and then went straight at it. Was Grace right to keep the girl here at home with her? Would it not be better for Viv to get a different job, branch out, as he called it with a wave of his hand? 'Girls these days don't have to sit and wait for a man.'

'You can't mean you approve of what goes on,' said Grace, with a fixed look.

Freeman laughed. 'Well,' he said, 'sometimes I don't, but on the whole I believe young women today are maligned. All that tommyrot in the newspapers about the twenties roaring to their end and standards declining. Some of the rich, certainly, behave badly, but you mustn't start thinking it's universal, Grace, and denouncing the bright young people. Women are not going back to being tied to their mothers' apron strings.'

'How can you say that, when I allow them –'

'Yes, yes, Claire and Julie are free enough and young Isobel spends her time in the clouds. I'm talking about Viv. She needs brightening up. Now, is it any life for a personable young thing to bike to the library and back every day and do a bit of dressmaking and help her mother in the garden?'

Grace was offended. It was a new sensation to be annoyed with Father Freeman, whose approval she needed. By nature, she was still the beauty who could 'get anybody', which now that she was older meant she could get their agreement, approval, admiration and respect. She had forgotten how cross she used to be with her husband who had the impertinence to argue and find fault.

'I don't think you are being very fair,' she said, her cheeks still an uncomfortable pink.

He felt contrite, looking at the pretty middle-aged face. He was fond of Grace who hadn't a gleam of imagination. She had a good heart, was a good Catholic and in many ways was the salt of the earth. He must try to get her to see sense. Relaxed in the quiet Chinese room, he made some kind of apology which Grace, eager to smooth over any kind of trouble, quickly accepted. He asked her to play to him.

She went to the piano. Insensitive to most of what went on, seeing only her point of view, sulky when faced with anything to do with sex, implacable to a husband who had longed for her forgiveness, Grace at the piano was another person. She rarely played anything cheerful and her touch had in it some heart-rending quality, as if her fingers, Freeman thought, were on the strings of your heart. She played herself back into self esteem and was far away when he rose to fill his glass – he was encouraged to behave as if this were his home – and tried to resist the melancholy her music brought to him. He fixed his mind on the problem of Viv. He loved the young. He respected them. He did not like to see a girl turning into a woman destined for loneliness.

When Grace closed the piano she was relaxed and cheerful.

'That was perfect. Will you play at the little party I am giving at the Metropole next week?'

Seeing her surprise he laughed. It was his fiftieth birthday, he said, and some good friends were throwing a party for him. Of course the Bryants must come.

'Those two daughters who now spend their time getting up to heaven knows what in London. And the little dreamer upstairs. And Viv. You must all put on your glad rags and do me credit.'

Grace was not sure it was the thing for a Catholic priest to be given a party at the Metropole. The hotel was infamous as a place for illicit weekends. It was also the choice of anybody needing a contrived divorce; people made jokes about it. But she accepted gracefully when it was time for him to leave and walked with him to the front door. He climbed into his car, roared the engine and drove away down the bumpy lane, his rear light a good deed in a naughty world.

She liked to say Father Freeman was 'an important part of our lives'. He had helped Claire to get her secretarial job in Harley Street. He had introduced Julie to one of his wealthy women friends through whom she had been given occasional work as a mannequin at Michou's in Bruton Street. He encouraged Isobel's painting. But Grace did not approve of that. Isobel was to be a secretary and must keep her nose to the grindstone. Father Freeman, however, bought a painting of Isobel's for five pounds and hung it (not draped with a rosary) in his study.

Grace did not know, as she watched the tail light disappear

round the corner of the lane, that the priest was ignorantly playing destiny.

The girls were delighted to hear that FRF – his nickname among racier friends for Father Francis Robert Freeman – was being given a birthday party. They assembled at Woodlands, queued for the bathroom, borrowed each other's silk stockings and scent. The chatter upstairs along the passage leading from one bedroom to another sounded like a flock of starlings in a tree.

Five women could not fit into the Austin Seven. Grace drove the two younger girls and Viv and Claire went by train.

The summer had been hot and the grass in the Brighton crescents and squares was brownish. People too. The big hotels facing the sea glittered with lights and when Grace and her daughters were in the entrance hall the band was playing 'Don't Bring Lulu', which made Julie laugh.

Freeman had arranged to meet them in the bar, and before making her way there Grace looked her daughters over. She was vain of being the mother of four presentable young women, and decided that tonight they did her credit. Claire and Julie sometimes dressed alike for fun to underline their nickname. They wore white organdie, short in the front, dipping at the back, with frilled sleeves showing off sunburned arms. Isobel was in green which suited her dark hair and Viv, dressed up for once, wore a coffee coloured chiffon which had been Grace's. It had been taken in and shortened to fit her slender small figure. She looked pretty enough, thought Grace, whose eye then returned to Claire, the blonde beauty very like herself.

The dance music was loud, the ballroom crowded both with dancers and couples sitting at tables. The head waiter showed them to the adjoining bar where a group of perhaps twenty people were gathered, drinking champagne. Francis Freeman strode over.

'My favourite five.'

There were a good many introductions. The priest's men friends – most of the group were male – brightened at the sight of so many pretty women. Julie was tickled to recognize some of the characters she had seen at the greyhound racing track. She thought they

28

looked deliciously evil and why did FRF always win when he took her to the races? 'I must just pop into my club,' he would say, and return to whisper the name of a greyhound on which wise Julie would stake her money. It never lost.

Claire was singled out by a young man who played Rugby for Sussex, Isobel remained with her mother and her host. His arm was round her shoulders while he talked to Grace and introduced them to some friends who had been in his regiment in the last war.

'Bill Black, he was with me at Arras,' he said, as a tough-looking man wrung Grace's hand, 'And this is Dolly Johnson, our Colonel.' A man with a white moustache and twinkling eyes also shook hands.

Viv was slightly adrift from the introductions and the jokes. She sipped her champagne, feeling shy. How often, indeed always, when she came to parties she wished she was at home. The hotel was elaborate and expensive and noisy, and FRF's friends were not her sort. But who was her sort? She'd recently parted from a young Welshman who had violently kissed her in his parked car outside Woodlands; she had had to fight him off and he'd been so angry. Such incidents made her miserable. She envied her sisters their self-possession, even little Isobel. She loved her family. She had never loved anybody else.

'Miss Bryant?'

A large figure loomed. 'Father Freeman says I must introduce myself to you.'

The accent was foreign. His name, he said, was Carlos Santander; he had arrived in England only two or three days ago and she must take pity on him. He smiled, showing large and beautiful teeth.

Viv gave a nervous laugh and said surely Father Freeman was looking after him. He replied easily, looking at her with very dark eyes in which admiration was as clear as if he had spoken it aloud. His presence seemed to overshadow her. He was pleasing, confident, male, and had about him a kind of mystery. She had never met anybody like him. His face was heavy, spade-shaped, his features strongly pronounced, a big nose, thick lips which looked as if he did not find it difficult to smile. Yet he had, when in repose, a sombre air. Most of all his eyes, black as ink, affected her. Thinking to escape, Viv looked around. The priest, glancing in her direction, nodded and grinned with a gesture of approval, pointing at her companion. Carlos Santander saw and laughed.

'You see, *he* wants you to take pity too. Would you like to dance, Miss Bryant? You look as if you enjoy dancing?'

It was true. Viv was light as a feather and danced perfectly, but rarely did so, since she soon lost her men through her dislike of being kissed. As a result she had not danced for months. She and Carlos Santander left the bar and walked into the ballroom. The floor was crowded and shiny as glass. Santander put his arm round her and led her into the first movements of the quickstep. They were perfectly matched. He had the heavy man's grace and lightness of foot, Viv followed him as if they had been partners for years.

Seeing them in the distance the priest was pleased. He liked Carlos and they were old friends. They had met in Spain in 1919. The war was over and Francis had taken it into his head to go to a Spanish monastery for a week's retreat. On leaving the monastery, he visited Barcelona where he met the Santanders and was entertained at their enormous house. On a later occasion he returned for a holiday as their guest. He and Carlos developed a real friendship; there was something very attractive to Carlos in this unlikely English priest, this racy man so different from the black-coated over-zealous clerics who filled the streets of his native city. Carlos travelled a good deal. He was worldly in the best sense of the word, and he took a fancy to England, visiting the country quite often and never missing the chance to stay in Brighton with his English friend.

On the evening of his arrival this time, Freeman had informed him that his fiftieth birthday was the following week.

'Will there be a celebration?' enquired Carlos.

'As a matter of fact there will. My old messmates have decided to give me a party. Good idea, really, for they do have a habit of dying off. In a few years time, Carlos, there won't be any of us left.'

'Why should they die?' enquired Carlos politely; he had

forgotten the war that was called Great. It had never been part of his life, or that of his country.

'One or two have an odd bit they mislaid in France. A leg. A lung. That kind of thing. Others still have the jitters, poor so-and-so-'s. One of my old friends has become a schoolmaster. He still bursts into tears on November 11th when they play anything a touch patriotic.'

'He loves his country,' said Carlos gravely. Freeman gave him a look of affection, muttering 'not exactly'.

'It's rum,' he continued. 'Up until three or four years ago, nobody who was in it would talk about the war. Even me. It was just there in our heads and now and again it was embarrassing, like when my old mate started to blub on Armistice Day. But it's the new decade very soon. 1930! Things are on the move. All the high jinks were a reaction, I've often thought, a crazy dance to forget the noise of the guns. What's good is to meet a new generation who don't remember the war and don't care either.'

'Do you mean that?'

'Oh yes,' said the priest. 'Yes I do.'

It was during this conversation and an excellent fish meal in one of Brighton's best restaurants that he talked about the Bryants, and – on an impulse – about Viv.

Carlos Santander liked the English. He liked cool English women, abrupt English men, the lush greenness of the fields, the social events which, through one or two introductions, led him to Ascot and Goodwood. As a Spaniard he was without the snobbery of the English which, shocking and entertaining, was in full view. He saw that they divided their own people into sections, like cutting a cake into slabs.

He was only mildly interested when his friend the priest described the Bryants and particularly the eldest girl. Francis Freeman had not mentioned her looks, merely her gentle nature and when Carlos saw Viv in the Metropole bar he thought her quite beautiful. She was small and fair and golden and shy. To his astonishment he fell in love. Scarcely two months after their first meeting in Brighton, after several dinners with him and having

31

introduced him to Grace, Viv told her family that she was engaged to be married.

They were poleaxed. What did that worldly foreigner see in old Viv? Even Grace had a moment of jealousy, followed by a hasty satisfaction that Viv's suitor was a Catholic and a friend of Father Freeman's.

The engagement, costly ring and announcement in the English newspapers were followed by letters to Grace from Señora Santander.

'My mother, of course, writes in Spanish. I will translate,' said Carlos, arriving at Woodlands one morning of early summer bringing an incomprehensible packet of compliments.

'Come and sit next to me, Carlos,' said Grace, patting the sofa. 'And let me hear everything.'

Carlos had already skimmed through the letter and decided on censorship.

'In Spanish, it will sound elaborate,' he said. 'She greets you and sends you God's blessings and many salutations to Viv, and –' smiling as he read, 'wishes to assure you how happy she is that her only child is uniting himself with a young English lady who is of the True Faith. Etcetera,' added Carlos. There followed one or two paragraphs of prayers and religious references, which the Señora had the knack of making sound like threats. Carlos omitted those.

'My mother is old,' said Carlos frankly. 'Alas, she does not feel strong enough to make the journey to England, much as she regrets it.' More etceteras followed, before the letter returned to good wishes and his parent's 'eager longing' to have the pleasure of meeting her new daughter-in-law.

The letter finished with blessings to Viv, and to Grace.

There was also a sentence or two, heavily censored by Carlos, on the subject of Grace's divorce. 'On my knees I am praying that your dear husband will see the light and return again to you and Holy Mother Church.'

Grace was pleased with the letter, which Carlos forgot to give her. He was a realist, and how did he know that one day Grace might not meet somebody who could speak Spanish?

32

The wedding was fixed for the beginning of September, and the time of the engagement rushed by. Soon the wedding gifts began to arrive. Viv decided that Isobel, by far the most excited of her sisters, should have the job of opening the presents. Grace demurred. 'After all, Viv, they are for *you*.'

'Ma, she enjoys it so. Have you seen her face when she opens parcels?'

Isobel's delight was not in the predictable packets from big London stores, containing trays and cocktail shakers (there were three of those, to Carlos's amusement). There was also a very large cheque from Francis Freeman and a small one from the girls' father. What kept Isobel running to the post were parcels from Spain.

'Another one, miss!' said the cheeky post boy, staggering up the path with a wooden crate or a great square cardboard box sealed and covered with Spanish stamps.

Isobel, who had a hammer and a saw-edged kitchen knife ready in the hall, would yell, 'Come on, Viv, or I'll start!' The future bride and bridesmaid would drag the parcel into the dining room. Isobel prised open the packages, after having removed any nails. Out came the strangest of gifts. Wrapped in sheet upon sheet of cotton wool like an Egyptian mummy was a vase covered with twisted yellow and blue leaves through which grinned the face of a devil. There were carved boxes with an exotic scented smell, coffee cups which looked as if they were made of gold, and a rosary which *was* gold, with real pearls surrounding the crucifix. There were a good many statues of saints, some of porcelain and some made of glass. There was a boxful of very old cobweb-fine lace.

Isobel had never enjoyed unpacking so much in her life. Claire and Julie were amused and pitying. When alone together they wondered what their sister was going to do with the junk.

'Expensive junk, too,' said Claire.

'I suppose one could cut up the lace and sew it on one's knickers,' said Julie.

Carlos was staying for convenience in a country hotel not far from the town and arrived at Woodlands every morning. Viv, who

33

had given up her job, was on the lookout for him and rushed down the path to throw herself into his arms. Where was the girl who had struggled to escape from young Englishmen in their Morris Minors? Clutching his hand, Viv led him into the house. He always said the same thing.

'Has anything arrived from Spain today?'

'Oh yes, do look. So beautiful.'

Everything from her lover's country was beautiful to Viv. Beautiful and exotic. Her commonsensical blue eyes were blurred by sexual attraction; she did not know the man she had fallen in love with. As for his country, to Viv it was the music of Carmen, the disturbing paintings of El Greco and, far removed from those, Hollywood films in which girls in black lace mantillas wore roses in their hair and flirted from behind black lace fans.

Three months after the evening when Carlos had seen Viv in the Metropole bar, he married her.

When Frank Bryant (his presence insisted upon by Julie) took his eldest daughter on his arm and led her up the aisle of St Gregory's, and her bridegroom stood waiting, Carlos was as strange to Viv as a rajah or a Red Indian brave. She was linked to him only by passion. She was in a state of ecstasy as a saint might be who had somehow reached the Divine Presence. She was made mad by love.

The Nuptial Mass said by Francis Freeman was long. When she thought about it afterwards, Viv remembered nothing.

The reception for nearly two hundred people was given in a marquee on the lawns at Woodlands. Grace's luck held. It was a beautiful day and the sun still shone down when laughing crowds pursued the couple, showering them with real flower petals picked by Isobel early that morning. They watched the car drive away. Viv and Carlos were still waving.

'Well, Grace, happy?' said the priest, brushing off some white petals Julie had thrown at him.

'Oh yes, Father, and we have you to thank for everything!' said Grace, turning a radiant face. It was, she added, a miracle that entirely due to him Viv had found a wonderful husband.

*

Carlos had warned his bride about the Spanish heat, but her imagination had not grasped its intensity. By the time they stepped out on to the platform at Barcelona, she felt as if she had been stunned.

'You will learn in Spain, *mi amor*, to move very slowly,' said Carlos. The porters certainly did as they came to wheel away the enormous amount of luggage. Viv's new husband accompanied her, smiling, solicitous, out of the station.

She was very tired and very happy. It seemed in harmony with the fierce heat, the drifting crowds, that Carlos should settle her into an open carriage drawn by a tired horse. The driver whipped the poor animal, who meekly set off along a boulevard blessedly shaded by trees. Viv had thought when she first saw Paris on her honeymoon that it was the most fascinating city in the world. But Barcelona was much much more strange. She had never imagined so great a port, lined with sailing ships, a procession of masts vanishing into the distant heat mist; and right up against the quay the huge shape of an ocean liner. Paris was glamorous but not utterly unfamiliar. Here there was nothing she could recognize. Donkeys went by, their backs loaded with vegetables covered with nets. The men outside wine shops drank from skins as they had done in the time of the Gospels. One little boy, wearing nothing but a vest, was curled asleep on the pavement beside his mother who sold roses from a giant basket. They passed fountains tiled in turquoise, great sombre churches, and streets so narrow that there were open bridges built from one side to the other.

Carlos took his wife's hand as she exclaimed and wondered, removing the thin suede glove which was glued to it with sweat, and put it to his lips.

He was a man who loved and despised and needed women. He was spoiled and generous hearted and proud as Lucifer. He had never done a sillier thing than to fall in love with this mild little English miss. But there was something in Viv's physical appearance, her small neat body, her little English breasts, her metallic voice, her courage, the blue eyes at times so like her mother's, fixed as if on some inner vision, and most of all her almost crazy sexual

35

reaction to him, which turned his bones to water. She was shy, and shyness was something which, as a Spaniard, he could not comprehend and found comic and moving. He looked on her as an emperor might do who had taken a bride from some country which he had decided to annexe. The queens of the past had wept for weeks until they understood their duties. Viv, too, would accept what was coming to her. And then, if difficulties appeared, there was the delight of their lovemaking. He knew that whatever Viv found difficult in his country he could banish with one thrusting embrace.

Like the captive queens she so much resembled, who had been married for reasons of state, Viv spent the first weeks in a state of shock. She had scarcely realized – had Carlos told her? – that his mother lived in the huge, elaborate and over-furnished palace. It seemed like a palace to Viv after Woodlands. The house was called Nueva Casa de los Arboles Naranjas – the entire courtyard was set about with orange trees. It had been built in the seventeenth century in an elaborate pinnacled style with cloister-like open balconies. It looked as if nobody had purchased a new piece of furniture for two hundred years. It was in the richest part of Barcelona and had once been the home of a duke.

The Señora received her kindly. Carlos's mother, big and heavy, still dark haired at sixty-five, was waiting to take over her adored son's new wife. Her own husband had died years ago, and she ruled the huge old house as she'd done since *her* mother-in-law had fortunately died. Carlos's mother came of a noble family, had been beautiful once and was very fat.

'How happy I am,' she said, when Viv and Carlos entered a vast room stuffed full of statues, paintings and ivory crucifixes, 'how happy I am to have a daughter.'

All this in Spanish, translated with lack of hurry by Carlos, who walked over to his mother, kissed both her hands and, Viv thought with a shaft of irony, comically went down on both knees.

Viv faced up to the realities with matter-of-fact guts. As well as a mother-in-law, other inhabitants of her new home were a silent and antique great aunt and a silent, very young, distantly related cousin. Viv was flabbergasted. She could not tell Carlos what a blow it was not to be alone with him. And she was still dizzy with love.

Concepción Santander was not a bad woman. Her heart was in the right place; she genuinely wished to see her son happy. It had been as great a shock to her as she was to Viv, when her adored Carlos decided to marry a young woman of an alien race. Knowing nothing about them, Concepción disliked the idea of the English. Viv had learned of the great English victory of the Armada in the prim convent. Concepción as a girl had been taught that the weather alone had ruined the expedition, the great winds had blown and scattered the ships, or the English would still be in the power of Spain.

Viv knew from the outset that she was not going to win her particular Armada with her mother-in-law. All meals were taken together. Concepción sat at the head of the huge carved black dining table, the young Asunción on her left, Viv on her right, the old aunt at the end of the table where she could be served most easily. Occasionally another distant cousin, brother to Asunción and looking like Christ in a Spanish painting, was also present.

During the meals, Concepción dominated. She was more garrulous than any woman Viv had met. She talked and talked. Viv was not without linguistic talent and now applied herself to her husband's language. Soon she was able to understand and later speak a considerable amount of Spanish. She saw that Carlos's mother, kindly enough, was a staggering bore. Grace's sometimes overlong tales seemed the acme of wit to Viv as the weeks passed and every day she was verbally battered at the dining table.

A boring woman, perhaps more than a boring man, imprisons her audience through their own politeness. Only somebody very impatient or very brave will shut them up. Like the sufferer in the legend who has been bitten by the tarantula spider and must dance until he drops, a bore will continue talking, talking. Concepción talked her family, young Asunción, the ancient great aunt, Carlos and Viv into the ground. Carlos crumbled bread and occasionally shot Viv a sexy look which revived her for a moment; but only for a moment. By the end of every meal the family had been squashed into a pulp.

37

Escaping after the agony of mealtimes, Carlos took his wife on expeditions. The teeming city was filled with churches and palaces, with statues set in niches in every crowded street, with toy markets and long promenades and wooden kiosks where people who had not learned to write employed the services of letter-writers. Carlos took her shopping and bought her silk dresses so fine she could thread them through her wedding ring. He took her to a fan shop, and bought her an exquisite eighteenth-century fan, painted on white chicken skin.

Viv was determined to become part of this new life even though another woman commanded her home. The civilisation around her appeared unchanged for centuries, the people grave and religious – she'd never imagined there were so many priests in the world. She looked about her with awe, and blessed every day the fact of a husband, exciting and to-be-adored, in whose embrace she felt faint.

Like opening a locked door, Viv began to learn Spanish. Once she could speak a little, she made small changes in the household, particularly in the food which, at her suggestion, became less heavy. Sometimes she dared to venture into her mother-in-law's talk with a pretty confidence; she even managed once to make a Spanish joke at which Concepción laughed and Carlos looked proud. She was resilient and she loved Carlos with her whole heart.

Imagination had never been Viv's strong point. Brave as a last-ditch soldier or Horatius at the bridge, Viv did not know, did not guess, that what she was up against was not the reign of a tedious elderly woman who was dominating but at least good hearted. She was not up against the heavy food and the heavy house. Her enemy was Spain.

'What are we going to do today, Carlos?' said Viv one July morning which was hotter than ever. He was shaving, his handsome head bent to look in a silver-framed looking glass in the bedroom. He always shaved in the bedroom after Viv had told him that she liked to watch. 'What about driving up Mount Tibidabo? You said the view is wonderful from there.'

She was sitting up in their bed, rightly called a *cama matrimonial*,

38

made for coupling and somehow symbolic of the groans of childbirth. It was richly carved in dark wood and so weighty that, like marriage, it was immoveable. Viv had seen the little maids brush under it by lying flat on their stomachs.

Unsuited to the elaborate brocade hangings, the holy pictures most of which were tragic, the heavy furniture and heat, Viv sat against her pillows wearing pink, fresh as an English rose. Sex made her prettier than she'd ever been. She looks almost edible, thought Carlos. He finished shaving and slowly wiped the blade of his cutthroat razor.

'Alas, *mi vida*, I cannot take you out today. There are friends to see.'

'Friends? Can't we have them to dinner?'

'I'm afraid that is not possible.'

Viv gave her tinkling laugh. What could he mean? Why couldn't his friends –

Carlos sat down on the bed, and took one of her hands, encompassing it with his own large broad one so that it was imprisoned like a captured white butterfly. He explained carefully. In Viv's country he had seen how free and easy it had become to entertain people in the home. Young women invited their friends, parents entertained, he had heard the phrase 'open house'. It was hospitable and impressive. But here in Spain, it was not so. The home was sacred, the life out in the street was something different. He had many men friends whom he met in the cafés. Respectable women did not – Viv sensed that he meant were not allowed to – go to these places.

'We talk. Of business or politics. It is not very interesting, *mi vida*, and certainly not to you. But it is the custom. That is why I can't take you to Tibidabo today.'

'Then tomorrow?' She felt a chill in the hot scented room.

'Perhaps. Perhaps.'

Viv was not sure she believed her husband's story that Spaniards went to cafés to meet their men friends. She nervously wondered if there was more behind the feeble alibi. She asked herself, with a sudden pain like a stab wound, if he had a mistress, somebody from

39

before his marriage with whom he was already reviving the liaison. After all he was in his thirties and must be very experienced.

In bed in Paris during the two blissful days of the honeymoon journey, Viv had once asked him about his past sexual life. He had put a finger against her lips as if she had asked him to break some sacred vow. It seemed men never spoke of such things to their wives. At the time, armoured by a happiness which was going to keep her safe against suffering for ever, Viv accepted her husband's law. Now she was frightened.

When Carlos had gone, kissing her tenderly goodbye, Viv bathed and dressed and set off in search of the only member of the family who was near to her own age: Carlos's young cousin.

Asunción was in actual fact a cousin many times removed from the Santanders. She came from a small village in the province of Castellón. The family were poorish, and the generous wages paid by Carlos for her work as his mother's companion were posted home every week to her parents. She was a strange looking girl. Her pale face was narrow and lengthened into a long chin. She had a high bony nose and slanting eyes. She was ugly, but she was arresting. You couldn't ignore Asunción's looks, they resembled the medieval virgins in the smoke-darkened paintings in ancient churches; they were mysterious. She rarely spoke but smiled very sweetly. She did everything her commanding mistress told her in silence. Now and again, when Viv happened to catch her eye, she thought she saw a friendly gleam.

Concepción Santander stayed in bed until midday every morning except on Sundays. She read holy books or sent for the many servants. Viv had heard her haranguing them and, since the huge house was spotless, often wondered why. Knowing her mother-in-law was safely out of the way, Viv walked the length of the open upper-storey cloisters and found her way to the room where Asunción did the family mending.

The room, hot, whitewashed, was as bare as a cell. The girl sewing at a table looked very startled.

'The Señora is still in her room,' she said.

'Yes, Asunción, I know. It is you I have come to see.'

More startled, Asunción stood up and pushed forward the only other chair, after removing a pile of beautifully repaired sheets.

Viv sat down.

English to the depth of her soul, Viv could see only one way of doing what she'd come to do and that was to be blunt. She said she was 'troubled'. She had decided on the choice of word beforehand. Asunción would do her a kindness if she could explain – Viv repeated what Carlos had said about men in Spain meeting by themselves without women.

Putting down her sewing, the girl turned her long solemn face to her visitor. There was a silence. A fly imprisoned against the window gave a series of desperate buzzes. Viv went to the casement and shooed the insect to liberty.

When Viv returned to her seat, the Spanish girl drew a breath. She had scarcely addressed a word to the English bride since her arrival several weeks ago; she found the foreigner rather disturbing. Asunción had her own worries and sensed, because the two girls were of an age, that Viv's were going to be larger than her own. Here was the first of them.

Speaking in simple Spanish, as if to a child, Asunción explained that her cousin had spoken the truth. Men never invited other men to the home.

'You will see many cafés when you know the city better, and will see, also, the many many men who will be sitting there,' said Asunción.

'But what do they *do*?'

'They talk, of course. My brother, also, he is in the cafés all day when he comes here to stay in the Nueva Casa. They talk.'

'But what about?'

The girl's reply echoed Carlos. 'Oh, about politics.'

'Why cannot they talk of such things here in the house?'

A shrug was all the answer.

'And how can there be so much to say, after all?' enquired Viv, anxious to understand.

'Because our country is not happy. They talk also of their business, I suppose. I do not know. They talk,' said Asunción with simplicity.

41

Viv digested the far-from-enlightening information.

'What do the women do?' she asked, relieved and half smiling.

'Oh, we like to walk. It is pleasant in the Ramblas at the time of the *paseo*. Would you perhaps ...' a hesitation, 'like to come with me?'

'Very much!'

At Viv's enthusiasm the young girl said, 'What about this evening?'

So it happened that Viv went out for a walk with another girl. It was not a country ramble with her sisters, a walk with Grace to the shops, a stroll along the beach at Brighton with Father Freeman, but the walk which was part of the Spanish day, the *paseo*, when the streets were packed with people on their evening promenade.

Viv admired the Ramblas. Broad boulevards like those in Paris, they had been built by the same architect. They were rather dusty, but pleasantly shaded by trees. She had been taken along the Ramblas a number of times by Carlos in a horse-drawn carriage. Now she walked. The streets were astonishingly crowded, the people swarmed like bees and Viv saw that here was the real social life of the country. In England you asked people to play tennis. In Spain you took to the streets. How elegant the women were – even the poorer women wore pure white frilled blouses, brilliant skirts, silver earrings. And strangest of all, the women walked together; there was not a couple, a man with a girl, in sight.

Asunción did not talk much but pointed out a crowd around an open shop selling birds in wooden cages, and great baskets of red roses in the flower-lined *rambla* – Las Flores. She was more animated than Viv had ever seen her, and now and again her enigmatic almost noble face smiled, not at anybody in particular but at her own thoughts.

Viv noticed an odd thing, and not only about Asunción. The girls who walked by talking animatedly, displaying their beauty, their sparkling dark faces and brilliant eyes, never looked at the men who passed them in the street. As men approached, the girls dropped their eyes. They might have been Victorian governesses. To Viv this was all the more strange because the femininity was so

42

flaunted. As they gracefully walked, in their elaborate clothes, the girls swung their hips like dancers.

Asunción, too, never looked once at the passing men. Viv did not follow her example, but looked in English interest and curiosity at some of them. They reacted with stares and even grins. They made it plain they thought less of her because she had looked directly at them.

'Asunción.'

'Señora?'

Viv considered and dismissed the idea of asking her companion to call her by her first name.

'Explain a little more to me if you would be so good. Do Spanish people *never* entertain in their homes? In my country we do, all the time.'

After a pause, as if deeply considering a difficult subject, Asunción said, 'There could perhaps be a cocktail party?' She pronounced the word as if it were Chinese, and Viv couldn't help laughing.

That night in the comfort of the matrimonial bed, with Carlos blessedly returned and a tedious evening meal with Concepción over, Viv suggested the cocktail party. Carlos gave her a smile and kissed her. Reading his pitying expression she knew she was not going to win that little battle.

Slowly, over the weeks and months, the Spanish way of life, the Spanish heat, the Spanish character, defeated Viv. She had arrived with a good supply of English energy, from a cold climate, from a middle-class upbringing which during the decade just ending had given young women liberty and a lot of fun. She was 'emancipated' to use the cant word, but in its true sense. Her free spirit, blinded by love, had chosen to enter a cage. And a cage it was. One of its worse aspects was the insupportable interest Señora Santander had in Viv conceiving a child. Carlos had done nothing to prevent Viv from becoming pregnant, and although Julie had strongly advised a visit to a woman doctor – 'She's *so* good and won't embarrass you, you shy old thing' – Viv had not taken her sister's advice. She had faced whatever the future was about to offer starry-eyed – the loss

43

of her virginity to the man she worshipped, the new but ancient country of her adoption, the probability of conceiving a child.

Carlos enquired once – he was modest to the point of neurosis about her monthly periods – and Viv confessed that 'nothing has happened yet'. He kissed her hand and patted her cheek and was quiet. Often loquacious, amusing, expansive, he had moods of silence which Viv, comparing him to Asunción, thought must be a Spanish trait. To be subjected to questions about her periods by her mother-in-law offended and outraged her. She did not show that she was angry except by a Grace-like thinning of the mouth and abrupt icy replies. Anybody English, thought Viv contemptuously, would know that what I actually mean is 'mind your own business'. But Concepción threw her dark eyes to the ceiling and said, 'Not yet? Alas, alas.' As the months went by, and it grew late into the Spanish winter, she looked at Viv almost with hostility. She thinks I'm incapable of having a child, thought Viv, leaving the drawing room abruptly after another barrage of insupportable questions. She looks on me as a brood mare; it's disgusting.

When disturbed or not happy, she always went to talk to her one friend, who was as usual at the sewing machine. Outside it was raining heavily and the room where Asunción worked was very cold. When she saw Viv she stopped working, and gave her rare transforming smile.

Viv sat down. She was not as pretty as she had been during the flowering time when the philtre of sex had transformed her. She looked thin and, because she was much indoors, as pale as Asunción. There was a new trait in Viv, she was nervous.

'Shall we go out for the *paseo*?' Viv was in need of company and literally forgot the beating rain.

'I'm afraid I cannot, Señora.' She paused. 'I have had a letter from my mother.'

Viv clutched at any thread to lead her out of the labyrinth of her own unhappy thoughts.

'I'm so glad. How is she? I know how you look forward to news from your home.'

'She is well and she sent me this,' said Asunción, smiling again.

She held out a gold box, open to show an array of oval-shaped sweets.

'They are turrón. You must have some. No, no, more than those,' emptying into Viv's palm three or four from a box which scarcely contained a dozen.

The sweets were made of marzipan and were sweet indeed. While Viv was eating them, the girl watched her with intense pleasure.

'Ah. You enjoy.'

'They are delicious.'

'You must have more,' said Asunción and would have given her the boxful if Viv, whose Spanish was now fairly fluent, had not made a speech about the fact that Asunción's mother would not be happy unless her daughter had at least half. The girl laughed, and they finished the sweets off together.

There followed one of Asunción's lengthy pauses. She carefully folded a darned sheet.

'I have something to tell you. I am to go back to my home. It is arranged.'

'For a short holiday?'

'Oh no. For always.'

Dismay shot through Viv. She had not realized until this moment how much the presence of this quiet enigmatic companion meant to her. Asunción was her lifeline. She was young and she was a girl. She wasn't an elderly woman cross-questioning her about her monthly periods, or an antique, over-religious, near-silent aunt. She wasn't an irresistible autocratic man who seemed, as time went by, to have become a marauder. She was a friend.

'I go in three months. In May,' said Asunción. 'In three months, yes, I shall be with my mother and father and my brother. My family.'

She wore a smile filled with love.

Viv was never sure – yes, she was sure – that Asunción leaving the Nueva Casa was the reason that she made up her mind that she, too, must go. It seemed incredible, downright absurd, that because she was to lose her little ally, Viv should find she could no longer bear her married life. Yet it was so.

She loved Carlos. She was afraid of Spain. She could never settle

45

here. She would always be a foreigner to them, she did not belong. She discovered that there was no word in their language for 'wife'. To her mother-in-law, the old aunt, the servants who kept Viv at arm's length, to anybody she met, she was Señor Santander's woman. And not even the woman who ruled his house.

There was something impenetrable in Carlos. He was two people. The powerful lover. The absentee. He was excessive in both, but as time passed the second part of him was uppermost. Sometimes when she lay in her bed and watched him dress with the care and grace of an aristocrat, she thought, he's the handsomest and most alluring man I have seen in my life. He was so strong, so composed. She knew, she saw in his heavy face, how far away he was from her. Many times, for all his courtesy, he was indifferent. When she had been sure of herself, before English energy and confidence had drained away, she had asked him why he had said, 'The politics in my country are difficult.'

He turned round from looking at himself in an oval pier glass.

'We are an impossible people,' he said with sudden anger. 'We are priest-ridden and decadent. We have thrown away the pride of the past. We are corrupt. Who can govern us? We are a disgrace to ourselves.'

The fire died in his eyes. It was as if he had momentarily forgotten to whom he was speaking. He shrugged and turned back to the glass.

The days for Viv dragged by until at last Asunción, radiant and silent, had packed her trunks, been formally embraced by the family and hugged by Viv. Asunción's eyes shone with tears. Her brother, still looking like Christ, with his beautiful hair and classic face, arrived to take his sister back to Castellón.

It was not Viv's imagination that after her one Spanish friend left the house, Carlos grew more morose. There was less lovemaking and he scarcely ever laughed. His absences grew. Even his mother who never criticized him looked disapproving when he announced at dinner that he would be away again.

'I will not be here for two days. Perhaps more, perhaps less. I may return on Friday, or perhaps not.'

'*When* shall we expect you, Carlos?' broke in Viv.

He said calmly, 'If I come, then I come. We will see.'

It was the style of conversation which had once made her giggle and now affected her so much that she wanted to scream. His favourite way of ending a conversation about his absences would be the incomprehensible, 'If not, not.' There had been a time, there had been many times, when she had thought to change it. To change him. Now she did not waste her hopes. With Asunción gone, she began to thirst for home.

CHAPTER THREE

Nothing was resolved during the fish-and-confession lunch. The air was not cleared, and Grace's idea of gathering the family together so that Viv could, so to speak, put her case and be given absolution, signally failed. Viv and Julie knew that it would, Viv from pain and Julie from instinct. Isobel was silently miserable throughout the meal. She hated to be disturbed, and her eldest sister's unhappiness did just that. It took her thoughts away from painting.

But Claire, listening to the story of the strange marriage, came to a decision. She did not tell her mother (whose side she was naturally on). She wanted a free hand. Waiting until the family finally left the dining room and went off on their own devices, and for the thousandth time wishing the telephone was not in the hall, Claire rang a Brighton number. When she heard FRF's voice she said almost inaudibly, in case anybody came down the stairs or out of the drawing room, 'It's Claire.'

FRF got the point at once.

'Trouble?'

'Yes. But not mine.'

'Want to come to Brighton and see me?'

'Not easy at present. You couldn't come to the Burrell Hotel, I suppose?'

'Of course. I'll buy you dinner.'

'Not easy either,' Claire spoke with regret. They arranged to meet at half past six, and Claire rang off.

48

She borrowed her mother's Austin, lied about where she was going, and drove to the Burrell, reflecting on all that had happened. Claire, as conventional as Grace, whose looks she had inherited, had found Viv's rash act almost incomprehensible. She herself had a good many admirers, nicknamed by Julie 'Claire's SM's'. Suitable men. They were suitable because they had pleasant manners, good jobs, spoiled her and were slightly upper class. Claire spent a good deal of time reflecting on whom, among the SM's who telephoned, wrote, and took her out and about, she was going to choose as her husband. She was the girl who when offered a tempting tray of chocolates took minutes to decide which she would enjoy the most.

She had had a determination, an obsession, about getting married, since at fifteen she had come home from school to announce to her startled family that she was engaged to the doctor's son. He had even bought a Woolworth's ring. 'Claire's Big Romance' became a family joke and, although she had little sense of humour, even Claire saw now that it had been funny. Yet she had not changed all that much from the schoolgirl with her blue eyes fixed upon marriage. It was to be her career. It was to be *it*. At present there were three men whom she was keeping in doubtful hope.

Of course she was a virgin. No man would dare to ask Claire to go to bed with him. Her virginity matched her white satin evening dresses, her white silk nightdresses. Loving Julie and often jealous of her, Claire refused to believe that her sister had affairs.

For all her natural egotism, made worse by being beautiful, Claire was devoted to all her sisters and at present, putting her own future aside, she was genuinely troubled about Viv. It was, she thought, a mess and a muddle.

The Burrell was an out-of-town country hotel with a gothic style of interior decoration, phoney panelling and carved arched doorways and inglenooks. There was a pleasant garden and a swimming pool.

FRF was waiting in the lounge. He smiled at the fair-haired figure who came in, carrying one of those large silly hats which were fashionable that summer. Girls wore them occasionally but more often used them as props.

49

'Like a drink by the swimming pool?'

'Lemonade would be nice.'

Claire drank only at weddings and then one glass of champagne which she never finished.

The priest ordered the drinks. They walked out into a garden of well-mown lawns, early roses and the winking blue rectangle of the pool. They sat down on two vacated chairs by the bright water. There wasn't a soul about.

'And what's the trouble?' asked the priest.

His world was filled with trouble; he was used to it. Old women turned to him in loneliness and grown men asked him what had become of their Faith. Young unmarried girls, God help them, came to Francis Freeman when they were pregnant and young boys when they lost or could not get work. And there were the many drunkards who rang the presbytery bell or with whom he talked in filthy apartments in the Brighton slums. To the priest, the appalling suffering drunkards inflicted on their women and children was disconnected with his own pleasure in a double Scotch.

Claire said in her flat little voice, 'Viv has left Carlos.'

Freeman gave a whistle. He looked astounded.

'He hasn't been unfaithful. So she tells us, and one supposes she would know. She just hates Spain. Carlos is out all the time or away, and ... she just hates Spain.'

He wanted to swear. What had made him think Santander would be a good husband? I ought to stop playing God, he thought. It was so tempting and always a mistake. In this case it could turn out to be a tragedy.

'Of course she must go back to him,' said Claire.

'Are you sure about that?'

'Father! She's a *Catholic.*'

'Yes, yes. She's also your sister and I haven't heard a tenth of the story yet.'

Determined to be fair, Claire tried to remember all Viv had said earlier. The picture she painted, some of which Freeman recognized from his own experience of Spain, was not a hopeful one. He saw Viv's marriage against a background of harsh sunlight and the

50

excesses of speech and silence in the Spanish nature. He thought of their religion too. The gloomy churches, the harsh bells, the scores of unfamiliar saints whose statues, holding symbols of terrible martyrdom, wheels, hatchets, stood in the aura of burning candles. He imagined Viv on Sunday, kneeling by the mother-in-law, both women in the requisite black veil. These were images he could have conjured, ought to have done, before he introduced Carlos to the Bryants. He was stricken at his part in what had happened.

'I quite see,' finished Claire, 'that it's a bit much to be forced to live with one's Spanish mother-in-law. Impossible, in fact.'

He looked at her curiously. He thought, I really believe if it had been you landed with the elderly Señora, you would have got rid of her.

'We'll have to explain to her that she must go back.'

By 'we' she meant the priest.

'I wish I had your certainty,' Freeman said slowly.

If she had imagined calling religion to her aid was going to solve anything, she was wrong. He talked a little and questioned her more. He was less than his humorous self; in repose his face looked set.

He finally said, 'I must do some thinking.'

'And praying?'

Looking at Claire just then he saw that for all her sophistication she still believed that his dog collar and a few words with the Almighty were going to do the trick.

'We all will,' he comfortingly said.

As it happened, it was not Freeman who made any kind of decision about the wanderer returned, it was Grace. She had not been feeling well recently. Although she would have preferred to put this down to shock over Viv, it had started a week or two before her daughter reappeared. She'd had splitting headaches. The idea of getting away and at the same time giving a little comfort to Viv appealed. She suggested they should go for a motoring holiday to the Lake District.

For their stick-in-the-mud mother to consider anything as revolutionary as leaving home and driving long distances was hailed by her family with approval. Even Viv thought it was the first cheerful thing that had happened to her for months.

Mother and daughter left on a sunny Sunday in late June. Viv could not help noticing the bright faces of the sisters assembled to see them off. They clustered at the gate, waving goodbye. Viv guessed that the prospect of having Woodlands to themselves was delighting them. They had never had such an opportunity before. Did she hear the word 'party' in the air? Grace never gave parties.

Mother and daughter set off into the bright early morning. Grace concentrated on the driving; her headache had returned but she was accustomed to fighting it off and this holiday was for Viv's benefit. She hoped a few days of peaceful Cumberland might bring her daughter to her senses: Grace planned one or two gentle talks about marriage. Driving tired her and Viv knew that, but her mother resolutely refused to allow her to take the wheel. She always preferred to be in command.

They left Sussex and eventually reached the Great North Road. The hours passed, the stop for lunch in a pleasant roadhouse was soothing. The car went well and as they drove North, skirting the great manufacturing towns, there was not much traffic. They talked little. Grace, thought Viv, could be as silent as Asunción had been but not so mysterious. When she did say a word or two it was to trot out comforting clichés.

'That farm over there is quite big. Why doesn't the farmer re-thatch his roofs? Of course thatching's so expensive. I suppose that's the trouble.'

'Did you see the AA man? He forgot to salute.'

They spent a night in Leicestershire at an unremarkable hotel. Grace was snappish and looked pale, but it was useless for Viv to repeat her offer to drive on the following day. The next morning, satisfactorily early, saw them again on the Great North Road. The countryside slowly but steadily changed. There were no more gentle fields, no more smoke-heavy towns, it became rougher and more dramatic and in the distance, on high rounded hills, boulders were scattered which resembled flocks of sheep.

Viv enjoyed the journey. She was content to remember that every mile took her further away from Spain. Now she was safely in

England, how often in her thoughts she used the word safe! She determined not to brood over Carlos. She was not going to think about him. He had proved he was not a husband in the way she, and every other Englishwoman, thought of that comforting word. He had shared nothing. He had simply disappeared, returning 'perhaps', or 'if not, not'. Had she ever truly loved him? Or had it been an infatuation, by which she meant sexual passion? She refused to remember the nights when she had cried aloud during his lovemaking and begged for more. She resolutely turned her inward eyes away from their two figures, locked, exhausted, utterly united.

It seemed to Viv that her love had been like a plant in a pot, covered with green leaves and buds, burgeoning, moist, cared for, scented, healthy. Now, poor thing, after a year of merciless, austere and incomprehensible Spain, her love had died. It had died and dried in the Spanish sun and there was nothing left but desiccated sticks as sharp as thorns.

The sun, brilliant but not cruel, shone straight in their faces as evening fell.

Grace suddenly said, 'There's the hotel. That's the entrance.'

She swerved sharply to drive through narrow gates and up to a hotel no bigger than a small country house, set on high sloping lawns surrounded by trees.

'Thank goodness we're here. My head's worse,' she said.

She climbed out of the car with difficulty, haggard and ashen. Viv was concerned. Her mother's headaches had been part of the Bryants' youth and the only thing to do with the sufferer was to put her to bed, curtains drawn, a bowl of cold water beside her and a flannel, wrung out so that it did not drip water when draped across her throbbing forehead.

A youngish man received them in the hotel entrance hall, having sent a porter for the luggage. He was concerned too, and accompanied them upstairs to their rooms. Grace's bedroom was quite large and comfortable. Just what she needs, thought Viv.

She soon had her mother lying down, the necessary bowl on a table nearby. She sat in the darkened room to keep her mother company.

Grace gave a little groan. 'I wish you wouldn't stay.'

'My dear Ma –'

'No. Don't. Go and have some supper. You know I prefer to be by myself.'

'Are you sure?' asked Viv doubtfully.

Grace shifted slightly and readjusted the flannel.

'Don't argue with me, Vivien.'

Unwillingly, Viv went to her own room, had a bath, changed, then looked into her mother's room again on her way down to dinner. Grace had not stirred. Viv wrung out the flannel and replaced it on her forehead and Grace wrinkled her nose, waiting for the drips. But Viv was careful that none came.

Viv crept out and went downstairs. The hotel offered good plain food, rather Scottish in character although they were in Cumberland. There were a dozen or so other visitors, and a low buzz of voices. Unaccustomed to eating by herself, she was lonely. Her thoughts returned to the House of the Orange Trees; she was too tired to keep Carlos away. She tried to imagine how it would be if she ever returned – she couldn't think he would forgive her. It was days since she had made the terrible decision to leave and she would never have been able to do so if she hadn't kept, from sentimentality, some English money. Claire had given it to her before she left on her honeymoon.

One hot Spanish morning Viv had slipped, trembling, from the house and taken a taxi to the station. She had not received a word in answer to the letter she'd left for Carlos. He is glad I've gone, she thought. She felt so sad.

After the meal she went into the drawing room. There were comfortable sofas and flowers, the atmosphere of a private house, even to a row of shabby books. She found a copy of *Kidnapped* and was reading the first page when the young man who had received them on arrival came over to her.

'Miss Bryant. May I have a word?'

Something in the quiet voice struck her.

'Could we perhaps ...' He indicated that they should leave the room.

Viv was surprised and annoyed. Was he going to ask for money on account? Slightly blushing, she followed him. The other visitors took no notice, but Viv frowned when they went out and he carefully shut the double doors behind him.

'Would you step into my office?'

'Really!' Her blush deepened.

He did not reply but took her into a crammed room with a typewriter, telephone and a good many metal filing cabinets.

As he turned round, she was suddenly terrified.

'Miss Bryant. I don't know how to say this but –'

He swallowed and started again, 'But I am afraid – your mother is dead.'

Her whole face turned from red to white. Colour drained away like water.

'Don't be stupid.'

She held on to the desk, swaying. The man's formality left him. He sprang towards her and caught her in his arms, afraid she was going to faint.

'I'm sorry. So sorry. I went up a moment ago when the chambermaid called me. I have sent for the doctor. I'm so sorry,' he kept saying, 'I can't tell you what a shock –'

'You're mistaken. She's got a migraine – she …'

'I wish that were so. I'm so very sorry. Will you come up with me? I don't think you should go alone.'

Supported by a perfect stranger, she went into a hotel bedroom to find her mother lifeless.

Viv did not cry. The doctor arrived almost at once. There were consultations. Pauses. Viv sat in the bedroom, her mother on the bed, the flannel removed from her forehead, her fair greying hair for a while still damp. The doctor confirmed that the lady had died and later the diagnosis was of an aneurism.

'To die like that is a great blessing,' the doctor told her during the night. He held Viv's unresponsive hand.

All kinds of people touched her, spoke to her, embraced her. She never remembered them afterwards.

Part Two

CHAPTER FOUR

Harold Mason's lanky figure and beaked face under a snap-brimmed trilby hat could be seen over the heads of the passengers on the platform. He, with the eyes of love, saw a thin fair girl dressed in black. He'd never seen her in the sombre colour before. The trappings and the suits of woe became her; she looked frail. Harold often hoped that deep down she was. She came up to him and allowed him to kiss her.

When they separated he began, 'Oh, poor Julie –'

'No, Harold. Don't be sympathetic or I shall howl like a dog. It makes me feel ill to think about Ma. Look, I'll tell you quickly what happened. It wasn't an accident, like you said on the phone this morning. She died suddenly of an aneurism, whatever that is. Apparently people can. She was up in Cumberland with my eldest sister Viv. The reason I rang was to ask if you could take me to Hornsey.'

'Of course.'

Julie always wanted something when she telephoned him. And he was always glad to hear her voice. He had driven her across London to Hornsey a number of times; the journey was long and when they arrived at their destination he was not allowed to stay with her, but asked to call back for her later. He had discovered a pub where he could sit and read, longing for the time to be up so that he could fetch her and be with her again. The chains of love round Harold were heavy. He would do anything she asked for the chance of her sitting beside him in the car, smiling at him

59

sometimes, perhaps allowing him to touch her hand. The tedious suburban drive, the boredom of hanging about in a smelly pub, it was all worth it to see her. To sit close. His heart continued, falsely, to hear a promise she never made.

He was tall and hunch-shouldered, with short black hair, a Ronald Colman moustache, a job in the City, parents who lived in Wimbledon (to whom he had never introduced Julie as he thought they would bore her) and a taste for jazz. Like most of Julie's pick-ups, she had met him on a train to London after he had spent a week's holiday in Brighton. An arresting young woman had thrown herself into a corner of his fortunately-empty compartment and when he offered to lend her his newspaper, any excuse would do, she responded with a grin. Julie, like Kipling's Kim, was the friend of all the world.

But Harold's first joy in the fascinating odd-looking girl soon disappeared; Julie was impossible to pin down. Delighted at any and every invitation, she broke most of her dates. She was elusive, obliging and utterly unreliable. Her daring laugh haunted his dreams. He had fallen in love with her on the day, on the hour, when she sprawled untidily in the corner of the train compartment and stared across at him with engaging curiosity.

He wanted to marry her. He dared not say so. He could no more stop hoping for Julie than his father could halt the weeds crowding into his Wimbledon garden after the rain.

Now he settled her in his car – few of his friends owned a car, he was very proud of it – and they set off on an endless cross-London journey. Julie accepted a cigarette. She lit it, he noticed jealously, with a new lighter he'd never seen before. He guessed (correctly) that it was 22 carat gold.

'Ma's the first person I've known who has actually died,' Julie said, smoking thoughtfully. 'I don't count the girl at school who died on holiday.'

'What happened to her?' He was relieved that he did not need to go on being sympathetic. It made him shy, and anyway he had never set eyes on Julie's mother.

'Her name was Fenella something. She and her aunt were staying in Sicily, and there was a storm and they were both carrying umbrellas.'

'And ...?'

'And,' said Julie, trying to keep a level voice, 'they opened them and were blown over a bridge. We made up awful rhymes at school: "Auntie and poor old Fenella, both opened a handy umbrella ..."'

She began to laugh, then said 'Oh hell' and started to sob.

She kept saying, 'Take no notice, don't take any notice', while Harold tried to catch hold of her hand. She pushed him away, crying and scrubbing her eyes until they were red-rimmed.

'I'm okay now. Tell me about your work in the City. Talk about stocks and shares or something. Please. Be really boring.'

Her tears rent his heart. When unflappable people wept it was much, much worse.

They finally drew up at a small house in a row of small houses with wicket fences and bits of gardens. Some of the gardens were cared for, some were a wilderness. The house Julie was visiting had an over-smart garden – the lawn had practically been hoovered. Straight rows of Julie's most hated flowers, scarlet salvias, burned all round it.

She jumped out of the car. 'Give me an hour. And thanks, Harold.'

All Julie's charm was in the gesture as she leaned towards him, smelling of French scent and gave him a brief kiss.

Harold drove to the Lord Napier and went into a too familiar saloon bar.

The front door of the house was opened at Julie's ring by a woman who did not smile on seeing her.

'Hello, Connie,' said Julie, 'I'd like to see Pa, please.'

'He's busy.'

Julie's stepmother had given the identical reply ever since Connie and Frank Bryant married. Julie was the only one of the sisters who called to see him.

If it is true that divorced men, if they remarry, choose the same physical type of woman, to such an extent that a much married man will have a series of wives closely resembling each other, Frank

Bryant was the exception. His second wife was short and stocky to Grace's stately height. Her hair was dyed, her jaw was big, her eyes hazel and calculating instead of a somewhat vacant blue. Connie was a senior teacher at a big local grammar school for girls. In Hornsey she was admired and deferred to and this gave her an attractive authority. She knew she was popular. Frank Bryant was the only man who had discovered how exciting she could be in bed.

Connie's very faults, excessive jealousy of his previous life, rudeness to the only daughter with the guts to keep in touch with him, and a habit of denigrating Grace to other people ... Frank liked all those things.

He always disagreed with her about Grace – which was only fair. But he was flattered, and Connie made him laugh. Julie thought her 'a rude cow' but was accustomed to the glare and the manner, and simply walked into the cramped house and without more ado shouted 'Pa!'

Her father appeared from the front room where he had been working. He had retired from his engineering firm the previous year, but they still consulted him and paid for his knowledge with ungenerous cheques. The miserly amounts always made him grin and exclaim 'God bless my soul'.

'There you are,' he said, seeing his daughter, and held out his arms. She flung herself into them. Connie turned on her heel and marched back into the room where she had been marking exercise books. Piles of them lay on her desk. No sooner was one lot completed than another appeared, as in a nightmare. Connie waited for father and daughter to go and then slammed her door.

'Come into the back,' said Frank. He put his arm round Julie's shoulders and they went down a passage to a smallish room with French windows overlooking a slightly larger garden. It was as well cared for as the front but with roses instead of salvias. He shut the door. It was always like that, thought Julie. Two doors between Connie and herself. Fortunately.

He sat down and patted the sofa beside him.

'How's my favourite lass?'

He was big and ruddy, familiar and kind, sensible and lost to her. She took one of his great broad hands, held it tightly in both of her own and gasped, 'Ma's dead.'

She told him in two sentences. In the last few days she and the other girls had said the same thing to friends, over and over again. But it was infinitely worse telling him because she knew he had a corner of love for Grace somewhere. He had treated Grace badly, and she in turn had been as merciless as Connie. Everybody was to blame. When he heard the news he shuddered. His eyes brimmed.

'Oh Pa. Don't. Please don't! It's such ages since you and she –'

'What's that got to do with it?' He released his hand, pulled out a handkerchief and blew his nose with a trumpet noise. He scrubbed his eyes just as she'd done in the car. They had gestures in common.

Sitting close, they talked about Grace. Frank understood Julie by instinct more than knowledge, and knew not to let his grief show again. He knew Julie was afraid of such things. He remembered her as a child when they were on a steamer going to Greenwich, and the tide in flood. Eyes enormous, she kept saying, 'Oh Pa, I know I shall fall in.' She was a mixture of the reckless and the cowardly and the riptide of grief terrified her.

'So what's going to happen to you girls?' he said, when they had ceased to talk very kindly of Grace. 'You'll be wanting some help from me, I shouldn't wonder.'

'Of course we won't.'

'Is – I mean was – your mother badly off? I managed to give her a bit, of course, but her family were against her after the divorce, and I think her Dad cut her off. I never knew how she was fixed about things. She was very close.'

'Ma thought it common to talk about money.'

'That's true. And she liked a secret, Grace did.'

'I'm sure she didn't have much,' said Julie, 'It was torture trying to get a fiver out of her.'

They both laughed.

'I must come to the funeral, Julie. You'll be sure to let me know? The others –' he always spoke of the three like that, 'won't like it. They gave me the frozen face at Viv's wedding. How's Carlos? I liked that chap.'

63

'Oh! You don't know! Can I have a cigarette?' Smoking furiously, she told him about Viv's marriage.

Her father looked grave. Being with him, conscious of him, gave Julie a sort of comfort. He had thick white hair which grew like a brush straight up over his head. You could run your fingers across the top and it bent like wire or heather and sprang up again. He had steady grey eyes and a Northern accent. And the Yorkshire virtues and vices. He was plain-speaking and honest. Red blood flowed in his veins and when Grace's lack of interest in sex chilled him, and Connie Holt set out to catch him, she found it only too easy.

Hidden in his big solid body was an Anglo-Saxon romanticism, a poetic soul, a tender foolishness as well as an intense pleasure in sex. Connie responded to every one of those things; she relished them, and was moved as Grace had never been by the contradictions in Frank. She was infinitely clever in his arms. He was haunted by a bad conscience at losing his children, but somehow Connie was the reason that he never saw them after the divorce. She had him in thrall. She was possessive, jealous, amorous. He had the strong man's weakness and when it came down to it, he fell in love.

The story of Viv's troubles worried his Yorkshire conscience too. Was it his fault in some way? His bad example? Viv did not know that two men, her father and her priest, took on the responsibility for her broken marriage.

When Frank said to Julie that he must be partly to blame, she shouted, 'Pa, you really are a fool!' and burst out laughing. Connie came into the room.

'What's the joke?' she asked, with a look of plain dislike.

'Nothing, nothing. Golly, I must fly. I've got Harold waiting. I bet his car's outside again.'

'I did see a car hanging about,' from Connie. 'Want to ask him in?'

Julie did not bother to answer the ridiculous invitation.

'I must fly,' she repeated, gave her father a convulsive hug, scarcely said goodbye to Connie and ran out of the house.

After she had gone Frank told Connie of Grace's death. His wife was struck dumb: at Julie's laughter, at the unexpected gift from fate, at her own confusion of feelings. She did not know that Julie was already missing the only person in her life whom she could shock and whose disapproval she had enjoyed. Connie in her turn was going to miss her rival and her enemy.

'What happened?' asked Harold, who had been patiently waiting. Julie had been a long time.

'He was upset.'

'He left your mother though, didn't he?' Harold was negotiating a crowded high street.

'So he did, and shut up.'

But she relented and allowed him to buy her a lobster mayonnaise dinner at a smart restaurant facing Victoria Station. The orchestra was playing 'Ukelele Lady'. The restaurant was empty, waiting for theatre audiences later on.

'Thanks for looking after me, Harold,' Julie said, as she caught his yearning eye.

'Any time, Julie. Any time.'

The old Bryant order of precedence, each girl lining up to wait her turn, Viv first, Isobel last, did not hold during the days after their mother's death. The sister who became temporarily the head of the family was Claire. Everything was organized by Claire, and very well too. Viv, as Claire pointed out not unkindly, was something of a broken reed. Viv was inclined to agree, although Isobel had rushed to her defence.

'It's true. I don't seem to be much good at coping. And I'm so grateful to Claire for getting everything done.'

Claire immediately looked pleased and self-deprecating, and took up the baton again with a will. It was she who decided that the girls must wear black. Some of their clothes were taken to the dyers. All four sisters then appeared 'like female undertakers' said Julie, wriggling into a tight black skirt; a good many of the clothes were somewhat shrunk. It was Claire who took over the organization of the funeral. She invited a hundred and fifty people – friends who lived locally, relations the family had not seen for years – to the

Catholic church. Telephoning, letter-writing, she forced her sisters to help. It was Claire who chose the hymns and went into Brighton to the most expensive florist to choose beautiful wreaths. The sisters each sent a wreath and were obliged to write their own message on it. They did so one evening in silence.

How strange, thought Isobel, as she carefully wrote, 'Darling Darling Ma, how I miss you and always will', I am writing to the dead.

The evening before the funeral when Claire was counting the acceptances, ringing the caterers and making sure that everything had been thought of, Julie came into the drawing room.

She said casually, 'I've asked Pa.'

Claire turned round very suddenly and said in a cold sharp voice, 'What have you done that for?'

Julie folded her arms. 'You planned to leave him out, did you? And did any of you remember to tell him that Ma is dead? *I* did. Have you thought of him once since it happened? And now he's not to come to her funeral. Sometimes, Claire, you make me sick.'

The twins glared at each other, looking very alike. Viv and Isobel said nothing, which annoyed Julie more.

'Well,' she burst out, rounding on her eldest sister, 'You're very quiet all of a sudden. Have we no opinion from you?'

'I suppose Pa ought to come,' said Viv, after a pause.

'Isobel?' Julie was mustering allies.

'Yes. I think so. And anyway, poor man –'

'Don't talk rot!' burst out Claire, angrily. 'Poor man indeed. Ma couldn't stick him. He deserted us. She always said he broke her heart. She wouldn't want him at her funeral. Don't you believe one should respect the wishes of the dead? I shall ring and tell him not to come.'

She went out into the hall and picked up the telephone, but Julie, in a melodramatic gesture which made her think of a heroine in a film, slammed her hand down on the telephone.

'Oh no you won't. He wants to come. I went to see him and he wants to come. He's our father, Grace's husband, and you're going to be civilized about it. Family wars are hateful. Anyway, I rang FRF and he agrees with me.'

66

Silence like thunder greeted this announcement. Claire was still furious, Julie triumphant. Nothing more was said and fortunately Julie went out that evening. Claire did not speak about her defeat, but was very sharp with the other two.

The funeral went off almost too well. Had Claire worried about her father's behaviour? Had she thought in her middle-class way that his presence would be an embarrassment? He arrived at the church in good time, darkly dressed, rather distinguished, and with a black tie. He looked serious and solid and, in a way, grief-stricken. Even Claire could not fault him. When the four daughters trooped up the aisle in the wake of the coffin, the bridesmaids of death, Frank followed at a slight distance.

Afterwards, at the reception at Woodlands, Claire only caught sight of him once, talking to Julie. He did not say goodbye when he left.

With the funeral over, a strangely busy series of days followed. There were innumerable letters to answer. Claire, who forced the others to help with these, felt extraordinarily tired when every-thing, at last, was done. Her poor mother's clothes had been given to the church, the old-fashioned bedroom tidied and emptied, the smell of Grace's lavender scent gone because the upstairs windows were open all the time. A sort of lull, a loss of purpose, came over the house. Everybody felt it. Viv was wrapped up in herself again; Isobel reluctantly agreed to return to her shorthand and typing classes. Julie lounged about, saying that Michou's at present had offered her no work. Claire was glad, one weekend, to take their mother's car and drive to Brighton. It was a sultry August day and she had arranged to have supper with an old schoolfriend. She called in at St Gregory's and found FRF at home.

'You're in luck. I was just off to call on one of my old ducks,' he said, taking Claire up to his study, untidier and dirtier than ever.

Claire wrinkled her nose. 'Doesn't Mrs Duffy ever bring a duster into this room?'

'Over my dead body. She can waste the parish money on Vim and furniture polish anywhere else. She can clean the altar brass until it blinds me. But she keeps out of here. I told her – just let me catch you crossing the threshold.'

'It is absolutely filthy,' said Claire, flicking at a chair with her suede gloves.

'No harm in a bit of dust.' He blew on a pile of prayer books, raising a small storm. Then he looked at her questioningly.

'Well, Claire? Come for some religious advice? Or would it be for a glass of my best sherry?'

'Neither, thank you, FRF. I'm having supper with Peggy and Jim and they don't –'

'Drink. I see. So if you arrive ponging of sherry they'll think you've taken to the bottle.'

He poufed himself a whisky and they sat down, Claire somewhat gingerly. He leaned back in his chair – it sagged and bulged – and studied her. Neat as a lady-in-waiting. He admired her. She was not his favourite, but she amused him and he approved of her strong will. Since Grace's sudden death he had often remembered that trait of Claire's with relief. The girls needed somebody with sense.

'How are things at Woodlands?'

'Not good. My sisters keep going round like chickens after their heads have been cut off – still running. Does that really happen? Don't tell me, FRF, it is very disgusting. Anyway, they're totally disorganized and Viv is the worst.'

'Does that surprise you?'

'I suppose not. She will have to sort herself out, though. I'm sure she'll go back to Carlos in the end.'

'Will she?'

She looked disapproving. She had imagined that Grace's death would alter what she considered was the priest's shocking laxity about her sister.

He lit a cigarette and watched the smoke curling up in a straight line.

'What do you know about the marriage, Claire? As a matter of interest?'

She was on her mettle. 'Not enough. But the facts are there.'

He drew on his cigarette. He was sardonic and self-sufficient, the

68

last person, thought Claire, you could imagine as a priest. He was as handsome as an actor. Whatever you expected was never what you got from FRF. That was a strong part of his attraction. Or had been until now.

'I'm not going to argue with you, Claire. So poor Viv is in a bad way?'

'Yes. Quiet and inward looking and pinched in the face. Julie's getting over the first shock. One can almost see her recovering, although I've asked her twice when she's going to start doing her mannequin work again and she only shrugs. She ought to go to London and see them,' said Claire in the respectful voice she used when talking of employers. 'She's now developed a new admirer who is apparently over forty and divorced. Imagine. I don't know what one can do about Julie. We used to be such friends.'

'Let her rip for the present.'

Claire stared at her well manicured nails.

'Yes,' she said, meaning the opposite. 'Then there's Isobel. She keeps bursting into tears and rushing out of the room. I don't think I've ever seen anyone cry as often as Isobel does.'

'Not very sympathetic, Claire.'

'Father, she wallows. It isn't as if she and Ma were particularly close. I'm sure she got on Ma's nerves. All that stuff about wanting to be a painter – poor Ma had to hide the paint-box sometimes to force her to do her homework. She and Ma were never really comfortable together. Isobel just wasn't Ma's type.'

Which makes it all the more admirable that the child still mourns, thought the priest. All he said was, 'So, what happens next?'

'We must get back to work. I've started again, my boss was very good about my weeks off. Isobel's at college, and about time too. And I've told you about Julie. Which leaves Viv. She'll have to write to Carlos and –'

He held up his hand. 'Leave that bit.'

'You shock me sometimes, FRF.'

'I'm glad to hear it.'

After a moment she turned to practicalities, which made her

69

more comfortable. 'We've decided to keep Woodlands for the moment. At least it's somewhere for Viv and Isobel to live, and Julie and I are always back at weekends and sometimes during the week. We've no idea if we can go on affording the house. Did our mother have any money? Probably not. You remember how she went on all the time about being broke ...?'

A pause.

'If we do have to sell, where does that leave Isobel? Viv's twenty-nine and, yes, yes, I know you want me to shut up but she *can* go back to her husband. Julie and I could share inexpensive digs somewhere, I suppose, even if we do fight. Isobel's the problem. So young. And young for her age. Every time I think about how things are, I come back to Isobel.'

'I somehow don't think you are going to need all that worry over Isobel,' he said.

He went over to straighten the rosary round one of his photographs. It was of Isobel herself. Recently he had added studies of all four Bryant girls. Isobel looked out at him with a merry smile. As for Viv in her wedding dress, she was seen through the fashionable mist of a photograph by Lenare. He straightened her rosary too. Apart from veils, lilies, white satin, there was another element in Viv's picture. It was bliss.

He returned to the empty fireplace and stood with his legs slightly apart, grasping his glass. Sunlight from an arched window high above his head danced with dust.

'Don't make important decisions yet, Claire, about Woodlands or anything else. Not until you've talked to that fellow, is his name Russell?'

'Ma's solicitor. He's coming tomorrow as it happens. We haven't seen Ma's will, of course. He's bringing it with him. He said there'll be various things to settle.'

'Like Grace's jewellery.' Freeman smiled. 'One of my old ducks died and left me all hers. Poor old dear, she had nobody else to leave it to. It's over there in that velvet box. Damned if I know what to do with it. Stuff my old friend probably wore when she was doing the polka. I suppose I'll have to sell it and give it to the church

70

building fund. Take a look.'

He indicated the jewel box which had been on his desk for three months. Claire looked more cheerful. She took out the items one by one and laid them on the desk in front of her. Link bracelets, gold bangles covered in seed pearls. Big half-hoop rings of rubies and garnets. Brooches shaped like stars. Mourning brooches enclosing photographs of men and women who were long gone. Earrings too.

Claire sat playing with the treasures like a magpie picking over the brightest.

'Well, what would you like?'

'You don't mean I can have something?'

'One item. Don't want to make you greedy or annoy the others. Take your pick.'

Deliberating, hesitating, Claire finally chose a pair of opal earrings.

'Aren't they bad luck?' he said, as she fastened the little greenish stones at the end of gold chains in her ears. They gleamed with blue and orange fire.

'Not for me. My birthday's October and opals are my birthstone.'

She shook the jewels, smiling and awaiting his approval.

'Very pretty.'

'*Thank* you, FRF. They're lovely!' Claire admired them in a tiny mirror in her powder compact.

'Now stop primping. I'm glad you called in this evening, it saves me a journey to Woodlands. I have a shock for you. Brace yourself.'

He need not have bothered to give this advice. Nobody could be more poised than Claire, who had returned to his disreputable chair. Most people, certainly her sisters, would have reacted to the warning by worried looks and questions. Claire, enhanced by opals, merely raised her plucked eyebrows.

'My shock,' he said, 'is to do with your mother's money.'

'You mean there isn't any. I'm not surprised. So the only thing we can do —'

'On the contrary,' he interrupted, 'I estimate there is a great deal.'

She gave a little laugh.

'That can't be true. You know how she grumbled about it. She

71

used to have kittens every time the telephone bill came in. She really did go on about the cost of almost everything, FRF. She must have told you how she worried.'

'What has that to do with having money, Claire? You're supposed to be a worldly young thing, you go out and about. Surely you know by now that it is the rich who shout over the gas bill. Some of my old ducks will scarcely buy themselves a pint of milk. One poor soul slept with two thousand pounds in gold sovereigns sewn into her mattress. She lived in a tumbledown old house with a leaking roof. It was the lumpiest mattress you can imagine, and the undertaker only discovered the money because the stitching was coming undone.'

'We're talking about Ma,' said Claire.

'You do like to stick to the point, don't you?' he said approvingly. 'The fact is I suspected for a long time that Grace was comfortably off, and more recently that she'd become wealthy. When I touched on the subject, of course, she became quite indignant and denied it. I imagine a lot of money to Grace was merely seen as a nest egg in case of hard times. You remember when your grandfather died?'

'Of course. We never knew him. He didn't approve of Ma's marriage and apparently he got even worse when poor Ma divorced Pa.'

She looked at him strangely; she was sure he had his facts wrong.

'Yes, yes, we know all about that,' said the priest impatiently. Poor Grace, how boring she had been over both her husband and her father. Sympathy was essential to her, she fed on it and was never satisfied. Hungry for a listener, did she ever hear a word the listener said in reply? Grace had bored Freeman about her father casting her off, and later about Frank leaving her. For the first few years Freeman had been very kind. It had never been enough. She could not forget. Could not forgive. Kindly, hospitable, soft-hearted to her friends, Grace was completely unforgiving. Now and again the priest, half from duty and half from mischief, pointed out that to refuse forgiveness was a sin. Grace looked straight at him and said outrageously, 'I forgave Frank long ago.'

72

She made the same bold and patently untrue statement about her father. Freeman had noticed time and again that she behaved to Frank as her father did to her.

'Your grandfather had a good deal of money,' he continued to the silent and tensely attentive Claire. 'Copper, remember? After he died, Grace inherited, although she wouldn't speak about it. But she let things slip sometimes which made me guess she had become wealthy. She also put her affairs into the hands of a clever broker and I had a strong impression that your mother's money in the last few years had been breeding.'

Claire looked blank. It was her expression when she was thinking furiously.

He watched her with interest. In his curious life, riches and poverty were the white and black queens on the chessboard. He knew rich and dubious people, rich and honourable people. He knew men whose money-morality was probably appalling and they were the ones who made him laugh. They were certainly the ones who gave him tips at the greyhound stadium. He also visited houses which stank of dirt, no better than Victorian hovels, where mother, father and half a dozen children ate only one meal a day.

He did his best – he himself was not poor – but there were many cases where charity was not enough. What was needed was to right wrongs. The going was tough. Despite or because of his religion, he did what his conscience told him, but refused not to enjoy himself. He once said to somebody – was it to Grace? – 'I believe God meant us to be happy.' At the time he thought it sounded glib. Yet he half believed it still.

Watching the beautiful girl, with her blank eyes in which pound signs invisibly shone, he wondered about the effect of money. In a sudden unexpected prayer, he implored heaven that the Bryants would not be harmed by so terrible a gift.

'Well?' he said.

She did remind him of her mother. Claire smiled without humour.

'We'll just have to see, Father, won't we?'

'And there's a big chunk of philosophy.'

73

The family solicitor had been chosen by Frank years ago; he was correct and prissy and exact; people felt they could trust Robin Russell with their lives. The same could scarcely be said for the broker whom Grace had employed after the divorce. Arthur Glossop – Russell found it difficult to bear this man – wore too much brilliantine on too much hair and had an ingratiating smile. But he was clever and quick-thinking and already, at the age of twenty-nine, having some success. Grace had met him by chance through Father Freeman at a dinner dance at the Grand Hotel in Brighton. Glossop had made a fuss of the stately middle-aged beauty; she could not help being rather flattered.

She asked the priest later what he would think if she gave the management of her financial affairs to Glossop.

'Robin Russell is so boring and I never understand a word he says.'

'Steady as a rock, Frank used to say.'

'But shouldn't one keep an open mind?' said Grace, who never did any such thing.

Freeman rubbed his nose. He looked dubious.

'I've met young Glossop a number of times and I often think he'll go far. But he does remind me of a door-to-door salesman.'

'You mean he is not a gentleman?'

'Oh Grace,' he said, laughing, 'I mean you might find his advice on the rash side. You don't like risks.'

She bridled.

'Everything he told me at dinner the other night sounded very convincing. And of course I will consult Robin Russell before I do anything rash.'

She liked the word.

'I don't see why you shouldn't give him a chance, in that case.'

The Bryant girls had met Robin Russell now and then when he came down from London to see their mother. She would give him lunch or tea and was always pleased to see him. They had never set eyes on Arthur Glossop. Russell telephoned Claire to suggest he should bring the broker with him on his visit to Woodlands. After the appointment had been made, Claire decided that all her sisters must be present. And wear black.

74

'Not again,' groaned Julie, who had been contemplating a visit to the dustbin with her funeral dress.

'Claire is right, it will look better,' said Viv, entering the dining room at breakfast time.

Claire gave her elder sister a rare look of gratitude.

Julie made a hideous face. This morning she was in a jazzy suit and looked the part of a Mayfair mannequin.

'It's the last time I shall ask you to do this, Julie,' said Claire in righteous reproach.

'Okay. Cool down.'

When Isobel heard she was to wear black she said, 'Oh, poor Ma, poor Ma,' in a choking voice and rushed once again from the room. Viv followed to comfort her. Claire, left alone behind the coffee pot, could have knocked all three sisters' heads together.

She was glad she hadn't mentioned what FRF had told her about their mother having money. There was no point in raising their hopes – they would only be tiresome if things came to nothing. Besides, the news, good or bad, was arriving this morning on the 10.30 train.

The quartet gathered in the Chinese drawing room to wait for the solicitor. Black suits them, thought Claire, as well as being a gesture of respect. They sat around in attitudes typical of them, Viv staring into space, Isobel covertly turning the pages of a book on Whistler, Julie collapsed on to the floor.

'Do get up. This isn't a cocktail party.'

'Keep your hair on.'

Julie scrambled good-naturedly to her feet. Her sister only really annoyed her when they discussed their father.

Of the four, Julie was the least affected by Grace's death. Viv had been shattered anyway and the loss of her mother was simply a further darkness in her heart. Claire felt weighed down with responsibility. Isobel cried. This left Julie, friendly and selfish, funny and feckless. She had jumped into a new love affair with a forty-year-old divorced man, George Silver, on the day after the funeral. She hated things which made her heart reverberate and the lazy world-weary George did not touch a string. Claire had met Silver and disapproved.

75

She looked critically at Isobel who had shifted her position, the book still on her lap, and was dangling her legs over the edge of an armchair. Her skimpy black dress had slightly shrunk from being dyed and Claire could see a petticoat hem, torn, and a suspender. She went over and pushed her back into a sitting position. Isobel did not protest but looked surprised.

'Your petticoat needs mending,' said Claire in a schoolmarmish voice.

'Sorry, I caught it on a nail.'

A guffaw from Julie, 'How could anybody –' Then the four girls stiffened like dogs hearing a door slam or a familiar voice. It was a taxi stopping at the gate.

Claire went to the front door, returning a moment later with the short figure of Robin Russell. He wore gold spectacles and his clothes were of the expensive Savile Row kind which only an expert eye recognizes. Russell greeted the sisters and introduced his companion, the rangy and ingratiating Arthur Glossop, who grinned and said in a slightly comical tone, 'Ladies!' Russell shot him a quelling look.

Everybody sat down and Viv fetched coffee. Russell talked for a moment or two to Claire while Glossop stared round the room with unabashed curiosity. He spread his papers busily on a small Chinese lacquer table in front of him. Julie could see he was dying to speak first. Russell forestalled him. He, in turn, opened his despatch case.

'We are here, of course, to talk about the late Mrs Bryant's will.'

He droned through a few bequests. To the local church. To the daily help. Five thousand pounds – Julie shot Claire a startled look – to the Reverend Francis Robert Freeman. Then came the real news. The solicitor told them just how much, as the phrase went, their mother had been worth.

The two men stayed for over an hour and after the first staggering announcement and discussion about the bequests (Grace had also left the priest her French clock), it was Glossop's turn.

He had been looking forward to taking the stage and did so with

76

the ease of a man far older. He explained the reason for the very large sums of money their mother had left. It was due to investments in American shares. These had risen sharply for the last two years and she had invested a good deal of her capital in the United States on his advice. 'I flatter myself,' he said once or twice. He smiled too much. His manner was over-confident, but Claire at least saw that he had something to be pleased about. He had taken their mother's money, as FRF had said, and made it breed. He'd invested with daring, and it had paid off wonderfully.

The talk went on for too long; Viv began to long for the two men to go. She wanted to be with her sisters. She wanted to sort out her thoughts and hear theirs. At last Robin Russell stood up, shook hands all round, stopped Arthur Glossop from getting into a jokey conversation with Julie and hustled him out into the hall. A taxi, ordered by Claire earlier, was waiting. She went down the path to see them off.

The moment the front door shut, Julie gave an errand boy's whistle. She spread her arms wide.

'We're rich! We're rich!'

Viv and Isobel were so solemn that she burst out laughing.

'You look as if you've been socked on the jaw.'

'That's how we feel,' said Viv.

All Isobel did was pick up a pencil and twist it round and round, her mouth slightly open, showing her small teeth.

'Fifty thousand quid each,' said Julie. 'And boy, am I going to splash it around.'

'I didn't exactly understand Mr Glossop,' said Viv.

'Nor me,' said Isobel helplessly.

'What is there to understand? Ma inherited a lot of cash from our grandfather, and she never told us, of course. She moved brokers and – amazingly enough – put her affairs into Glossop's hands. He advised USA bonds. They've shot up like fireworks.'

'Mr Russell said,' put in Claire, returning sedately, 'money is absolutely flooding all over America. A sort of gold rush. Even people who were quite poor are making fortunes. Ma's money in American stock is worth five or six times what it was.'

'Rich, rich, rich,' said Julie, doing a dance step.

Claire gave a slight smile. The money, she said, would not come through at once and they'd all have to go to London to sign various papers.

'We will be able to draw on the bank, of course.'

'Aha. That's what we'll do,' from Julie.

Claire sat down. She was amused, happy and relaxed.

'Well, girls. What do you all think?'

'I can't get used to it,' said Viv.

'It makes me feel peculiar,' said Isobel.

'It makes me feel swell,' said Julie.

CHAPTER FIVE

Like sunlight creeping across a wide, dun-coloured landscape, like honey dripped over sour fruit so that it glistens with sweetness, money began to change things. Woodlands was to be sold. With it would go their mother's stately ghost, whom Viv was sure haunted the front bedroom where Grace had lain in her husband's arms, reared his four daughters and spent her final years like a widow.

Of the four, Viv was the saddest to give up her old home. Claire was busy with her own affairs and seeing a good deal of a favourite admirer, Stuart Lockton. Julie was mostly in London, and Isobel – who felt it unsuitable to hide in her room and paint – was under everybody's feet. The day before the move she came dolefully up to Viv, who was in her bedroom making lists, to announce that she wouldn't be around to help with the move.

'Claire is going to stay with Mrs Buffett tonight. She says you'll be glad to have her out of the way.'

'Oh but –' began Viv, glad of no such thing.

'So I rang Mrs Buffett and asked if I could stay too for a few days. I couldn't bear to be here when they –'

'Of course you can't,' said Viv, inwardly shocked at being left with no help at all.

Claire, a tower of strength after Grace's death, had dropped the reins. To be in charge of packing cases did not interest her and Stuart Lockton did. She had stayed on at Woodlands, but was out almost every night, dining, dancing or going to films. She returned

79

with boxes of chocolates and a self-satisfied expression.

As for Julie, when she did make an appearance, she was at her silliest.

Viv had dreaded the arrival of the vans; she was lonely, tired and sad. She could scarcely believe how quickly the ordeal was over. The family home, familiar as her own skin, melted away before her eyes. The removal men – there were four – were professionals and moved terrifyingly fast. Room after room literally vanished, was carried out, dispersed, and gone.

Her own trunks and boxes had arrived months late from Spain and she had sent them ahead to a flat she had taken in Chelsea. When the Carter Paterson vans finally rumbled away, she went through the echoing rooms for the last time, sat down on the windowsill in her mother's bedroom and wept.

She could not bear to go straight to London, and telephoned Francis Freeman. He was pleased.

'It's time I talked to you,' he said heartily. Climbing into the taxi for the station and refusing to look back at the deserted house, Viv wondered if the priest was going to tell her to go back to Spain. She was not afraid of arguments, but depressed.

For the hundredth time, while she stared through the train window, she saw the differences between the hedged Sussex fields and those of the land she'd married and deserted. Had she taken some part of that country into her bloodstream after all? She thought of Carlos and Spain every day and night of her life.

She had received one letter from him, written in Spanish. The burden of the letter was that he did not understand what she had done.

'I can only think that you became at the time a little mad, and will come to your senses,' he wrote. 'It is not my intention to travel to England and fetch you back to my country, Vivien. You know where your duty lies.'

There was not a word of love.

She leaned back against the cushioned seat and thought of him with helpless longing, as a prisoner might think of a feast. Her looks, her unremarkable English looks, delicate as a watercolour, were gone. She was pinched and tired, fair hair lank, red coat draining any colour there might have been from her cheeks. How dull and grey the day was. Spain came back again like scent. Mountainous yet fertile, swept by winds from the Pyrenees which gave a clarity like diamonds. The streets of Barcelona smelled of dust and flowers and the sea.

Brighton, on the contrary, smelled of fish when she left the station. She did not take one of the hearse-like cabs lined up outside but decided to walk. A wind, not from the Pyrenees but the Channel, had teeth, tearing through her coat and gnawing at her hands in her fur-backed gloves. It tried to wrench off her close-fitting little hat.

St Gregory's was a ten-minute walk down steep streets. The gaunt church and presbytery stood on the edge of a slum. Viv was frozen. Hurrying failed to keep her warm. Crossing a road clanging with trams she made her way through the churchyard of a handsome Anglican church, a kind of minor cathedral, then walked up a street past the college where girls like Isobel clattered down the steps. Viv realized with a start that it must be already one o'clock. She had had no breakfast, having spent an hour before the removal vans arrived searching for Julie's diary and Isobel's wristwatch, the loss of both having been telephoned by their owners with wails, earlier. Viv had found the things but forgotten breakfast.

Mrs Duffy opened the presbytery door. Viv was the only Bryant girl the housekeeper respected. Claire was stuck up, Julie no better than she ought to be and Isobel 'half daft, if you ask me'. But Viv was approved, and shown in with a 'good afternoon'.

'Visitor's come, Father,' shouted Mrs Duffy through the study door.

'There you are. You look perished. Didn't you take a cab?' Freeman asked accusingly. The room was so hot and so fuggy from cigarettes that Viv felt giddy. 'Take off your coat and sit by the fire. Let me give you a drink. Well, child, I'm glad to see you. I thought you'd given up your confessor.'

'I haven't been to confession –'

'I'm not talking about the sacrament. I'm talking about you

81

telling me nothing about yourself. We haven't set eyes on each other since your mother's funeral.'

'Claire organized everything for the funeral. She does things so well,' said Viv oddly.

'Mmm,' said the priest.

He poured a sherry and they sat on either side of a fire which had been lit at seven that morning. Nothing was changed from Claire's August visit except for the fire. The jewellery box was still on the desk and so was the dust.

'Staying to lunch, Viv? Mrs Duffy does the chops half raw, but her mashed potatoes pass muster and when I heard you were coming I asked her to bake an apple pie. Surprisingly enough, she can do that.'

'I'd like to stay very much. But I didn't mean to put you out.'

'Why not? That's what a priest is for. Being thoroughly inconvenienced.'

Viv sat in the chair he always offered his guests. It faced his own and was marginally less disreputable, although the cushion which had been yellow was faded to a dirty grey. Many people had sat in that chair. Drunken Irishmen cursing their women and interspersing obscenities with calling on the Almighty: 'The Holy God knows, Father, I never laid a finger on her.' They were believers who split their lives into two, crowding to Mass stinking of beer falling on their knees to pray, and returning home to hit their wives across the face. Such men were given short shrift by the priest. They listened to him. Sometimes.

Today he had a different kind of visitor.

He had not seen any of the sisters since news of their money had broken over their unsuspecting heads. There had been excited telephone calls from Julie and businesslike ones from Claire and his own congratulations. Then silence.

'I left Woodlands this morning,' Viv said, putting her sherry down carefully on top of a pile of newspapers. 'I did feel sad. The others weren't there. They'd all gone. The moving men were so quick. It was terrible in a way.'

'They always do the job fast.'

'I wished it had been slower. I could scarcely take it in. Ma's Chinese furniture going, and horrible spaces on the walls as the pictures were carried out. And I found one of her hairpins.'

'My dear child.'

'I know. I'm sentimental. I wish I was like Claire.'

'People often say they wish they were like somebody else. It isn't true. If the Archangel Gabriel appeared,' said the priest, gesturing to the door as if Gabriel would certainly enter in a human and not an angelic manner, 'you'd not agree to take on your sister's character.'

'I suppose not.'

'And?' he prompted. For there was more.

'I did hate leaving Woodlands. I did feel sad. It was losing Ma all over again. All our lives until now belonged in Woodlands. We grew up, we came home from school, we spent our hols there,' she said, using schoolgirl slang. 'We learned to ride our bikes round and round the house, do you remember? All the time I was in Spain I used to think "at least Woodlands is still there".'

Her voice expired. Conscious of being studied she looked away, fixing her eyes on the bottle of sherry. 'Augustin Blazquez' said a fine gold label, 'Jerez de la Frontera'. She had seen the same label, read the same words, in the Casa Nueva. She met the priest's eyes eventually.

'You're disapproving, Father.'

'I was thinking a young woman who loved her husband would scarcely find it a relief to remember she could always go back to her family.'

He deliberately used the word love.

'I did think it, though. I did think of Woodlands when I was in Spain. I'm sure Ma told you what happened when I was there, I mean how it was with Carlos and me. She hated me leaving him, didn't she? She kept saying, "It will come right. I shall pray". As if that ... oh, sorry.'

'We will overlook your lack of faith in prayer for the moment,' he said dryly. 'And how do we know Grace was not right? What about Our Lord's parable of the unjust judge who gave in eventually to an importunate woman because she nagged at him? If a bad judge behaves like that, Our Lord said, how much more kindly will Our Heavenly Father be when we ask for things. You mustn't blame Grace for asking.'

'I know,' said Viv in a humourless voice. She had lost her power to smile. My hat, he thought, she must be a trial to those lively sisters. What's come over the lass? I will not believe Carlos ill-treated her.

He had a sensation of helplessness when faced with the mess people made of their sexual lives. He was a priest. Fond of women, he had voluntarily given up that part of life, had chosen the priesthood after struggling for months with the appalling gift of a vocation. It had happened in 1915 after a year in the trenches. Freeman had been one of the first volunteers, joining the army in the heat of August when the last blind patriotism played its music to the crowds. Freeman, half Irish, was in London. A man about town, a time-waster, a success with women, a lover of some, a name on society lists. 'We must have Francis, he's so amusing.'

He had fought in the dreadful battle of Ypres when the Germans first used poison gas. He had been gassed, although not as badly as many of his regiment. Invalided back to England, he'd joined a seminary, and begun his training as a priest.

Who said a vocation was a welcomed call from heaven? Freeman had detested the idea, argued himself sick over it, rejected it, jibed at it in his head. 'You! A priest?' His struggles had been useless.

The Great War was history now, and the years which followed had been, still were, the dancing twenties. The brittle attitudes, sparkling and shallow, of the men and women who were not the very poor, seemed to the priest to be the antithesis of the words of the Cenotaph. Lest we forget, said the white column. Let's forget, said the dancers.

All this was ending. The new generation, Viv's generation, carried no unbearable memories. And no nostalgia either for the golden Edwardian afternoon.

Such thoughts did not help him with the quiet little figure sitting at his fireside.

84

'Did I interrupt you, Viv?'

'No, FRF. I just stopped talking.'

'Can I make you start again?'

At that moment, with her genius for bad timing, Mrs Duffy put a grey head round the study door.

'Meal's up, Father. I'll be loving you and leaving you. Sure you can manage?'

It was Mrs Duffy's question requiring the answer 'Yes'. The priest and Viv listened to steps thundering down the stairs and the slam of the presbytery door.

'We'd better go down, Viv. The dear woman leaves it on the table to congeal. Can you swallow a bite?'

She murmured something graceful. He had often noticed her beautiful manners; she meant them too, which was rare.

They went down the staircase to a gloomy high-ceilinged dining room. It was hung with a large print of the Miraculous Draught of Fishes, something which in the past had tickled Julie. A white tablecloth (at least that was spotless) was laid with places for two and there were two plates on which reposed the half raw chops; there was a dish of overcooked sprouts and another of creamy mashed potatoes.

Freeman ate a generous amount, Viv almost nothing. But during the meal, as the winter light filtered through the curtained windows and she was alone with an old friend, she began to talk.

He listened, trying to hear what she said and what she did not. She was modest and never spoke about lovemaking. He had not expected that she would. But from what he could gather, that, at least, had been satisfactory. Apparently nothing which happened in some large carved bed in a large carved house in Barcelona had brought her running home. She had fled from Spain itself: its extremes, its fanatical religion which the priest had seen for himself; it was as fierce as its reverse, a violent atheism. The worldly-seeming man who had carried Viv away to be his bride had not considered the shock of *his* world on her. She was an ordinary young woman under her mother's thumb, a domesticated little creature whose biggest adventures were Hollywood films, part-time

85

work in a lending library, and fending off sexy young men. Perhaps that had been her charm for Carlos – her sedateness.

Viv described the city where she had lived. She spoke of it with a mixture of nostalgia and distaste. 'The streets are so narrow. The houses almost touch each other.'

'But there are the boulevards, Viv.'

'You cannot walk there with your husband. Nobody does. Besides, he was always away.'

'Surely you could have persuaded him –'

'I couldn't. He didn't know what I was talking about. Carlos here in England and Carlos in Spain were not the same.'

She talked of Señora Santander although she omitted the woman's questions every month at the time of Viv's periods. But Freeman with his Spanish friends could guess that too.

'Oh, FRF. It was so like a prison. I couldn't breathe.'

'Did you tell him so?'

'Often and often. He only kissed me and said, "you will grow to love my country". I detested it.'

'Strong words.'

'True, though.'

'And do you detest poor Carlos?'

'I don't want to see him again. He would only try and get me back.'

'I expect he would. So you don't love him, is that it?'

'I don't know.' The tone had a kind of casual despair. '*He* took me there. Left me there. He never said "there is no Spanish word for wife".'

'Isn't there?'

'No. It is "woman". Carlos Santander's woman.'

As she tried to describe the eighteen months she had spent in the Casa de los Arboles Naranjas, she did to some extent succeed. What she told him was different from Grace Bryant wringing her hands about a broken marriage and the disgrace of yet another Catholic in the family being divorced. Grace had been basic, her morality simple. Frank had betrayed her, as she called it. Viv's troubles had none of Grace's certainty or venom and no boring recital of her wrongs. The break was amorphous, there was nothing to catch on to. Carlos was away or out too much. He had discounted his young wife's unhappiness. He'd expected her to behave in the Spanish way and then vanished to the cafés 'to talk politics'. This seemed the sum total of his sins.

Yet, thought Freeman, one could understand the young woman now talking dispassionately of a suffocating life.

When they left the dining room, she insisted on carrying the dirty plates to the basement kitchen, stacking them and leaving them covered with a clean tea towel.

'I suspect you're a treasure,' said the priest, teasing her.

Back in the study, piling on the coal, he said, 'In the good old tradition of the letter on the pin-cushion I suppose you left Carlos a letter explaining your decision?'

'Yes.'

She was uncomfortable. She felt a coward, which the priest wished her to do. At the time all she'd wanted was to flee, terrified that Carlos's embrace could so easily stop her.

'Would you like me to write to him? Tell him I've seen you and you're in good health. That kind of thing?'

'If you think it's the right thing to do.'

'My dear child, that is not the point,' he said impatiently. Why was it that people constantly marched up to him and dumped the scales of justice into his hands? Let alone popping a mitre on his head.

'I'm willing to bet my bottom dollar that since you left you haven't sent him a line.'

Viv replied thinly that Carlos had written and she had answered.

'His letter was horrible. So cold.'

Freeman bit back the desire to shout 'What did you expect?' Pride was the essence, the bones, no, the soul of the Spanish people. Their pride was absolute. It was flawed and magnificent. Viv's desertion was unforgivable because it made Carlos look a fool. What garbled story had he told the friends with whom he spent the long Spanish evenings?

'Yes, I shall write,' said Freeman.

87

She appeared slightly brighter. She had spent two hours in the company of a man who, despite his priestly disguise, was wise and unshockable. He hadn't said he'd pray for her either, and the parable mentioned earlier had been said in a racy way.

'Father –'

'For Pete's sake, Viv. FRF, please.'

'FRF. There is something more to tell you.'

'About your sudden riches?' he said, rallying her. 'Didn't Claire tell me on the telephone that you're thinking of taking a flat in town? You can expect a visitor from Brighton. I must admit I shall be intrigued to see how you girls get on with all the cash Grace poured over you.'

'I'd love you to come and see me. I'll give you the address. But there is something else.'

She hung fire.

'And what's that?' he asked, challenging the silence. He could not for the life of him read what was in her face.

'I'm having a baby.'

'Ah.'

His tone was odd. She was not sure what he had expected, but in her mind it seemed to Viv he gave a satisfied kind of exclamation like a man who saw a game of patience coming out.

He allowed himself a pause. Looking at her very kindly he realized that since she had arrived he had noticed a slight physical change in her. He had put it down to strain but now he saw it was not only that. She looked out of focus, her fine features slightly blurred. It was interesting, it was curious; he had seen it before in pregnant young women.

Viv had clearly come today to tell him just this. In the old familiar infuriating way, she was dumping the scales into his hands again, for all the world as if he were balanced on the top of the Old Bailey. He was to argue with her now, was he? Persuade her she was bound to return to the city of ships, boulevards and gloomy churches? To the imprisoned life, a harem of a life, where her English soul thirsted to break windows? He knew two things: he was incapable of urging that course of action, and probably the girl

88

would never go anyway. She still sat and looked helplessly at him for judgement.

Women, thought the priest, are rarely helpless. In any case, Viv was rich.

'I take it your expecting a baby is going to make no difference to anything, Viv?'

'Do you think –'

'*You* tell me,' he said, handing back the scales.

Viv's face was pleading. He hardened his heart.

'No. It won't make any difference,' she conceded, speaking slowly.

'I thought not.'

She looked into the fire, showing a charming profile, short nose, small chin, a swathe of brownish fair hair.

'Well, well,' he said. 'Despite the sad state of affairs, I must congratulate you. I'm delighted for you, my dear child. Great stuff.'

He came over and gave her a kiss.

He would have been amused to know the effect of their interview on his visitor. He had fairly dumped her problems back into her own lap and simply been pleased that she was pregnant. Yet she felt more cheerful than she'd done for months.

The flat which Viv had chosen as her new home was in a smallish modern block in the King's Road in Chelsea. Some of its rooms had a view of treetops and sky which was what had decided her. She felt she could be happy there – eventually. The apartments were called Roper Court. Many streets and pubs referred to one of Chelsea's most famous and enigmatic residents, Thomas More. Margaret Roper was the favourite daughter who had waited in a rowing boat under London Bridge, to catch her father's head when it was thrown down to her, after it had been stuck upon a pole among the heads of traitors.

Viv hadn't known the historical bit, it was Isobel who had remarked upon it. The youngest Bryant, when not devouring the lives of painters, preferred the most romantic forms of history.

The November day which had begun with the Carter Paterson

89

vans outside Woodlands, and shone dully over St Gregory's, was over when Viv arrived at Roper Court. As she emerged from the lift and crossed the landing to her own front door, she had an idea that she could hear music. She hoped she was mistaken. She put her key into the lock and pushed open the door and the music grew loud. Julie's voice was singing a refrain: 'Hullabaloo-loo, don't bring Lulu, she'll come by herself.'

'Viv's here!' called Isobel's voice, and suddenly, dazzled by bare bulbs – none of the lights yet had a shade – Viv found herself surrounded by sisters and visitors. Six faces and six smiles.

'House-warming party,' cried Julie.

Lines of packing cases had been pushed together to form a long table covered with a cloth. There were bottles, glasses and candles in saucers.

Bustled in by Julie, given a cocktail by Isobel, offered a cheek by Claire, Viv was overwhelmed by welcomes in her own new home.

'We knew you'd feel lonesome,' said Julie, putting on another record, and 'How did it go?' from Claire, arm in arm with Stuart Lockton, and 'I'm so glad you're here at last' from Isobel, pressing her hand.

Viv was so tired. Pregnancy made her tired, and it was a long time since she had found her mother's hairpin in the Chinese drawing room. She tried to smile and look cheerful. She laughed at one of Julie's jokes. But Julie was already a little drunk and was soon performing a kind of shimmy in the middle of the uncarpeted room. Isobel was dancing with a young man Viv did not know, and Claire sat decorously on a packing case, flirting with Stuart Lockton, the man Grace had approved of as 'the most suitable of any who has taken you out so far'.

Gramophone music filled the unfurnished room. The lights were exhausting. Everybody but Viv was having a good time. She found another packing case, this one pushed up against the wall, and sank down on it. Isobel came up accompanied by the stranger, who was ruddy faced with the physique of a boxer.

'Viv, this is Patrick. We met at a party last night. He's a journalist, aren't you, Patrick?'

90

'Half a one,' he said, grasping Viv's hand.

His voice was not Irish to match his name but North Country; its accent reminded Viv of her own father. He was ruddy as a countryman, friendly, and with slightly bloodshot green eyes.

'I've heard a lot about you, Viv.'

'Oh good,' said Viv, faintly smiling.

He was about to add something but the record changed, he lifted his head and said, 'Aha, a quickstep. Would you excuse us?' and scooped up Isobel. They began to fly across the bare floor.

Julie lounged over.

'Good party, mm?'

'A lovely idea.'

'You don't think that at all. You're all out. God, we're a lot of witches. I don't know how you stand us. Look, we'll go. Patrick and Isobel can come with us. George and I are going on to the Gargoyle and Claire can get rid of Stu. Come to think of it, you won't get rid of my twin. She's cadging a bed from you tonight.'

Pale protests from Viv, guilty at breaking up the party so soon, were swept aside by Julie who, the moment she decided upon a good deed, carried it out at once. Her own escort, the elderly George Silver, was told to say goodnight. The gramophone was slammed shut and the records without their paper covers left all over the packing case table. Isobel and Patrick were interrupted in the quick step and Stuart Lockton came over to say a brief good night.

'Good luck with your new home, Viv. May I come again?'

'Please do. Please do.'

It seemed to Viv just then that Stuart Lockton was the only real person in the room. He was solid.

Claire accompanied the group as far as the lift. Viv heard the door clang and the receding sound of Julie's laugh.

Claire reappeared, walking slowly. She sat down, yawning.

'I suppose I ought to get a cab. Mrs Buffett said I could put up there again tonight.'

'Or you could stay here,' said Viv, knowing it was what her sister was waiting for.

'Oh, can I? Yes, I suppose I could. But we'd better clear up first.'

They stacked plates and carried glasses into an empty kitchen, as Viv had done at St Gregory's.

Viv felt giddy with tiredness. She wandered into the bedroom she had chosen for herself. Somebody, it had been Claire, had made up the bed, and grateful and worn she collapsed on top of it, not bothering to turn back the bedcover. Later Claire tapped on the door.

'Can I come in?'

'I'm sure it was you who made up my bed. That was kind.'

'Oh, it was nothing.' Claire looked delighted at being thanked. She unscrewed her opal earrings and sat down at the end of Viv's bed, swinging the little jewels on their gold chains to and fro.

She turned to Viv and they exchanged the smile sisters sometimes give each other. A mute conversation. A kind of chord.

'Wait until you see the house Julie has bought. She's off her head,' said Claire.

'Is it very large?'

'More than that. It's peculiar. Gruey,' said Claire, her word for sinister. 'Somebody told me it was built in 1650 or something, but Stuart says it's much older. He said it's early Tudor and bits are Norman. It's called Dysart House. It used to have a different name but some horrible man lived there in Charles the second's time, he started the Cabal or something, and murdered lots of people in Scotland. He was loathed. Goodness knows how many rooms the house has got. And little half staircases and attics and cellars and panelling everywhere that's so old you can put your finger in the cracks. And rats –'

'Oh, Claire.'

'Definitely mice. Pattering their disgusting little feet over everything and dancing in the passages and leaving – well, you know what they leave all over the place. Julie's thrilled with the house. She says it's a joke and now she can put up all her friends and most of her enemies.'

'Perhaps that's what she wants.'

'I daresay.'

When Claire spoke of her twin, she was wistful and annoyed. She envied but disapproved. As if Claire, thought Viv, could have run away from school, split her bridesmaid's dress up the back at a cousin's wedding by jumping a fence, broken her arm when, visiting one of Grace's sniffy friends, she decided to shin up a tree and ... and what had Julie done since she had grown up? She certainly went about with dubious men. Did she also go to bed with them? Viv preferred not to know the answer to that question.

She was suddenly glad of Claire's company. In both their thoughts was the deserted house which for the first time in thirty years was empty of Bryants. Viv's invisible self went back to Woodlands and walked through the rooms as they had been until early this morning: Grace's piano in the drawing room, Chopin on the music stand, and the piano stool filled with all the music she used to play. There was Beethoven and Mendelssohn and old songs which Grace and Frank had sung together before the Great War. Grace never threw things away. Except her love, thought Viv.

'I suppose I ought to go to bed,' said Claire. 'And you need your sleep after the move. It's nice of you to put me up.'

'Why not stay here for a bit? Until you decide?'

'I'd love to,' said Claire, too promptly. She gave a little laugh. 'Actually I have decided, Viv.'

'Where to live?'

'Who to live with.'

She waited for her sister to be shocked and Viv wasn't.

Claire was piqued. Virtuous from conviction, Claire thought girls who went to bed before marriage were whores – her own word for them was tarts. The subject fascinated her. In her teens she had enjoyed the eighteenth- and nineteenth-century French novels in which beautiful girls took the road to ruin after a high old time in Paris. Manon Lescaut. Marguerite Gautier. Sappho. Nana. All except Sappho had come to a bad end. Julie once pointed out that of course they had, since women in the past couldn't get away with it. That was understood; they were victims. The men, naturally, got away with everything. Listening to Julie's theories, Claire would look down her nose. The punishment of female immorality was deserved, and to have lovers outside marriage ought to be

93

condemned. It was also the sure way to lose any chance of a husband.

Claire was playing with the blanket, running her fingers up and down as she did when practising scales. The tiredness in Viv was so heavy that she scarcely knew what to do with her limbs. She looked at her sister with exasperated affection, wondering if she had the energy to break the news about her pregnancy. With FRF's support there was no reason to dread Claire's easy-to-predict reaction. But oh, thought Viv, I am tired.

'It's very quiet here, considering we're in the middle of London. Your flat's not at all bad, Viv.'

'I like the sky. And the tops of the trees.'

'Julie's only a step away down the road.'

'Isobel is supposed to be going to Mrs Buffett tonight, but Julie's taken her off to some nightclub or other. I hope that's all right.'

Claire looked annoyed.

'Julie's perfectly capable of coping with Isobel.'

'But she's such a baby.'

'She is nineteen. Quite old, really.'

Viv did not bother to argue. Should she postpone telling Claire the news? In the criss-cross pattern of friendship, annoyance, jealousy, rivalry and love, let alone blazing rows, between the sisters, Viv was usually at ease with Claire. Perhaps Viv loved Isobel the most, although when she married Carlos she realized she had lost her. She'd seen it in Isobel's face on the wedding day when she was leaving for Spain. But Viv had been too selfish and too happy to care then.

Claire stopped playing an invisible piano.

'I have some news.'

Viv, about to blurt out 'So have I', stopped herself in time.

Claire gave a surprisingly impish smile.

'I'm engaged to be married. Stuart asked me last week and I said yes. I haven't mentioned it until now because of the move.'

Viv blushed with pleasure, leaned forward to hug and was offered a flawless cheek. She asked the right questions. How long had she known she would accept him? When had Stuart popped the question? With every engaged girl's keenness to bore, Claire went into the details, not of romance, not even a recitation of Stuart's virtues; she said they had decided on a 'pleasant house' just outside Lewes. She and Stuart had discovered it by chance, there were marvellous views of the Downs from some of the bedrooms and the garden was quite pretty. They would marry in four months' time when Claire had had time to get everything organized. There was so much to do.

As clearly as if she had shouted it at the top of her voice was the fact that Claire intended to live at Roper Court until her marriage.

'It's so kind of you to have me. I couldn't possibly get anywhere of my own, could I? I'd been thinking and thinking about whether to accept him; he's been keen on me for ages.' Claire's favourite description of love. 'But of course before we heard about Ma's money I would have had to save for ages for my trousseau. Now it's all changed and – well, Stuart is very nice.'

'I'm sure he'll make a wonderful husband. He adores you.'

'He does, doesn't he?'

In the carpetless room, in a flat not yet turned into a home, with her own uncertain future and an aching heart, Viv had a moment of truly forgetting herself. She looked at her sister and thought Stuart Lockton was lucky. Claire had not fallen in love as if she'd fallen under a train, like all the heroines, all the idiots. Claire would not walk up the aisle feeling she would certainly die of happiness, and look through her veil to see the broad-shouldered grave figure of Carlos waiting for her like a god. Claire would be safe; Viv never would be again.

Claire was still talking about her new house and then, to Viv's perplexity, about horses. None of the Bryants had ridden, although Isobel had been enamoured of two donkeys on the Brighton beach called Cheddar Cheese and Flying Fox. When Grace stopped her from having a fifth ride on one or the other, she wailed for an hour.

Riding was a new line for Claire.

'Stuart says of course we will ride. It's a blessing there are stables.'

'Surely the poor horses won't be able to manage to get up the Downs?'

95

Claire giggled and told her not to be a fool.

She yawned again. Said she really must go to bed. Viv looked rather tired, added Claire munificently.

'I haven't looked into the spare room,' said Viv. 'Have you sheets and things?'

'Don't fuss, darling.'

The endearment was rare among the sisters except when Viv used it to Isobel.

I can't tell her tonight, thought Viv. Long after Claire was asleep, she lay thinking about the child growing inside her.

She continued to feel a lassitude, a slight sickness, and it was Claire, delightedly moving in for the time being, who offered to help – which meant to organize – Viv's flat at Roper Court. Claire thoroughly enjoyed the task. Rooms were soon furnished with various pieces from Woodlands, and new furniture chosen with thought and taste. Two or three times a week Stuart Lockton came by train to London, escorted his fiancée out to dine or to a theatre, saw her home to the flat in King's Road and then returned to Lewes by the last train. Claire took these visits as her right. It was only natural that Stuart should do the travelling.

Apart from being that delightful character – the newly engaged girl – Claire enjoyed spending Viv's money and being gratefully thanked. She was clever and economical; she discussed prices, consulted lists and generally behaved as if Viv's £50,000 were her own. She was in a good mood from morning until night. One evening after dinner with Stuart, she returned to find Viv still awake and reading in bed. Claire entered the room, her long crimson taffeta evening dress making a swishing noise, her face brilliant. She stretched out a pale hand.

'My ring.'

Platinum set with diamonds and shining black onyx in the newest fashion; everything squared and square-cut.

'We're different from our parents, aren't we?' Claire was gazing at her own hand. 'Do you remember Ma's thick wedding ring? And all those half hoops she used to wear. So ugly. Which reminds me, we haven't done a thing about dividing up Ma's jewellery. I must ring Julie and Isobel.'

Approved of by Claire and with reservations by Viv, the youngest Bryant had recently accepted Julie's suggestion that she should live with her at the newly acquired ancient Dysart House. Neither girl had visited Roper Court since this arrangement and Viv supposed they were getting on well, since no news must be good news.

To think of a task with Claire meant to do it at once, and the morning after discussing their mother's jewellery she telephoned the solicitor and her two sisters.

'Julie? Can you come round this afternoon with Isobel? We're going to divide up Ma's jewellery.'

'What fun. George can come too.'

'We don't want anyone else. Just you two.'

'Oh pooh. Why can't I shove George in another room? He's easy. He can wait for me. He and I are going out on the tiles this evening.'

'I don't care where you are going, just bring Isobel. We're not discussing our private business while one of your hangers-on is in the flat,' snapped Claire. She had taken against George Silver, not much older than Stuart, because Julie always referred to him as 'more ancient than God'.

Julie sighed loudly over the telephone, then giggled and said it sounded a hoot, but what were they supposed to do with the stuff anyway?

'You don't suppose any of us could *wear* Ma's things.'

Robin Russell was in charge of Grace's jewellery. Their mother had left it with the solicitor some months before her death. She had retained nothing but her gold watch. It struck Viv like a blow on the heart that nobody, not even Claire, had noticed that.

Julie and Isobel had not been to Roper Court since the packing case party. They arrived at five on a cold December evening, wearing new furs, and in Isobel's case a scarlet woollen cap with a bobble on top. Both girls looked bright cheeked from the icy weather and in good spirits. Apparently, thought Viv, they were getting on. Isobel dashed over to her.

'Julie's given me a real studio! And I've got canvasses. Patrick came with me to Reeves in the King's Road and I bought some oils and loads of the best brushes, and beautiful thick paper and pastels, and I think I'm going to art classes. The joy! Not having to – well – to hide my drawings.'

She looked happy. She looked young.

Julie roamed about the flat admiring or criticizing. She laughed at the white telephone.

'Up to date at last!'

Both Julie and Isobel had been spending money. Claire had been doing the same, but it was Viv's money and on chests of drawers. The other two were wearing stylish clothes; clinging woollen dresses and expensive shoes. French scent hung about the room. Who said, thought Viv, money did not make you happy?

Claire gave a conducted tour round the flat, shamelessly pointing out that all the arrangements had been her own. Isobel returned to sit with Viv and chatter about painting while Julie telephoned George.

Punctual as usual Robin Russell arrived. He was easier with the Bryants this evening. Not only was he free of Arthur Glossop, but when he had to visit a house of mourning he was always nervous. Since he had been a young man, he'd never come up with a satisfactory way of behaving to clients after somebody had died. Sympathy sounded false; he usually retreated into a snappish chill. But now, looking at the four heiresses, he was relaxed.

'Your mother came to see me in chambers, let me see, it was in March, and said –' his voice dropped to solemnity but he caught Julie's scornful glance and continued in a normal tone, 'She said she had been thinking about what she called her bits and pieces. I suggested a list deposited with us, in which she made her decisions as to which daughter should have which piece of jewellery and so on. She disagreed. Her actual words were "the only fair way is by turns".'

'She meant you bung it all on the table and we grab a diamond, turn by turn. That's right, isn't it, Mr Russell?' from Julie.

'Perhaps "grab" is not the word,' he said with a slight smile.

'Oh, I shall grab. I don't expect the others will. Rather fun, though. Shall we begin?'

After a word or two suited to a solicitor's responsibilities, he produced two jewel cases. The girls knew them well. They were of worn leather, the initials G.M.B. in almost effaced gilt.

He unwrapped, arranged and emptied the little velvet boxes which contained the trophies of Grace's life. There were two wedding rings which had belonged respectively to her Quaker parents. There were bracelets which had circled the wrists of women in the 1850's, symbols of love and slavery. There were rings, earrings, lockets, and old gold chains the knots of which Grace had never untangled. Dully shining, the jewellery lay on the dining room table, reflected in its dark polished surface.

Julie and Isobel were childishly amused and took more or less anything which was nearest to them with remarks like 'I must have that huge locket. A picture of Grandpa. Ripping.'

Viv chose things which reminded her of her mother.

It was Claire who held up the proceedings. She poured over the golden pile, picking up and rejecting in a way of which Robin Russell approved. He thought Julie and Isobel absurd and he had never much liked Viv, she was too mousy. But the radiant blonde who gave such attention to the serious matter on hand was his kind of woman.

The game was finally finished. Each girl had a little heap of jewels in front of her. Russell asked for their signatures, was offered a cocktail and regretted he must refuse. He had a train to catch.

Viv took him to the front door and thanked him. When she returned she found Julie wearing gold chains and loading her wrist with bracelets while Isobel neatly packed rings into velvet boxes. Claire had disappeared to her room with her booty.

'That was rather a lark,' said Julie, 'Though what to do with it all? It isn't as if it is worth selling.'

'Don't try to shock, Julie. It is quite boring.'

'I know what you're thinking,' said Julie, wide-eyed, 'That we ought to keep all this rub– all Ma's things – because it would have hurt her if she'd guessed we'd take it round to the pop shop.'

99

'I was thinking it would be nice if you acted out of character sometimes.'

Viv sat down. Julie, quick to react to what was fair, ran over and knelt by her chair.

'Sorry, sorry. I know I show off. I'm so used to men thinking I'm the daring young woman on the flying trapeze. Sorry.'

She took both her sister's hands and gave them a hard squeeze and just then without meaning to, Viv came out with, 'Julie, Belle. There's something – I'm expecting a baby.'

Both sisters cried in unison '*What!*' They blazed with pleasure.

And then Claire came back. 'What's all the noise about? I thought you weren't interested in Ma's things.'

'Viv's having a baby!' shouted both girls again in unison.

Framed in the doorway, Claire froze.

'Yes, I'm pregnant,' said Viv weakly.

Claire came in, shutting the door as if from the ears of non-existent servants. She went to a chair on the far side of the room. The trio waited. Julie interested, Isobel nervous, Viv indifferent.

'How long have you known about this?'

'A week or two.'

'Why didn't you tell me?'

'Why should she?' countered Julie. 'It's nothing –'

'To do with us. How very sisterly you are.'

'Oh do stop behaving like a magistrate. Viv is having a baby. Let's drink to that.'

Claire replied calmly that it was wonderful news and she congratulated Viv. Then, sure enough, she asked, 'Have you sent a telegram to Carlos yet?'

Here goes, thought Viv. It is not only Julie who never acts out of character. She said, mildly enough, 'I'm afraid I am not going to tell him.'

The argument which followed ran on exactly the lines Viv had expected. Claire marched, so to speak, into the light, thrusting her flag centre stage – it flew the yellow and white colours of the Vatican. Viv must be so happy. And this news solved everything. She could sell the flat as soon as possible. Claire almost saw her on to a boat train, there and then. 'It's wonderful,' repeated Claire. 'Carlos will be so very glad to take you back.'

'Take her *back*?' repeated Julie sharply. 'He didn't throw her out. She left. And who can blame her?'

The rhetorical question is often a mistake and it was on this occasion, as it gave Claire a further opportunity to say her piece. Her sister was in the wrong. Viv, her haggard appearance now explained, lay back with a cushion behind her head and an expression which made Claire want to shake her. She had behaved like a perfect idiot. First, she had rushed off and married a foreigner whom she scarcely knew. Then she had rushed back home and left him. And now she announced that she was pregnant. Claire's thoughts did not enter the conjugal Spanish bedroom – she avoided thinking about other people's sexual activities. What she respected was a bit of common sense.

She knew the trio were waiting for her to speak so that they could chorus their disagreement.

'Nobody is to blame,' she said in a somewhat saintly voice. 'Viv certainly isn't and nor is Carlos. I'm sure he is still devoted to her. Viv, you've had a rotten time but having a baby makes all the difference. We're Catholics, Viv. You must go back to him.'

Viv said very slowly, 'FRF doesn't think so.'

CHAPTER SIX

Julie was a butterfly. Or perhaps a grasshopper. She darted from place to place, from friend to friend. She was impulsive and incapable of second thoughts. The offer to have her youngest sister to live with her was made so carelessly that for a moment Isobel scarcely believed she meant it. But Julie laughed and said that of course she did, while the emotional Isobel was too grateful and looked as if she might cry.

The liberty of her money intoxicated Julie. Up until now, with her good looks and her work as a mannequin in Mayfair, she had collected a number of smitten young men, and been taken sometimes to the parties which were now the rage of London. Parties were what Julie enjoyed, and where she shone the most. When she bought a house, her first thoughts were that now, instead of only going to parties, she was going to give them.

Her sister Claire, her friends, her lovers and her rivals all declared, when they heard which house she had bought, that she was off her head. She agreed. It was crazy for a girl of twenty-four to be the owner of Dysart House. That was the point. Dysart was the first and greatest symbol of her money.

Having seen a weatherbeaten 'For Sale' notice in a certain courtyard, Julie had walked into the estate agent's. The tall, balding, irritable-looking man behind a desk had eyed her with disfavour. She looked like an art student.

'I'd like to see round Dysart House,' announced Julie,

controlling a desire to sit on his desk. Grace had often told her men disliked the habit. But it was tempting.

Mr Bernard frowned. Yes, she was a student, up to the usual practical jokes. One of the Bright Young Pranksters.

'I am afraid that is not possible, madam,' he said, returning to the papers in front of him.

'I don't see why not. It's for sale and your name's on the board, which I might add, is lopsided. Quite difficult to read really, and absolutely weatherbeaten.'

'Madam —' said Mr Bernard, shutting his eyes in a martyred way, 'I am very busy.'

'Too busy to show me Dysart House? What you mean,' said Julie with an annoying grin like a schoolboy's, 'is it that you don't think I have the cash. Okay, ring the bank manager. See? I brought a letter. Just in case.'

She handed it to him. Mr Bernard put on his glasses and, as Julie told Harold later, 'That wiped the smile off his superior mug'.

She had seen the house ten minutes ago when walking down the King's Road, and a hunger had come over her. It was a familiar feeling; she had it sometimes when she saw a dress, passed a theatre, even occasionally when she met a man.

Mr Bernard went to fetch some large and somewhat rusty keys. His good manners were now in evidence to the pretty young woman who pranced beside him down the King's Road.

'So you just happened to notice Dysart House?'

'Well ... you can't see much of it, can you? Hiding behind those magnolias. And the wistaria writhes all over it like a snake.'

'Very old, that wistaria.'

'I pushed my nose through the railings.'

'1685, those railings.'

'I can imagine. Everything's gorgeously old. Has the house got a ghost by any happy chance? We could have evenings trying to raise the spooks.'

The estate agent showed her round the house, from the cellars where stone arches proclaimed the ruins of a convent, to attics with cobwebs thick across windows which had not been opened for years. The house was a maze, a mystery of unexpected staircases and sudden doors, large-windowed stately rooms and little parlours panelled like the inside of a cigar box. Julie did not listen when he intoned measurements. She did listen when he informed her that the place had belonged to the Earl of Lauderdale who, he was sure she would remember, was called 'the coldest friend and the most violent enemy that was ever known'.

Julie wanted Dysart House.

'You will naturally wish to consult your family,' said Mr Bernard, shaking hands and giving her the smile reserved for potential customers. He was not sanguine: he'd had so many people looking over the house. In the end they never purchased.

'I'll have it,' said Julie. 'My great friend, his name is George Silver, will do the things. I'll have it, Mr Bernard, so could you take down the skew-whiff "For Sale" notice?'

With her gift for producing the man needed for the moment, she telephoned George. He owned property: houses in Richmond, shops in Streatham. He owned the Brighton hotel where he had met Julie one evening when she called in for a glass of champagne.

Amused by her unlikely choice, Silver visited Dysart House and went over it from the filthy attics to the mould-smelling cellars. He ordered a surveyor's report – it was very bad. Julie didn't care. Armed with the report, Silver negotiated, through Mr Bernard, with Dysart's owner, an eighty-year-old Earl in need of cash to spend his remaining days in Cannes. The old lord was pleased to hear that at last he had a customer, but very cast down when George Silver offered a far lower price than had been set on the ruinous house. But the owner accepted because it was the only offer he'd had, and London fogs gave him bronchitis.

Contracts were exchanged and George went through the documents like a watch-maker with a magnifying glass screwed into one eye. He was attracted to Julie and, at present, would do anything for her. When Dysart eventually became hers, he was amused to see the ingratitude of the young.

With Isobel in tow, Julie moved into her magnificent house. She excitedly telephoned everybody: Claire (sniffy) and Viv (kind);

104

Harold was round with flowers an hour later. George was there of course and a new French friend Claude, and a lot of pretty girls, some of them mannequins and some in London society. Dysart woke with a start from the sleep of centuries.

For a butterfly Julie had strong ideas about the look of things and, helped by Isobel, bought up most of the furniture department at Peter Jones, some antiques in the King's Road and a four-poster she saw in Petworth which cost double its price because it had to be transported in an enormous van. The business of furnishing the hungry old house occupied Julie and Isobel for some weeks.

Viv had mourned the loss of their old home, but Julie was too entertained to give Woodlands a thought and as for Isobel, she was in a trance of gratitude. She had been scared when Woodlands was sold. At nineteen how to face the enormity of wealth and solitude? There was no Grace to disapprove, and no Grace to lean upon; Julie's 'You've *got* to come and live with me in Dysart!' was her lifesaver.

It was Isobel, poking through mildewed books which the Earl had left behind, who learned about the squat crooked-floored, cracked-panelled, money-eating house. It had been built in the early 1600's on the ruins of a nunnery destroyed during the Reformation. It had belonged to unremarkable members of the nobility until the time that Elizabeth, Countess of Dysart, and her second husband, the Earl of Lauderdale, had bought it. Isobel found descriptions of both of them – Elizabeth, a red-headed beauty, 'restless in her ambition, profuse in her expense and of a most ravenous covetousness. A violent friend and a much more violent enemy.' As for her second husband, he was unscrupulous, crafty, licentious and had a will of iron. 'A great gorilla of a man with uncouth body and a shambling gait, a massive head crowned with a disorderly tangle of red hair.'

Julie was delighted with the previous owners, and returned to the subject constantly in their first weeks in the house.

'Both red-headed. But he's the one I want to see. I'm sure he must haunt. Why haven't I seen him?'

'I should look out if you do,' said George Silver, who had called

105

in, bringing two bottles of gin. 'He was a famous lecher.'

'Imagine sleeping with a ghost,' said Julie with relish.

Isobel joined in the laughter, but when, on many nights, Julie was out at nightclubs and would not be home until dawn, Isobel hid under the bedclothes. In daylight Dysart was haunted by the living. George Silver, of course, and Harold with red roses. Julie thanked him with panache, 'Too thrilling', and went out into the kitchen where the roses were thrust into buckets, saucepans and jugs. The poor things never made it into the living room. Julie threw her eyes heavenwards.

'Why doesn't he bring gin, like George?'

'Don't be ungrateful,' whispered Isobel, busy unwrapping.

'I can't start being grateful to Harold!' hissed Julie. 'What for?'

More men than women came through the 1685 cast-iron gates and rang the bell at the weather-beaten, nail-studded front door. George Silver, whose work was either carried out on the telephone or at the Dorchester, arrived at Dysart one bitterly cold day to be shown in by a shy servant in a too-large cap and apron. It was just like Julie to hire a character from the first act of a West End comedy. In the drawing room, where a good fire burned and the brocade curtains shut out the end of the icy day, was a stranger. The young man, who had been sprawling by the fire, got to his feet and in a free and easy way announced, 'I expect you're looking for Julie. She's scampering round the West End buying more clothes. Isobel's upstairs in the studio, if you've come to see her. Name's Glossop. Arthur.'

He tendered a card.

'Silver,' said George, taking it and sitting down.

The man on the other side of the fire gave him a grin. His manner reminded George Silver of a friendly dog. Dogs were optimists, whereas cats were pessimists, every last one of them. A dog bounded up with the certainty that you were a friend. A cat waited to scratch. If you refused a dog some of your dinner, his face retained the beaming certainty that this mouthful or the next, or the one after that, was going to be for him. Arthur Glossop had the same expression.

106

'Julie has told me a lot about you, Mr Silver.'

'Indeed?'

'About your help over the house, and how she could never have managed without you. A tower of strength.'

George negligently smiled. He was forty-five, big, bulky, easy, moneyed. He liked sex but was not hag-ridden by it. He never hurried over an affair. You could not make a rose open faster by messing about with it, the thing was to give it plenty of sunshine. Dysart House teemed with men but George did not mind. Julie collected them like the grass seeds which cling to your coat when you walk through a field in midsummer. If she went to a party alone she would go on to a nightclub with two men. If she dined with friends she invariably met new admirers. She had to fend off married ones who telephoned the next day.

'I promise you, George, I don't do it on purpose.'

He did not believe her.

But the gregarious young man in the cheap suit was not exactly her style.

'Julie's a regular corker, isn't she?' said Arthur Glossop.

'In what way?'

'Likes risks. She reminds me of somebody walking along the balustrade of Battersea Bridge.' Arthur Glossop had seen her do it. 'Frightening her friends. This old place is a risk. Must make a big hole in her pocket.'

'I daresay she can afford it.'

'Oh, she can *afford* it,' said the young man with a knowing grin. 'But we never have enough of the stuff, do we? That's always been my motto in this old world. If you can't be bigger than the other fellow, you'd just better be richer.'

George chuckled.

'The fact is,' said Arthur Glossop confidentially, 'She and I are partners in a manner of speaking. You saw my card?'

'A broker,' said George, finally understanding. 'Can you be the reason, Mr Glossop, for the Bryant family's good fortune?'

Arthur Glossop was delighted.

'I don't like to boast, but yes, I've been some help. I met the late

107

Mrs Bryant some time ago, and she was good enough to employ me – through my firm, of course, but I'm the chief executive. I give financial advice and that kind of thing. To tell you the truth, Mr Silver, I'm a gambler. Not cards or roulette or that kind of rot. Stocks and shares are my game and I've had some success. Quite a bit in the good old USA. You wouldn't believe,' he warmed to the attention of the older man. 'You just wouldn't believe what's happening over there. It takes the cake. There are hundreds of thousands of people who know nothing about finance and are simply gambling with their spare dollars. Stocks and shares are going up like –' he gestured wildly – 'like a thermometer in a heatwave. It's a thrill. A real thrill.'

'I've heard about it from my American friends,' murmured George Silver. 'They're calling them the Boom Years. Everybody's making money.'

'They certainly are. And that's where I come in.'

'Investing Julie's money?'

'No, no, Mr Silver, not just Julie's or her sisters'. I'm advising a lot of people at present. My family. Close friends. Colleagues at work, and so on and so on. Making their money work for them.'

He gestured expansively.

'I like to think that I can help,' he finished.

Refusing to indulge his companion, George lit a cigarette and Arthur Glossop, robbed of more interest or compliments, explained that he had come about some new American bonds on the market.

'Very juicy. I want to give Julie and her sisters a chance to be in on the act. I am buying a big slice myself.'

'Then she's sure to,' said George lazily. 'Didn't you say you and she are already a sort of team?'

'She's a changeable young lady. That's my trouble.'

George remarked that Julie hopped about like a frog in a lily pond. The frog, on cue, burst into the room, arms full of the inevitable parcels. When did Julie return empty-handed? Her face was poppy red from the cold afternoon.

'Hi, Glossop,' Julie never called him by his first name, 'Will you ring for cocktails? George, darling George. Guess what? I've bought a car which looks like a yacht. A great big open yacht. A Sunbeam. Come out and see it. Shall we drive to Brighton and back tonight?'

From the first day she moved into Dysart House, Julie had jumped into the fashionable whirl of parties. She juggled skilfully with the men who were in love with her: the ratty but adoring Claude, a student from the Sorbonne; the middle-aged and world-weary George; the worshipping Harold always there when wanted and usually when he was not. There were other men, rich, attractive, a miscellany of swains. If she went to bed with one or other, nobody knew which and Julie wasn't saying. She and her friends spent their time with a recklessness very like the way in which Julie spent her money. If a place was fashionable, Julie was there on its opening night. If a party was the thing, Julie was the guest who left last. She threw, as the saying was, innumerable parties and poor old Dysart trembled to the beat of jazz. Immune from the painful self-consciousness of many young girls, Julie wrapped her thin arms round her partners and led them into the dance. George, dancing her round the Gargoyle nightclub very late one evening, sang 'Poor little rich girl, don't drop a stitch too soon'.

'Oh pooh!' was the scornful reply.

Whenever she could coax or bully her, Julie dragged her youngest sister along on these outings, but Isobel was growing steadily more reluctant to live Julie's Life of Riley. Despite the possibility of meeting Lauderdale's lecherous ghost, she preferred to remain at home.

With the kind of extravagant gesture which typified her, Julie gave her sister one of the most beautiful rooms in the house for a studio. Julie was free now from bus fares, trains to Victoria and the need to cadge beds from her friends. She was rich. Isobel's most startling inheritance was the time to paint.

She had been scribbling, drawing, painting and throwing away her efforts since she was five years old. She had been a star pupil and won the prize for drawing every year; but when she left school her mother flatly refused to allow her to go to college and study art.

It was a waste of time. What Isobel had to do was to learn shorthand and typing and get a decent job as a secretary. Her sisters interceded. Grace was adamant.

'If she wants to paint, what is wrong with the evenings and her bedroom?'

The north windowed room on the second floor at Dysart had been converted into a perfect studio. Julie was enchanted with her role of art patron, and would have covered the oak planks with inch-deep carpet and the walls with yellow silk, apart from buying her sister an easel, a Liberty's smock and a velvet tam-o'-shanter, but Isobel stuck in her toes. The floor which remained carpetless was soon splashed with paint. The walls were whitewashed, and the only comfort was the coal fire, replenished by the maid toiling up with full buckets. Here, in a domain entirely hers, Isobel started to work, wondering, now that the obstacles had gone, whether she had talent after all.

Julie's slave Harold had introduced Isobel to Patrick Quin, who worked variously for local and national newspapers. From the first, Patrick became Isobel's only steady admirer. And it was he who told her she ought to go to college.

'Perhaps they won't accept me.'

'Don't be naive.'

'They must turn down scores of people.'

'Not somebody who can do that,' he said, pointing at a drawing she had just completed.

During the week following the wildest excesses of parties which had said farewell to the old year, Isobel took his advice. She went to the St Helier College of Art, within walking distance of home and enrolled for her first term.

The teacher was elderly and critical and her fellow students, she thought during the first weeks, much cleverer than she was. Nobody was very friendly either. Returning from college on a pouring wet evening, she went upstairs to the studio to find Patrick by the fire, his shoes drying on the fender.

'There you are. I've been waiting half an hour.'

'I wasn't expecting you.'

'You should have been. Your woman's intuition.'

He liked to tease. Her face was so pretty and so solemn. She stood by the window and the rain beat against it in waves as if it were the sea. The windows, larger than many in Dysart, were a godsend to an artist. They overlooked a garden untangled by the hand of winter, showing only bare trees and sodden grass. The light was fading fast.

Patrick wriggled a toe, wondering if his socks were dry yet. He turned to study her again.

He wanted to take her in his arms, pick her up — she was small and light as a bird — and push her down on the shawls heaped in the corner. He wanted to learn the secrets of her thin little body and to make those dark eyes, so unlike her sisters', swim. All he'd been given so far were schoolgirl kisses.

'May I smoke?'

'If you must.'

'For a woman who stinks of turps I don't see how you can object to a ciggy. Anyway, mine are Three Castles, handmade.'

'All right. But keep still. I'll sketch you before it's too dark.'

'If you must,' he countered, slapping his pocket, and producing an expensive green packet of cigarettes.

Isobel often sketched or painted him, she had bookfuls of haphazard unfinished work. Patrick could never understand it. Journalists didn't start and stop, scribble a few lines, then snap their notebooks shut. They didn't keep unfinished stuff unless it was going to be useful later on. Writing was to be published, facts to be used. He was a good reporter who enjoyed his job and had ambitions to become part of a real newspaper, by which he meant a national. He was an artful interviewer, interested in every single thing about the man or woman who was his subject and his victim. His ruddy face and bluish eyes were full of sympathy and mischief. People liked him and talked to him frankly. He made useful friends and never wasted his work or his time.

Not like Isobel, who drew and painted, sighed, destroyed her work or shoved it away. *Her* subjects developed neck-ache and felt foolish into the bargain. He certainly did.

111

'Turn your head to the left. That's better. Patrick, your nose is the oddest shape.'

'Somebody bashed it when I was at school.'

'How horrid boys are. Did it hurt?'

'I'll say. It poured and poured. You should have seen my opponent's face when he was splashed all over with my blood.'

'Why didn't you use a hanky?'

'What did I want a hanky for? I howled and bled all over him. It made up for the pain. Do you realize noses are particularly sensitive? Like feet.'

'Of course I do and you're not as clever as you think you are. Do keep still or I shall make your nose even worse.' She continued to draw, to stare, and to draw again. Now and then she looked crossly at the window where the winter day was on its deathbed.

'Imagine you deliberately bleeding all over that poor boy. Sheer spite.'

'That's right.'

'I wonder if you'd bleed all over *me*,' said Isobel. She scarcely noticed what she had said. She wore the concentrated expression that came when she was at work. Her bottom lip, full and moist, caught by her teeth as if she were about to bite it from anxiety. At last she sighed and threw down the pencil. 'No. You can *not* look. If you said anything about it I'd only be sick.'

'Oh, you sensitive plant, you.'

She was full of self-doubt. The astonishing luxury, both of a studio and of time, worked against her hope. At school in Sussex the teachers had been proud of her. 'Very good, Isobel. Very nice indeed!' The teacher at Chelsea, a distinguished artist himself, scarcely spoke to his students except to tell them what was wrong. On one horrible morning, looking at Isobel's sketch of a pot draped with a woollen cloth, he exclaimed, 'No! no! no!' Later he showed her how to draw weight – but irritably, as if he thought it was something she should already know.

'Why am I trying to paint?' wailed Isobel when she had hidden away the sketch and they were descending the stairs towards the sound of Julie's gramophone and the usual masculine laughter.

112

'There are so many great artists who achieved unbearably beautiful things.'

Patrick had no time for such talk. He was looking forward to a cocktail.

Isobel leaned on him more than she would admit. She saw him almost daily; he would arrive after work, tug at the bell and come up to the studio two stairs at a time. He was soon the most important person in her life. She confided in Patrick and quoted Patrick to Julie, who didn't much like him. She drew Patrick. She kissed him good night.

She thought often of Viv, her pregnant eldest sister but found little time to visit her. She never felt exactly comfortable with Claire who was the most like their mother. And Julie, to whom she owed so much, was never ready to talk, uninterested in her painting and usually surrounded by noisy friends.

It was Patrick who became the person to whom Isobel felt she could at last show her work. He was encouraging, jokey and affectionate.

'Work is the answer to your problems. Stick at it,' he said.

He had become used to being her model. Sometimes he wrote his interviews, smoked or read the newspaper while Isobel sketched him. At the start of her painting life, everything was grist to her mill. The window of the studio, the cat who appeared from a shop in the King's Road, the maid with the coal bucket, the angle of a door, the oval shape of her own childish face in the mirror. She spent hours in a trance of painting, and although her pencil drawings grew in confidence, her oils were hit and miss. She often took a rag and wiped the whole thing away after working at it for half a day. She began to see that she over-romanticized. Gritting her teeth she told herself she would *not* paint like a little girl.

Apart from college and time spent with Patrick, and haphazard meals with Julie and her set, Isobel went to museums. The geniuses of the past refreshed and disturbed. Sometimes, standing face-to-face with a Turner or a Rembrandt, she would heave a sigh as long and tragic as that of Hamlet parting from Ophelia.

Walking home from St Helier through the foggy streets of

winter, she always saw lights in Dysart House. She opened the iron gates which screamed rather than squeaked and went down a path filled with dead weeds. There was music coming from the house. And indoors was Julie, and George Silver, and Harold, and the Frenchman Claude, and a scattering of girls who giggled and sprawled.

'Belle! Come and hear the latest!' shouted Julie, sitting on George Silver's lap. 'George, tell about what happened last night at the Embassy.'

Isobel stayed to listen and pretended to laugh, wondering how soon she could escape upstairs.

'She's off again,' said Julie, scowling when her sister left them, shutting the door behind her with what Julie considered to be pointed care.

'Is she going out?' asked Claude, who thought Isobel tedious because she rarely addressed a remark to him.

'Up to the beastly studio.'

'You gave it to her, Julie,' remarked George lazily.

He began to stroke her hair. She leaned back against him, almost purring.

'I know. I know.'

'And what is she painting up there in the studio you now wish you had not given her?' enquired Claude.

'I don't know. She never says,' said Julie, for once less than her sunny self. Isobel offended her.

'Doesn't she show you?' enquired Harold, surprised. He was not going to be left out of the conversation. He felt agonized while Julie was sitting on that middle-aged man's lap. And he disliked the French boy who was a conceited know-all.

'My father,' put in a girl called April sitting on the floor among the gramophone records, 'paints water colours. We have to troop into his study to admire them. Torture. Then he gets them framed and they're all over the house.'

'Poor you. I do remember Isobel used to show us her scribbles when she was a kid. Rather fun, they were. Pretty.'

'Oh, if it is only "pretty" she should give up,' said Claude.

114

'Do tell why!' said Julie.

Glad to get her attention, he began to make a speech about 'real art'. The door of the drawing room opened and Patrick's cheerful face looked in.

'Hello, all. Isobel back from college yet?'

Julie sat up, removing George's arm which was draped round her neck. She did not know why among the men who drifted in and out of Dysart, Patrick Quin was the one she had no time for. He got on her nerves. Was it something about his self confidence? Or because he did not seem to be aware that Dysart was hers?

'I presume she is up in the studio, and very boring she is. You can tell her so from me. And while I'm on the subject, shouldn't you ring the front door bell before you march into my house?'

He stared at her, ignoring the young Frenchman who gave a high pitched giggle. The rest of Julie's friends pretended not to listen.

'Oh, I *do* apologize,' said Patrick, in a voice of such sarcasm that Claude gave another more nervous giggle. 'The front door was ajar. I had no idea that I was so unwelcome. I am, I might point out, a friend of your sister's.'

'We can scarcely miss that, can we? I repeat, Isobel is a bore, stuck up in the studio. Tell her I said so.'

'Everything is "boring" to you, isn't it?' he said. His eyes were bright with malice.

'*Dieu*, how rude he is,' from Claude.

'I'd thank you to stay out of this,' said Patrick loudly, turning on him. He couldn't stand the young Frenchman.

Julie sprang to her feet, blushing with annoyance.

'Get out. I'm fed up with you marching in and out as if you owned the place. In future if you want to see Isobel, you can just meet her somewhere else. Go on, get out.'

For a moment the appalled audience waited for him to swear at her. He glared, then gave a laugh and left the room, slamming the ancient door so viciously that he split one of the panels.

Nothing lasted with Julie. She went up later to tell Isobel she was sorry. Patrick did still occasionally come to Dysart, but fell into the habit of taking her away from her work, to drive her to a film or out to an inexpensive meal. When he returned her to the house they stood in the freezing porch and kissed.

'Come up to the studio. Gladys has made up the fire. I told her to.'

'How jolly it is to have money, hey ho.' He put his hand through her thick hair.

'I seem to have got used to it. Money, I mean.'

'I've noticed.'

'Every morning,' she said, snuggling up, 'I wake and have a moment of being scared and thinking what's going to happen? And then I remember Ma's money and I know I'm safe.'

He stroked her hair again. A faint light came from the street through the trees in the courtyard. All he could see was the outline of her pale face and pools for eyes.

'You look very beautiful.'

'Oh good.'

'That's the wrong answer. You're supposed to say, what, this old thing, meaning the fur coat you're wearing.'

'I can't. It's brand new.'

'And would you say, as a matter of interest, that *you* are.'

'Brand new? I suppose I am.'

'I'm not, Isobel Bryant.'

'What does that mean?' she said, smiling in the dark.

'It means I want you. And I have the impression that your answer is going to be "No".'

She opened her eyes wide but not with surprise. He'd declared the same thing before, when they'd lain chastely kissing in his car.

'I suppose I do mean "No",' she said, and caught her lip in her teeth.

Peace between the sisters had been declared but Julie was still irked by Isobel's obsession with the damned painting and called on Viv at Roper Court to grumble. She found Claire as well, the sisters cosily having tea together. Julia felt quite an exile. At her complaints, both Viv and Claire were sympathetic.

'Isobel's always been excessive,' said Viv.

'And you can't say it isn't your fault, giving her a studio,' added Claire.

'How was I to realize she'd go off her head, holed up in the beastly room for hours at a time? How was I to know that was going to happen? I mean, when we were at Woodlands, when did Belle paint?'

'Now and again for an hour if Ma let her.'

'And if she went on longer Ma hid the paints,' added Viv. 'I remember Isobel found them in the music stool.'

'Last night,' announced Julie, pouring herself a drink from Vivien's cupboard, 'she painted the entire night. I went into her room in the morning to borrow a mag and the bed hadn't been slept in; I heard a noise from her studio and there she was looking like death warmed up. Sort of grey and the room like an ice box and paper all over the floor. Our sister is a case. If that's being a painter, God preserve me from a bit of canvas.'

They discussed Isobel's aberration for a while, but nobody came up with a solution. Viv did suggest she could call round and see her, but Julie shook her head.

'Of course, come any time but it won't make a blind bit of difference. I'm clobbered with a lunatic in the place. Oh God. If only she'd cheer up sometimes and come out to a party like everybody else.'

Claire and Viv couldn't help laughing. The subject was dropped.

The two elder girls had been living together at Roper Court comfortably enough. Despite her Catholic principles, despite her desire to interfere, Claire had been forced to accept Viv's pregnancy and do nothing to persuade her sister to return to Spain. It was not sisterly affection but practicality which kept her in Viv's pleasant flat, while her own plans advanced army fashion.

The chance of seeing Julie, a rare visitor and her favourite, was too good to miss. Claire launched into talk of the wedding, her new home, her plans and herself.

'I'm quite excited about the house, Julie. I've been going down to

117

Lewes every week to see about various changes. Our bedroom is too small and I'm having a wall knocked down. It is a tremendous improvement, much more spacious. Then there is the kitchen, one *must* have a decently sized one or we'll never get a cook to work for us. I'm not bothering yet about the garden, but Stuart has some good ideas. He's always wanted a garden of his own,' she added sentimentally.

She forgot that his parents owned acres of garden and her future mother-in-law was an expert on old fashioned roses.

Claire then sprang up and went to get 'the groom's gift to the bride': a tiny, modern, diamond-encrusted watch still in its leather case.

'Not to be worn until the honeymoon.'

Julie duly admired and Viv, who had heard talk of the watch for breakfast, tea and dinner, said nothing.

Consulting a notebook Claire went through various matters she wished her twin to help with: Julie was to be a bridesmaid but so was Isobel. Would Julie please organize her?

'Cripes, you don't imagine I could drag her out of that den stinking of turpentine to have a fitting, do you?'

'Someone has to.'

'Do your own dirty work. Anyway she listens to you.'

'Oh. Well, I suppose she does.' Claire dearly loved a compliment. She went on talking and Julie, sitting on the floor, thought her sister had definitely become worse. She began to doubt if Claire would ever be fun again. Julie wondered, not listening, if Claire ever talked about anything but the wedding and her trousseau and her beastly house. When they had shared a bedroom as girls at Woodlands, quarrelling regularly, Claire had sometimes shown a fascinating insight, flashes Julie never expected. And how she and Julie used to laugh. Perhaps it's all Stuart's fault, thought Julie. What can she see in the stodgy old thing?

He appeared later, bringing with him a spattering of raindrops when he removed his coat, pink carnations for Viv, and a kiss for his future bride who assumed a nesting pigeon look.

'Here's a stranger,' he said, as Julie stretched a thin braceleted

118

arm in greeting. 'What brings you away from the splendour of Earl Lauderdale's haunted mansion?'

None of Julie's men treated her as if they were her uncle or her schoolmaster. She was too kind not to react.

'I haven't seen the old reprobate yet. I live in hopes. I thought I saw a brocaded robe, the skirts of one anyway, the other night at the end of the passage and rushed down to look. No luck.'

Viv shuddered.

'I'm afraid of old houses. Carlos's house is as old as the hills. When I was alone upstairs I was often sure there was somebody in the room whom I couldn't see.'

'It wouldn't be a Scottish lecher everybody detested. Carlos's house would have a priest. White face, eyes burning in their sockets and a huge black hat. He'd be straight from the Inquisition,' said Julie.

'Do shut up,' from Claire.

'They never speak about the Inquisition,' said Viv seriously. 'At any rate, not to me.'

Stuart looked at her and smiled.

'Of course they don't!' cried Julie, 'That's a bit of their past they'd rather forget.'

Viv did not reply. Was there no other subject, when ignorant English people spoke of Spanish history, but the Inquisition and the Armada? Recently she had tried to avoid mentioning her husband's country. What did her sisters or her friends know about it?

'Stuart, I'm sorry to hurry you, but you know how punctual one has to be at the Brookes',' said Claire, getting to her feet. 'Everybody will arrive early, and if we are even five minutes late Lady Brooke will have started the meal. So embarrassing.'

'Don't much care for soup,' said Stuart. He liked his future sisters-in-law and was enjoying a drink and a gossip. As he was bustled out of the room he looked back, to give Julie and Viv a grin of helpless resignation.

'She's got him under her thumb already,' Julie remarked when they had gone.

'Perhaps that is what he likes.'

119

'How can he? Men and women should be equal.'

'You don't believe that. Not with all those slaves you have hanging about.'

'*I* don't make them into slaves! They only hang about because they want to get me into bed.'

'Who is the latest victim?' asked Viv with a tired smile.

'Ah,' said Julie, who enjoyed talking about the subject. 'I met somebody the other night at a Babies' party. Most people have stopped giving those, you know, they're beginning to be out of date. But this was fun. It was in some huge house off Belgrave Square and I had a sleeping suit with suggestive buttons all down my bottom and my hair in rags. And a huge dummy on a ribbon round my neck. This new chap, his name's Syd, wore a nightshirt and a bib and looked so sweet. He has curly hair. He's a bookie.'

She waited for her sister to exclaim. But it was only Grace who would have done so – Julie sorely missed her disapproval.

With no reaction from Viv, Julie went on. 'Syd's been in jug. In Brighton, and guess who bailed him out.'

'FRF?'

'Right first time. I bet Syd's the one who gave FRF those tips when we went dog racing and always won. Claire and I went once while we were still at school and I won so much I had to pour my winnings into my school hat. Syd's very good looking. Regular features and he's sort of smart, even in a bib. I asked him to teach me the tick-tack.'

'Did he?'

'Gracious, no. He said it's a trade secret and if I learned I'd ruin the business.'

A silence fell between them. Julie looked round, vaguely wondering where she had put her shoes. It was a treat to be with Viv and not with a man. Recently George had, at last, asked her to bed. She had not yet made up her mind. And Claude was being a nuisance. He got hold of a ladder from somewhere and climbed into her bedroom last night. When she'd seen his stupid figure at the window it was all she could do not to give him a shove from the second floor into the garden. Then there was Harold, whose second

120

name, thought Julie, should be hangdog. Even her young sister was getting on her nerves.

She looked over at Viv who was staring into the fire.

'How's the future Santander? You're a bit pale. You ought to use rouge.'

'Should I? The future Santander is jumping around.'

'How peculiar.'

'No it isn't. I feel as if I'd never not been pregnant. I'm so used to it. I float around a lot of the time in a kind of dream.'

'I've noticed.'

'The only snag is having to sleep on my side. Poor bump, I can't squash him or her by lying any other way.'

'I suppose not.' Julie had lost interest. A sudden thought struck her.

'I say, talking about going round in a trance, I'm sure you haven't done a thing about your dress for Claire's snooty wedding? Would you like me to help? I could take you to Michou's, he'd find something all flowing and billowing. Or isn't there a shop called Treasure Cot where we can get you something snazzy?'

'I don't need any more maternity clothes. I have lots.'

'I'm talking about the wedding. We must have you looking, what's that word people always use when girls are preggers? – radiant.'

'Claire says I can't come.'

'She *couldn't* have.'

'I thought it was rather sensible of her.'

For the moment Julie was speechless. Then she began to splutter, leaping to her feet and walking up and down the room. Their sister must be mad – Julie's description for anybody who behaved badly – Viv could leave everything to her, she'd tell Claire a thing or two!

'I'll soon make her see what a pig she's becoming.'

Viv, touched by her champion, was loath to seem ungrateful, but inclined to disagree with her sister.

'I'm too big now, Julie, and too lackadaisical to go on a long train journey to Lewes; let alone standing around talking to people I don't know.'

121

'But *we'll* be there!'

'I know, I know, but when you think about it you'll see that Claire is right.'

'I shall never see Claire is right. When I get married – and I probably never will – I shall insist on you being in the front place in the church even if you are expecting triplets.'

'I don't see how I could manage that,' said Viv, and they laughed. Julie accepted that her strong arm in battle was not needed after all.

Viv did not mention that somebody had already wanted to fight for her. And he would have won.

Earlier that week she had been alone in the flat, feet up, reading of all things, a Spanish novel. Chiming with her resolve not to talk about Spain was the desire not to lose that language. The front door bell rang, and when, stately and stout, she answered it, there was Stuart Lockton.

She was surprised. 'I thought you and Claire were supposed to be meeting at a sherry party in Sloane Street.'

'And I take it Claire has already left?'

'Half an hour ago.'

'Ah. So Claire's there and I'm not,' he said cryptically.

He followed her into the comfortable unpretentious room, and looked about with approval while Viv took his coat and draped it round a chair. He liked the gesture. They sat on either side of the fire for all the world like a well-married couple. It was cosy and quiet too. Viv smiled.

'Stuart, you're an unexpected pleasure, but I don't think I quite understand. Do you mean you've decided not to go to the party?'

'I'll tell you a secret. I hate 'em. Always have. Sherry is disgusting stuff if you drink more than a glass and a half, it goes straight to the liver. And I don't know any of these people she's so keen on.'

'Claire said they were second cousins of yours.'

He gave a dry kind of smile. 'Well,' he said, 'yes they are distant relatives but it was Claire who dug them up. 'They're too smart for me; I'm afraid I told Claire a white lie. Said I was on a difficult case and would be late at the party. Probably not turn up until it finishes.'

'Oh.'

'I decided on a little subterfuge. I never get the chance to talk to you alone.'

'Oh,' said Viv again.

'A small lie at times is not be to despised,' remarked Stuart, warming his hands. She noticed his signet ring was engraved with a crest, almost effaced. His hands were large and pale, elegant for a man who was sturdy and stocky. Viv felt easy with him as if they had always been related. She knew he liked her, even that he admired her. He was a strong-looking, relaxed, reliable kind of man. She did not know very much about him except Claire's facts: the 'good' family, the parents who lived on the other side of Sussex, his work as a country solicitor. Viv perceived other things. His thoughtful face was impressive at times, and so was his mouth which tucked into a straight line when his face was in repose. His voice was low and good to listen to. It was so calm. Above all, he gave an impression of kindness. She could not imagine him leaving a wife for days in the prison of solitude.

'Now, Viv,' he said matter-of-factly, 'I'm here to talk about the wedding and all that fandango.'

'But everything has been arranged, Stuart. Down to the last carnation for the ushers' buttonholes.'

'So it has, so it has,' he said with a certain wonder at his fiancée's talent for organisation. 'I'm not talking about all that. But about you.'

There was no guile in Viv's dealings with men. She saw at once what he was getting at.

'I'm not coming to the wedding, Stuart.'

'Why not?'

'Because of him or her.' She lightly patted her stomach.

'What has your condition got to do with it?'

'Oh, you know ... I get stupidly tired. And Lewes is a long way. Well, it seems so at present.'

'I shall send a car for you.'

'November's such a chilly time.'

'What's wrong with a fur rug?'

'Stuart –'

'Yes?' he said sturdily, adding 'You haven't met my mother and father. They'll like you.'

'I'm sure I would like them.'

'Well, now? A car purring at the door. A damn great rug to wrap yourself in. And your nice face at the church.'

He upset her. She wasn't used to somebody like this.

'No, Stuart, I shan't be there. Not only because of what Claire thought –'

'Leave Claire to me.'

'Stuart,' she repeated his name almost desperately, 'I wish you'd stop being so kind. Ignoring what Claire wants – and it's a bit mean of us to do so – I would truly prefer not to come. I am too tired. Silly, isn't it? I shall think of you both so much on the day. I just want to be here and – and hear about it all afterwards from Julie and Isobel.'

He turned this over.

'I see.'

'You do, don't you?'

'I see I'm not going to persuade you,' he said. 'I like to win, Viv. You've disappointed me.' He shook his head at her, half in disapproval, half in regret.

'I've failed,' he said, rubbing the end of his aquiline nose. 'I was certain I'd make you see how very much I want you with us.'

'Dear Stuart.' She leaned forward and patted his hand in a gesture she had never used to Carlos.

A few weeks after the wedding, while the couple were still on their honeymoon in Paris, and the weather was bitterly cold, Viv's baby was born.

She had made the arrangements herself, discovering that such things are not difficult if you pay for the best. A friendly midwife moved in the week before the baby was due. A sympathetic if snobbish doctor was to attend Viv.

124

The baby took twelve hours to make his appearance, and Viv told Nurse Sallis that none of her sisters was to be told that she was in labour.

'Are you sure, Mrs Santander? Next of kin like to be informed.'

Nurse Sallis had tactfully not enquired about husbands.

She was big, efficient, and had a face with laughter lines round eyes and mouth.

'Nurse, I'm quite sure. I really don't want any of the three to know until after the baby has arrived.'

'If that's what you prefer,' said Nurse Sallis peacefully.

Promised 'a lovely cup of tea afterwards,' bent double with backache, and grateful for Nurse Sallis, who was elderly and strong and funny, Viv at last, with her help and the late appearance of the doctor, produced a bawling son.

It was only after a long night's sleep, and following a little breakfast the nurse had coaxed her to eat and Christopher Pablo having had his first meal, that Viv asked Nurse Sallis to ring her sisters. Their numbers were in the hall by the telephone.

'And there's a Brighton number. Father Freeman, a great friend. Would you be very kind and ring him too?'

Isobel arrived first, hands full of daffodils, eyes dark with excitement. Nurse Sallis opened the door.

'You are not to stay long, Miss Bryant. Ten minutes.'

'Why? Why? Isn't she all right?'

'Of course she is, but we had a night of it. Go along, she's waiting for you,' said the nurse who, like Mrs Duffy before her, thought 'here's a ninny'. Pretty, yes, but a halfwit.

'Viv, Viv, why didn't you tell us it was coming!' was Isobel's cry as she ran into the bedroom to find a sister, whom she'd imagined at death's door, sitting up and looking eighteen years old.

Viv put out a hand and Isobel blindly clutched at it and burst into tears. Her sobs were so loud that Nurse Sallis put her head round the door.

'Does she always carry on like this, Mrs Santander?'

It was Isobel, laughing and crying at the same time, who replied, 'I'm so stupid. I know I'm being stupid but I'm so happy.'

The nurse was accustomed to emotion at the birth, and went over to Isobel, taking her to see her new nephew fast asleep in his cot. Isobel wiped away more tears with the back of her hand and sniffed a good deal. The doorbell pealed again, and Nurse Sallis went to answer it for the second time. There was Julie, with a vast gold basket filled with fruit, attended by two men, one carrying a boxful of half bottles of champagne, the other a barrowload of red roses.

'I take it you're another sister?' said Nurse Sallis, who put this one down as a 'little madam'. 'Come in. But I'm afraid I must ban your friends. Nobody but close family allowed on the first day.'

'Oh, oh, can't they come in for two secs?'

'Sorry, Miss Bryant.'

The men in question, Claude and George Silver, did not care a jot that they were forbidden to see mother and child. It was Julie on whom their eyes were fixed. They went in relief to the sitting room where the nurse soon provided coffee.

As for Julie, she burst into the bedroom more noisily than Isobel, plumped down painfully on Viv's feet, then sprang up to press the roses in her arms and run over to the cot.

'He's funny! He looks exactly like a parrot.'

'Of course he doesn't,' from Isobel.

'Julie's right,' said Viv.

Did she imagine, through the congratulations, a certain coolness between her sisters? They scarcely addressed a word to each other, directing all their remarks to Viv. Julie opened one of the half bottles and drank most of it herself, Viv and Isobel refused. She went over to study the baby again.

'He's dribbling. What a comical face, I'm sure he's going to be a boxer.' Finally, 'I ought to go, George and Claude are taking me to a new film.'

She went over to kiss Viv, returned to the cot to whisper 'Bye for the present, little parrot', and went out.

They heard her calling, 'George? Claude? Come on, you two, or we'll miss the beginning.'

The usual lull followed her departure. Isboel sat with her arms folded across her breast in an attitude which Viv had once said was that of a buried crusader. The nurse looked in, decided the daft one was not tiring her patient and left them together.

Viv moved a pillow behind her head. The light from the gas fire threw aureoles. They were deceiving, a golden glow over the sad fact of a fatherless child. Every time she looked towards the cot with its bows and frills and thought of the parrot baby with his Spanish nose and black eyes, she had a sensation of joy and sorrow.

She thought for a moment, then said, 'Belle. What's the matter between you and Julie?'

'Rather a lot.'

'You've fallen out?'

'I don't fall out, Viv, you know I don't. Julie's bored with me. I get on her nerves. She can't stick Patrick either, so what with him coming to the house and me holed up in the studio painting and never joining in the larks, she thinks me the biggest bore of all time.'

Isobel was quoting.

'But you seemed to get on so well at first. And Julie doesn't mean her explosions.'

'Of course she does. She always says what she thinks. People imagine she's being amusing or temporarily huffy, but it's the truth with Julie all the time. She couldn't pretend to save her life. I can't stay at Dysart much longer, Viv. She's quite blunt about it. Yesterday she said "Anyway you've got just as much money as me, more now I've bought Dysart, so go and buy yourself something somewhere."'

'I'm so sorry. What about Patrick? How does he feel?'

'He doesn't like her any more than she likes him. When they're in the same room they make jeering remarks pretending they're jokes.'

'Not very comfortable.'

'Awful. I hate it.' Then in a rush. 'There was a row yesterday morning because I was painting late the night before.'

'How late?'

'Oh, pretty late.'

127

'Come on, Belle.'

'Most of the night, actually. I wasn't due to go to college and after working hard I slept into the morning and Julie came up to my room. She wanted help with one of those stupid parties she keeps giving. This one is to be a Dickens party, everybody in Victorian fancy dress. She came bursting in and I just couldn't wake up. She got hopping mad. She kept saying "What's it all *for*?"'

'Meaning your painting?'

'Of course. And Patrick too. None of her friends do a stroke. Joan and Mirry and the Hornton girl and Evelyn Bennett. The men are just the same, except Harold is messing about on the stock exchange and George Silver owns houses. The rest do nothing.'

'Like us.'

'They can't all have private money, Viv. They're not posh, like the Lady Things and Lord David Whatsits in that column in the Daily Mail. I think most of them live on tick.'

The door opened, as Viv had begun to hope that it would, and Nurse Sallis came in, commanding obedience. Isobel was banished.

CHAPTER SEVEN

Spanish pride was not a myth. In the sixteenth and seventeenth centuries the Spanish had been masters of the world. They had founded the first great empire since the Roman legions marched along the arrow-straight roads which they themselves had built. The Spaniards had once been great and it showed in their bearing, their shadowed eyes, their enigma and their philosophy.

Carlos Santander was as proud as Lucifer, and for the first weeks he did not admit to his family that Viv had left him. Only his mother knew. Viv had returned on a visit to England, and after that there had been her mother's sad demise. She was staying on to be with her sisters. It was all very natural. When people enquired about his absent wife, he was polite and no more, and since close family matters were not discussed with outsiders, the matter was put aside.

But the weeks melted into months. Apart from one, to Carlos, despicable letter which Viv had left on her departure and his own arrogant reply – eliciting a cold one in return – nothing more had been exchanged between them.

He truly did not understand what had happened. He was a thoughtful inward-looking man who enjoyed some solitude and some company. He was dignified and had a heavy charm. In sex he was passionate, almost wild. Since Viv had gone he'd found a beautiful very young Spanish prostitute whom he visited two or three times a week. But that had nothing to do with his feelings for his lost wife. Viv had made a sabre cut across his soul.

He had a traditional Spanish nature: intense, individualistic, he found it difficult to put himself into another man's mind, and as for doing so with a woman, it was impossible. Viv's betrayal, he decided, must have been a form of hysteria; yet he'd never thought the English hysterical, they seemed a cool sensible race. On his visits to London or to see his old friend Francis Freeman, they had seemed very pleasant foreigners often glad to laugh. Carlos liked that. Their manners were good, and he liked that too, for his were of an old-fashioned kind. Their woman were intriguing with their fair hair and their shyness.

He loved Vivien Bryant deeply and uncomprehendingly. He had taken her back to his cave, the stuffy baroque house in Barcelona, and dumped her there. He had been happy to think he had won her, happy to remember her now and then when he sat in endless talk with his friends. Her passion in lovemaking had been a revelation. At first he had found it unbearably exciting to stir her just a little. Instead, he found himself answered by fire.

Into this simple delight of the strong man and the imprisoned and beloved woman, had crept, step by step, insidious inch by inch, a kind of darkness. At first it was nothing to be worried by, easy to brush aside, to flood with the light of his pleasure in her, his spoiling of her, and – when absent – his forgetting her. But the darkness grew between them and even Carlos could not ignore it. His nature knew the dark. A Spanish writer, apostrophizing his country, cried, 'One half of thy face fiesta, the other misery.'

Meeting Viv's growing misery, he countered it with silence, reserve, disdain. He was proud and would not beg. He was a man and would not submit. His pride was as much part of him as his skin; remove it and he was flayed.

After Viv was gone, he confided in a priest – his family knew scores of priests in Barcelona, amiable men in shabby black, glad to be given dinner at the house. One priest who had known him for years, an unworldly old man very different from Francis Freeman, sorrowfully told him he must 'go in search of his woman'. Carlos burst out in angry refusal. Then he bought a train and steamer ticket.

The priest, good soul, protected Carlos's pride. He did not imply that a man who loses his wife for no apparent reason also loses his dignity. He simply counselled 'a denial of self'. And when Carlos told his mother what he had decided, she said gravely, 'Yes. You must go. Your choice, my son, was wrong. But it is now your duty under heaven to get your wife to return.' One way and another, Carlos felt his journey wholly admirable.

After much thought he made up his mind not to telegraph that he was coming to England. He travelled for nearly three days and caught the last evening steamer to Newhaven. The sea was flat and calm, and he fetched up at the port at nearly midnight where he persuaded a taxi driver, for a large sum, to drive him to Brighton.

The moon in a starry sky made the little country to which he had come look pleasantly mysterious. He liked it because it was so un-Spanish. The small houses, the often sad weather, the famous London fogs, and another kind of mist – the hypocritical charm of the middle classes. But even the moonlight tonight, with its eerie magic, could not make the countryside look as magnificent, as dramatic, as Spain.

The cab was as ancient as any in Barcelona but in slightly worse condition; it ground its way through the slums of Brighton. The man had to stop three times for directions until, with a shudder of brakes, he at last pulled up at St Gregory's. Carlos sprang out, took his heavy bag, paid the driver and added a generous tip. He was given a salute. The man had been a corporal in the Great War.

He drove noisily away.

Carlos rang the bell, waited, and rang again.

A window opened above his head, and a recognizable voice shouted, 'Now, now, Liam, if it's drink you've taken and it's my absolution you want, you can go and boil your head. Off with you to your long-suffering wife. You can come to confession tomorrow after work, yours and mine. But just you see you're in time at the factory in the morning.'

'Father Freeman. It is I.'

The priest's glossy black head caught a reflection of moonlight as he peered down.

'Carlos? By all that's wonderful, what are *you* doing in Brighton? Wait a sec, I'll be down directly.'

In less time than it took Carlos to square his shoulders and grasp his bag, Freeman had flung open the door and welcomed him with outstretched hands.

'Come along up. What a late visitation. Why aren't you in London?'

Carlos followed him up the stairs and when they arrived in the study said in a puzzled voice that he would scarcely be likely to go to London, since Woodlands was much closer to Brighton. He would hire a car tomorrow, or take a train. He had come first 'for a little counsel'.

The priest felt winded. It was clear that his friend knew absolutely nothing of what had happened. As far as he was concerned, the girls, still with little money, were living at their old home.

Except when shouting at drunken parishioners, Freeman was not a man who dashed straight into a conversation; he preferred a pause. After a moment or two of silence he said without emphasis, 'You didn't know Woodlands has been sold?'

'*Sold?*'

'A big change has happened in the Bryants' lives. When their mother died, she left a great deal of money.'

It was Carlos, this time, who paused. Freeman had no idea what he was thinking.

All the Spaniard finally said was, 'Indeed.'

'Come on, Carlos, it was a tremendous stroke of luck for the girls, wasn't it?'

'Yes. I suppose so.'

'They're very wealthy now. Odd, isn't it?' said the priest, keeping the under-emphasis. How mysterious marriage is, he thought for the thousandth time in his religious life. You can guess and question and draw conclusions, but when it comes down to it, you know absolutely nothing after the door of marriage shuts on two people; you're outside the house. What had this serious man done to drive Viv away? Viv's own explanation had not satisfied Freeman.

But who was he to judge or understand?

'I would have written to tell you the news, my dear chap, but I imagined you would hear from Viv.'

'She left me one letter. To which I replied.'

And a damned cold reply it was, remembered the priest, but could not find it in his heart to blame him.

'So Vivien is living in London,' Carlos said. 'I must go there.'

'But you'll stay tonight with me. I can't have you arriving in London on the milk train.'

They continued to talk but it was clear that after the first shock of learning his wife was now rich and no longer living in her old home, Carlos did not want to speak about Viv. Freeman was relieved. In his hands just then was a precious, treasured, living, breathing fact: the birth of a son to the sombre man making conversation. Freeman could not tell him about the child: it was not his secret.

After thinking for a little, he enquired about Spain. He knew from many previous talks with Carlos and from his own observations that it had recently been a divided and unhappy country.

Carlos shook his head wearily. 'In my city, Primo de Rivera is hated,' he said. 'Don't they know he is the best leader they will get in today's Spain? Barcelona is filled with working class anarchists – the riots were more than seven years ago but they are never forgotten. Of course the people are right to loathe the Army who shot them down in their hundreds and would do so again. But there is nothing but hatred in our streets.'

Freeman wanted to know more about the Spanish dictator.

'A cheerful man. A patriot. He has brought some prosperity to Spain and his heart is generous. He's very brave. But his party has no prestige. It cannot last.'

'What will happen then, Carlos?'

'God knows.'

The note of melancholy which had been with Carlos since he'd spoken of Viv, grew worse. Freeman tried to bring a touch of optimism into the conversation. Once Carlos did smile.

'You can't help liking de Rivera even if he is no leader,' he said.

133

'For weeks he works like a dog. Then what do you think? He disappears for two or three days.'

'But where to?'

'On a kind of orgy, I'm afraid. Drinking, dancing with the gypsies. Also lovemaking ...'

Carlos's voice had a ring of approval and meeting the priest's eye, he laughed.

At last even Carlos, a night bird, was tired and they went to bed. Freeman showed him into a room which he kept for his rare visitors. The chaste bed was covered with a white honeycomb quilt, and one picture, a cheap print of the Sistine Madonna, hung over an unused fireplace filled with a paper fan.

In the days when they'd lived at Woodlands, the Bryant girls used to sleep in this room. On the toss of a coin, one girl took the bed, the other had to make do with an uncomfortable camp bed. Sometimes it went wrong, and tried to fold itself up while still occupied. According to Freeman he had come to wake the twins one morning and found that the bed had closed up and cut off Julie's head.

'Fortunately I popped it back at once. No harm done,' he'd said. It had become a long-standing family catchphrase.

Early the following morning, Carlos was up and bathed and had to endure one of Mrs Duffy's English breakfasts. It always astonished him that the English could like leathery toast, rubbery scrambled eggs, bitter orange jam and strong red tea. He longed for coffee, fragrant coffee, its scent floating up to his room from the kitchen of the Casa de los Arboles Naranjas.

Having thanked his host, promised to keep in touch, and been given the Roper Court address, Carlos caught the Brighton Belle train to London.

It was curious, it was irritating, to visit a totally unfamiliar place where, he had been told, his wife had now made her home. Money, he thought, changed so much. It changed people and it changed the way others saw them. Viv's lack of anything but the fifty pound cheque her mother had given her as a wedding present had swelled

Carlos's heart. He had liked his woman having nothing. He was far from wealthy but it pleased him to see her pleasure when he bought her things. He had loved her wonder and naiveté. One of Viv's qualities very dear to him had been that she was a simpleton. She was unworldly, as Claire and Julie were not. She had dreamed her way through her one-day-a-week work as a librarian. Her interests had been domestic, limited. As for money, the main part of her salary had been dutifully surrendered every week to Grace. Her mother had claimed a large donation towards the family house-keeping. On one occasion Viv had told him this, explaining why she could not afford more clothes for her trousseau.

'Of course Ma needs what I can give her,' Viv innocently said. When she mentioned the amount, Carlos held his tongue, seeing that it had been far too much.

Now she was wealthy. He could not get used to the idea. He was wounded that she had never thought to tell him of her inheritance. Although it meant she was now comfortably off, and it wasn't necessary for him to worry over her welfare, he felt, not relieved, but robbed. He had lost for ever the heart-rending pleasure of giving.

The King's Road was not a district Carlos knew. It was somewhat down-at-heel, with lines of miscellaneous shops and old houses which were as shabby as many in his own city, but with little romance about them. There were no impressive buildings, no squares, except one far too cramped for his taste; the whole area had an artistic and seedy air about it. It did not suit his idea of Viv. He frowned when he arrived at the modest block of flats with 'Roper Court' over its doorway. He noticed the windows were latticed in a pretence of the Tudor style. That must make the rooms dark, he thought.

Arriving at the top floor of the building he had a sudden flood of expectation. He forgot dignity, embarrassment – everything. He was going to see her again.

The door was opened by a girl in a painter's smock. Carlos gave her a tender grin.

'My dear Isobel!'

135

She blanched.

'Carlos – I –'

'Who is it?' called a voice he would know in his grave, and coming slowly down a passage holding a bundle in her arms, the long shawl trailing, was Viv.

She halted as if turned to stone.

Both girls, Isobel at the door, Viv clutching the baby, were unable to move. But Carlos did. He ran towards his wife, wearing an expression so beautiful that Isobel fled, rushing away in the opposite direction to her bedroom and slamming the door.

The couple did not see or hear her go.

Viv's grasp of the baby was so tight that he gave an angry cry which turned into a wail.

She said absurdly, 'You've woken him.'

'Is he yours?'

It was to Carlos's eternal credit that he did not say or think 'Is he mine?'

'Of course he's mine,' said Viv crossly, bouncing the child up and down at which the wails grew louder and she had to raise her voice.

'Oh come in for goodness sake, don't just stand there staring.' She threw open the drawing room door. She vanished and, after a few minutes while Carlos stood listening to the wails as if enchanted, she reappeared.

She was plumper than he remembered. Her hair was shorter and curled at its edges like a little golden cap. Her cheeks had regained their colour after the first moments when, like her sister, she had paled with shock. But what he noticed most was her bosom: her breasts were very large, making her slender figure top heavy and giving her a curious importance. She was no longer the little creature he had captured and imprisoned. There was an authority about the bosom as if it should be pinned with medals.

'How did you know where to find me?'

She was polite and cool.

Still suffering from shock, joy, and an emotion he had not known existed in his soul, he said, 'Francis Freeman told me. I stayed with him in Brighton last night. I landed in Newhaven and was on my way to Woodlands.'

'To Woodlands?'

'I did not know it had been sold. I did not know anything.'

Viv looked straight at him.

'And FRF told you about Kit.'

She saw by the frown that he did not understand and said impatiently, 'Kit. Christopher. My baby.'

That possessive pronoun, he thought. What did I do to this girl that she treats me so? Pride tapped him on the arm and when he ignored her, gave a tug at his sleeve. He resisted her still.

'Kit,' he said slowly. 'No, he did not tell me about Kit. I suppose he thought that only right. He did tell me where you lived, of course. And about your family inheritance.'

'Our mother left us a lot of money.'

A pause.

'Did you not consider you should have told me you were *encinta*?'

'I didn't want you to know.'

'That's obvious. But was it fair?'

'Oh, if we're talking about *fair*. Was it fair of you not to tell me Señora Santander would share my house?'

Carlos was not intuitive about women. He revered them but did not understand them, and their very mystery was part of their power. Yes, they had their own power and he must have his. But now every tendril of intuition was alive and trembling. He saw she was determined to set him against her. She was afraid of him, afraid of his rights over the child. God knew he had those and did not intend to use them. He actually pitied her.

He could smell the scent she had used when they lived together and another scent, light and faint which he did not know was baby powder.

He sat quietly, but his senses shivered. How long could he stay? How long would she give him? He was far from his world, with its indifference to the awful bondage of time. Viv's nature demanded the actual. The 'Where are you going and when will you return?'

The 'I can spare you five minutes'. To Carlos time was something that, if you were wise, you evaded: 'If we meet, then we meet. If not, not.'

When he and Viv had been married – was he already seeing that in the past? – she'd used her English slavery to time and attempted to make him a fellow bondsman. She'd failed. It was only when they had been blind with passion that the hours had meant nothing to her. She had not known there was a clock in the room or in the house when she was in his arms. Now it was Carlos who heard the clock on the mantelpiece.

She did not seem nervous. She sat there in her plumpness, enhanced by the magnificent bosom of the nursing mother. She appeared to be waiting to see what would happen next. If her heart pounded, as his was doing, she didn't betray it by a flicker. Carlos had his first vision of the English as calculating and cold.

'I think we should talk, Vivien.'

'What are we doing now?'

He gave a forced laugh.

'I am talking and you are not. I have never understood why you ran away.'

That touched her on the raw.

'I didn't run, as you put it.'

'You crept out of the house, you did not even have the help of your maid.'

'She would have told the Señora.'

'Might it not have been better had she done so?'

She said impatiently, 'Do you believe that? Do you imagine that a scene with the Señora' – she would not call her anything else – 'would change anything?'

'Very well. Your mind was made up. Since you were strong enough to leave me, Vivien, surely you could have been strong enough to stand up to her until I returned home?'

She said in surprise, 'I am not afraid of *her*.' And it was his turn to be surprised, for he was in awe of his mother. 'Why should I be afraid of the Señora? She's very dominating. She can't bear not to be the centre of attention, she'd fight tooth and nail to stay in it.

138

She didn't frighten me, but I hated what she did. She was like a spoiled child. I was lucky to have a cup of tea with you alone.'

His expression was not its relaxed, contented self. He looked strained and older.

In a deeper voice he said, 'You were jealous of her.'

Viv's face did not soften. She gave a sigh.

'No. I was not jealous of her. Scarcely of you either, Carlos. It was just that I couldn't live with you any more. I tried. I did try. But I couldn't breathe in your world. There was nothing in it, not a single thing, that I could bear.'

Carlos did not believe her. He sensed, with invisible tendrils of desire for the familiar yet changed body, that she was still his.

'Are you saying that you cannot bear me?'

Viv appeared to wonder for an instant if she had gone too far. She was more affected by his presence than she dared show. They were both physically conscious of one another but unlike Carlos Viv did not betray it. Had she forgotten how handsome he was? In a way she wanted to lean forward and touch him, to melt against him as she used to do, to feel again as she used to do. The sensation hurt and stirred her.

The distant wail of the baby came through the door. Like an animal hearing a sound which meant danger, she sprang to her feet.

'I must go. I have to feed him. Goodbye,' she gabbled, and before he could collect himself or protest or speak, she was gone.

He heard a door slam somewhere.

He rubbed his chin, then took out his cigar case, lit a cigar and drew on it. Acrid smoke rose in the room which until then had smelled only of scent and a bowl of lavender.

He sat still, legs crossed, reflecting. Time again tormented him; how long did it take to nurse a child? Viv would return after that and ask him to go. By her very demand, his case would weaken. He could lose whatever round he had gained a moment ago.

Smoking thoughtfully, his nerves calmed down. Before leaving, he looked about at the room, thinking how it differed from the Casa de los Arboles Naranjas. There were flowers in tall jugs, fresh English chintzes, shelves of books which had not been imprisoned behind glass. In front of the fireplace was a screen he vaguely recognized. He forgot he had watched Grace painstakingly stitching its sentimental picture of a cottage and a gardenful of hollyhocks.

He walked over to the window to look out at the tree tops. They shook in a slight breeze, turning from green to silver. He had made himself calm again, he thought, as his black eyes watched the trees. He had found no answer to the conundrum of why Viv had left him; but something new had happened, there was an ache inside his heart, a pain he had never felt before. He needed to see his son.

He stabbed out the cigar in a silver ashtray which until then had glittered with empty cleanness. I shall come back, he thought. She can't refuse me that.

Viv was in her bedroom, sitting in a nursing chair which had no arms while the baby sucked and kneaded her bursting breast with his fists. She must keep calm. Calm. Like Carlos, she took a deep breath and waited for her thoughts to settle. Like Carlos, she looked across at the swaying trees. She must not be upset, it could affect her milk. When she heard the front door shut, and the clang of the lift door, she closed her eyes in sheer relief.

Out in the King's Road, carrying his hat and stick, Carlos walked by dingy shops which sold antiques only just visible through dirty windows. He scarcely saw where he was going. He missed the two or three attractive young women who looked at him with feminine interest as he went by. Accustomed to Barcelona, where the girls dropped their eyes like nuns, he was missing a good deal.

He thought intently, and finally decided on his next move.

At the Royal Court Hotel in Sloane Square, he took a quiet room on the first floor and rang his friend in Brighton.

'Good,' exclaimed Francis Freeman at once. 'Good of you to telephone. How did it go?'

'I saw her.'

'And?'

'I only saw the child from a distance.'

'Surely Viv did not prevent you!'

'No. It was not like that.'

140

'But she wasn't exactly welcoming.'

'Alas, FRF.'

A little pause.

'How can I help you, old chap?'

'I have been wondering if you have Claire's telephone number?'

'Of course. But I should be careful if I were you.'

'I don't understand you,' said Carlos, who liked Claire.

'I mean she is a somewhat enthusiastic Catholic.'

'My dear Father Francis!'

'Now, now, Carlos, it's no good taking that line with Mother Church. You can't tell me you're much of a churchgoer. When did you last go to Mass?'

'At Christmas, always.'

'I've seen you Spaniards on Holidays of Obligation. All the women praying their heads off, and all the men outside on the steps, talking about the bullfights.'

'Well ...'

'You see?' said Freeman, laughing.

'But I am still a believer.'

'Of course. The reason I am warning you about Claire is that she is inclined to be more Catholic than the Pope. Wouldn't Isobel be more help?'

'I don't imagine so,' Carlos recalled the ashen face of the youngest Bryant. 'She will not be on my side.'

Neither of them mentioned Julie.

'Yes,' Freeman said, after a moment or two, 'Perhaps you're right to talk to Claire. If Viv will not listen to you, there's a chance she might listen to Claire who reminds her of their mother.'

It was a cobweb of hope, and even while he was talking Freeman could see how the precious stuff could be torn. Yet Carlos might reweave it like the patient spider. But was Viv to be cast in the role of fly?

Problems, sick parishioners, and a late appointment to play billiards filled Freeman's day. But he did not forget Carlos and in his thoughts travelled to Lewes with him to meet Claire.

As it happened, when Carlos spoke to Claire she said immediately that she would come to London. She'd be at the Royal Court hotel in the early afternoon.

'You can give me tea. It has to be Lapsang Souchong.'

The tinny little voice gave him a feeling of relief.

The Bryant girls, thought Carlos, standing up to greet the third of the bunch in the last few hours, had changed. Isobel had become older and better looking – he'd remembered a gawky half-child at his wedding. Viv was disturbingly altered. And now here was Claire, walking with the slight sway which had become natural to her, coming towards him. She was as slim as ever but no longer merely pretty. Claire had developed style. She wore a white dress patterned here and there with pale green, a floating white summer coat, and a charming hat, the brim folded back from her face, and decorated with small bunches of silk flowers. She smiled at him, holding out her gloved hand.

'How nice.'

It was nothing of the kind but Carlos took her hand and kissed it rapidly, then settled her in a comfortable chair and ordered tea.

'I must not have any milk,' said arrow-thin Claire to the waiter. Her voice, warm the moment before, was as hard as nails. The waiter bowed politely and left. Carlos, who treated intimate friends, servants and beggars with the same grave courtesy, and regarded the poor as especially noble, tried not to notice. Other countries, other manners. But Viv had never behaved in that way.

'Well, Carlos?' said Claire, looking at him with her slightly staring eyes. They were of a blue so brilliant that Carlos, who had forgotten, was startled all over again.

She continued calmly, 'I'm so glad you decided to come to London and make everything all right again. What do you think of the baby? Isn't he sweet?'

'I have not seen my child.'

She looked shocked.

'Not seen him! But you said on the telephone that you went to Roper Court this morning.'

'So I did. I saw the child in the distance. Then Viv took him away somewhere. And she and I talked.'

142

'And she wasn't very nice?'

'Not exactly.'

'I am so sorry.'

He brooded for a moment or two.

'I think she tried to explain why she ran away,' he said. He always described his wife's action to himself like that. It made her sound like a schoolgirl.

'Perhaps the explanation doesn't really matter,' Claire comforted. 'Husbands and wives quarrel occasionally. Stuart and I do. But things are always settled later.'

They were settled, as in most cases with married couples, in bed. Stuart was crazy about her, thought Claire with complacence.

Around them the English families, well-dressed women, tweedy men, one or two bored children, talked in low voices. Nobody laughed loudly or burst into an argument. The atmosphere was subdued, like the dim looking glasses on the walls.

'What did Viv actually say, Carlos? Forgive me for seeming curious. But we never understood what it was about.'

He gave a Mediterranean shrug.

'I can only suppose she was not happy in my country.'

'But she married *you*. Not Spain.'

His pride was stung. Who was she criticizing? Himself, or the country he loved and castigated?

She had offended him; yet there she sat, innocent of any intention to hurt, merely as baffled as he was.

'Claire. What do you advise?'

She felt a wave of power just then. Like all the Bryants including poor lost Grace, she had been impressed by Carlos, by his male confidence, his foreignness, his mystery. To have this handsome giant, he really was very big, asking her for help gave her a charitable thrill. She determined to do her best. And in any case it was cruel of her sister not to allow him to see his son.

'I've had an idea,' she said. 'What about us going to call on Viv together? I'm staying the night with Julie in Dysart House – Stuart thought it too tiring for me to return to Lewes by the late train. Why shouldn't we call in to see Viv on my way to Chelsea? When I

143

rang, Julie was thrilled to know you were in England by the way, and asked you to dine with her. So you could come with me after we've seen Viv. Unless, of course, Viv asks you to have a meal with her.'

'She won't do that.'

Claire could have made a sympathetic reply to the four low-spoken words, but the waiter had arrived with the tea.

'Oh,' said Claire, 'good.'

She waited until everything was set before them and did not thank the young man. Carlos knew he was Spanish when he said something about the water jug being very hot, and gave him a smile. It was returned with swiftness, warmth and no gratitude.

When the waiter was out of earshot, Claire asked, 'Would you like me to come with you?'

'Very much. But should we not telephone Vivien first?'

'She might make a silly excuse, she can be so tiresome. No. We will just call round. All I shall say,' said Claire, warming to her act of charity, 'is that I happen to be in London today and have popped in to see the baby. In any case,' indicating a neat package, 'I have knitted him a matinee jacket, so it's a good chance to give it to her instead of posting it. I shall say we met here at the Court, you invited me to tea, and I was amazed, to say the least, that she hadn't given you the chance to see Kit.'

He listened as a lion might do to the squeaking mouse about to gnaw through his bonds.

'I shall shame her into showing you the baby,' added the mouse.

She drank her tea, expecting Spanish effusion. She was filled with good nature and perfectly certain her plan was excellent. At that moment he was in her power and he knew it.

He said gently that she was very good, and perhaps her idea would work; he was not sure Viv would consent to see him again unless Claire came along. He could no more help his courtesy to her than he could help his black hair and heavy features and Spanish lisp. But he wished he had never called up this bright angel of self righteousness.

Having settled, to her satisfaction, the matter of a fractured

144

marriage and a father refused the sight of his newborn son, Claire changed the subject. She talked sociably about her wedding, repeating now and then, 'We were so sorry you could not be with us. It was such fun.'

They set off for Chelsea slightly after five o'clock in a soft sunshine. Claire remarked that it was a good time to call.

'You seem very sure that she'll be there.'

'One always feeds a child at six.'

'I see. I did not know.' He connected nothing with clocks.

Claire, glancing at him under her eyelashes, was glad she was doing her bit. He looked serious and preoccupied. Now they were actually walking towards Viv's home he was regretting more than ever that he had asked for her help. This was Viv's sister – their blood tie was as close as you could get. Sisters were full of instincts he knew nothing about. But he never doubted their mutual devotion.

Once when he had first met the Bryants, Julie had said laughingly, 'We are always getting furious with each other. We quarrel like cats. But when we're attacked by other people we form a square like the soldiers in the last century. You know? The British square.'

Am I attacking them? thought Carlos.

The King's Road had a certain raffish charm, it was not unlike a village; he understood why both his wife and the unpredictable Julie had chosen to live here. Carlos thought they reached Roper Court rather too soon. Claire had walked swiftly, not matching her pace to her companion's preferred Mediterranean stroll.

At Viv's front door it was Claire who pushed the bell and Isobel who again answered.

She did not look so shattered this time, but widened her large eyes, muttering 'Claire!'

'Yes, as you see, Belle, Carlos and I met at the Royal Court,' tinkled Claire. She smiled casually and taking Carlos with her moved into the hall almost before Isobel had time to step aside. It was Claire who shut the front door. Before another word was spoken, Viv appeared from the drawing room. Seeing the visitors she went scarlet.

145

'Viv, hello,' said Claire, advancing to offer her cheek which Viv was forced to kiss. 'As I just told Isobel, Carlos and I have been having tea at the Royal Court. I'm staying the night with Julie, so I thought I'd bring along the matinee jacket I've knitted for Kit. Stuart was so impressed that I've taught myself to knit.'

As sociably as a hostess at a difficult dinner, practised at getting her own way, Claire manoeuvred everybody into the drawing room. She had the gall to say, 'Do sit down, Carlos, that's Viv's most comfortable chair. I should know, I always make Stuart sit there.'

But Carlos was not looking at the chair.

Propped on the sofa between cushions like a small idol, long silk dress sewn with lace frills artistically arranged, small head with its cap of dark hair against a minute white pillow, one fist vaguely moving, was Christopher Pablo Francis Santander aged four and a half weeks.

Claire, undismayed, continued to chat, exclaiming over the baby, how he had grown, and asking Isobel patronizingly about her painting, 'Did you do that little sketch on the bookcase? I must say it isn't bad, and I do like the frame.'

Isobel was forced to answer. But she was watching Carlos. And so was Viv.

Unaware of the three women in the room, he stood looking at the tiny scrap of humanity. He stared with a kind of incredulity, very still. Then he did a strange thing.

He went over to the child and knelt down.

Isobel swallowed. Claire frowned. Viv shut her eyes.

The big man knelt on the floor by the sofa, put out a hand which seemed enormous, and carefully took the minute waving fist. He murmured something in Spanish which even Viv could not hear. He took the tiny fingers white as milk and unfolded them and examined the creases of birth, which resembled the creases in the petals of flowers, released from protective sepals and opening at last. He looked at the tiny face and unconsciously frowned because the baby frowned. He would have lifted his great hand to caress the small head but Viv, opening her eyes, said sharply, 'Don't touch his head. The fontanelle isn't closed yet.'

146

He turned, uncomprehending.

'It's a little space in the baby's head covered with a membrane. It closes later,' said Isobel. She couldn't bear to look at his face. So tender. So wounded.

'Oh. I did not know.'

Isobel spoke again, scarcely realising what she was going to say.

'Do you want to hold him?'

Avoiding Viv's eyes, knowing she must have stiffened, Isobel picked up the baby with newly acquired skill and put the silk bundle in his arms.

With a sound like a sob, Viv ran out of the room. Something went out with her; a tenseness.

'Sit down with him,' said Isobel. 'Give him a rock or a bounce. He likes that.'

Awkwardly, Carlos sat down on the chair which had been chosen for him by Claire and began to bounce the little creature gingerly in his arms. Isobel stood watching with approval; Claire rayed with satisfaction.

'I'll just have a word –' she said and left the room.

The bemused man and the young girl were alone.

Claire found Viv in her bedroom standing with her back to the door looking out of the window.

'Now Viv –' began Claire.

Viv started round.

'How could you? How could you bring him here? What did you think you were doing?'

'What's for the best.'

'For Christ's sake!'

'Don't swear, it is not like you. And nor, I must say it whether you like it or not, is the way you're behaving. Did you really think it was right not to allow Carlos to see his own son?'

'What I think or don't think is nothing to do with you.' Viv turned her back on her again.

Claire saw what she had to contend with. She picked up various moral weapons and remained looking at her sister's back calmly enough. In emergencies Claire was never rattled. But what emergency apart from the tragic and unexpected death of their mother, had she had in her short life? A doting husband, a rich home, and an inheritance for good measure; money unearned and unexpected.

'Viv, I want to talk to you. Please turn round.'

Viv did so, her face a study of antagonism.

'You can't shut your husband out of your life,' said Claire with awful reasonableness.

'I have done.'

'Until now you have certainly tried. But don't pretend you are happy because it's obvious that you aren't.'

'It is nothing –'

'To do with me. Of course it is. I'm next to you in age,' said Claire quoting the precedence Grace had dinned into them from birth, 'and now Mother has gone, who else is there to tell you a few home truths?'

'I asked FRF.'

'Oh yes. He told you that you must decide. But that was before Kit was born. And anyway how could you be fooled by what he said? FRF saves his hard words for drunks and prostitutes. He hopes for the rest of us. Hopes we'll use our religion and our heads. He certainly hoped it of you, although –' she held up her hand to stop interruption – 'I have not discussed you with him once. Not once. Don't try and get out of it like that or think,' added Claire sarcastically, 'that he'd be influenced by me. Not in a million years. What I'm saying is that you've got to have Carlos back. You've got to. He loves that baby. We all saw it just now and if you didn't, it's because you deliberately closed your eyes so as not to see how he looked. Poor man. He's a born father.'

'He was not a born husband,' said Viv very bitterly.

Claire had no answer to that. She sat down and returned calmly to the attack.

'Surely you can give him a second chance?'

The silence was so long, perhaps a full minute, that Claire literally thought she was beginning to win. Viv had turned away again. Still with averted face she suddenly burst out, 'I can't.'

148

'Oh Viv.'

Her sister in a sudden movement turned back to Claire who saw with a stab of something like horror, that Viv's face was twisted in pain.

'He doesn't understand,' she said in a shaking voice. 'He won't accept that I can't live with him again. I can't. And I won't let him have Kit. Claire, if you don't leave me alone, I shall be sick.'

It could not last. The moment of joy when Carlos sat holding his little son for the first time, the gentle support of Isobel, even Claire sitting with her sister and rallying the forces of Mother Church.

Everything petered out. Carlos left and when he returned to see Viv again she nervously agreed that he might sometimes see his child. She could scarcely bear the quiet way he took that; in future he must make appointments to be a father.

Then he left for Spain.

Isobel had been stirred by the drama. She was on fairly good terms with Julie, now that she was living with Viv and safely out of Dysart.

Meeting Julie in the King's Road by chance one day soon afterwards she explained all that had happened. Julie came down heavily on Viv's side.

'I can't understand why you went over to Carlos and Claire,' she exclaimed. 'Viv must do what suits her.'

'She looks miserable.'

'She's perfectly all right,' declared Julie. 'It's her decision after all. She's got that comic baby and she's got some cash and she's shaken the dust of Spain off her feet. What's wrong with all that?'

Hands in the pockets of a voluminous coat, head crowned with a tiny hat dotted with diamanté, Julie looked stagey, which was the idea. Autumn was coming. Isobel had forgotten to buy anything warm, and was wearing clothes which were too thin. She hunched her shoulders.

'We're not going to agree. There's no point in talking about it,' she said, 'I just wanted you to know the news. Despite what you say Viv is in the dumps. I'm sure she was more affected than she admits

149

when Carlos turned up. Poor Carlos, you have to admit, Julie, he is very beautiful.'

Julie leaned back and burst into unkind laughter. Whenever she did this it grated on Isobel who felt that something in her sister was against her. What she had said about Carlos was the truth, but when Julie was in this mood, usually at her worst in front of an audience, there was no way of reaching or sharing. Isobel made an excuse and said she must go.

Julie hailed a taxi and vanished to wherever she was going to get up to heaven knew what. She had looked very white in the face and Isobel wondered if it was drink. All those bottles of gin at Dysart ... Isobel could not understand the lure of alcohol. Puritanically she avoided it. One single cocktail affected her painting.

Feeling disturbed by Julie she walked back to Roper Court. To paint needed peace. Yet doing it was not peaceful but frustrating and exhausting, eating up the time like a starving beast. To approach the task, to go into Viv's spare room, smaller and more modest than Dysart's magnificence, took an effort. Isobel always dreaded seeing what she had done yesterday. It was invariably worse than she hoped.

Viv was not irritated by her young sister's passion for painting, but she did think her behaviour extreme. She disapproved of her disregard for food, indifference to her appearance, her habit of working when she should be asleep, and a general lack of common sense. Julie was unconventional, a show-off who entered a room in a 'look at me!' way; Viv could understand that. To enjoy herself was Julie's career. But Isobel could be downright idiotic.

Viv also noticed that Patrick, Isobel's one close friend, appeared to get on her nerves. He was the only person to whom she showed her paintings and drawings, yet she resented his down-to-earth personality and shameless criticisms – 'you're not on form today, Isobel', Viv heard him shout while he was sitting for her. Viv believed Isobel was in love with the man. Once Isobel had said 'he's the enemy of the life of the spirit'.

Viv had only smiled and Isobel said quickly, 'You think that's pompous.'

'No, I don't. A bit solemn, perhaps,' Viv had replied.

Patrick enjoyed teasing Isobel who found it hard to laugh at herself. He mocked her attitude to her religion.

'For a good RC you're very broad-minded about your sister's moral sin, as you'd call it.'

'Which sister? Which sin?'

'Aha. Did you think I meant Julie? We won't go in to *her* sins, you're much too young. I'm referring to la Señora Santander who refuses her husband his conjugal rights.'

Isobel went red. She was what he called a 'constant blusher'; her cheeks burned easily. He loved to annoy and looked with satisfaction at poor Isobel's crimson face.

'I see you'd prefer not to discuss the secrets of the Spanish bedchamber.'

'Do shut up.'

He often tried to take her opinions and prejudices by storm. He came riding up armed to the teeth. He was never content to sit around in her studio unless she was painting him, which tickled his vanity. He persuaded her to go to theatres, movies, meals and galleries. If she demurred he would say 'call yourself an artist'.

'I never call myself any such thing.'

'Whether you do or not, that's what you're trying to be and artists need to look at life. You can't frowst away in your studio like a monk.'

'You mean a nun.'

'Don't be so literal.'

He used her affection and her time and dissipated them. Yet in some ways he replaced what he wasted, giving food to a mind hungry for such things; for the galleries hanging not canonized work but that of new painters, for plays reflecting the times, and for books. He affected her and that's what he meant to do.

He had returned to his campaign to get her to bed, but his patience was beginning to wear thin. There had never been a girl on whom he spent so much of his charm. He also lavished money he could scarcely afford, and a good deal of somewhat mocking devotion. In his way, he was in love with her but not romantically.

151

Isobel wrote poetry and he thought it mawkish. When they cuddled and she whispered sentimental speeches about her feelings for him she sounded like a schoolgirl.

But he wanted her. She was rounded, slender, young as a rose just budding, her breasts small and neat; her eyes melted, her pretty mouth was often slightly open. How much longer, for God's sake, must he hang about in her studio or take her to films during which, in the dark, he clutched her hand with his own sweaty one? He was not used to aching for women; when they responded he was energetically sexy and, in a good mood afterwards, inclined to joke.

The drama of Carlos's appearance was over and normal life resumed. Viv was nervous but absorbed in her baby. Isobel had begun a series of drawings of mother and child and was cheerful when she and Patrick met in the evenings after he had returned from his newspaper. She decided not to show him the drawings, but put them into a folder and piled books on top of it. When he did not ask to see them, she was offended and relieved.

It was early summer in Chelsea, a time for sprawling on the grass in the park or going for evening drives in his third-hand old motor to Hampton Court. One Saturday, hot but not yet dusty, he persuaded her to come with him to the country. 'I know a pub on the river. You'll like it.'

He had decided privately that the long frustration had simply got to end. He was going not to beg but to take.

He arrived with his usual punctuality, looking attractive and tough, 'like a cowboy', as Viv had once described him. Isobel laughed because round his neck, tied like a casual scarf, was one of Kit's clean nappies. Viv had lent it to him recently to dry his hair after a shower of rain. He had liked the nappy which was soft and pliable and asked if he might keep it. Viv was amused, wondering if it was a symbol. But her mind ran on nothing but babies.

The pale cloth tied to resemble a sportsman's white scarf suited him. Isobel, conscious of the look of everything – a beloved man, a flower, a cloud – said so.

'You look like a tennis champion.'

'That was the idea.'

They drove through sunny London, leaving it behind at last and taking a road which now and again ran close to the Thames which brimmed after heavy spring rains.

The trees were freshly green, the air pleasantly cool. Isobel had dressed up, relinquishing the daubed smock and, at Viv's insistence, wearing a silk dress of turquoise and dark blue and her mother's sapphire ring. When she caught Patrick's eye, they exchanged smiles.

The place he had chosen for a meal was an ancient hotel, once a posting house, with a restaurant opening on to lawns going down to the river and a gardenful of roses. It was all very pretty and smart and Isobel exclaimed that he was extravagant to spend his salary on her. Patrick said yes, wasn't he? He guessed the bill would be painful, but, squeezing her arm in his, thought wasn't she worth every penny?

It flattered Patrick that the restaurant was full, that, having booked a table he was shown to it by the head waiter. The food was good and Isobel at her most engaging. For today she had put aside her self absorption. She listened to him attentively and asked about his career plans, something she usually forgot but now appeared eager to hear about. She leaned her elbows on the table, unconscious that other men looked at her with interest. Patrick was proud to be her man.

When the meal finished, he said, 'Shall we go for a walk?'

'Do let's. The buttercups are out.'

She would say that.

They walked arm in arm down a lane high with early summer weeds, smelling sweet and rich and buzzing with insects. Soon Isobel cried, 'Patrick, just look!'

And there was a field so crammed with buttercups that it was a great sloping sweep of dark rich yellow. On the far side of the field was a high hedge. Patrick, who had sex on his mind, saw that the field rose slightly, then fell again. There must be a nook there where they could lie down. The countryside was deserted and filled with sunshine.

Threading their way through the flowers they arrived at the

place he had mentally chosen and sank down on a counterpane of buttercups. Isobel looked up at him as he embraced her. He kissed her mouth, opening it wider, and pressed her small firm breasts. Then he said in a low whisper, 'I want you, lovely one. I must have you. *Now.*'

She tensed and began to protest, gently at first, then more wildly. In the struggle her blue skirts were tugged up to her waist and wrenched down again. Tears streamed down her face. In his angry frustration he began to swear.

'All you are is a little bitch who likes to tease. To hot me up and cool me off. I might have known it from the start.'

'Stop, stop,' sobbed the girl. 'Don't be so cruel – you know I've never m-made love and I think it's wrong to do it and – stop!' she dragged herself away as he began to caress her in a kind of fury. It was all hideous and the worst part was her choking sobs. He scrambled to his feet, buttoning his clothes. He looked down at the figure melodramatically stretched among the squashed flowers.

'Hell, don't cry like that. It isn't a bloody tragedy.'

She lifted a mottled face.

'You don't love me.'

'For Christ's sake what have I – oh for Christ's sake.'

'Don't swear, I hate it.' She sat up sniffing, and said dolefully, like the child she still was, 'Now you won't want us to be friends.'

He gave a sarcastic laugh, to his later shame. They returned to the car and to London in a sullen silence. When he drew up in the King's Road Isobel, without a word, hurried away, head bowed.

She threw herself into her work. She arranged to attend classes at college four times a week. She disappeared into her bedroom/ studio to paint. She asked Viv if she could sketch her with the baby, and while she drew and Viv sat quietly with Kit in her arms, Viv thought once or twice she saw her sister's eyes brimming.

Viv did not say a word about the noticeable absence of Patrick during the last few days. There must be trouble of some kind but it would blow over. If Isobel did not want to confide, why should she?

154

Viv felt for her and knew that some things – many things – were better left unsaid.

The following week, the sun which had shone over the buttercups intensified. It rayed over the city which sweltered in the sudden heatwave. The girls in Chelsea wore their thinnest clothes; London became unexpectedly European; there were even parasols about. A favourite summer gag was used in Fleet Street – an evening paper showed a front page photograph of a girl in a swimsuit frying eggs on the pavement under the headline 'Phew!'

Isobel returned from college, fanning herself with the brim of her straw hat and let herself into the flat. She called, 'Viv?'

'I'm in here.'

The drawing room windows were wide open, the tops of the trees motionless, the door propped open with a cushion. The baby was on the sofa as he'd been on the day his father had seen him. Isobel thought that every day the little creature seemed to alter, grow rounder. He was peering short-sightedly at his own fist.

She sat down beside him and spoke in the voice she kept only for her nephew, 'Aren't you the lovely baby? Aren't you just the lovely boy?' She tapped the minute fist hoping that, as it sometimes did, it would make him give a knowing smile.

It was only when she glanced over and saw her sister's troubled expression that she said nervously, 'What's happened? Has *he* come back from Spain again?'

'No, no, Carlos won't be here for three months,' said Viv in an odd voice. Isobel's perceptions fastened on another he.

'I suppose Patrick came round,' she said, hope springing.

'No,' repeated Viv, and then reluctantly, 'It was Julie.'

The light died in Isobel's face. She turned back to the baby, and tapped his fist again. This time he smiled.

'Isobel. There is something I have to tell you. Patrick has gone to live at Dysart House.'

She waited for her sister's burst of crying. All her life Isobel had wept often and easily. Now nothing happened. Isobel stared, not at Viv but over her shoulder. Viv saw she was filled with hate. For the man and for the sister who had stolen him. She went straight out of the room and out of the flat.

The evening was hotter than ever but she did not cross the street to be in the shade. She walked steadily down the road through the loitering crowds towards her sister's ancient kingdom of a house. She did not think at all, she simply moved.

Dysart was looking its exquisite self, with its leafy two hundred-year-old trees in the courtyard, the paving stones sprung about with ferns. The front door was open and a dog Isobel had never seen before, a kind of rough-haired wolfhound, lay on the step; she had to step over it but it neither growled nor stirred.

There had always been music in Dysart and there was a gramophone playing now, and the low noise of men's voices, then her sister's voice followed by laughter. Isobel pushed open the double doors into the drawing room.

Everybody stopped talking.

Julie was sitting on George Silver's lap and George, who liked Isobel, gave her a sort of wave. Two girls, rich looking, very young, were sitting on the floor; Harold was at the gramophone and the French boy sprawled nearby. And there was Patrick.

Seeing Isobel, everybody chorused 'Hello' except Patrick who drew on his cigarette and looked at her without expression.

'Come in, Belle. Come in and sample Claude's new cocktail, it's absolutely disgusting,' trilled Julie.

'I want to talk to you,' said Isobel in a loud voice.

'Talk away. Here I am.' Julie snuggled up to George Silver. She wore a dress of pale creamy silk which shimmered as she moved. She was as bright as the garden outside the French windows.

'Not here.'

Isobel's face, her voice, had no effect on Julie who cried, 'Mysteries, mysteries. As a family we go in for them. Is that what makes us so intriguing?' She gave Patrick a wink, climbed from George's lap, said to her guests, 'Go on drinking!' and swaggered off behind her sister.

'And where are we supposed to go?' she enquired. She had shut the drawing room door and now regarded Isobel warily.

156

'Where you like. There?' Isobel pointed towards the kitchens which led one from another into a stone floored scullery.

'Nobody's around upstairs at present,' said Julie. 'Shall we go to my room?'

Shrugging and making a face, she led the way up the stairs and down a corridor where, in the seventeenth century, men had walked, candles in hand, to seductions or to plots. Julie's bedroom door stood open. There was a vast and rumpled bed. Seeing it, Isobel shuddered.

But she began quietly enough. 'How could you? How could you ask him to live here?'

'He hates his digs. He says they smell of cats.'

'You don't even like him,' said Isobel, voice still level. 'You did it to spite me.'

'Why should I spite you, Isobel? You are an ass. All I did was say he can stay here for a bit. You know what scads of room I've got and as I told you, his digs stink.'

'You don't even like him,' repeated Isobel, her voice rising when faced with Julie's insouciance.

'I do as a matter of fact. Like him, I mean. When he popped round and told me you and he had separated I didn't see why on earth he shouldn't be rescued from the cats' pee.'

'*He* doesn't like *you*,' said poor Isobel. She had come in fury. Now she felt lost.

Julie threw herself down on the bed, sprawling and showing black lace knickers.

'Look, Isobel, don't make a scene. You and Viv are a couple, aren't you? First Carlos. Now Patrick. He's told me all about you and him, you know. How you wouldn't have him – no, don't butt in, let me speak for a minute. Don't think I blame you for not sleeping with him –'

'Holy Mother of God.'

'For crying out loud, Isobel, you sound like Ma! I'll say it again. Why should you sleep with him if you don't want to and he doesn't attract you or something? And since *you* don't want him I can't see why you should object –'

157

Isobel's eyes, always large, were now enormous.

'You've already been to bed with him then?'

Julie gave a vague gesture.

Then Isobel lost control. She rushed over and slapped her sister so hard across the face that she knocked her on her back. She plunged her fingers into Julie's short waved hair and tugged as she did as a child when teased by Julie beyond endurance. She tried to scratch her face but Julie, wiry although as light as Isobel, managed to roll away, shoving her sister aside and kicking herself free. With another attacker Julie might have laughed. She'd done that once or twice when slapped and insulted by would-be lovers. But this was her sister and Julie was infected by the same rage, as she more or less fell off the bed.

'What a little cow you are!' she burst out, picking up a chair and holding it feet forward like a shield. 'You don't want him. He's been dancing round you for months with his tongue hanging out, asking you to make love and you won't. As I just said, I don't see why you or any woman should give in if they don't want to. You don't want to, do you? But you can't bear me to have him. What sort of a person does that make you? Mean spirited. Mean. My God I'm not surprised you aren't Pa's daughter.'

The silence that followed was like a gasp.

It was Julie who broke it. Her eyes filled with tears, she put down the ridiculous weapon of the chair, and rushed over gabbling, 'I didn't mean it, I didn't mean it, take no notice of me, I'm the one who's a bitch and a fool.'

She tried to catch hold of Isobel but her sister pushed her aside without violence and ran towards the door. Julie, still weeping, ran after her. All Isobel kept saying was 'I must go,' over and over again.

She fled down the stairs and through the courtyard and out into the burning street.

CHAPTER EIGHT

It was never Julie's habit to warn Frank Bryant beforehand of her sudden visits to the Hornsey house and when he heard the bell and opened the door and found his third daughter on the step he was not particularly surprised.

'The bad penny. Con's not here today, you'll be glad to hear. Come along in with you. I'm in the back garden.'

Julie threw her arms round his neck and kissed him. He smelled of tobacco and Lifebuoy soap and when she pressed her face to his bristly skin she was a child again. He shooed her through the tiny house into a garden the size of a pocket handkerchief. One tree, a lilac, gave a patch of deckled shade. He had drawn a deck chair under it and had been reading his newspaper.

'Sit yourself down and I'll fetch another.'

Julie obeyed him.

Wearing black cotton with thin straps showing arms browned in Dysart's garden, she looked pinched. Frank, on the contrary, looked the way he often described other people – bonny. His shirt was rolled up to show brawny arms. His hair, greyish yet still fair in places, was bleached on top by the sun. He liked to garden and the borders of the suburban lawn were crammed with old-fashioned hollyhocks, foxgloves, delphiniums and dark orange seeded marigolds. He came out of the potting shed with another chair and set it up facing his daughter, then lit his pipe and drew on it comfortably; but he was aware of her silence and lack of mirth.

'You've come sooner than you usually do. Wasn't it April when we saw you last? Yes, it was, I remember it poured. Now it's only June. Any reason for your appearance this time?' He thought she looked poorly.

'I came for advice.'

'Bless my soul.'

'Don't laugh at me.'

'Well, you are a bit of a Dismal Desmond this morning. You're usually so merry and bright. What is this advice I'm to give and you're not going to take?'

He was unlike any other man Julie had known in her life. Her lovers were ghosts compared to him. They were men she could fascinate. Not Pa. They were at her mercy. Never Pa. Even her sisters' men were sexually aware of her; Stuart and Viv's magnificent Carlos. You could always tell when a man saw you in that way. As for Isobel's Patrick, her latest lover and an energetic one, he pleased her body but not as much as his presence made her conscience miserable. Bloody hell, thought Julie; the phrase which covered everything from sins to hangovers.

Frank continued to smoke and look at the garden. He knew perfectly well the girl would break the silence eventually; it was his old trick and always worked. He was glad Connie wasn't around today. Con could be a right bitch and was so jealous of his daughters; it was partly her fault he'd lost three of them. When did he see Viv? When Claire? How was Isobel growing up? Now he came to think of it, both his wives, Connie and poor Grace, had been jealous cats.

He did not regret marrying Connie. She was a good wife, far better than Grace had been, not stuffy, not giving herself airs and a good passionate bedfellow. But he regretted his girls ...

Julie said at last, 'I think I've come to make my confession.'

'Well, I'm damned.'

'Don't laugh, Pa,' she said again, and just then she looked stricken.

'What have you been up to, girl?'

'I told Isobel you aren't her father.'

He was thunderstruck. He sat looking at her as if, like in the old stories, she had suddenly turned from beautiful woman into serpent. He glared at her for so long that she burst out, 'Please don't. Please don't.'

'I must say, Julie, you've shocked me.'

'I know.'

'What the devil made you do such an awful thing?'

'I never meant to.'

'That old song,' he said with a contempt she'd never heard in his voice before. 'Never meant. Isn't that the worst kind, not to mean to do wrong? To do harm? What did you do it for?'

Julie tried to explain what had happened. She told the story badly, she was too used to being queen and empress, seductress and fascinator. The role she was forced to play of penitent Magdalene sat ill on her thin shoulders. She had never been on her knees except in church, and even then her mind was always crammed with distractions. She told him about Patrick. She spoke about Isobel. She did not make excuses but stated the facts in a slangy miserable mutter. He smoked and asked no questions until she finally came to the row, the fight and what she had blurted out.

He stared at his plimsolls.

She waited.

'You've done it now,' was all he said.

'That's not much help, Pa.'

'My good girl, what did you expect when you turned up here? I absolve you in the name of the Father and the Son? I can't forgive you, you didn't do it to me. How does poor Isobel feel about what you told her?'

'She won't see me.'

'Did you imagine she would?'

A thrush landed on the fence, started a song and changed its mind. It flew away.

Despite her father's expression, she felt very slightly better; it was as if his condemnation was a medicine she must take to be cured. She hadn't discussed her crime with any of her men, least of all with Patrick, busy making love and making jokes – he was in fine fettle since they had become lovers. When Julie went to see

161

Viv, Isobel was noticeably absent. Viv was angry and cold. *She* knew.

She made Julie feel worse when she was leaving by saying in a voice of ice, 'Don't you *dare* tell any of those men about Isobel. It's her business that she's illegitimate, that our mother had an affair and all that. You just shut up. Don't salve your conscience by telling the whole thing to a lot of stupid men who hang round you. They'll be only too pleased to tell you it isn't your fault. Well it is. So hold your tongue.'

Apparently sharing Viv's opinion, Frank Bryant said, 'Discussed this with anybody else?'

'Only Viv.'

'Who told you off right and proper?'

'Yes.'

'What about your twin as you call her?' Julie said nothing. Since Claire's marriage, the two had drifted apart. Julie minded and told herself that she did not. Claire rarely telephoned her and had disappeared into the life of a young upper-class wife, a somebody in the county with dogs and horses and snobberies to match. Julie didn't make a move towards Claire, who was too wrapped up in her own new life to notice.

'What about Claire?' repeated her father.

When he was with Julie he felt the tie of blood. How strong it was and how often he forgot it. Busy with Connie, busy with reports still sent to him by his own firm, enjoying a quiet steady life, he only thought about his daughters now and then. But with Connie absent and this child of his close to him, the strange strong familiarity took over. And all the old grief at what he'd lost.

'Claire's making her number in Sussex,' said Julie. 'She's taken to the county. Dogs, horses, she even gets her picture in *The Tatler.*'

He gave a slight snort.

She looked at him quickly.

'You're not furious with me any more.'

'I suppose not. One can't go on fuming at somebody when they do something wrong. Not if they're sorry.'

'Oh, Pa, I am.'

'Let's say you're uncomfortable and you don't like yourself much at present. I suppose we'd best see what can be done to make things better.'

'I could say I'd lied. That I'd made the whole thing up to hurt her. When we were fighting that time.'

'Fighting,' echoed Frank Bryant. 'That's a pretty spectacle I must say. As for the suggestion of pretending it was a lie, you're daft.'

'What do you mean?'

He shook his head at her obtuseness.

'For a clever young woman, you are a fool. Did you think Viv wouldn't tell the poor child the whole story after you'd blurted it out like that? If I know Viv – God knows I wish I knew her better – she'll try and smooth it over, explain that Grace must have been unhappy at the time because I'd been having a bit of a fling myself. Your mother, you know, was having her revenge. Or maybe she wanted to know what infidelity felt like. I've never understood what happened really. It wasn't in Grace's nature. However, the thing was done and little Isobel on the way and we made the best of it that we could.'

'That was wonderful of you, Pa.'

'Don't be dafter than before,' he said, knocking out his pipe on the sole of his shoe. 'I wanted her back. I didn't mind about the kid. Rather liked the idea after I was sure she wasn't hankering after its father. That old stuff is all dead and forgotten. What matters is Isobel.'

'But what can I do when she won't see me?'

'Thought of writing?'

Julie was genuinely surprised. She belonged to a growing section of people who apart from signing cheques never put pen to paper. She said to friends if they went away, 'You know me. I never write.' She said it in self-congratulation, sharing with her listeners the kind of person she was, just as idle women might say, 'You know me, I never cook', and mean ones, 'You know me, I don't give money to beggars'. Her friends accepted that Julie would never write to them. If they wrote to her it was because they loved her.

'Well?' he prompted, 'what about writing her a letter? It's the best

163

thing in a case like this. If you saw her you'd only put your foot in it again like as not. She must be feeling as raw as a bit of beef. From what you tell me, she's a sensitive little thing.'

'Yes.'

'And a good little painter.'

'I don't know about that.'

'You don't, do you? You could buy one of her things sometime when you're both on speaking terms again and bring it to show me. I'd like that. I do remember her lying on her stomach drawing with pastels when she was a little scrap, four years old. Don't remember thinking she showed any talent. Mostly houses and stick people. However, back to my point. You must write to her and say you are sorry. Tell her you are very sorry and you take the blame for breaking the silence which her mother begged me to keep. I'm shocked, incidentally, at Grace. How did you girls learn about it?'

'Mother never told us. We found it in some papers in her desk. Viv hid them from Isobel.'

'I see.'

He was glad it had not been Grace. He preferred to like his first wife, even to love the idea of her.

'So,' he said encouragingly, 'You'd better write a really good letter.'

A bee went buzzing by. It was quiet and hot and there was a scent of flowers. Somebody over the hedge called, 'Morning, Mr Bryant. Isn't it a duck of a day?'

A thin faced woman with her arms full of dried washing peered through the trellis. There were greetings and a joke or two. Frank and Julie waited until the woman disappeared indoors.

Then Julie said, 'Pa.'

'What is it now?'

He had forgiven her. He supposed he ought not to have done so easily, but there it was. She was his child and she was sorry. She looked peaky.

'I suppose ...' her voice expired. She pulled off a little hat and it left a red mark across her forehead. She ran her fingers through her hair making it ripple. She was prettier without that damned hat. He

164

did not react as all Julie's men did, to her unfinished sentence, her thin beauty, her wistful face. He relit his pipe.

'I suppose,' she said at last, 'you wouldn't help me write it?'

'If you like,' said Frank Bryant. 'Now I think about it, I'm not sure you'd make much of a fist of that letter.'

To have one shock which sets you reeling can sometimes be borne. You get back on your feet, give yourself a shake, dust your clothes and persuade yourself that you are lucky it was not worse. Isobel had had three. She'd lost the man she was half in love with in a humiliating rupture. He had left her and walked away straight into Julie's arms. Finally came the worst blow of all to a sensitive young woman, she had been told with deliberate cruelty that she was not her father's child.

After the fight with Julie, Isobel went to bed for an entire day with a headache so intense that Viv was alarmed, remembering Grace. She sent for the doctor who had attended her when Kit was born.

He spent some time with the sufferer who had been in her darkened bedroom for over twenty-four hours. Viv walked up and down the drawing room waiting for his verdict and trying to keep calm. She felt she could never speak to Julie again.

The doctor came in at last.

'You must not upset yourself, Mrs Santander. There is nothing seriously wrong with your sister,' were his comforting words. Viv found herself suddenly sitting down. Her legs had given way.

The doctor, Henry Varley, was sixtyish and wore morning dress to call on his patients as if on his way to Goodwood – a magnificent suit with satin lapels and a black pearl pin in his grey silk stock.

'What has happened,' he said, 'is that Miss Byrant has had a series of shocks. Of course you know all about those. In a less steady young woman they might well have caused a nervous breakdown. But in this case –'

'I never thought Isobel was steady,' said Viv anxiously.

'Oh yes. Oh yes. She paints, does she not? I noticed one or two canvasses in her room. There's talent there. Artists, Mrs Santander,

165

have natures of steel. They have to or they'd go to the wall.'

He talked for a moment or two about his collection of water colours. Social chat was a part of his job. He then returned to his patient. Was there migraine in the family? Ah. He'd thought so. Isobel's symptoms were classic; he could show Viv a picture in one of his medical books which illustrated migraines. The sufferer saw things distorted or with pieces missing in the vision. Migraine usually caused vomiting which was of course because of the eyes. Nothing need be done for his patient but to keep her quiet, give her plenty of rest, aspirins and tea, and not too much sympathy.

'The artistic temperament may be hardy but it is self indulgent. If you're too understanding she'll have a crying fit which won't do the headache any good. I will be back tomorrow at about this time,' finished Dr Varley. He picked up his black leather bag. Viv noticed that his initials upon it were lettered in gold and beneath them was a small family crest. She took him to the door and he bade her a formal paternal good night.

Her sister was still flat on her bed. The pillows had been thrown on the floor and the curtains tightly pulled, keeping out any gleam of the golden afternoon. The room smelled of Isobel's lemon eau de Cologne. Memories of Grace came back to Viv in a harrowing wave.

'Has the doctor gone?' asked Isobel in what even Viv thought a dying duck voice.

'A moment ago. He says you must rest and keep quiet and have aspirins. I'll make some tea.'

'I couldn't drink it.'

'Of course you could. Don't be silly,' said Viv, following instructions.

Isobel surfaced, propped herself on one elbow and managed to swallow the aspirins and drink the tea. She asked Viv to open the curtains, 'but only a teeny bit'.

Within two days she was herself again. She was nineteen, and despite anger and misery, the thought of painting, like an uninvited guest at a wake, kept coming into her mind. She was still drawn looking and quiet, thought Viv. But at least she set off punctually for college.

166

At the St Helier, Isobel had a good many acquaintances; she was sociable enough and perfectly willing to talk to people. But she made no intimate friends. Unlike the rest of the students, she disliked talking shop. They gathered on the steps of the college, or clattering out of class at four o'clock, trooped off to one of the quaint little Chelsea tea shops, to discuss nothing but work. They were noisy and facetious, earnest and critical. They dismissed many of the great masters, past and present, and each had one particular artist whom they 'worshipped'. It was usually an obscure painter whose name had a satisfactory mystery about it. Isobel didn't want to be part of all that. She was half bored and half afraid of her fellow students.

Since coming to London she had made only one friend, and that by chance. To avoid the tea shops on a day when Viv and the baby were out visiting, she had gone into a cheap ABC on a corner of the King's Road to have tea by herself. It was there that she met Larry Daniels.

The place was crowded and there was only one vacated chair at a table by the window where a man was having his tea. Isobel shyly asked if he would mind if she joined him. He stood up and said, 'Delighted.'

She could scarcely avoid answering, when he made a remark or two.

He was short and undistinguished looking, a plain young man, his face colourless, his hair ordinarily brown with one deep wave over his forehead. He had grey eyes and his smile was infectious, his voice, tinged with Cockney, rather ugly. But he was friendly and natural, he was not a painter, and in his eyes she saw such admiration that Isobel was pleased.

They fell into the habit of meeting at the ABC shop, never by arrangement but at roughly the same time. Larry was always glad to see her. 'Hello!' he would exclaim, jumping to his feet as she came into the steamy place, which in the afternoon smelled of buttered toast.

Isobel knew he was attracted. She did not want to think about that.

167

When she went into the ABC after her return to the St Helier, Larry jumped up so fast that he knocked his chair over.

When they sat down he burst out, 'Where have you been? I thought you'd left the college. I didn't know how to find you. You aren't in the telephone book. I've been at my wits' end. Are you all right? Have you been ill?'

His concern made Isobel want to weep with self pity. She explained that she'd had a bad migraine and had been 'kept in bed', implying relatives and doctors. Larry exclaimed again. He had had headaches as a child, not a real migraine but 'splitters just the same'. They had always made him sick.

'Poor, poor Isobel!' he said.

Things were different that afternoon. Isobel's days of absence gave a reality to their friendship. It was more intimate, it was warm. Isobel, touched by the fact that he had actually looked her up in the telephone book, gave him her address. Until now they had scarcely talked of where they lived. She told him about her sister and the baby and Larry listened to every word with eagerness. It was as if by telling him a few facts about herself she paid him the greatest of compliments.

When they finished tea he asked tentatively if he could walk with her as far as her home.

'Don't think I want to be asked in,' he said. 'In any case I couldn't accept. I have to be at the theatre by half past five.'

'Do you go to the theatre often?' said Isobel, imagining that it was necessary to get there early because he was queuing for the pit.

'No, no, not a real theatre. The Essoldo. The cinema,' he said, laughing.

'What film are you going to see?' She was not offended that Hollywood this evening was replacing her.

Larry laughed again, pleased by the misunderstanding. 'I don't go to the cinema, Isobel. I work there.' Before yet another wrong impression, that perhaps he was the technician in charge of the projector, he explained.

'I'm called an assistant manager but that's only because my boss thinks by giving me a grand title he can pay less. I have to put on a dinner jacket every night and see the queues in.'

'Golly.'

He was quite unselfconscious about his job. 'I'm on hand in case the public wants anything. Suppose somebody doesn't feel well for instance. Then occasionally there's trouble in the ninepennies.'

'What sort of trouble?' Isobel asked, eyes wide.

'Drunks, mostly. Fortunately that's only on Saturdays.'

She was still full of wonder and interest.

'Did you choose that sort of work because you want to run a cinema yourself one day?'

'Oh no. I do it for the money. It was the only job I could get and I bought the dinner jacket at a pawn shop. I go to college too. Not the St Helier, I go to the Poly. I'm taking Matric.'

He was full of surprises that afternoon. They walked back along the King's Road in an evening dull-skied and promising rain. Encouraged by his companion, whom he thought by far the most beautiful girl he had met in his life, he explained that he'd left school at fourteen to help his mother when his father had died. He'd worked in a wholesale butcher's 'to pay Mum's rent'. Now with his Chelsea job he could afford to give her more.

'Mum agrees with me that a night job means I've got the chance to finish my education. Don't imagine I'm not grateful for my job, Isobel. The work isn't hard and the manager is a nice chap, very proud of the Essoldo; he doesn't think there's another cinema to touch it. And the pay is not bad. The only trouble is I have no nights off.'

'But there is always Sunday,' said Isobel, thinking of quiet Sundays in Chelsea with all the streets empty, the shops closed and time to paint or wander along the embankment at low tide.

'We work on Sundays, too,' he said, smiling. 'They pay overtime.'

They continued to meet and their friendship to grow. He confessed his impossible dream of getting high marks in his examinations, getting some 'real' job where he could make something of himself. His aspirations were vague but when he talked of the future, his grey eyes shone. She liked him very much. Every time they met now, he walked home with her to the doors of Roper Court,

169

insisting on carrying her portfolio of drawings. Not for nothing did Larry work at the Essoldo where the American films endlessly showed clean-cut young college boys accompanying their girls on Graduation Day.

One day in early autumn when they were more pleased than ever to see each other, and Isobel had hurried to get to the ABC early so that she would have more time with him, she told him about Julie.

She had already described her three sisters and Larry remembered details of each one of them. Once they had walked past Dysart House, and Isobel said, 'That's my sister Julie's place.' Larry, looking at the mansion hidden among the trees, found it difficult not to whistle. Isobel's aura, rich and mysterious, grew stronger than ever, surrounding her like a glow.

Why did she decide to tell him about the thing which lay like a stone on her heart? Because he was her friend now, her only true ally.

She hadn't been able to speak about it to anybody else after her first sobbing outburst to Viv. She had not mentioned it again to her sister. She, Isobel, was the only outcast. It was true that Viv and Claire never saw their father but that wasn't the point. They were not bastards. They were not the result of some affair of her mother's, her birth lied about because, she supposed, Grace hadn't had the guts to leave Frank Bryant. Sometimes Isobel, brooding about herself, forgot the other three.

Now sitting at the tea table she burst out, 'Larry, I've got something to tell you.'

He nodded; it was natural to be confided in by Isobel.

She described her quarrel with Julie, omitting Patrick from the story and saying she had got on her sister's nerves when she'd lived at Dysart House; she had painted too much and joined in too little. In the end there had been a terrible row. She repeated what Julie had told her. She could not look at Larry while she was speaking. When she finished at last, she lifted her head and met his eyes. Would he cease to admire her? Had she embarrassed him? After all he was only an ordinary London boy, he was not sophisticated. Larry, like everybody else, would let her down.

'Of course, you've got to find your real father,' he said.

Isobel stared.

'But that's what this is all about, isn't it?' He was delighted with her awful secret and continued, 'What a marvellous story. Do you know anything about him? Perhaps that's where your talent comes from.'

'I don't think I have any talent.'

He really laughed. 'None of the false modesty. Look, you must have already thought of this, but perhaps your dad is a famous artist? Didn't you tell me the other day that Augustus John lives around here somewhere, and that he has loads of illegitimate children? Maybe you're another of them. You've got to find out, Isobel. Don't you see how exciting it is?'

Like a swimmer floating in the water, shouting up to her as she stood on the top board to 'dive, dive', he seemed to be saying how easy it was. It was almost as if he had already done such a thing himself. There was something boyish, matter-of-fact and extra-ordinarily comforting about him. The very idea of illegitimacy connected with Isobel fascinated him.

'You'll have to find out all you can from your eldest sister,' he said as they were walking home. 'Isobel?'

'Yes?' was the doubtful answer.

'What a story!' he exclaimed, 'Viv –' Larry had not met any of her sisters and was on first name terms with all three, 'Viv is sure to know more. After all, how did they find out?'

He grinned at her, carrying her along with his own enthusiasm. When they parted he said as usual, 'Same time, same place?'

'Of course.'

'I shall be dying to hear the news.'

'Oh Larry.'

'Don't be silly,' he said, looking at her with a caressing shy look, 'I can't wait!'

Isobel had to wait before she spoke to Viv. You couldn't, she thought, cross-question a woman who was breast feeding. She put her head round the bedroom door and there was Viv in her pose of Madonna with child. To calm her nerves – she was tensely excited –

171

Isobel fetched her sketch pad, returned to Viv's room and sat down. Viv glanced up, smiled, and looked down again at the baby. There was no sound but the loud sucking. Once he snorted and Viv laughed tenderly.

As Isobel drew, she could see Carlos, invisible yet strangely real, kneeling beside the little boy.

At last the feeding was over and the baby carried away to his room where the windows opened on to the view of the poplar tops. He was already asleep, bloated with milk. Buttoning her dress, Viv came back to Isobel who was still sketching.

'Come into the drawing room. That chair's as hard as nails.'

'It is,' said Isobel. She shut her book and followed her sister to more comfort and the ordeal to come.

Discussing it with Larry, Isobel had decided not to tell Viv what she had in her mind; she was to go on her search in secret. She was still too wounded to argue, and very conscious that what she was going to do was totally her own business.

She managed a casual voice.

'Viv. I want to talk. About something we've both been avoiding.'

'You mean Patrick?'

She had seen Julie with him in the King's Road two or three times, driving in Julie's showy Sunbeam car. She had thought her sister more culpable because the man, to Viv's prejudiced eye, looked coarse.

'No, I don't want to talk about Patrick,' said Isobel, coolly enough. 'He's yesterday. I mean the other matter. About –' Her voice expired. 'About my – my real father.'

Viv waited a moment.

'Are you quite sure you want to talk about it, Isobel? Surely it will only hurt all over again? After all you're our sister. It doesn't change anything that you found out what you did. When we all discovered the paper –'

'What paper?' said Isobel too quickly.

But Viv was concerned and did not notice.

'Didn't Julie tell you when she was shouting at you, poor Isobel? What we found was your birth certificate. And a letter from Ma in

172

an envelope where she kept a lot of little things, locks of hair when we were babies and a poem you wrote once and our baby photographs. And there was a letter from Pa.'

'What did it say?'

'Just that all was to be forgotten and forgiven. That kind of thing.'

'Can I see it?'

Viv turned the request over as if it were dangerous. She wondered, she often wondered, what matter-of-fact Claire would say. Yet why shouldn't Isobel see the things? They were far more 'yesterday' than her romance with that young reporter. For all her habit of bursting into tears, (perhaps Dr Varley was right) Isobel was the strongest of the four.

'Are you sure it won't upset you?' asked Viv.

'Julie upset me. This is only fact. A bit of paper. The truth.'

'If you really think ...' murmured Viv and went to the bureau. She foraged about in a drawer beneath the bureau's writing surface and pulled out a sheaf of papers fastened by a rubber band. There were records of Grace's investments kept over the years, and a copy of her will. There was a prayer or two; who had given her those? Finally the letter which had astounded the sisters. They had stuffed it out of sight when Isobel had come into the room at Woodlands.

Viv handed it to her.

It was written in their father's level old-fashioned handwriting, on a piece of notepaper with the address of a Glasgow hotel.

My dear Grace,

Your letter of two days ago to hand. I must admit what you tell me is a shock. I would never have believed it of you. But you were very upset over the Anny business and although I promised I would not see her any more, I suppose the trouble affected you.

You tell me you are two months gone, following an affair with a man called William Clanfield at Ockrent and that this happened when during my absence you were staying with the Vernons. You say, you have not yet told Clanfield and, as you

173

put it, 'will leave me to decide what should be done'.

Grace, I have thought long and hard and since you beg me to 'have you back', I will do so. We will let bygones be bygones. I agree to say the child is mine. Everybody will take that as perfectly natural. After all, we already have three and our friends know us as a 'happy' family.

Under these circumstances, I will bring up your child, boy or girl, as my own and will treat him or her like the others in every way. I give you my word. But your way of writing, Grace, is somewhat hysterical as if you trusted nobody. I understand your state of mind and want you to keep this letter. It is my solemn contract to bring up William Clanfield's child as our fourth Bryant. In exchange I want your solemn vow that you will never inform the man that you are carrying, and will bear his child.

I do not intend to speak about this to you. I prefer we treat the matter from now on as closed.

We must resolve to do our best for all our children.

Your husband,

Frank.

Isobel read the letter through twice, then handed it back to her sister in silence. Viv put it back into the bureau.

She looked earnestly at Isobel to be sure she wasn't going to start crying or retreat into another migraine. She appeared quite calm. Behind the blank expression, Isobel was repeating names to herself. William Clanfield. Ockrent. Where was Ockrent?

'You are not going to get upset again, are you, Belle?'

Isobel gave a slight laugh.

'No. I wouldn't go through all that again. I've got used to the idea now. Besides, it's different reading Pa's letter than having the thing yelled at me during a spiteful row.'

'Do you mean that?'

'Yes, Viv. I do.'

The following day was cloudless and very hot and Isobel set off, Viv imagined, for college. She might be late home, she said, she

174

wanted to go to the National Gallery after her art class.

In fact she took a bus to Paddington and a train to a place called Kingham in Oxfordshire.

Early that morning when Viv was feeding the baby, Isobel had crept into the sitting room and found an English atlas. Ockrent was marked in tiny print not far from Kingham.

She was excited. She was on her way to an adventure which would end the hurt inflicted by Julie, the waves of mystified unhappiness and most of all the bruises to her self respect. She had Larry to thank for this brave journey.

The train windows were open and although smuts blew in so did the sweet air. Every cornfield was ripening not to the colour of gold as the poets described it but to the soft brownish tint of biscuits. Isobel stared out, trying to visualize what her father would look like – supposing, oh supposing, she was lucky enough to find him. She thought about the art teachers at college, many of them artists in their own right. Colin Cleves, with a snappish manner and a square ugly body. Oh please, not a man like him. Paul Haddenham, attenuated and effeminate, who taught etching and had a habit of fatuously agreeing with any student who made any suggestion whatsoever. Not one like him, either. She was perfectly certain now that the father she was on her way to find was an artist. How else had she inherited her longing to paint? Frank and Grace hadn't any interest or skill in artistic things. Her own gift, if gift it was, must come from somewhere. Her father would be dark, surely? With luck he would be handsome. A bohemian sort of man, probably working in his studio in the garden. Was he married? She hadn't thought of that.

She made up her mind if she *did* find him today, she was not going to say who she was. Not at first. She would make an excuse, say she'd lost her way or something. Then she could come back on a second visit.

Perhaps he left Ockrent years ago, she thought. Then I must somehow find somebody who knows where he is.

Her spirits rose with every mile further into the sunlit country. I never had a real father, she thought, and I'm on my way to find one.

175

After all Pa left us when I was much too little to know him, and William Clanfield is my own blood. Nobody is closer to me than he is.

There wasn't a soul on the platform when she arrived at Kingham. Somebody had watered a bed of French marigolds which spelled KINGHAM in deep orange knobs even to the extent of a flowery full stop.

The ticket collector, small as a sparrow, said, 'Good morning, miss. Nice day again.' Isobel had never visited Oxfordshire before and thought his accent much softer and more attractive than the Sussex intonation. When she smiled at him, he grinned back showing a noticeable lack of teeth.

'I'm going to Ockrent,' she said. 'Is it far?'

'Matter of two miles and a bit.'

'Then I can walk.'

'You'll have to, miss. No cabs at this time o' day. Won't take you long seeing as how you're young and hearty.'

Isobel rather agreed, she felt both those things. The porter gave her colourful directions.

'You'll see a pub on the corner, The Bear and Staff, you go straight on past it, see? There's a bit of a riding school on your left, the Major runs it, you go on along past him, and turn at the signpost and walk on to the village a good two miles. You won't be able to miss Ockrent Church. There's a pub, too, The Custard Pot, but you won't see that, it's round a corner.'

Isobel set off. It was very very hot. Hedges hiding thorns sprang high on either side of the road. The ditches brimmed with meadowsweet and ragged robin, and thistledown floated in the still air. Birds sang from little stunted trees. It was not a wooded place; there were no green tunnels to shade the road which snaked its way along under the beating sun. This is a pilgrimage, thought Isobel. She felt brave and nervous and strung up and filled with starving curiosity.

What was it about a father that became so enormous, so all-absorbing, because you had never set eyes on him? She could not remember longing for her other father after he'd left the family

176

home. She did not remember crying over his absence and she was pretty sure Viv and Claire hadn't done so either. They must have been influenced by Grace. They had never tried to see him again. And although Julie did, it was only showing off, thought Isobel cruelly. Everything Julie does is for effect, even hurting me.

She was unfamiliar with such deep country. Woodlands had been on the edge of a small town, Brighton an elegant city, and Chelsea near the busy heart of the capital. I suppose the people who live here think we are townies, she thought. I don't envy them. I wouldn't want to live anywhere so lonely. Perhaps my father chose the country because he's a landscape artist. She occupied herself during the second mile of the walk recalling landscape exhibitions in Bond Street and at the Royal Water Colour Society.

Ockrent was scarcely more than a cluster of houses and a too-large church with mossy gravestones in the recently mown grass. There was the usual village shop with the usual enamel ice cream sign outside.

Isobel stood hesitating by the church gate. Ought I to find the vicarage, she thought? They'd know if he's still living here. She wandered about for a few minutes and then came to a small handsome Georgian house at a short distance from the church. It was of golden Cotswold stone, perfectly square, with an enormous holly tree at the gate. A brick path led up to the house and on either side were beautifully kept velvety lawns and high clipped beech hedges. It must be the vicarage, thought Isobel. And then her heart turned over, for at the side of the house was a sort of cottage with one window greatly enlarged. She felt quite faint. Her father's studio.

She walked up the path to the front door. A short pretty woman, sunburned and freckled, came to the door and said pleasantly, 'Yes?'

Isobel was half prepared for her. The stepmother. Her father's wife. She said, somewhat hoarsely, that she was very sorry to be a bother but she was looking for somewhere to lunch and the porter at Kingham had said there was a pub nearby.

'The Custard Pot? Oh, you don't want to go there,' said the

177

woman, smiling. 'It isn't exactly – look, do come in for a moment. It's so hot. Could I give you a glass of lemonade?'

She thought her visitor, remarkably pretty, looked uncomfortably warm.

'We're in the garden. Come on through.'

She led the way through an exquisite old house, paler and lovelier than Dysart, white panelled and filled with light. Beyond an open door was the vision of a garden as radiant as the one Alice had seen in Wonderland.

An elderly man was sitting on a garden seat under a cherry tree. When the lady introduced the visitor he stood up and welcomed Isobel, pulling a rustic stool into the shade.

'You have a wonderful house,' Isobel said.

Her heart was beating so much that she felt she would choke. She looked at him hungrily. He was thinner and older than she had imagined.

'Yes, it's a good old place,' he said affectionately, as if talking of a horse or a dog. 'It's been in my family for a year or two. Two hundred years to be precise. John Ockrent. Glad to know you. We have the same name as the village, you see? My ancestor built the village for his pains, the cottages were for his labourers. You'll see the "O" on the front of most of them.'

'Ockrent,' repeated Isobel faintly. To make miserable assurance doubly sure she added, 'Do you paint, Mr Ockrent?'

'You noticed the studio,' he said, laughter creasing the sides of his eyes. 'No. no. My wife does. Rather good flower studies. I put in the big window for her last year, she said it is quite a help.'

'It's more than that, it's a necessity,' said Mrs Ockrent, arriving with a tray, glasses and the clink of ice.

The trio talked for a while. Mrs Ockrent had daughters of her own and had taken rather a fancy to the over-heated young stranger who'd appeared out of nowhere. She hospitably suggested giving her lunch. Isobel refused – 'Oh, but I couldn't trespass –'

'My dear child you'll do us a favour. With our children away, we're as quiet as that church,' said John Ockrent, gesturing towards the spire visible through the trees.

178

They went into a dining room as beautiful and plain as the house. Isobel decided that it would surely be safe to ask these kindly strangers if they knew anything about her father. She would say she had heard about him from a friend and wanted to meet him. Would it sound unlikely? She waited until they had taken some iced coffee back into the garden under the cherry trees, and then came out with a prepared sentence.

'I wonder if you know somebody who used to live here? An old friend of one of my friends, actually. I believe his name is William Clanfield.'

John Ockrent chuckled.

'It looks as if he has a few successes even now, eh Mary?'

His wife smiled back.

Isobel managed, 'Is he a painter too?'

Her heart was knocking against her ribs.

'A painter? No, I don't think so,' said Mary Ockrent in her pleasant way. 'He runs our little shop. He's a nice man. In fact, the best grocer for miles, everybody says so. You ought to pop in this afternoon. I'm sure he'd be glad to hear from your friend. And from you.'

'He always has an eye for a pretty face,' added Isobel's host with old-fashioned gallantry.

Half an hour later, taken to the gate by Mary Ockrent, repeating her thanks over and over, Isobel said goodbye. Mary Ockrent gestured towards the houses.

'The shop is opposite the church. He makes his own ice cream, it's delicious. Try the chocolate one.'

When Isobel had rounded the corner and was out of sight, she sat down on the grass verge. She felt rather ill. Where was the artist who would take her into his studio, where the father she had come to find and from whom she had inherited the tormenting desire to paint? And what had her mother been doing chumming up with a grocer, thought Isobel snobbishly? Grace, a snob as well, had gone to bed with 'the best grocer for miles'.

I'll see him, thought Isobel. I'll see what he's like. And then catch the next train home and forget this ever happened. She stood up, brushed the grass from her dress and crossed the road.

The shop was dark and smelled of soap and herbs. On the polished counter was a big jug of cornflowers, not exactly arranged, just stuffed in anyhow, but vivid the same.

There were shelves of packets and tins and bottles, boxes of the earliest apples, punnets of raspberries with a handwritten label saying 'morning picked'. There were jars of pear drops and acid drops and whirls of liquorice studded with pink hundreds-and-thousands. There was a box of sherbet surprises.

Standing by the shelves rearranging a display was a very handsome man. His black hair was curly, thick and slightly flecked with grey. His face was sunburned, his lips thickish, his eyes a dark-fringed grey. He had the manner of a man whose good looks have been with him since he was a child, a kind of easy self-assurance. A spotless fawn-coloured cotton coat was worn over his suit.

Seeing the girl he smiled.

'Good afternoon, Miss. What can I do for you?'

'Mrs Ockrent said your chocolate ices are very good,' stammered Isobel.

The man saw her embarrassment and looked pleased. His voice deepened.

'Mrs Ockrent is very kind,' he said, the Oxfordshire burr as strong as that of the porter at Kingham station. 'She's a great lady. You'll be a friend of hers?'

'Not really,' said Isobel, refusing the borrowed glow because she knew the lady of the manor.

She stared at the man who, incredibly, had created her. Only someone refusing to accept unpleasant truth, Claire for instance, would pretend William Clanfield was not magnificent to look at. He was so big, so easy, his hair so thick, his confidence so sure. It was as if the whole of Oxfordshire, his pride probably didn't stretch further, belonged to him because of his male beauty. He was a good grocer, good at his job. He fetched a cornet full of chocolate ice cream, saying 'the wife makes it herself'. He gave it to Isobel with a smile in a large capable hand.

On the wall behind him was a looking glass, sent to the shop by

180

Reckitt's Blue whose slogan 'Blue as the Sea' was lettered round the enamel rim. For a split second Isobel caught sight of her own face and that of her father reflected together. The resemblance was unmistakeable. The same nose. The same texture of curling hair. The thick lips. For an insane moment she thought, 'He *must* see.'

But William Clanfield was chatting about the weather, 'good for the harvest, good for all our farmers'. He took Isobel's proffered sixpence, put it into the till, closed it and then, rounding the counter, accompanied her courteously to the door.

Forced to lick the cornet like a six year old, Isobel said a muttered goodbye. She did not turn round but went as fast as the heat would let her along the blazing road. She wondered if he was watching her. But why should he?

The sense of excitement, of destiny, which had possessed her from the moment she'd set off this morning was dead. So was the man who had lived in her imagination. She could see him still, the famous artist drawing her into a studio crammed with his work. She could hear his voice, filled with vitality, as he talked about painting and shared with her its troubling gift.

Toiling back to the station, licking the ice which had begun to melt, Isobel had to let the vision go. Like Prospero releasing Ariel she must cry, 'Be free, and fare thou well.' All she'd found at the end of her travels had been a total stranger. What was the Biblical phrase? The fruit of his loins. She did not feel she was. She had seen the resemblance in the looking glass; nose, hair, a dent in the centre of his chin reproduced in her own. For a moment she had marvelled that he did not see who she was, but you only see what is in front of you. What William Clanfield had been looking at was a stranger from London buying an ice cream. I wonder if he's completely forgotten Ma, she thought. Sex with men can be like that. Julie had once said, 'Like a ram in a field. A single night, one ram and eighty sheep.'

The London train was not due for half an hour. She sat on the station, uncomfortably hot; there was no shade anywhere except in a stuffy empty waiting room.

She stopped thinking about William Clanfield and turned

181

instead to her mother. Isobel had thought her all of a piece: loved and looked up to when Isobel was a child, loved and slightly laughed at as she began to grow up. Grace had no surprises. She liked to tell her daughters that her upbringing had been strict. She was very much a lady. Very precise. Her change of religion when she'd married Frank Bryant had suited her. She became rather pious.

Thinking about her mother more deeply than she'd ever done before, Isobel saw a similarity between Grace's husband and her lover. Neither had been what Grace would term a gentleman. I suppose those were the men she was attracted to, thought Isobel. Did Grace feel superior because the men had brawny arms and rough hair and rough voices and an animal strength? The thought was an uncomfortable one.

But Grace's coarse tastes had brought *her* into the world. If Ma hadn't been like that, I wouldn't exist, she thought. The idea of her own self, her body and mind, her love of painting, her whole living youthful being simply wiped out, gave her a sensation as if she had gone into a trance.

She arrived home late, let herself into the flat and went to find Viv. Her sister had come back from a walk in the Royal Hospital Gardens. The baby, lying on his back, was energetically bicycling with bare dimpled legs.

'Viv –' Isobel waited for the effect – 'I saw my father.'

Her sister, about to fasten a safety pin, all but stabbed her first born.

'Which father?'

'My real one. William Clanfield.'

'*How did you find him?*'

Isobel sank down on the bed beside the baby who stopped cycling for a moment, eyed her and then continued his airy journey. She explained that she had remembered his name from their father's letter, and the name of the village where Grace had met him.

'I knew there was the probability that he didn't live there any more. But that's where I went.'

182

Viv was so fascinated that she could scarcely bring out the words, 'Who is he? What's he like?'

'Good looking. His nose is the same shape as mine.'

'Start at the beginning.'

Isobel did. She longed to talk and Viv's attention was of the kind she thirsted for. She described her journey, meeting the Ockrents and asking about William Clanfield.

'I was so positive my father was a painter. A kind of Augustus John with a lot of – of illegitimate children. If not John himself then somebody like him. A bit of a genius.'

'And?'

'He's a grocer.'

How Julie would have laughed. Viv didn't. She put out her hand and the baby grasped one finger.

Isobel said, 'It's quite funny, isn't it?'

'No. Did you like him?'

'Not much. Not at all. As I said, he's still very handsome; it was quite a shock looking at him at first. I am sure he's vain of his looks and I suppose his effect on women. He sort of gives you a treat by being charming. He has an Oxfordshire voice like a gardener on the stage.'

'That sounds rather nice.'

'But he wasn't. The whole thing was so stupid. I mean, I was. All that thinking it was Augustus John and there was this man – my father! – selling biscuits and home-made ice cream. I had made up such rubbish about him.'

'But what did you feel for Mr Clanfield?' persisted Viv. She gave the man a certain dignity.

Isobel bit her bottom lip.

'I should have felt something, shouldn't I? The great discovery scene. The end of *Winter's Tale*. Beautiful reconciliation and tears. I didn't feel a thing. I could see we were like each other. There was a real resemblance. But that was all. I didn't feel a thing,' she repeated.

'You're taking it very calmly.'

'I don't see how else I can take it. I never want to see him again.

183

What would be the point? Do you think I ought to go to Hornsey and see Pa?'

Viv couldn't help smiling.

'You can't spend your days trekking off to find fathers. You never wanted to see Pa until now and nor – to my shame – did I. I daresay he feels the same about us. We've grown apart. Leave the whole business. Get on with your painting.'

Isobel agreed. But fathers had become an absorbing subject to her and she wondered whether not having a father explained something lacking both in herself and her sisters.

She was tired from the hot day and the long journey, when she dragged herself into her studio to work. Might it not exorcize the phantom father with his garden studio and torrent of talk, his tender paternal welcome, his non-existence, if she tried to draw him? For an hour she attempted to sketch what she'd seen in her mind's eye. The man would not come. He appeared and disappeared on the page, the dark hair right, the eyes wrong. He glared out at one stage with the look of a murderer. Then changed, losing the wickedness and becoming vacuous. It was as if the ghost, to torment her, stood messing about with her pencil, taking it from her hand, whispering that he could draw and she couldn't. In the end, in disgust she tore the sketches to bits.

The following afternoon Larry was waiting in the ABC. He saw her the moment she came into the shop and sprang up, blazing with interest.

'*Well?*'

Isobel was braced to tell the anti-climactic story. She dreaded mockery, she hated to be laughed at. But Larry forgot to drink his tea and listened as intently as Viv had done, asking more or less the same questions.

When she finished the story he sighed.

'So that's it, is it, Isobel?'

'I suppose so.'

'No great painter. Hard to believe, knowing you as I do.'

'You're prejudiced.'

184

'Yes. I am.' He looked at her with admiration, affection and a tinge of sympathy.

'You aren't shocked, are you, Larry? I suppose it does sound heartless, not wanting to see that man again.'

'But why should you?' he exclaimed. 'What is he to you? You owe him nothing. You hoped he was going to be somebody who could share your life and he just isn't. You owe him nothing.'

She thought, I owe him my life, but did not say it aloud. Could you owe such a thing?

Larry walked home with her, squeezed her hand tightly and said, 'I think perhaps I'm glad at the way it's turned out. Do you know – I'm rather ashamed to admit it – I believe I was going to be jealous of Augustus John.'

Almost forgetting the drama of yesterday, Isobel had supper with Viv by the windows open on to her sister's favourite treetop view. The summer poplars retained their deep green, the turn of the year was still far off. The door was open and a faint breeze came into the room. There was a sound in the hall, a kind of flick, of something dropping through the letter box.

'Evening post,' said Viv. 'I'll go.'

She came back carrying an envelope and said in a flat tone, 'It's for you. By hand.'

She passed the letter to Isobel. Who could mistake the enormous handwriting which hurried across the envelope?

'It's from Julie,' Isobel said, and stared down at it.

'Aren't you going to open it?'

The writing paper was so thick that it scarcely folded and there were four pages; Julie's enormous scrawl took up a great deal of space, only two or three sentences to a page. It had no beginning, no 'Dear Isobel'. Like the handwriting itself, it flew.

> You must forgive me, Belle, though I don't see how I can forgive myself.
>
> I'm horrible sometimes and I was then and I'm very very sorry.
>
> I can't say I didn't mean to hurt you, that would be a lie,

185

because of course I did. And you tugged my hair nearly out by the roots!! But now I can't bear to think of what I did. It was disgusting.

Please forgive me. Will you? Will you? If you do, come and see me. I'm too cowardly to come to you. I've told everybody not to come this evening, in fact I said they could all get to hell out of Dysart. You're the only one I want to see.

Oh do come.

J.

Isobel passed the letter half folded, it sprang open in Viv's hands.

Neither of the girls could know just how long that impulsive document had taken. The essence of Julie, her very nature, was in her words. There had been a good many arguments between father and daughter and it had been Frank who'd forced her to write that she had meant to hurt Isobel.

'To pretend any different would be bloody silly.'

Ignorant of her father's part in it, Viv thought the letter so like Julie. Julie at her best.

Isobel sat forward, her arms round her knees. The long walk from Kingham in blazing sun had flushed her cheeks and burnt her nose. She looked like a clown.

'I'll go now,' she said suddenly, and ran out.

Dysart House was deserted. There were no cars outside and the place was silent, not a squeak from a gramophone. The front door was on the latch. Even before she pushed it open Julie came running and flung herself into Isobel's arms. They hugged and laughed and of course Isobel began to cry.

'I'm so glad. I'm so glad. Don't be afraid you'll meet Patrick, I sent him packing last week, isn't he impossible!' Julie put her arms round her sister and led her into the house.

'Oh Belle. I've so missed you. Viv all maternal and Claire all county. Who is there but you?'

186

CHAPTER NINE

If people with money are interested in it, they study the stock market and fill their cupboards with annual reports. After which they settle down to worry about other things. Love, health, anxieties, spring up like weeds in any garden, however well kept.

On a winter day in London Julie arrived very late for luncheon at the Carlton, and caught sight of Claire deep in talk with a sober elderly man on the other side of the restaurant. Before Julie could dart over, Claire and her companion had left.

Julie teased her about the meeting later and her sister said coolly that 'it happened to be a man I know who works in the City'.

'Poor you. He looked just the kind to talk about his job.'

'He did, as a matter of fact.'

'What agony.'

Claire looked sphinx-like and changed the subject. She never talked about her money, just as the other three never thought about theirs; it merely pumped like heartbeats into their bank accounts.

In the summer of 1929 Claire came to London to be presented at Court, and the sisters gathered in Viv's drawing room to admire. She wore white slipper satin and a tiny veil fixed with three feathers in her fair hair. She looked ravishing. Stuart, in velvet knee-breeches and spectacles, bore the vision away to Buckingham Palace. Early in the autumn – Claire's timing was impeccable – she became pregnant.

Absorbed in their own affairs, the Bryants scarcely noticed newspapers full of stories about the United States boom: a tidal wave of prosperity in which every American, with a new passion to invest, was making large sums of money in a positively magical way. As Arthur Glossop had said the previous year, 'You can't go wrong if your cash is in the States.'

Then out of a clear October sky, the bottom fell out of the Wall Street stock market.

The crash was so spectacular that it pulled everything down, small banks, big banks; the famous skyscraper suicides began. 'You have to stand in line to get your window to jump out of' was the black joke made by the comedian Will Rogers.

In England nothing too dramatic happened; the country had not had the huge market boom and although the newspaper comment was sober, it was not hysterical. The feeling was that the United States, always ebullient, would pick itself up soon. The Bryant girls felt a passing twinge of sympathy for the Americans who were suffering, but it was all very far away. The New Year came in, a new decade too, with parties.

Viv and Isobel decided against going to Julie's party to welcome in 1930. It was to be a fancy dress affair and Julie, in a whirl of fantastic plans and extravagances, scarcely noticed that her sisters refused what all her friends, and a good many strangers, were eager to accept. Viv peaceably said that Kit was teething, and Isobel declared she couldn't leave Viv alone on New Year's Eve. They contented themselves with a glass of champagne, and the music from the wireless.

'We'll wait until Big Ben stops striking, then we'll make our resolutions and go to bed,' said Viv.

At the reverberating sound from the great clock the two girls kissed.

'Happy New Year, darling.'

'And to you and Kit.'

As they drew smilingly apart the telephone rang.

'It'll be Julie, pixillated with champagne and wishing us a happy New Year,' said Viv. Secretly she was afraid it might be Carlos. He had already appeared at the flat twice since Kit had been born, asking quietly if he might 'sit with the boy for a while'.

Viv had, of course, agreed. She had been so nervous that the first time she simply sat alone waiting for him to leave. He looked in and said 'Thank you'. And that was all. But on his second visit, serious and somehow formidable, he stood in the doorway.

'Vivien, may we talk?'

'Please. I'd prefer not.'

Giving a shrug, he left.

Now she picked up the telephone certain she was going to hear the Spanish voice. Instead a man with a faint echo of Cockney said, 'Mrs Santander? Glossop here.'

'Hello, Mr Glossop. A happy New Year.' What on earth could the man want tonight of all nights?

'Thanks, thanks. To you too.'

He waited a moment and as she said nothing, he added, 'I wonder if I could call round and see you and the other ladies?'

'Of course, Mr Glossop. Sometime next week?'

'I'd like to make it tomorrow afternoon if you don't mind. Could you get your sisters to be present?'

'I'll try,' said Viv, mystified. She rang off.

The following morning, she telephoned Julie to be answered by a voice from the dead. What was Viv thinking of? Didn't she realize it was only eleven o'clock? 'I wasn't in bed until five, for God's sake.'

Cutting through the groans Viv explained. Julie, still groaning, recovered her good spirits enough to agree. 'If I must, I suppose I must. Oh, my head. That telephone bell just now was like a blow with a shovel.'

'How dreadful,' said Viv unsympathetically.

In Sussex, Claire, not suffering from a hangover, was plainly cross.

'Of course I can't come dragging up to London at this time' – she was heavily pregnant – 'Stuart would never allow me to do such a thing.'

Since Stuart never refused Claire anything, Viv made a face. But she could only accept the verdict and say she would telephone Claire later to tell her what Glossop wanted.

189

'It'll be about the American shares. I will ring him myself.'

'Okay, if you prefer that. Or perhaps Stuart could speak to him.'

Claire gave a sharp, laugh.

'I wouldn't dream of it. I manage my own business, thanks very much.'

'Claire is distinctly snappy,' remarked Viv to Isobel who was sitting with the baby on her lap, rocking him to and fro and murmuring her litany of praise, while the baby smiled back at her.

'Claire's often snappy. She's much worse than she used to be. She has nothing to react against. It's "yes, yes, yes" all the time from poor Stuart. She reminds me of an overfed horse.'

'Isobel, she's not all that big –'

Isobel gave an exasperated laugh. 'I didn't mean physically. I mean her nature. She's like a horse which gets no exercise. There she stands in the stable, munching bag after bag of oats and in comes Stuart with more. It's so bad for her. When is she *ever* even contradicted except by us? And how often has she seen us recently since the swanky visit when she was going to Buck House?'

Claire, thought Viv, got on Isobel's nerves, as Isobel used to get on Julie's. She sighed inwardly. Did a bunch of women always scrap? Perhaps the days when all four had been in sisterly harmony had never existed except in her own imagination.

Julie arrived in the early afternoon more or less punctually, looking like a ghost.

'Death warmed up. Just avert your eyes,' said Julie, shuddering at her reflection in the mirror on the wall. She lowered herself, supporting her head, into a chair and proceeded to describe the evening's adventures.

'Fancy dress at Dysart – you were dotty not to come. You could have brought Kit, dear little scrap. He could have come as a baby, couldn't he? I was an Indian squaw, I looked pretty marvellous, and darling Peter wore his blues from when he was in the regiment, and George Silver was Bonny Prince Charlie and old Harold came as Dracula. Heaven. Well, we left Dysart eventually and went to the 43, you know, Mrs Meyrick's dive and all we were doing was drinking the tiniest gins when in came the police. Huge feet tramping all over the place. What do you think? They arrested Mrs Meyrick.'

'Who's she?'

'Viv, really! She owns the 43 Club, and the poor sweet had been in jug three times for selling drink after hours. Well, that's her story, but George says to his certain knowledge she was nabbed for bribes to the police. I thought we were for it, but Peter, who can be nippy when it's an emergency, poured our drinks into a huge flower pot in the corner. It thrives on Scotch. Then we began to dance, and a sergeant came up and said 'You can stop all that, sir and madam', and the poor band had to grind to a halt and Mrs M. got hustled off into the Black Maria. People cheered. I mean they were on her side; they whistled at the police and did a bit of booing.'

Her eyes sparkled.

When Arthur Glossop arrived he looked in almost as bad shape as Julie, face white and smeared with fatigue, black rings under his eyes. His suit was a mass of wrinkles. He did not seem the same flamboyant character who had given them the good news at Woodlands.

'Mr Glossop, you look as if you need the hair of the dog,' said Julie, indicating a bottle she had brought with her. But to their surprise he said, 'No, thanks very much, and no, no tea either. Nothing, thanks awfully.' He had picked up his slang from people like Julie. He sat down like a man who has been on his feet too long, put his dispatch case on his lap, opened it, did not take out any papers and snapped it shut again.

'I'm afraid my sister Mrs Lockton, who is expecting a baby, is not well enough to travel to London at present. She said she will be telephoning you,' murmured Viv.

He was scarcely paying attention.

'You have read about the Wall Street Crash, ladies,' he said.

They looked at him without shock.

'Collapse. Panic. Disaster,' said Glossop.

Viv and Isobel remained calm. It was Julie with her aching head who used her wits.

'Are you saying the crash affects *us*?'

191

'I'm afraid so. I'm very much afraid so.'

'How much have we lost?'

'Yes, how much?' Viv had begun to understand the young man's haggard face.

He opened the case again, and this time brought out some papers. They were dirty and fingered.

'A lot. That is –'

'Mr Glossop, how much?' repeated Julie loudly.

And he proceeded to tell them.

When he finally stood up to go, Viv showed him to the door and managed to cut short his farewells; she could see he was going to repeat everything he'd already said over and over again – that he was horrified, that he had been skilfully advised in New York, that he himself had invested his 'life's savings' (he was not yet thirty), in the same corporation which lost Grace's fortune. Kit began to cry as Glossop babbled on and Viv, exclaiming, 'Goodbye, Mr Glossop, I must go, that's the baby', hurried away.

She picked up the child, wrapped him in his shawl and carried him for comfort into the drawing room. Julie was sitting astride the sofa, swinging long legs, her face filled with drama.

'Girls! Do you realize we are penniless?'

She said it with a sort of relish and couldn't help laughing at Viv's expression. Isobel fiddled with a gold bracelet, thinking about other people who had no private money. Larry Daniels, for instance. He could manage. He did manage. She was already trying to look ahead. It was Viv who wailed. What was to become of them? What was to become of Kit? She had lost all her money and so had they, but *they* had no children.

'Claire's in the same boat,' said Julie, legs still swinging. 'She's having a baby too. Of course she's got Stuart, he's her insurance, isn't he?'

'Stuart told me he had invested in the States as well. He said how clever Glossop was,' said Viv faintly.

'Oh God!' cried Julie. The drama continued to enliven her. She was at her best at moments of crisis.

Viv sat cradling the baby, Isobel continued to push her bracelet round and round.

'I think Claire guessed it was going to happen. She said something about the Wall Street Crash on the telephone,' said Viv.

'I must ring my twin,' Julie went out to the telephone in the hall, leaving the door wide open.

The two sisters listened.

'Claire?' began Julie. 'Me. Glossop's just gone. Not a bloody penny left. How about *that*!'

A pause. Apparently Claire was bemoaning the tragedy. The sisters waited.

Julie spoke in a totally different voice, 'What?'

Another pause. More talk from Claire.

Julie said 'yes' a number of times, and 'I suppose so' once. Then 'Okay. 'Bye', and put down the telephone. She returned to the waiting girls.

'Was she very upset?' asked Isobel. 'Claire minds about money.'

Julie did not return to the arm of the sofa but sat down in an upright chair and crossed her legs. She lit a cigarette.

'She hasn't lost a bean.'

There was a chorus of disbelief.

When the exclamations died down Julie said, 'But it's true. *Wouldn't* she just? Wouldn't she just take her lump of Ma's money and consult somebody else. Apparently she did not like Glossop, so why didn't she tell us? She's invested in land in Sussex. Some of it bringing her in "one or two quite reasonable rents" as she puts it. She's fine. She's comfortable. And she's got other investments which she says she's "very satisfied with". She's got the laugh on us. And on poor Stuart too. He must have lost a packet. Why didn't she tell him?'

'Perhaps she didn't know he'd put his money into American stocks,' said Viv.

'Of course! He hadn't told her. Crumbs,' said Julie.

A long silence fell. They were almost disinterested in their sister's duplicity and good fortune. They were sitting in the company of a grimy stranger called poverty.

193

'We'll have to borrow from her,' said Julie suddenly.

'No, we can't,' said Viv and Isobel in unison.

Julie gave an exaggerated shrug; she intended to squeeze money out of her twin somehow.

Eventually Viv poured some drinks, and Julie went to telephone her most recent admirer.

Viv and Isobel heard her back to her old self, crying 'Fearful news, Peter! I'll have to get an itsy bitsy bit drunk again tonight. Will you keep me company?'

She returned, her face again lit with the drama of the thing. Giving them impartial hugs and making meaningless remarks such as 'It'll come out right in the end' and 'It's worse for the Americans, isn't it?' she left them, whistling a new tune, 'Happy Days Are Here Again'.

Without her strong and unrealistic presence, Viv and Isobel talked. Viv fetched her bank book. They did sketchy arithmetic. 'We'll have to sell the flat,' said Viv. 'Oh Belle, what about the baby?'

Isobel felt old just then. They made pitiful plans. A stranger listening would have wondered at the change that Glossop's visit had made: Isobel was the protective one now.

After a night of broken sleep she went off as usual to college. She had paid for the rest of the term and must get her money's worth. She worked hard and scarcely talked to fellow students who were their usual noisy selves when the art master was out of the studio. Isobel kept looking at her watch, wishing away the time until she could see Larry.

The weather was cold, dull, a solid sky of grey as Isobel went towards the familiar ABC shop on the corner of the King's Road, its windows filled with loaves, large and small, and lines of jam tarts and doughnuts.

She had a sensation almost like joy – the certainty that Larry would be there. Her world was turned upside down but Larry would be there. It was her first happy thought since Glossop had left Roper Court last night, with ruins behind him.

There was Larry, eating a toasted tea cake. He stood up.

194

'Sorry to begin, I'm starving. I've been doing an essay since dawn and I'm not satisfied with it, it's no good. I didn't dare stop for lunch.'

He pulled out her chair, waited until she had sat down, then said to a waitress, 'Usual, please, miss.'

It took Isobel three sentences to tell him what had happened. He was appalled.

'My dear girl. I'm so sorry. So sorry. What can I say?'

'Nothing. Just be nice.'

'Isobel.'

He covered her hand with his. She liked him touching her and turned her hand over so that they could grip.

'Viv and Julie and I are like those poor men in New York. Jumping out of skyscrapers.'

'If you do, I'll be on the pavement to catch you.'

She gave a weak kind of smile.

'I want to ask you something.'

'Good.'

'We need jobs. Julie may be able to get back as a mannequin, but Viv can't work because of Kit. I've got to.' She looked at him.

'Larry, what at?'

He was the one who could answer such a question. He worked at the Essoldo to make a living, send his mother some money, give him a chance to pass those examinations he was set on. Poverty of sorts must have made him wise.

She had never lacked for anything in her short life. At home at Woodlands until she grew up, her mother had been on the mean side but there had been plain and nourishing food, warm dresses for winter, cottons for summer. Iced lemonade in cut glass jugs when they played tennis. Tureens full of home-made soup when they came home from frosty morning walks.

To be in need was something Isobel had imagined as only happening to 'the poor' to whom she gave pennies when she saw them sitting on the pavement or selling boxes of matches at street corners.

Until she was eighteen she had known the protected and

comfortable life of a daughter from a family with no financial strains. Then her mother's riches had come down in a great glistening flood covering her daughters with gold dust. What now faced three of them was strange and new.

She is part of the times now, thought Larry. He had a capacity for pity and a fellow feeling for the unemployed who came to London, who wore their medals from the Great War and stood in little groups playing the haunting music of the cornet. 'We Fought For Our Country', would be chalked on a board beside them. Soon to be effaced by the rain.

Isobel looked at him anxiously.

'But you're a painter,' he said at last.

She was desperately disappointed.

'But who'd employ me for doing that? Poor Viv must move out of Roper Court and we'll have to find rooms somewhere. Oh Larry, I've got to work!'

They sat in the steamy shop, racking their brains for a means of livelihood. Each made suggestions which the other turned down. It was finally Larry who came up with the idea that perhaps Isobel could be an usherette in a cinema.

'There isn't a vacancy at the Essoldo, or you know I'd talk to Mr Levine tonight. But I could ask him if he knows any other cinemas that need a girl. He's a nice man, he'll listen to me,' said Larry.

'Oh thank you!'

Her large eyes were wet. She laughed and rubbed them.

The thunderbolt which was about to blow Roper Court's rich domesticity to kingdom come did not appear to have done its fell work on Julie. Sell Dysart House? What a lark. She was not attached to places as her sisters were; any new idea, even a desperate one – perhaps more than ever a desperate one – amused her. Dysart had been great fun, but, as Noel Coward sang, 'the party's over now, it's time to say goodnight'. She enjoyed expensive clothes, but those might still be managed if she returned to being a mannequin. She had only played at the career at Woodlands; now she would see if she could take it up as seriously as Julie could take up anything.

196

What was meat and drink to Julie was drama. The thrill of being rich on Monday and penniless on Tuesday. She used the busking ex-servicemen who rent Larry's heart as a metaphor for herself.

'I'll be playing in the gutter soon. I'd better learn the ukelele.'

Her men, to do them justice, rallied. George Silver took her out for a series of comforting lunches and dinners. Her old slave Harold suggested that he would pay for her to learn shorthand and typing. He could get her a job in his office. The prospect of Julie in tight black skirt and white blouse, notebook on her knee, thrilled him; he was hurt when she laughed.

'Harold, use your loaf. Can you imagine your dizzy friend learning *anything*?'

Wearing the black fringes which much became her, Julie set off to look for work two or three days after the bombshell, taking a bus. The open Sunbeam had been sold for cash.

Mayfair was its graceful self. The streets and squares looked rich, women in furs and tiny hats entered or descended from taxis. Julie walked from Piccadilly to Berkeley Square, arriving at the pillared mansion of the French designer Michou for whom she had previously worked on occasion. She knew the woman who employed the mannequins, a sweet-voiced, hard-eyed, white-haired sixty year old called Mary Hawthorne.

Julie walked up the marble steps and in through heavy glass and gold doors, sinking into carpets emblazoned with Napoleon's golden laurel wreath, the 'N' replaced by an arrogant 'M' for Michou. She wandered up to a young woman whom she did not recognize, sitting at a French Empire desk, and asked for Madame Hawthorne.

'You are here for the spring collections?' said the young woman whose name was Erica.

'You could say that. I'm looking for a job. I used to work here.'

The welcoming smile vanished from Erica's face.

'You'll have to wait.'

'Okay. Can I borrow your *Vogue*?'

Julie sat down in a high-backed red velvet armchair.

Madame Hawthorne appeared rather sooner than might have

been expected – she was on her way to the changing rooms. Erica was glad to see her employer. This girl, out of work, had no right to sprawl like that or look so pleased with herself. Even Julie's rippling fringes were an annoyance.

Greeting Julie coolly, Madame Hawthorne said, 'Come into my office, Miss Bryant.' Erica was amazed. She did not realize that the girl had the right beanpole figure, the long silken legs, needed for showing Michou clothes.

It was to Julie's advantage that being broke had brought with it no humility. She had no sense of being one down, and Julie's personality had been set at the age of ten when the nuns at her school had described her sadly to Grace as 'bold', meaning confident, courageous and sometimes funny. Grace had vainly tried to instil the commandments of high suburbia into her second daughter. 'Never show your ignorance', 'Never speak about money', 'Never tell people how much – or how little – you have.' Julie had not absorbed these. She smiled at Madame who had taken her seat at a desk decorated with one or two silver-framed and signed royalties.

'I don't think I told you, Madame,' she said. 'May I, by the way? Oh thanks,' lighting a cigarette from a case encrusted with opals, 'I don't think I told you that our mother left us great wodges of money when she died last year. My sisters and I were frankly staggered.' Mary Hawthorne's brain was working fast. Was this girl a customer after all? Had that fool Erica misheard when she'd muttered that Julie Bryant was looking for a job?

Magnificent in her way, she was about to make the usual welcoming speech to customers when Julie added blandly, 'The dough's gone. Kaput. Lost in the American crash. Rotten luck, isn't it?'

Madame Hawthorne bowed. Erica had not misheard.

'I was wondering if there's any work around. You once said you quite liked the way I look. I heard you because I was changing behind the screen and you didn't know I was there,' confided Julie. 'It's always fun to overhear a compliment.'

'I believe I added that you were unreliable and impertinent.'

'You have a good memory, Madame.'

'I need it.'

Mary Hawthorne stood up. Julie, waiting to be told to leave, stubbed out her cigarette, unaware of Madame's wince, in a silver ashtray. She also stood up, the fringes rippling with every movement. The elder woman looked her over, noticing the leanness, the grace, the sunken cheeks – she would have looked unhealthy if she had not appeared energetic. There was a great deal of vitality there.

'We will see. You may come in tomorrow.'

Looking for a job during the first months of 1930 was something which Isobel never forgot. As good as his word Larry managed to get her some introductions to cinema managers. For weeks, between her art classes and time spent helping Viv to look for somewhere to live, Isobel kept appointment after appointment. She travelled to cinemas all over London. She visited Egyptian picture palaces, newly built in their glory, with painted pillars and sphinxes and vast cinema organs which rose to music and flashing rainbow coloured lights. She went to old theatres now transformed into cinemas but retaining their garlanded cherubs dancing along circles and galleries; hiding behind plush curtains were the boxes where men and girls had flirted in another age. She went to offices at the back of brand new concrete buildings and had to walk up seventy stairs. If you were looking for work you were never allowed to use the lift.

She kept fifty-three appointments throughout the slowly breaking London spring until she finally got a job.

Larry heard of the vacancy by chance; a girl he knew who worked as an usherette was leaving to get married. Isobel had scraped together a little money from what was left in her bank at the end of the Easter term, to pay for one day a week at the St Helier. It was here that Larry appeared at midday, an unheard-of-occurrence. He was in the entrance hall when Isobel, in a paint-daubed smock and summoned by the porter, came running down the staircase.

'Larry, what's happened? Are you ill?'

'No, no. There's a job I've just heard of.'

He whispered it to her. Porters, taxi drivers, people like that made him nervous. He hurriedly gave her the details and when Isobel hugged him with delight, he went red with embarrassment. Was the college porter looking?

Behaving for once like Julie, Isobel took a taxi. In Leicester Square she entered the most fantastic dream factory of them all, the Empire cinema. In the foyer, ankle deep in thick carpet and with Joan Crawford posing four times larger than life on the walls, Isobel asked an usher for Mr Rose.

The young man looked bored – he had been coping with the same question from young women all the morning. He showed her the way to a back office.

It was miserable, it was inevitable, that there were fifteen other girls waiting to see Mr Rose. It was always the same; Isobel had never kept an appointment for work which had not meant joining a mass of other young women after the same hungered-for job. Young or not so young, fresh and pretty, or spotty and greasy-haired, fidgety or still as statues, they sat longing for a weekly salary, a torch and the privilege of speaking the refrain, 'This way, please'.

Unlike her confident sister, Isobel expected nothing. She had begun her search for work faintly hopeful, but the fifty-three appointments, the fifty-three refusals, had destroyed her belief that anybody was going to employ her. She was pessimistic. She was sad. Could she become a servant? Even the register offices were crowded with applicants. Could she become a nursemaid? She was clever with young Kit.

At last it was her turn. She entered a small but richly comfortable room. A man behind a polished and empty desk, with nothing on it but a photograph of his plump wife, said, 'Sit down, Miss – what is your name?'

'Bryant.'

She handed him the card which she had been ordered to fill in when she arrived. It bore the usual betraying confession. He studied it for a moment.

'No experience of being an usherette, I see.'

'I'm afraid not, Mr Rose.'

Reg Rose was a big overweight man with an aquiline nose, a satin tie of blue and gold like an old school tie, melting brown eyes and frizzy dark hair. Isobel liked the way he looked and wished she could paint him. As for Mr Rose, he was amused at her failure to lie. She was the first girl this morning who had not invented experience which any fool could see through like a pane of glass.

'No experience, eh. So what makes you think you'd be useful? Do you know my cinema at all?'

'Of course!' exclaimed Isobel, forgetting nerves in her enthusiasm. 'We always say it's the best in London. And try to come as often as possible. When we were kids we used to have a family joke. You know how you always put on your trailers for a new film "Starts Friday"? That's what my family called the Empire. Let's go to Starts Friday, we used to say.'

Her look was totally devoid of disingenuousness. He rubbed his handsome nose.

'Another question. Have you taken in the fact that when the customer is wrong, he has got to be right?'

She looked serious. Yes, she said, she understood.

He continued to rub his nose with his middle finger. He gave a sigh. He was big and fat and the world was a sad place even for a girl looking like this one; perhaps more than ever for a girl looking like this one.

'Very well, Miss Bryant. You've talked me into it. You can start Friday. That'll amuse your family, mm?'

CHAPTER TEN

Both Stuart Lockton and Carlos Santander, dissimilar in every other way, had done one completely impulsive thing in their emotional lives – they had married a Bryant. In Carlos's case it had been a marriage of passion – sudden wild actions sprang from his hot nature and rich blood. It had not been like that with Stuart. He loved Claire in the way the reserved English can love sometimes, with a terrifying, romantic, unrealistic adoration. She was his goddess; when she agreed to be his wife his heart almost broke with happiness.

It was his worship for Claire which made him do a further thing which was rash, out of character and led to disaster. During the boom he moved his capital from sober English investments to America. It would never have occurred to Stuart to act in this way if he had not been affected by Claire's wealth. He wanted to run in tandem with her. Helplessly in love, he wished to pay for anything and everything his beautiful wife might want.

His American investments during the first year of their marriage brought in astonishing dividends, and this extra money he lavished on his wife. It was true that he doubted, had always done, whether she loved him much. Of course she said she did but it was always with a little laugh – she was not a girl for high emotion. She was as cool as a golden guinea, the colour of her hair.

She did not exactly return his lovemaking; she lay, so to speak, in his bed and under his love, her arms round him but never clutching. He was passionate, she was supine. There was a mystery about her which he found irresistible. He adored everything about her. Her slender figure, her tinny little voice, her hair like cornstalks, her smell, her clothes, her presence. When she was at home in his Sussex house, an old flint-built manor under the slope of the Downs, he was the man who had sold everything to obtain the pearl of great price.

Claire never talked about her money or what she was doing with it. She made telephone calls about business during the day when Stuart was at the office. She wrote any necessary letters at a little Victorian desk in her boudoir, also when he was at work. She was efficient and well organized and not to put too fine a point on it, secretive. She never discussed her finances with Stuart, or showed him business letters. In the morning at breakfast when the maid brought in the post, she would open this letter or that, say 'Oh good', and after the meal, trip away to file the letter in one of her desk drawers.

Like a messenger from Nemesis, Arthur Glossop telephoned to say he needed to see Stuart and should he come down to Lewes? Stuart, who had already begun to fear for his American bonds and stocks, said he would prefer to come to London. They could meet for luncheon at Stuart's club on the Embankment.

When Glossop arrived, he looked marginally worse than when he had faced the Bryants and Stuart did not need to guess that the news was as bad as it could be. All his investments were gone. He still had his position as a solicitor, of course, and thank God he owned the Lewes house. But there was less than a hundred pounds in his bank.

Returning home, he felt rather ill. He had asked his wife to meet him at the station and now wished he hadn't. How to tell her? There she was in the station yard – she never came on to the platform to meet him – sitting at the wheel of her modest Austin car, waving a gloved hand.

'Are you tired?' she asked, starting the car; she liked to drive and he liked to be driven. She negotiated Lewes without being aware that her husband did not answer. In any case it was a question she always asked, a kind of reflex. When they reached the country,

Kipling's 'blunt, bow-headed, whale-backed Downs' rose up ahead of them. Stuart looked fixedly at the familiar green shoulders.

'I have bad news.'

'I know,' said Claire. Then with a frown, 'Farmers are so stupid – that chicken shouldn't be wandering about in the road.' She put her hand on the horn and hooted loudly. Squawking, the bird fled into the hedge.

'How can you know, Claire?'

He spoke without his usual warmth. Claire liked to be right, as Julie did, and was too busy waiting to prove it to notice his tone of voice.

'You vaguely mentioned to me months ago that you were thinking of investing some capital in the United States. And now there's been the crash on Wall Street.' She had her eyes on the road. 'My sisters are in a real mess. How is it for you, Stuart?'

She did not say 'for us'.

He told her in a few short sentences. She made one or two comments. Had he been in touch with the American brokers? After all, he only had Glossop's word for all this. Why not speak to his old friend in the City, such a reliable man, and get him to find out anything that it was possible to discover in the aftermath of the crash? To have his wife, twelve years his junior, giving him such advice was difficult to swallow. But Stuart was no Carlos. The majestic and pitiful luxury of male pride was not in his nature. He listened to what she had to say and agreed to think about it. She knew he would do as she suggested.

She had only a few weeks to go before the birth of her baby and Stuart was against her going to London to visit her sisters. He said he would prefer her not to be jolted about. It was what Claire had wanted to hear: she liked him taking charge. Even if he could scarcely meet the household bills at present – their style of living far exceeded his salary – she agreed meekly to do what she had clearly decided to do. She contented herself with telephoning Julie, but she was out. Viv was also out but Isobel answered.

'Viv's gone to see the moving men. We're leaving next week. We've found something much cheaper.'

'Good.'

What do you mean, *good*, thought Isobel, you haven't even seen the place. Isobel was harassed at finding herself responsible for Viv and the baby, and frightened every morning by the post.

Claire's little tinkling voice came out with optimistic platitudes. 'After all, you say the new house is still in Chelsea. How sensible of Viv.'

Isobel felt raw. She could scarcely be polite to the rich sister and found an excuse to ring off.

In Sussex, Claire, with the satisfaction of a good deed done, went upstairs to have a mid-morning rest.

Isobel's life had utterly changed. It was she who had visited the estate agent to say the Roper Court flat was for sale. It was she who remained in, to show the officious little man round. She had suggested to Viv that she should take the baby out for a walk and Viv jumped at the chance. Poor Isobel dragged herself round other estate agents and eventually found a tiny house, a smartened up workman's cottage, in the furthest part of Chelsea, beyond the World's End. Viv did not like the place and nor did she; they could afford nothing else.

She had also begun her job. It consisted of standing in the dark for six hours every evening, flashing a torch at the feet of stumbling customers. She had to see, over and over again, the Hollywood delights which used to thrill her. She began to dislike Ronald Colman's whimsical style, and the sexy figure of Carole Lombard. The best moment of the week, apart from seeing Larry, was the pay packet. Every Friday she was given a brown envelope with her name written on the top in ink, containing a pound and a ten shilling note. The first time she tore open the envelope, Isobel thought of all the pounds which had flowed in and out of Coutts bank since Grace died. And now her own fortune had shrunk to thirty shillings.

On an impulse, Isobel rang Claire again.

'Sorry to ring back so quickly, but I forgot to tell you I've got a job.'

Claire sounded pleased; she was full of approval and twice said 'well done', but did not ask what sort of job.

'It means I have one day a week off which is today. Viv and I have got things pretty organized up here. I suppose I couldn't pop down to Lewes this morning? Just for a quick visit?'

Claire was delighted. Mean with money, she was the soul of hospitality, profligate with her time and her home. She loved to entertain. She loved above all to have her sisters with her, and since none of the girls ever asked if they could come, it hurt her. She said she would send a taxi to the station.

Hearing of the proposed visit, Viv looked pleased. She was always pleased when any of the sisters made a move towards another.

It was weeks since Isobel had seen her sister and when Claire came to the front door to greet her, her appearance was a shock. The child had grown suddenly and Claire looked top-heavy. Her face was thin, as if the future Lockton had used up all her beauty; she moved as slowly as an old woman. She proffered a cheek for Isobel to kiss.

'It's lovely to see you,' said Isobel awkwardly. Did one mention the baby? Julie would have done.

'You haven't had the chance to see the house, have you? I believe you only came for the wedding,' said Claire in reproach.

If Isobel was affected by her elder sister's altered appearance, the reverse was also true. Claire thought Isobel looked a mess. She had always had what Claire used to describe to their mother as an arty taste; she had never looked groomed even when she'd had money. Julie was a racehorse; she wore outrageous clothes and turned them into poems of style. But Isobel, even as a bridesmaid, had looked untidy and Claire recalled at the wedding reception having to whisper to her to comb her hair. Isobel had not done so.

Now the girl, in some kind of raggedy skirt and jumper, looked like a housemaid. But Claire was glad to see her.

As for Isobel, she'd forgotten that she loved Sussex, the long barrier of the rounded Downs, the sweet country smells, the old flint-built house with turf lapping right up to its walls.

There was no sign of Stuart but a good many signs of Claire's servants; she had three.

The girls had lunch in formal splendour in a dining room modelled on the fashion of the eighteenth century. The furniture was antique mahogany, the walls hung with oil paintings, silver on the sideboard; it was a room totally wrong for relaxed gossip. Isobel was constrained and Claire in a factual mood, eating grapefruit with the correctly shaped spoon, and boring her sister with information about plans for the garden and Stuart's decision to change the car. Not a word about the total disappearance of her sister's money.

She wants to pretend things are normal, thought Isobel. Well, they aren't.

Claire picked at a plate of cold ham and lettuce and delicately buttered a slice of bread, cutting it into tiny squares.

'Don't you want to hear our news?' said Isobel suddenly. 'You've been very clever about the cash, Claire, and we weren't. We're down to rock bottom. Not a farthing. Let me tell you what happened. Julie –'

'I know about Julie, I've rung her every week,' interrupted Claire, jealous of anybody else's closeness to her twin. 'She's gone back to Michou to work and is quite enjoying it. The dresses she's been modelling have been a big success with a South American woman who's very rich –'

'Claire. I am talking about Viv and me. I told you I'd got a job.'

'Yes. Congratulations.'

'Scarcely a subject for those. I'm working at the Empire.'

Claire did not know what her sister was talking about. She almost asked if Isobel were working for the government.

Isobel saw the puzzled face and said impatiently, 'The Empire Cinema. Remember it? I'm an usherette. They pay thirty bob a week.'

She had had an effect at last. Claire's eyes popped.

'Surely you could manage something better than that!'

'No, Claire, I couldn't. Clearly you have no idea of the crowds of women who go after every single job. I've kept fifty-three appointments and I only managed to land this one because the man liked me. It wasn't as if I had any experience.'

'What do you mean, he liked you?'

Remembering Mr Rose, the soul of probity, discussed by the usherettes for his devotion to home and family, remembering the large photograph of his wife on the desk, Isobel gave her sister a pitying look.

'You can forget your suspicions. He's a nice man and he knew I admired the Empire. Who doesn't? Anyway, you object to my job but if you used your nut you'd realize what I've been up against. What training have I got?'

'You can paint,' squeaked Claire.

Isobel gave a contemptuous laugh. It betrayed the religious way she felt about painting to denigrate it, but she'd had to set that against her need and Viv's. Did Claire expect her to paint on the pavement?

'Being an usherette isn't so bad. I got the job ahead of sixteen other girls and my salary's vital for Viv, I can tell you.'

Claire stretched out her hand and began to arrange the salts and peppers. They were Georgian silver and had belonged to the Locktons for a hundred years or more. They stood on little silver feet. Claire arranged two sets in two straight lines, like facing regiments of soldiers. She frowned in concentration, shifting them to get them exactly right. How well I know you, Claire, thought Isobel, with a spasm of the heart. She loved and disapproved of her. Claire always arranged the things on the table when she was embarrassed. Long ago at Woodlands Julie used to shout, 'Claire's at the cruet again.'

She finished lining up the salts and peppers and sat looking at her handiwork. When she spoke at last Isobel thought, hell, I should have guessed what she was going to say.

'Has Viv written to Carlos yet?'

'Of course not.'

'I don't see how you can say that. After all, this affects Kit.'

Isobel looked angry.

'You know very well how she feels. She left Carlos. She doesn't want even to talk about him; she only puts up with him seeing Kit because she has to.'

'But that was before –'

'We lost our money?' Isobel's voice rose in derision. 'I see. So now she's broke she's got to have him back. You don't understand *anything*.'

It was Claire's turn to glare. She was not angry, she was offended. She always prided herself on her affection for her sisters, her awareness of their problems, her natural involvement in anything that happened to them. Of course it was true they were stony broke and she was richer than before; but even over that, she'd hinted to Julie about selling the American investments; all Julie had done was make jokes. When is Julie ever serious? thought Claire, ignorant of the bitter division and subsequent reconciliation at Dysart.

She began to talk, rather sulkily and tentatively at first, and then with more enthusiasm, even kindness, about Carlos. She was interested in the idea of helping, through contact with Viv's husband. She stood up, top-heavy and stately, a woman from a Renaissance painting, and took her sister into the drawing room. Isobel was rather ashamed of her outburst; she couldn't miss Claire's kind intentions. She sat down in silence on furniture of downy comfort and listened. Claire was boring and well meaning. She was sure if Isobel thought about it, she'd see that the rift with Carlos must be healed and now was the right time. Knowing nothing about the marriage but her liking for her Spanish brother-in-law, her love for Viv and her desire to tidy things up, she talked on.

Isobel felt helpless. She saw she could never dissuade her sister from these views. There was an adamant core in Claire. You could talk and talk, as they used to do when they were children – Julie often yelled – but you could never change Claire's opinions if she held them strongly. The more you argued the more she clung. She had always disapproved of Viv's separation from her husband, and now money could provide the means to mend the sacrament broken by Viv. Claire loved her sisters in her own way. She talked and talked and now and again called Isobel 'darling'. Isobel saw with alarm that Claire was forming a plan of campaign.

'I think I'm the right person to help. After all, Carlos has always liked me.'

She spoke as if his affection had only been for her. Isobel nodded feebly. What was the good of protesting when Claire was in full flood? Yes, said Claire, with a slight smile, she knew she could help. She would write a nice letter to Carlos and explain everything.

'It would be wonderful,' she said, having talked herself into it, 'for them to be happy again.'

While Isobel still sat helpless, there was the sound of a car in the drive. Claire stood up.

'Stuart will be so pleased to see you.'

Pregnancy had stolen away Claire's beauty, but Isobel thought Stuart looked ghastly. He was an unhealthy yellowish colour, like somebody recovering from jaundice and there were liver-coloured marks under his eyes. He gave Isobel his usual greeting and made a few facetious jokes. But his attempts at appearing to be the hearty man he used to be only made things worse.

Isobel mentioned the time of an early train and said she would catch the bus to the station. Stuart offered to drive her. Claire did not protest in spite of his exhausted looks and it was Isobel who flatly refused.

'Of course you're not going to drive me when you've only just got home. No, Stuart, I've put my foot down. Look!' she said, displaying her small foot in a once-expensive Italian leather shoe. She won a smile from him, and goodbyes were exchanged. He insisted on walking with her to the bus.

With Claire's 'don't forget to tell Viv what we've decided' in her ears, Isobel walked with him down the drive and out into the road. She wondered whether he had taken the opportunity to be alone with her to tell her something. She was curious and concerned. But all Stuart talked about at the bus stop, until at last the bus rumbled down the lane, was delphiniums.

'I've decided to plant a dozen or so where Claire can see them from the French windows. If you keep an eye on them they'll flower two or three times a season. Good things, delphs. They give a bit of colour to a border.'

Isobel had intended to catch the fast train to Victoria and stood waiting for it to arrive. A fattish woman, very out of breath, puffed up to the porter to ask for the next train to Brighton. He indicated a distant glimpse of smoke.

'Next one in on platform two. You'd best hurry, missus.'

The poor passenger set off helter skelter up the steps and over the bridge to the Brighton platform and Isobel, on an impulse which she had no time to question, followed her. They both jumped into the train just as the whistle sounded. Her companion blew out her cheeks and mopped her forehead.

'Cor, that was a close one.' A few minutes later, from over-exertion, she was fast asleep.

Isobel sat in a corner and looked out at the twilight.

At Brighton station, she paid for her unexpected journey and set off down the once-familiar hill to St Gregory's. My luck is not running at present; I bet he won't be in, she thought. She asked herself why she'd bothered to visit Claire; but she knew why – it was because Claire was always so pleased to see her and was now cut off from her sisters more than just geographically. Rich Claire had given Isobel the impression of lacking something. But she had never been noisy and rash, a girl whom the very fact of youth fills with bliss. When Isobel had been twelve years old she used to run all the way to post her mother's letters at the end of Coppice Way, then dash back again from the sheer bursting happiness of being alive. Not Claire. She had been conscious of the way she looked, washing her hair, discussing clothes with her mother. Or hobnobbing with Julie, her favourite. No sprinting and flying for Claire. Why, then, did Isobel feel sorry for her?

Quickening her steps down the sordid street with its fish-frying-shops, pawnshops, ramshackle greengrocers and dirty-windowed shops selling second hand clothes, Isobel was anxious to get to her family's old friend.

'The Father's out,' said Mrs Duffy, the moment she opened the door. She wore a dubious apron and held a duster, although it was five in the afternoon. A smell of cabbage floated out.

'When will he be back, Mrs Duffy?'

211

'Couldn't exactly say, miss. I'm cookin' his dinner.'

'So he will be back quite soon?' Isobel persevered, thinking he would have to suffer the cabbage to come.

'He'll be back sometime. Don't know when. It'll be in the oven when he does. Are you wanting to wait?'

Isobel said she was.

She was shown up to the famous study and was there for an hour. A gothic-shaped clock musically chimed the tune borrowed from Big Ben. Da-da-da-*da* at the three quarters. Isobel sat in one of the collapsed chairs, having found a pencil and an exercise book in which FRF had scribbled some figures she was sure were not housekeeping. Greyhound winnings? In his attractive firm hand were the words 'Golden Lad', and further on 'Summer Lightning'.

Because when she held a pencil she could not help it, she began to draw. She chose the priest's chair, facing her own and in worse condition, and drew steadily. The clock reminded her of the waste of time. A voice shouted from the ground floor, 'I'll be off, then.' A door slammed. Isobel had almost finished the drawing, down to every crease and crevice and the bald patches on the cushion, when the study door was pushed wide framing a handsome black-clad figure.

'Isobel Bryant! Let me look at you. Stand up, stand up, child, I can't see you properly crouched there like a mouse.'

She laughed and jumped to her feet, pirouetting so that the skirt Claire had disliked flew out in a coloured circle of purples, browns and blacks.

'Good. Now what brings you to my study? What brings you to Brighton? Let's have a look at what you've been busy at.'

He took the book, looked at it smilingly and said, 'I'll buy it. Not a penny more than a fiver.'

'FRF, don't be mad!'

'Perhaps I shall sell it later for ten times more,' he said, taking out his wallet which was stuffed with thin white five pound notes. He handed her one and appropriated the book. Isobel protested, but weakly. The money would keep Viv, Kit and herself for days.

She watched the priest cutting out the drawing which he laid on his desk.

'I must have it framed. Well now? Julie rang me a couple of times so I'm au fait with the bad news. Not a peep from you or Viv.'

'And Claire?'

'Nothing from her either. Julie informed me with a good deal of bad language that her twin is rolling. Rather more so, since she's recently bought Kemp's Farm, a valuable piece of property. You know it? On the corner by that line of cottages.'

He remembered what people told him; it was his strength with garrulous parishioners or young girls. He fell into the collapsed chair.

'Want to stay to dinner?'

'I'd love to,' said Isobel with some nobility. The cabbage had made its demonic way under the door.

He burst out laughing.

'Mrs Duffy's cooking sticks in your gullet. It sticks in mine too. But she's a good soul. I won't impose the penance on you tonight – we'll go to the Albion.'

'But –'

'But nothing. We'll get rid of Mrs Duffy's offerings to the dog next door. Sammy resembles an ostrich, he'd eat a bag of nails. The Albion is the place for us, and Sammy will have time to bless Mrs Duffy's culinary skill. Come along. Do you feel you could brave the kitchen?'

Freeman, it seemed, had a routine line of attack for the problem of dinner waiting for him on his return to the presbytery. Isobel wondered what percentage of Mrs Duffy's cooking was dispatched in this manner. He wrapped up undercooked chops, unspeakable cabbage and a flabby piece of jam tart in a newspaper parcel. With Isobel at his heels, he went across his sooty back garden, through a gate and into a paved courtyard where, with deafening barks, he was attacked by a strangely shaped dog – the beautiful glossy black head of a retriever, dark as a seal's, a long thick body, a waving tail, and little legs no more than four inches high. The effect was of a canine submarine.

Seeing the parcel, Sammy was overcome with hysterical joy. FRF spread out the feast with remarks such as 'Here, boy' and 'Not so fast'. Sammy had almost finished before the priest removed the paper.

'His mistress says I overfeed him. Do you think she's right?'

The Albion, softly lit, purred with luxury, its great windows overlooking the blackness of the night sea; here was Isobel's reward for offering to eat Mrs Duffy's feast. Harry Preston, the hotel owner, known as the prince of friends and friend of princes, came over to greet the priest. He was short, bald, exquisitely dressed, and had a pink rose in his buttonhole.

'A joy to meet a friend of my favourite holy man,' he said, taking Isobel's hand. 'Waiter, a bottle of champagne for a beautiful lady who has done my hotel the honour of visiting us.'

When he had gone, after more extravagant compliments, FRF told Isobel that it was Preston who had recently persuaded the Prince of Wales to come to a big Brighton boxing match.

'He's changed the whole face of boxing,' said the priest approvingly. 'Suddenly it's respectable.'

'Do you go, FRF?'

'Now and then. Now and then.'

They drank their champagne.

Turning dark eyes on his young companion, he suddenly asked, 'What's the problem?'

She did not bother to deny there was one. The Bryants only came running when they needed him.

'Claire.'

FRF looked into his glass for a moment. Unless he decided for a short time to share the shocking luxury of wealthy friends, he dealt with human suffering. It was his métier. In the mornings he said Mass to people erroneously called the faithful. He spoke Latin words that had been used for nearly two thousand years, and gave Communion to men and women who made resolves and broke them an hour later. He believed in God and not in humanity, which was flawed and sad and repetitive and pitiful. The Bryant family were his Achilles heel. He had steered Grace through her divorce, given

214

her back her self-esteem. He had married Viv – a mistake – and Claire too. He had rejoiced when the girls grew rich and had wanted to see them the moment they became poor, but his parish would not let him go to London, and the girls never offered to come to him until now.

He was thoughtful.

How pretty Isobel had become. Grace had never been proud of her because she had been born on the wrong side of the blanket, yet in many ways she was now the beauty of the bunch.

'Claire's determined to write to Carlos and ask him to take Viv back,' blurted out Isobel. 'Take her back! He never let her go. And all Claire's thinking about is the money. Viv wouldn't take his money if he was on his bended knees.'

FRF was unimpressed.

'Not for Kit? Mothers worth their salt have no principles.'

'You always make jokes,' said Isobel, misunderstanding. 'She wouldn't take his money for anything. We can manage without her humbling herself to a man who didn't love her.'

'My dear child, that is not true.'

'Of course he didn't. Or he wouldn't have made her a prisoner in that awful house.'

The girl's simplicities bored the priest. She was now in full flood, indignation against Claire mixed with jealousy that her sister was the only one who had saved herself from the crash. He let her talk too much, he heard and did not hear her. He was thinking about Claire, who was not exactly the way her young sister judged her. It was true she was one for the money, as her mother had described her. She'd married with her head and not her heart. But she had chosen a good man and would come to no harm with Stuart Lockton. Yet there was more in Claire than the obvious descriptions. She had something of Julie. Not for nothing had they called themselves the twins.

His thoughts returned to the present problem.

'I'll stop her from writing to Carlos. Does that satisfy you?'

'Would you? Could you?'

'Of course. I'll do it in the morning.'

He expected her to relax. He looked at her pretty reactive face, waiting for a smile and an exclamation of relief, but Isobel was biting her lip.

'FRF.'

'I'm listening.'

'There's something else.'

'You surprise me.'

'Do I?' she said. 'I don't mean to burden you.'

'Of course you do. Shall we choose the meal and then you can burden me during the roast beef.'

The girl had the look he had seen in a hundred, perhaps a thousand faces in his work in the parish. A look of something like blankness when life comes up from behind to deal a blow which damn near breaks an arm or even a neck. He asked himself what could be coming next and decided it must be sex. A waiter appeared, carefully serving soup in little bowls with gilded handles.

They both waited until he had gone and then Isobel said, 'I met my real father.'

Freeman, about to take a first spoonful, practically choked.

'But who told you –'

'Julie. She got furious because I was angry over a boyfriend – that's all over now – and she suddenly shouted it at me and later she was sorry. She was in a state. Really sorry,' continued the girl, all solemnity. 'In the end I was glad she'd told me. I mean, the truth is always best.'

He let that go.

'So I kept wondering and wondering who he was. I couldn't get it out of my mind. In the end I got Viv to show me a letter from Pa and then I took the train. I didn't tell Viv of course, and went to the Cotswolds.'

He was as astonished as Viv had been.

'But your father might never have been there. He could have died. Or left the district long ago.'

'Yes. But he hadn't, wasn't. He was as large as life,' said Isobel, still solemn.

216

The priest scratched his chin. He took a step forward to see if the ground was firm under his feet.

'You're full of surprises. Start at the beginning. You found an address and took yourself off to the Cotswolds. Was it to Ockrent, a village near Kingham?'

'You knew.'

'Your mother told me about it years ago. I'm not divulging anything from the seal of the confessional, Isobel. As it happens, she told me here in the Albion one night just after she'd discovered she was expecting you. That's funny, wouldn't you say?'

'I suppose so,' she said indifferently, and continued. 'Pa's letter gave the man's name, of course, and mentioned the place which was Ockrent. I looked it up and it's near Kingham in Oxfordshire. So that's where I went. And walked to the village. Some nice people gave me lunch. You see ... well ... I'd spotted a studio in their garden and imagined –'

Freeman saw it all. She told him about visiting the shop. He was deeply interested.

'I never met him. Your natural father. What was he like?'

She paused for a while. He looked at her intently. A trick of nature had produced this girl sitting here in all her anxiousness. She had come to be, by chance.

Freeman had known scores of married parishioners who longed for a child, grieved for their empty arms and the years that had gone by without that irreplaceable blessing. Tragic cases. Unexpected ones too, when an ageing woman found herself pregnant, with great happiness to follow.

This girl had been unwelcomed, almost feared, the result of two or three sexual encounters by her mother whose own behaviour had shocked her to the depth of her soul. Poor Grace had been a fly in such a sticky web. The curious part of the story was that she'd done it from revenge. She had been humiliated when Frank Bryant foolishly confessed to one or two infidelities. She had prided herself on her looks and her capacity to hold a man; Freeman, hearing the phrase, had thought it sounded as if she were holding a leaping goat upon a string. After Frank had made his idiotic confession

217

Grace's pride had been in the dirt, and – with her daughters away – she had gone on holiday and at some village hop met a good-looking man.

They had made love in his cottage after the dance, and three or four times later in the afternoons. Freeman had asked what the village Romeo did for a living.

'I don't know,' Grace had replied. 'A farmer, I think, Father, I was mad. Crazy. I was so unhappy about Frank, I didn't know what I was doing. Yes, I was mad.' She repeated this a number of times; later in her mind it became true. She said it to Frank. It was Grace's face-saver, she had suffered from temporary sexual insanity.

And here is the result, thought the priest.

'It was a good grocer's shop, was it?' He could rarely resist teasing.

Isobel roused herself. 'It wasn't bad. The Ockrents said the shop was very popular and so was its owner. Everybody liked him.'

'Did you?' The same question Viv had asked her.

She met the question with candour.

'Not much. I had an impression he thinks all women are fools. No, I didn't like him.'

'And you were not once tempted to say –'

'Never! If he'd been a painter and that studio had been his, I couldn't have stopped myself. But not him. So pleased with himself. Patronizing, really. Now I keep thinking I'm so glad my other father agreed to let me be his. I'm so grateful.'

'You don't see him, though.'

'No. Viv and I don't. Nor does Claire.'

Resisting the desire to interfere – surely it was up to Frank if he wanted to see his daughters? – he said, 'And what do you feel about your mother?'

'I don't know. Not the same.'

'Are you judging her, by any chance?'

His black eyebrows met and she said hastily, 'We're not allowed to, are we?'

'Judge not that you be not judged. I see you're a good Catholic. I also notice you are not eating enough to keep a sparrow going. I'm

218

not going to make another parcel for Sammy. I think I will amuse you while you finish that roast beef. Then we'll get you an ice and you can tell me about your painting and your new job. And stop looking as if the world's on your shoulders. Remember? It is now on mine.'

It was always like that with FRF. His humour saved him from being too right, too good, too impossible to take in the flawed world. He hung rosaries round the photographs of movie stars. He now hung an imaginary one round the neck of the worried girl who obediently ate her dinner and drank champagne.

He accompanied her to the station in a cab and saw her on to the last train to London, putting her in the charge of a white-jacketed waiter in the restaurant car: the Brighton Belle worked late. He gave her the money for a taxi back to Roper Court, and kissed her goodbye as heartily as if she were ten years old.

Fed, comforted, tired and relieved, Isobel leaned out of the window and waved to him until the train curved away on its swift journey home.

Part Three

CHAPTER ELEVEN

The Twenties in Britain turned into the early thirties without the tragedies of Wall Street. People did not commit suicide; but they suffered from being out of work, demoralized and miserably poor. The little groups of ex-servicemen playing the cornet multiplied. There did not seem to be a street in the West End of London where thin-faced men were not standing, collars of their jackets turned up against the bitter weather, playing the sad music which came from their Northern land.

Viv's and Isobel's new home lay scarcely a mile away from the glories of Roper Court but a million miles from it in comfort and luxury. In a narrow street with no shops, a row of cheap little houses had been built in the early 1900's for £25 apiece, with scraps of front gardens and fences which now needed repair. Gladys Road was somewhere at the back of Chelsea, beyond World's End, and was all Viv and Isobel could afford. They told each other it was only a temporary home. And counting their money each week, like nine-tenths of all the people in England, they knew it was not.

The two girls made a sort of life for themselves and little Kit, now growing into a three year old, a thoughtful little boy romping but rather timid. And beautiful.

To be poor had to be learned like a role in the theatre, except that you did not take off the costume at the end of the performance. You played it for always. Poverty meant a narrowing of thought as well as action. For Viv and Isobel it clipped the wings of impulse. You had to think out your life and stick to its pattern; you could swerve neither to right nor left. The girls, naturally generous, could not afford to give, except the invisible gift of time, and even then their open-handedness must be limited, for the hours earned them their livelihood.

Both girls had jobs. Viv had begun to give music lessons to small children. She had started her career through an introduction from a friend of her more affluent days and her little collection of pupils was growing. Isobel continued to shine her torch in the darkness of the Empire cinema while the gigantic face of Garbo or Clarke Gable, Jean Harlow or Gary Cooper loomed on the screen. She had been given a two and sixpenny rise in salary.

Of the two it was Viv who took poverty in her stride. The years of her wealth had not had the same reality to her as to the others; leaving Spain, her mother's sudden death and her own pregnancy had given her no time to come to terms with possessing money. It had simply been convenient. In any case her nature was not an extravagant one. She knew Isobel fretted about going without. She helplessly sympathized. But if Viv did not worry over being poor and often literally forgot it, she had another overriding anxiety: Carlos's appearance in London to see his son.

He had told her he wished to see Kit four times a year and she had been forced to agree. It was painfully reasonable of him and his behaviour, courteous, punctilious, could not be faulted. But the visits were irregular. In his usual way he kept to no pattern and in consequence she was permanently on edge. Sometimes he sent telegrams. Sometimes he didn't. He would turn up after four months. Then three weeks later. The only thing about Carlos which was predictable was the hour of his arrival, four in the afternoon off the boat train, his arms full of parcels.

Kit loved him.

'Papa! Papa!'

He would rush down from the nursery, clutching a rabbit and put out his arms, rabbit and all, and Carlos would kneel and put out *his* arms. Viv always went away to hide from their happiness.

Carlos liked to take the little boy out for a walk in the Royal Hospital Gardens and sometimes in a taxi, the two of them went to

224

Kensington to sail a boat on the Round Pond. Carlos had produced an overlarge, exquisitely-made yacht bought in Barcelona; on the prow was the name 'Marie-Cristina'.

Viv's sisters had accepted the mess of Viv's life, although Julie once suggested a divorce. 'At least you'd get another chance, wouldn't you? Lots of suitable men around still, thank God.' The idea of divorce was repellent to Viv. She would never remarry and nor would he. It was against their religion.

One winter's evening in 1932, just before Christmas, Viv was saying goodbye to a new pupil, a rich child with no talent whose Jewish parents were passionate that she should be taught the piano. Opening the door to the frosty garden path, Viv saw a large figure in a black coat descending from a taxi.

'Goodnight, Mrs Schlegel. Goodnight, Amy,' called Viv, and then in a quiet voice, 'Please come in, Carlos. It's very cold.'

Mrs Schlegel, fat and friendly, cast a look of interest at the man who entered the piano teacher's house. Later she told her husband, 'Believe me, Lionel, there's something going on there.'

'How do you know it wasn't her hubby?'

'You didn't see him!' exclaimed Mrs Schlegel who had a romantic heart. 'She makes herself out to be a widow, but ...'

Unaware of causing titillating scandal, Carlos went into the tiny house, said good evening to his wife, and asked for Kit.

'We weren't expecting you. He's out to tea with a little friend and won't be back until six. May I make you some tea?'

Without the presence of the child, Viv was more than usually nervous. Every time she saw him again, she was affected by the way he looked and sounded. Her body melted sometimes and she would silently scream at it to stop.

He followed her into the sitting room where a small coke fire glowed: coke was cheaper than coal. In the corner by the window was Viv's upright piano, with a stool for her pupils and a chair at which she sat during the lessons. Sheet music for children, this one was called 'In the Wood', was open on the music stand. Amy Schlegel had been murdering the little melody, getting every third note wrong.

225

When she returned with the tea tray, Carlos had not sat down but was standing by the front windows. The lamplight was dim, and his broad figure loomed against the net curtains. The scent of cigars had come into the house with him.

'Do sit down, Carlos.'

He turned with a start – he had been deep in thought – and sat heavily facing her. A self-conscious silence followed. She poured tea and offered him some iced biscuits patterned with horses, dolls and gollywogs. He suddenly broke through the pause.

'Vivien, why did you lie to me?'

She almost dropped the plate.

'I haven't lied to you!'

She had gone scarlet. His face was set; he folded his lips which were as thick but not as innocent as Isobel's.

'You told me after the American crash that you had enough to live on. I believed you. You also assured me that you liked your new house and this district. When I questioned you, you were evasive. You made it clear that I wasn't to interfere. You even said –' he gestured towards the piano - 'that it interested you to teach the young.'

'But that's true!'

He ignored the desperate interruption.

'You didn't tell me you are in difficulties. I am very angry.'

The blush burned and burned. Looking miserably guilty, she began to deny that she was in any kind of difficulty.

He said harshly, 'I do not object to this place,' making a contemptuous gesture. He ignored her furious 'Oh thanks!'

'I realized you were no longer wealthy. But I did not know that you give these lessons because, how do you express it in English, you are stricken with poorness and have to pay for food. I allowed you your –'

He did not use the word pride, it was for men.

'I allowed you your attitudes. I know you dislike me. Probably hate me,' he added with an extreme of word and emotion. 'When my solicitor wrote to yours suggesting a settlement, the reply was insulting.'

226

'It was not meant to be.'

'Of course it was. Later I asked you two or three times if you were in need of money and you told me fairy tales. What I will not have is that Christopher should be in need. I have no doubt you give him enough to eat and go without yourself.' He looked at her drawn face. 'I will not allow that either. In future I shall put enough money in your bank for you to pay for necessities.'

'I don't want your money. I won't take it.'

'Indeed you will. And if you do not spend it, I shall ask Francis Freeman to discover this through your bank and he will come to insist that you behave like a woman of sense. You are a great fool, Vivien. You must pipe down.' He had collected the phrase from the priest and rather liked it.

'Now it is settled. And here is my treasure —' There were three rings at the door. Carlos was too polite to hurry out and embarrass Viv's friends. Frozen with expectation, he waited until the child came scampering in to throw himself at his father.

Carlos stayed too long. It was late and Kit must be put to bed. When Viv went up to Kit's cramped nursery, she found the little boy, face crimson with excitement, on the floor playing a card game with his father. At the moment she appeared, he cried 'He Garado!' in parrot imitation and slammed his cards down on top of his father's in triumph. Father and son laughed.

'I know, it is late,' Carlos said. 'Kit, your mother has come to give you your bath.'

Kit, now red for a different reason, wailed that his father must bathe him. The big man stood up, looking helpless, until Viv carried the wailing child out of the room.

She hoped Carlos would go. During the routine of the bath, talking and playing and getting splashed, she was tensed for Carlos to come and say good night. Nothing happened. Kit, wrapped in a bath towel, demanded to kiss Papa.

Carlos was in the sitting room, standing by the window as he'd done earlier. The curtains were not drawn and there was fog outside. He turned to kiss the child, muttering in lilting Spanish something Viv could not catch. The sound upset her, it was faintly

227

familiar; had he once whispered it to her? She carried Kit away again and was absent half an hour while she read to him. She finally turned off the light. Winning games had worn Kit out: he was already asleep.

As she went downstairs to the sitting room she thought, why doesn't Carlos go? Was he going to upset her again about money, even bully her? She did not feel strong enough to stand against him this evening. The day had been long, seven pupils, and Kit to look after and worry about, and now her husband was here. Isobel was out at the Empire. Viv was always alone and the evenings were lonely. But she would prefer a month of solitude to the man waiting for her.

'He is very beautiful,' said Carlos, turning from his study of the fog. She did not answer, except to say, 'I must pull the curtains. The fog comes through the cracks.'

'Why did you not ask?'

He was fastidious and set the curtains into straight folds. He came over and sat facing her, saying might he smoke? She could scarcely refuse and the scent of his Romeo and Juliet cigars came strongly into the room. He had torn off the band of the cigar and Viv remembered that she used to wear the little paper rings on her fingers when they had first fallen in love.

'I have something to say.'

'I thought you had said it.'

'That was important, of course. This also. I wish for you and Christopher to come to Barcelona.'

'Out of the question,' she replied quickly.

He shook his head. 'You think I am asking you to come back to me? Of course I am not. You have made it very plain over these three years that you hate my country –'

Oh, those 'hates'. He would use violent words.

'And since that is so why should you return to it? In any case –'

'In any case,' prompted Viv, sensing something behind the hesitation.

'In any case it would not be suitable for you to return as my wife.'

'You mean there's somebody else?'

'You know we never speak of such things.'

'Don't we? Then let's!' flamed Viv, changed from gentle mother by the aura of sex in the room.

She had thrown off the suffocating cloak of marriage to Carlos but in a peculiar way she still thought of him as hers, as she was obscurely his. She had twice had young men friends here at the little house in the lonely evenings who had begged her to go to bed with them. Viv had refused. She could not bear to. Now she glared at Carlos. Something in her usually passive face amused him.

'We are not talking about my life, Vivien, but about yours and my son's. I wish you to come for a short stay in Barcelona, not' – holding up his hand to stop her talking – 'to stay at my house. I would not dream of suggesting such a thing. Besides, my mother –'

'Oh yes. The Señora.'

She had been looking straight at him. Now something in his face made her drop her eyes.

A pause.

'So,' he said carefully, like a man sheathing a sword-stick and turning it once again into an innocent instrument for knocking small stones off a path. 'You and Christopher will come to Barcelona and stay at the Majestic for a week or two.'

It was reasonable and so was he. She was still nervous; he made her so. More than that, she was conscious of bitter-tasting resentment because he had another woman. She hated to think about it. And could not bear the idea of returning even for a short time to the city where his woman must be living. And then Viv remembered that she was dealing with a man of Spain. In his country in normal conversations people would say, 'If I come, then I come. If not, we shall see.'

'Very well, Carlos,' she said in her meekest voice.

He gave her, in place of surprise, the most heart-rending smile. It was so sad. In Carlos a smile was the tragic past and the uncertain present. Both love and separation were in it as he came towards her. She stood up, thinking he was about to leave and she would walk with him to the door. She would remark on the fog and tell him where in the obscurity he might find a taxi.

As she approached, like a wild creature waiting to fly and flee, he advanced in one long step, put his arms round her and embraced her. She stiffened her body against him. She meant to wrench away her mouth which his had found and opened, she meant to move her head and cry 'No, no'. But her body was a traitor. It had a long memory she had never been able to kill. He pressed hard against her, holding her powerfully, giving her a kiss which lasted a long time and to which she responded; she could not help herself. Finally, desperately, she broke away and almost ran into the narrow hall.

He followed slowly.

When she opened the front door the fog came in like a ghost. She did not cry out, 'Don't do it again', or wipe her mouth with the back of her hand. How could she when she had kissed him wildly in return? She stood trembling.

He merely said, 'I will see Kit tomorrow.'

She had not the nerve to ask him at what time and, typically, he never mentioned it.

The years which had changed Kit from a baby to a beautiful little boy, which had thinned Viv almost to emaciation, had made alterations in Isobel, though not visible ones. She still had the same vulnerable face, younger than her twenty-three years. She still had fits of dreaminess and fits of painting for long hours in her cramped bedroom studio. But she went without resentment every night by bus to Piccadilly to put on the uniform, the perky pill-box hat and neat patent buckled shoes and the heavy constantly-checked torch. She was now an old hand at the Empire. Other girls appeared and left, like the images on the enormous screen. 'Starts Friday' might have been supplemented by 'Goes Saturday', for the girls did go. They left to be married or to leave London and return to their homes in the Midlands or the North. They left to train as secretaries or to work in shops. Some of them became dancers in night clubs which paid them the vast sum of one pound a night, instead of one pound and ten shillings a week.

Isobel stayed. The work suited her. Mr Rose liked her loyalty and her apparent efficiency – she was not quite as efficient as she looked, and occasionally went into a trance so that customers tripped in the dark, in danger of breaking their necks. Unaware of her sins, Mr Rose approved of the one familiar face still there among a bunch of strangers.

'Evening, Miss Bryant. How do you like our offering for this week?'

'Thrilling, Mr Rose.' Isobel always said every film showing at the Empire was good. Most of them were.

'The public agrees with you, Miss Bryant.'

Reg Rose returned to his office, to refuse pay rises to three of his staff. Isobel's modest rise had been won because in one month four of his usherettes had vanished into thin air.

The change in her was nothing to do with the Empire, Leicester Square. It was to do with painting. In Isobel's teens, Grace had called her drawing a waste of time but when she had gone to live at Dysart with Julie, she was drawing and painting with concentrated passion either from models (her sisters) or from imagination. After talking to Viv she had done a series of pastels of an imagined Spain, the bell towers of a church, the iron gates of a great house, a giant statue of the Virgin carried in procession. To invent such scenes intrigued her, they came out of nowhere. When she showed them to Larry, he said they were fascinating but that she ought to specialize.

He had become a frequent visitor to Gladys Road. The days were gone when Larry, awestruck by the sight of Dysart House or the posh entrance to Roper Court, had treated Isobel as a member of some different species, a goddess descended from Jove's chariot or one of the gilded creatures living high in the air in *Metropolis* while the workers toiled in their dreadful fates below. Isobel poor was not like Isobel rich and he loved her the better for it. They were constant, united companions. He became a member of the little family, approved of by Viv and treated by Kit as an elder brother and playmate.

Isobel liked to use Larry as a model. He was a good one and sat

231

very still, absorbed in thought or bent over a study book. It was at the end of one of these sessions that he spoke about the Spanish paintings.

'I've been thinking about your work,' he said, closing his mathematics book. 'You're clever, Isobel, and the work simply pours out of you. But you go from one medium to another. Look at you recently, oils, water colours, pastels, pencil, and now coloured inks. It's a mistake. You'll never be well known if people can't recognize an Isobel Bryant picture. Look at Russell Flint. What does he give us? A lot of half-naked beauties. What does Munnings give us?'

'Horses' said Isobel, rather cross.

Larry, unimpressed by her expression, warmed to his subject, which he'd been thinking about for some time.

'What about Rossetti and the girls with red hair?'

'You may have a point.' She was cast down.

'Of course I have. Specializing's the thing. Believe me. That's what's annoying about my exams at present. I've got to get through Higher, before I can even begin to go deeper into anything.'

'When is the next dreadful exam?' asked Isobel, changing the subject because she wanted to think about it. Larry said it was in July and he had far too much revision to do.

'Thank God for the Essoldo. What would I do if I had to work during the day?'

Agonizing over his advice, she took it, comforting herself with the thought that she could return to Corpus Christi processions in years to come. Might she not even visit Spain? She began to concentrate on drawing people. Her portraits, of course, but also the queues outside the cinema in Leicester Square, the giggling girls changing into their usherette's uniforms. She sketched the man who mended shoes in a shop at World's End. He lived like a goblin in the basement and only appeared from below if you rang a bell. Most of all, Isobel painted her sister. Viv with Kit. Viv in the kitchen. Viv hanging out the washing in the strip of back garden. Viv asleep, her book fallen to the floor.

Dragging herself from her painting, Isobel ran for the evening bus, cramming on her hat and fastening her coat as she did so. The winter of 1933 was freezing cold and her coat was old and very thin. She always entered the huge cinema gratefully, as if going into a warm bath.

On the same foggy night that Carlos unexpectedly turned up in Gladys Road, Isobel saw her would-be lover Patrick again. She was in the auditorium before the last showing of the film at half past eight when two customers came into the gloom. The man handed her the tickets, they were the most expensive in the front row of the circle. Isobel noticed the woman's scent: it was very expensive and had been a favourite of Julie's during their wealthier days.

'That isn't Isobel, is it?'

Her sister was somewhere in the dark. To Julie's delight and Isobel's annoyance, this had happened a number of times before. She never trusted Julie not to talk loudly and behave in a very un-Empire-like manner. To dampen her sister's bubbling spirits, all she murmured was yes, it was Isobel and would they come this way, please?

She shone her torch in the direction of their feet. At that moment, the light caught the shoes of the man accompanying Julie and Isobel recognized them. Impossible but true. She knew those shoes. They were of ordinary black leather, far more worn than when she had seen them last, the toe-caps scuffed and dusty. But across one toe cap was a long sizzled and unmistakeable scar. It was the burn she herself had made when she dropped an electric iron on the shoes one afternoon at Dysart House.

'I'm with Patrick', hissed Julie at the same moment. 'Pat, my sister's carrying the torch for you. Good joke?'

'Hello, stranger.' A muscular hand groped out and seized hers, almost making her drop the torch. Isobel showed them to their seats and vanished into the dark with relief.

It was the last evening of the week's film, *Grand Hotel*. But Garbo, broken-hearted and wearing her ballerina's frills, did not move Isobel who had seen the film eighteen times before.

Somewhere out there among the serried seats were her sister and a man she had thought she loved. I wonder if they're watching the film or kissing, thought Isobel. Julie liked cinema embracing and often said she never saw whatever film she was taken to – 'I was rather busy!' was her usual excuse – a claim Viv and Isobel disbelieved.

Standing at the back of the cinema while the Hollywood figures moved on the giant screen, Isobel was interested in her own reactions. She had felt nothing just now when Patrick touched her. She had not even remembered the feel of his hand. The voice with its Northern accent meant nothing either. She didn't give a pin if he and Julie were locked in hungry kisses throughout the entire film. She didn't mind if later this evening they returned to Julie's temporary bed. Her sister now had no fixed home and spent her nights with friends; any friends. She moved good-naturedly when asked to go, and promptly found somebody else. 'I'm a gypsy,' said Julie.

At last the house lights went up, the organ thundered 'God Save the King' and Julie and Patrick came blinking out into the foyer. Isobel saw that her sister was growing her shingled hair. It was as smooth as brushing and brilliantine could make it, and she was wrapped in a big shawled coat – Julie was always cold. She came over to Isobel.

'I told Pat we'd be sure to find you. When do you finish this lark?'

'In half an hour.'

'They get their pound of flesh. What about coming to the Gargoyle with us afterwards? You'd like two women instead of one, wouldn't you, Pat?'

'I certainly would,' he said, dimples showing in his lively face.

Meaning to refuse, Isobel accepted. She telephoned Viv from the changing rooms.

'If you decide to stay with Julie, wherever she's putting up at present, let me know. Otherwise I shall worry,' said Viv who had been by the fire trying to recover from Carlos.

'I'm sure I shan't stay with her. It's always on the floor if one does.'

But when you guessed about Julie you were usually wrong. Julie told her sister, when she turned up at the Gargoyle Club, that 'somebody's lent me a flat. Wait until you see it. All white and mirrors, very rude, on the bedroom ceilings.'

Isobel had never been to the Gargoyle and when she arrived at the entrance there were a number of men in tails and women in long dresses and furs edging their way into the building. The lift seemed to be the smallest in London and Isobel was squashed between a man and a girl who talked over her head. Isobel was short and they were elegant storks who behaved as if she did not exist. She followed them down to the lower ground floor. The ladies' cloakroom was a jungle of mink coats and her own shabby coat was hung upon a satin hanger by a lace-aproned lady with the air of a duchess.

There was no sign of Julie or Patrick in the gold-glassed bar, and Isobel had to go down to a lower floor where members dined and danced. The room was as dark as the Empire, a deep midnight blue lit only by silver stars in the ceiling. A fountain played somewhere. Couples were dancing in the dark to the music of *Goodnight Vienna*.

Julie was on the lookout for her, and Patrick weaved his way through the tables and across the floor. He put his arm round her.

'Nice to see you, kid.'

At their table, Julie leaned her face on her hands.

'I'm thrilled we found you in the dark. Pat said we never would, there were oodles of girls in uniform, but I had one of my feelings. It'll be Isobel tonight, I said.'

She poured Isobel some champagne, and after a while – Julie never stayed anywhere long – said she must speak to the bandleader. 'He's in the glooms at present, poor sweet. Can't tell you why. I swore I wouldn't.'

Wandering across the floor with her mannequin's beautiful walk, she went up to the platform and stood talking to the dark man in a dinner jacket. He looked down at her, smiling and attentive whilst still conducting the soft sexy music.

'Your sister has been sleeping with that chap,' remarked Patrick

235

without rancour. 'God, this champagne is sweet. Where do you think they get it and how much for? My guess is they pay five bob a bottle and charge us ten quid.'

Isobel refused a second drink and said in a low cold voice, 'Why do you say things like that about Julie? I thought you were supposed to be fond of her.'

'But it's true, kid. She still goes to bed with him sometimes, between dress shows. They go to that flat she's borrowed. The all white one.'

'I don't believe you.'

'Don't if you'd rather not.' He was touched by Julie's innocent champion. 'That flat she's hanging out in is an eyeful, I can tell you. She invites all and sundry. Six bedrooms. Roy Stansfield, the conductor over there, real name Roy Sly, is a wreck after playing here every night until five. He revives in time to get Julie to bed between one and two, so she tells me.'

'Shut up. I'm going home.'

He looked at her over the top of his glass and grinned. He was as mischievous as Puck.

'Sorry. I didn't mean to hurt your feelings. I'd forgotten what a respectable little thing you are. Julie sleeps around. Most of us enjoy that. Haven't you succumbed yet?'

She did not deign to reply and he helped himself to another glass of champagne. He had accepted Julie's invitation to the Garbo film because he had been bored. Nothing was happening on the newspaper tonight. He'd suggested to the editor doing a piece on the Depression but was turned down flat.

'The numbers of unemployed are worse than ever,' Patrick had said angrily. The editor, rough and tough, merely passed him some figures. For those with jobs, standards of living were rising. Patrick was annoyed with himself for not knowing that and with the editor for not suggesting an alternative article. The very facts themselves grated against his thoughts – where did that leave one's views of this mess of a world?

Julie's reappearance was a minor comfort tonight. His affair with her, so hot at Dysart, had lasted only a few weeks until Julie moved on, taking up with George Silver again. She enjoyed the middle-aged man's relaxed spoiling and his way of not giving a damn about anything. Furious, Patrick left Dysart in a rage.

All that had happened three years ago. You could not make an enemy of Julie Bryant because she forgot why you were angry with her. They'd met again in the small world of Mayfair. Patrick had gone to a dress show at Michou, scarcely an assignment for an experienced reporter but the only woman on his paper was ill and he sulkily agreed to attend. There he saw Julie swooping across a crimson carpet in a crimson dress.

She was amused when he appeared after the show to invite her out to a meal.

'Hell and damnation. I'm going out with Tom.'

Or Dick or Harry, Patrick thought. But their friendship began again and when time and chance were in conjunction they made love.

Here was quite another kind of woman sitting at his table at the Gargoyle, cross with him, silent, shabby, and good enough to eat.

Julie reappeared.

'Sorry, folks. Really sorry. But Peter's turned up. He's been trekking all over town – wasn't it clever of him to look for me here? I can't exactly refuse. Pat will look after you, Belle. Okay?'

She went back into the crowd of dancers and was swallowed up in the romantic darkness. Patrick laughed.

'I've never been out with her when she didn't stand me up sooner or later for some chap on the other side of the room. Don't look so shocked. Haven't I got you?'

As a matter of fact he had not got Isobel at all. They danced, too close she thought, and he kissed her ear. Pressed into a crowd of scarcely moving dancers they caught a glimpse of Julie in the arms of a tall man with the air of a Guardee. She was looking up, he gazing down, both in a kind of dream. Isobel thought of Larry Daniels. He looked at her just in that way. She said, 'I really must go, Patrick. Could you get me a taxi?'

'Of course. I'll share. Where do you live now?'

Handed her worn coat by the duchess in the apron, who bowed

237

as if in prayer when Isobel put sixpence into a gold dish brimming with half-crowns, Isobel found Patrick waiting by the tiny lift. They were borne upwards, and out into the bitter cold of three in the morning. A line of taxis stood waiting to take debutantes to houses in Belgrave Square.

When Isobel gave the address of Gladys Road, helpfully adding that it was beyond World's End, the driver did not exclaim 'Cor!' but he certainly looked as if he might. The cab moved away into the empty streets.

Patrick opened his arms. In all politeness she could not refuse to snuggle into them.

'So you're living at the other end of nowhere,' he said, kissing the top of her dark head.

'We had to leave Roper Court.'

'I remember. You all lost a packet, didn't you? I was sorry good old Dysart was sold to Lord Garland. He's a nincompoop and owns a bloody sight too much of Chelsea anyway. I gather he heard the place was suddenly on the market and beat Julie right down in price. Funny girl didn't seem to care, from what I gathered.'

'No, I don't think she did,' said Isobel trembling with cold and not with desire. The streets were as deserted as if it were the end of civilization. Empty thoroughfares, locked shops, darkened houses blurred with fog. Not a burglar. Not a whore. Just the floating fog and the long vista of the King's Road with an almost invisible necklace of street lights.

'Don't let's talk about your sister. Don't let's talk at all,' he said huskily, and gave her one of his kisses. Isobel was out of practice. She had been on the way to seduction, or perhaps half way, when she and Patrick had been close at the time of her wealth and his infatuation. He used to kiss her until her head swam. Now the once longed-for embrace was not desired, his taste not remembered, his physical self not repulsive but forgotten. She did not want to stay in Patrick's arms and pretend what she did not feel.

He said in a low voice, 'Little Isobel.'

Oh bother, she thought, how am I going to get out of this? I don't want to offend him, he'll only turn nasty. He did before. He continued the long embrace, absorbed by his own pleasure and unaware that it was one-sided until Isobel gently moved away.

Patrick had also changed. He was no longer a man to call a woman names when she refused her sexual favours. He'd discovered that he could get almost any woman he wanted, he was a success in bed, and it titillated him to find that Isobel still resisted. Wasn't she Julie's sister? Surely she could not be the nervous virgin of the past? When she sat at a slight distance on the taxi seat, he took her hand and gave it an amicable squeeze.

'Where the devil do you suppose we've got to?'

The fog had grown worse. The driver had his head out of the window so that he could steer by the kerb. Icy minutes went by until at last he shouted, 'Gladys Road! Thought I'd never find it!'

Patrick jumped out and congratulated him. 'Good work, I don't know how you cab drivers do it. Don't you dare go, will you, or I'll land up in the Thames. I'm relying on you to get me back to Kensington.'

'Right you are, sir,' said the driver, pleased with his own success and the prospect of a fare which took him back to civilization.

Patrick accompanied Isobel through the gate and up the path to the house. He could scarcely see a thing. Kissing her without meaning, he said 'I'll phone', and was immediately swallowed up in the murk. As Isobel unlocked the door she heard the taxi slowly drive away.

Two of the sisters lay awake that night in a dingy little workman's cottage in the heart of the London fog.

CHAPTER TWELVE

'Girl wanted' was a notice which disappeared during the Depression. When Isobel, shopping on a cold Monday morning, saw it in the window of a shop she came to a sudden halt.

The notice in a small gilt frame was being pushed into the window by a middle-aged man. He gave it a final shove, withdrew inside the shop, and Isobel walked straight in after him.

He turned expectantly.

He was portly and balding; what was left of his hair, and his still-thick bushy eyebrows, were a rich ginger colour. He was smoking and removed the cigarette to say, 'What can I do for you, madam?'

He gave an expansive wave at his wares. Nothing but maps. They hung on all four walls, they leaned against his desk, they burst out of portfolios loosely tied with black tape. Town maps, county maps, railway maps, geological maps, military maps, maps of the distant past. The shop was the whole wide world.

'I'm afraid I am not a customer. I see you want a girl.'

'We always want those. Specially pretty ones,' was the roguish reply. He was playful and not lecherous. He straightened his face to a businesslike frown.

'Yes, indeed, I do need a young lady to work here. Mine left unexpectedly. Here one morning and gone the next. To tell you the truth,' he added confidentially, 'she gave me no warning. Simply took herself off to the Register Office yesterday and got married. Rash. Rash.' He paused. 'Damn it,' he finished, picking up his cigarette again.

'Would I do?'

He looked as Isobel for a moment or two; then gazed about for inspiration.

'I'm sure you'd do, young lady. The question is, would *I* do for *you?*'

Even Isobel whose only experience of a job had been three years at the Empire knew he was talking about money.

Delicacy or shrewdness, or both, made her say, 'What does the work consist of, Mr –'

'Draycott. Delford Draycott, known to friends as DD. I had the notion of calling my shop DD's, but I was assured that frivolity is not the attitude of people who buy antique maps. Nothing light-hearted about what I sell, Miss –'

'Bryant. Isobel.'

'Charming.'

They measured each other.

For the past few months Isobel had been growing steadily more resentful of the slavery of being an usherette. She had to work every night of the week and was home so late that unless she ran full pelt across Leicester Square she missed the tube or bus home. The map shop smelled of parchment. Of leather, possibly crumbling away. Of dust and Woodbines and Isobel's own Nuit de Paris scent which was cheap.

She's like Hebe, goddess of youth, thought Draycott. Who is she?

'So you are very kindly enquiring,' he said, as if unemployment did not exist, 'about the job here. It is as saleswoman and general help. A ray of sunshine. Holder of the fort. The fact is, Miss Bryant, I was by profession, and still am by nature, a hack. I am no longer an employee, but I still write. I go to Fleet Street to keep up my contacts. And so on. Holding the fort while I am absent is part of the job, and quite a sizeable part.'

Isobel looked respectful. She was thinking about money; a figure was burned on her brain as if by a red hot poker. Her salary was one pound twelve shillings and sixpence. She could not live on a halfpenny less.

'Mr Draycott –'

241

'Miss Bryant?' he enquired, speaking with the burning cigarette in his mouth and screwing up his eyes.

'Mr Draycott, I earn thirty-two and sixpence a week.' He looked very puzzled and Isobel's spirits dropped to rock bottom. It was obvious that he was going to offer her only a pound and she would not be able to accept. Yet how she longed to escape from the uniform, the repeated films, the chatter of girls about men, everything that had been her fate for the last three years and she'd begun to believe was her lot forever.

'That's an odd sort of salary,' he said. 'How did it come about? No, no, I am being impertinent, don't bother to reply, I beg. Let me see. I could pay thirty-five shillings a week, Miss Bryant, and every other Saturday off.'

She looked at him with enormous eyes. With the cigarette hanging from his lips he reminded her of a bookie at the Brighton greyhound track.

Before she could reply he said, 'It is not munificent. Far from it. But we both know times are not easy.'

'I'd like the job very much, Mr Draycott.'

'Do you mean it? Oh, first class. How kind. When could you start?'

'I will have to give a week's notice. I work at a cinema, the Empire, Leicester Square. But only in the evenings. I could start tomorrow morning.'

'Good gracious, young lady. Working at night and during the day as well. I wouldn't dream of imposing on you,' said Draycott, in the next breath accepting her offer.

It was agreed that she should begin the next morning. That night when she was leaving the Empire she asked to speak to Mr Rose.

'Leaving us at last, Miss Bryant?' he said with unflattering cheerfulness. 'No need to give me notice. I have a young lady in mind for the next vacancy.' He nodded and rang for his secretary. 'I wish you happy,' he added as an afterthought.

Viv was delighted with Isobel's news.

Larry was anything but pleased.

She met him, before her last evening at the cinema, in the ABC as usual. The shop had not altered in any way since the first afternoon they had seen each other there. The same tea urn steamed away, identical Chelsea buns were lined up in the same misted windows, the same door constantly swung open and shut, and what seemed to be the same customers sat huddled over their tea reading the racing results.

Larry, as always, was there first and Isobel ran over to burst out with her news.

'I've got a new job, Larry. Imagine! I'm going to work in a map shop in the King's Road. I'm giving Mr Rose my notice tonight.'

He looked perfectly furious.

'I thought you'd be pleased!' wailed Isobel.

'At not being told when you decide anything so important. Oh, I'm pleased all right. I'm positively thrilled.'

She tried to make excuses. She began to explain: it had been sheer luck that she had caught sight of the notice, if she hadn't gone in straight away the job would have been snapped up. She minded because he was hurt, and felt self-conscious at not realizing he would be.

He listened with a stony face. But after a while he relented. He knew she hadn't thought of him once when she accepted another job. He joined her pretence that he was not offended. He forgave her because of the way her dark hair sprang up on her forehead, because she was as selfish as she was lovely, and the only place he wanted to be was where he could touch her pale unringed hand.

As they walked home down the King's Road he caught sight of the shop.

'Draycott Maps. So that's it.'

'Quick, quick, we must cross the road.' She was wildly tugging at his arm. 'He'll see us,' she cried vehemently.

'Why shouldn't he? Isobel, you really are ridiculous.'

She was not listening. She almost ran under a bus in her eagerness to get away and Larry, laughing and annoyed, had to follow.

During the few angry words Larry had spoken about the new job before he cooled down he pointed out that she was sacrificing a painter's necessity – daylight.

243

'You've given up daylight for two shillings and sixpence a week,' he said sarcastically.

He was right and it was going to be a fresh source of anxiety. Yet Isobel was sure she'd done the right thing. The usherette's slavery had been going on too long. How could she ever meet any friends but Larry? During her first months at college she had avoided other artists, but the time went by and she had begun to like their company. She enjoyed talking shop. She visited one or two of their studios to eat bread and cheese, but most of their meetings and parties were at night when Isobel was wearing her red and gold uniform. She knew it was bad to bury herself in Gladys Road, toil off to the Empire and return dog tired. She needed stimulus. Perhaps Delford Draycott and a new pattern of life was going to provide it.

Encouraged by Viv who lent her a new white sweater for a new job, Isobel left Gladys Road punctually. Mr Rose and his minions had trained their staff with severity. The usherettes who were late were given three warnings – and then the sack. Isobel's punctuality had been exemplary.

Draycott had told her he did not open the shop earlier than ten in the morning because 'the chaps who buy maps' seldom made their appearance until midday. Ten o'clock meant time to have coffee, to arrange the merchandise, discuss plans and 'generally get ourselves going'. He would, he said, see her at the door of the shop, show her round and give her the set of keys which he'd left temporarily in his flat in the Gray's Inn Road.

Sheltered under her umbrella against heavy rain, Isobel crossed the road facing the shop. She could see nobody at the door and no light in the window. When she arrived the place was locked and in darkness. She sheltered in the inadequate porch and waited. Hopeful at first, she grew steadily more depressed. There was no sign of Delford Draycott. There was scarcely a sign of anybody. The workers had gone to their shops and offices an hour ago, the shoppers had seen the dreary wet morning and stayed indoors.

Looking up and down the empty road for the tenth time Isobel said loudly, 'Really!'

Still no macintoshed figure hurried along the wet pavement. When over half an hour had gone by she was thoroughly annoyed, took out an envelope and scrawled a message.

'I came but you weren't here. It is 10.40. I'll ring the shop at eleven. I.B.' She fixed the envelope to the door handle, splashed through the puddles and set off for Larry's digs in Markham Square.

She rang the outside bell marked 'Daniels' and he appeared, wearing a dressing gown and unshaven. Apologizing and bent under her umbrella, she began to explain, but before she'd finished he pulled her in out of the rain.

'Come and share my breakfast. God! Your feet are drenched.'

In the anti-climax following the earlier excitement at starting a new job, Isobel followed him upstairs. She had visited him here on a number of occasions and they'd kissed and there had been some passionate embraces up to the stage when Isobel said 'No'. Larry accepted that. He usually accepted everything from Isobel, even her forgetting him.

His room was under the roof with inward-sloping walls. There were books everywhere, school books and encyclopedias and tattered dictionaries and books of history and English literature, the armoury of the man determined to learn. The room smelled of books and the gas fire roared, sending a glow on to a rag mat made from old clothes by his landlady twenty years ago. Outside, the rooftops shone with rain. Here it was warm and cosy. The bed was unmade, like Larry, but the coffee was fresh.

'Your new boss seems to be one of the unreliable sort,' he said, handing her a big cracked cup. 'Never mind. Nice, having you here so early. I don't remember ever seeing you at this hour of the morning, come to think of it.'

'I'm sorry to land myself –'

'Don't be silly. Who else would you land yourself on?'

'Can I ring him in twenty minutes?'

'You can ring him every twenty minutes if you like, dear Isobel. He probably won't be there yet. When a man's late, he's late. Perhaps that girl who left him so suddenly got fed up with being locked out in the rain.'

'Larry! You don't think there isn't a job, do you?'

He calmed her down. Hadn't Draycott set the salary and even shown her where she was to sit? He continued to list proof of Draycott's probity and Isobel listened and agreed, growing more and more frightened. She thought with desperate nostalgia of the Empire, the man who came round with the pay envelopes, the sensation of belonging to a rich and powerful organization where if your uniform looked even slightly worn you were given another.

She buried her nose, the shape so pretty, into the coffee cup. He looked at her with love and hidden anxiety.

'I think I'd better ring,' she said.

'Here's two pence. The phone is in the passage by the front door.'

He did not suggest going down with her. He knew she'd prefer him not to wait beside her if there was no reply and if the news looked bad.

Isobel went down to a telephone installed by the landlady, into which the lodgers fed their money, painstaking penny by penny. She telephoned. She stood listening to the telephone ringing and saw, in her mind, the shop as empty as it had been when she left it. The number rang on and despair hovered over her. She was afraid of being without work, afraid of poverty. She did not know, because Viv had not revealed to her, that money was now coming from Spain into her sister's bank account. Viv was still struggling to decide if the money had hooks to it.

Half turning as if to face the spectre beside her, Isobel was about to put down the telephone when it gave a click. A voice said resonantly,

'Draycott's Map Shop.'

'Oh, Mr Draycott –'

'My dear Miss Bryant,' he cut in. 'How can I apologize? A mere matter of the tube dying at Charing Cross. We were left helpless in the middle of a tunnel. I considered getting out and walking to you, but the guard prevented me.'

She couldn't help laughing.

'That's a welcome sound. I hope I am forgiven. Where are you, Miss Bryant? Did you have to return home?'

Isobel said 'yes' from sheer relief. She needed time to recover from the shock he had unwittingly given her. She needed to stay a little by the fire with her friend.

'Come as soon as you can,' said Draycott, adding that he would put on the kettle.

Larry was on the upper landing and said at once, 'It's all right, I could tell by your voice. What happened?'

She explained, ashamed of her previous panic. He shut the bedroom door and they sat down together on the rag mat. Moved by her April face, he kissed her. Isobel responded. She was full of emotion. Such relief, such foolish hopeful happiness, and a stirring of desire she had never felt until this moment. They lay down and she put her arms round him and he pulled up her sweater and she did not stop him. She gave a luxurious expectant sigh. He made love expertly, tenderly, but his whole body trembled. She had never had a man before and he was very gentle, but his forehead was wet with sweat when it was over. He still lay on top of her and tried to roll away but she clung.

'I like you here. You're heavy. I like that.'

It was a tube train delayed somewhere near Charing Cross, and an employer who kept her waiting, which lost Isobel her virginity on a day of Chelsea rain.

Her boss, furiously smoking, was standing at the door when Isobel finally ran across the road. He welcomed her as if she were a long-lost daughter. He made a great fuss of her; he was so glad to see her that Isobel could not believe her luck in finding this eccentric employer. After coffee, which he insisted on preparing, he showed her round. The shop was smallish, with a cramped and untidy office at the back which overlooked a paved yard, dustbins and a high wooden fence. The walls of the shop were crammed, row upon row up to the ceiling, with framed maps. A desk on the left was piled with them, and so were shelves and drawers and the desk and chairs in the back office. Isobel had never been interested in maps, old or new, and felt overwhelmed. Was she supposed to learn about the things?

247

'Don't worry!' he said, interpreting the despairing look. 'The subject's much too large for you to take in at present. But you've noticed, no doubt, that I sell only maps of the British Isles? In business, as in art, my young friend, it is wise to specialize.'

Larry's dictum had popped up again.

Delford Draycott took Isobel on a tour, talking of a subject he enjoyed. Maps were children of their times, he said. By studying them you could tell the geographical knowledge of the period and its gaps. The older the map, of course, the less accurate. Map-makers used the knowledge of previous map-makers, copying the errors over and over again, not only cartographic details but the names of places. A hundred years after a first edition you would sometimes find the same mistakes.

'I've often thought it's not unlike the flaws in stamps,' he said. 'Some stamp or other comes out with a purple streak, and up goes the price. People like buying the early and wildly inaccurate maps, you know. My maps are a good investment,' he added cheerily. 'They go up in value because as the years go by they get more rare. They're not individual works of art and nobody knows how many of the old maps were printed. But only twenty-five per cent, probably far less, survive.'

He stared at an exquisite Tudor map dated 1599.

'Maps!' he said, apostrophizing to his own four walls. 'They were made for travellers and great landowners. Soldiers and sailors needed them for campaigns on land and sea. Shrewd men demanded them before purchasing property. The very idea of maps is ancient. The Romans had them inlaid on mosaic floors, the Chinese printed them on silk ...'

He was well into his stride when he glanced at his watch.

'Gentle heaven. I must be off.'

Taking his raincoat off a hook behind the door, he pulled it on and tied the belt tightly round his waist. He flipped a greasy trilby hat off another hook and tipped it over one eye. He looked the epitome of a middle-aged and rakish reporter.

'Got to get to Fleet Street pronto, people to see. Don't look alarmed, Miss B. If a customer turns up who seems to know more than you do and asks tricky questions, be your charming self, stall, and get his name and address. Tell him I'll ring this evening. Better still, if he's happy to browse around, I can be back in less than half an hour. I always give cab drivers double fare when I'm in a hurry.'

A lavish gesture with a nicotine-stained hand. He scribbled a Fleet Street telephone number for her, then paused at the door.

'You look most professional to hold the fort. Remember. Twenty-five minutes and I can be with you.'

The day went by, rainy and quiet; there was no further sign of her employer. No customers either. Isobel sat at his desk and turned over sheafs of maps, liking the noise of parchment, the delicate eighteenth century tracery of titles, the cartouches with their coats of arms. She learned nothing. She found a duster. Most of the pictures had half an inch of grey fluff along the tops of the frames. It was getting dark and after four when the telephone rang.

'Miss B?' said a now familiar voice. In the background was the steady noise of voices. 'You can shut up shop at five. Had any luck today?'

'I'm afraid not, Mr Draycott.'

'Never mind. There's always tomorrow to give us a smile, as Jack Buchanan likes to sing. One little task you could do for me. Telephone Lady St Just. Dear old character lives in Lowndes Square. She wants a military map published in the early eighteenth century after the Jacobite rising in Scotland. Her great-great grandfather, or was it great-great-great? was a colonel in the Parliamentary army. Those maps are rare but I've found her just the thing. Tell her I'll pop round to Lowndes Square tomorrow. She's in the book, her first name is Theodosia. Pretty, isn't it? Nighty night,' he added.

When Isobel telephoned she was answered by a superior maid who said her ladyship was out and she would take a message. Isobel replied that she would prefer to ring again. 'As you wish,' was the reply. The receiver was slammed down. Why are the servants of the nobs so rude? thought Isobel. I wonder if the nobs are the same. I must ask Julie — she used to know them by the Rolls-ful. She picked up a portfolio marked 'Military Maps, Scotland' and was turning over the thick parchment pages when the telephone rang again.

'Draycott Maps.'

'Isobel? You sound very professional. Sorry, I don't need a map today. It's Patrick.'

'Patrick!' she cried in surprise and added, half laughing, 'How did you know I was here?'

'I suddenly thought about you and rang Julie for your news. Well, Isobel? Can I buy you a drink this evening?'

It was so unexpected that she said yes. After telephoning Lady St Just and this time getting a quavering and pleased customer, Isobel locked the shop and went out into the rain.

She ought to be going home. On the bus she could sit and think about Larry, examine her own feelings since they had made love. Her head, her heart, were both full. She was not sure why she had agreed to meet Patrick whom she no longer cared about. She supposed it must be curiosity.

He had arranged to meet her at the Royal Court Hotel. It had been a frequent meeting place of the Bryants in their wealthy days, but Isobel had not set foot in there since the money disappeared. She knew she couldn't afford their price for a cup of coffee. It felt strange to go through the swing doors again, and not into the ABC shop. There was Patrick deep in an evening newspaper. Could he see through it? The second she came in, he stood up. She walked towards him, wishing with every step that she had not come.

'Hello, kid.'

He took her hand and gave it a squeeze and then, as if they shared some old-established joke, he laughed. His round face, with the long upper lip, the slightly monkey-like look, the eyes creased with amusement, had a sexy charm. Hell, thought Isobel, what am I doing here?

CHAPTER THIRTEEN

Lewes was one of the few English towns where an effigy of the Pope was still burned on Guy Fawkes Day. The townspeople were no longer concerned about the threat of the Papist church, but they did enjoy standing round the bonfire to watch a triple-crowned figure catch fire and vanish in puffs of unholy smoke.

Like the town she had adopted, Claire had become a traditionalist. She was no longer a girl living in a suburban-style house and catching the London train each morning to earn her living as a secretary. She was a member of the county now, the Sussex of flint-built houses, rolling Downs smelling of thyme, Saxon churches and country manners. For all her pretensions, Claire was strongly middle class and matched the times, sharing a romantic thirties patriotism which half believed Merrie England still existed. She looked on King George and Queen Mary rather as if they were beloved grandparents. Her attitudes suited Stuart who said little but looked approving.

Nobody was more pleased than Claire at expected or unexpected visitors and her hospitality made her popular: she was known as 'that nice Mrs Lockton. So pretty, too'. Women were not jealous of her golden looks. She liked masculine company but wives knew by instinct that she was not dangerous. Claire would think it vulgar to flirt with married men friends.

A year or so after her marriage Claire produced a fat little boy resembling her husband and named him Anthony Ward Lockton –

Ward was Stuart's second name. She forbade people to call the baby Tony but they did just the same and Julie, to annoy, called him Tiddles.

Claire was now the complete country lady. In the past at Woodlands her mother had once or twice allowed her to go riding but had soon stopped the treat, complaining at the price of seven and sixpence an hour. Claire now began to ride every day and Stuart, pleased with her progress, decided she was experienced enough to go hunting with him. Looking her radiant best at local hunt balls, Claire was sometimes struck by the atmosphere which appeared charged with sexual tension. Her friends swooped round the dance floor or drank champagne, laughing loudly in the bar. She wondered. She never heard a breath of scandal but everybody did look so healthy ...

Following the birth of Anthony, dumped on a starched nanny, Claire took time off before producing a daughter with a moon face and a nose like a lump of putty, whom she unsuitably named Clarissa, the fashionable name of the season.

Stuart surprised Claire by swooning over Clarissa. He was proud of the little boy and bought him a pony before Tony's legs were long enough to span its stout back. But the girl was his weakness. 'Don't make me jealous,' Claire would gaily say when Stuart took the child in his arms, shut his short-sighted eyes in a kind of ecstasy and planted kisses on the round baby cheek.

After Stuart lost so much money in the Wall Street Crash he could not sleep, lost weight and began to look haggard from anxiety and a kind of shame. But Claire was financially flourishing; she consulted her broker, paid some of Stuart's debts and placed a considerable sum in her husband's practice. He was overwhelmed with gratitude, which she found very satisfying.

Then a curious thing happened. When Claire's money began to call the tune he gradually stopped making love to her. She wanted to speak about it, but pride stopped her. She felt she would choke if she confessed how much she missed his lovemaking. It had been very important to her: a symbol of his adoration. It was true that he was wonderfully kind, he would do anything for her. He drove her anywhere she wanted; he allowed her to talk too much. For a quiet young woman, Claire became voluble; she enjoyed talking and was pleased when he agreed with everything she said. He scarcely ever made his old-style jokes.

He was not himself. Sometimes at the weekend he sat with a newspaper on his lap without reading it, simply staring into space. The least intuitive of all the sisters, Claire did not relinquish her boast at having rescued him. She often mentioned this to friends when he was present.

'I managed to pull the iron out of the fire,' with a little laugh, 'didn't I, Stuart?'

'Yes. You've been magnificent,' he would simply reply.

Claire rather liked talking about her success with her money. She never went into detail, she never told her listeners how much she had, how much she'd made; she was not outrageous. She punctuated any discussion of her achievements with a self-deprecating laugh. If she set her husband's teeth on edge he never showed it.

Julie arrived to stay for a night in Lewes during the winter after Clarissa was born. She looked as thin as a nail, wore extraordinary clothes and loudly wailed over her lack of money.

'I had a sort of mad idea and put my salary on a horse. There was this man at a party who made a terrific pass and then told me about a horse called Julie.'

In none of Julie's stories was there a gleam of success. She always finished losing her salary, or somebody else's.

After Sunday lunch Claire suggested a walk.

'Not me. I'm going to write a letter or two,' said Stuart drinking his coffee.

'Julie?' said Claire.

'*Must* I?'

'Your legs will atrophy if you don't take a walk sometimes.'

'I dunno,' said Julie, hitching up her skirt and displaying long silk legs. 'They're not so bad, are they, Stu? They keep in shape flitting down the cat-walk.'

'Julie,' said Claire sharply.

253

'Your husband's seen my legs before, haven't you, Stu? In my bathing suit.'

'Indeed I have, and a very nice pair too,' he said, and actually winked.

'Oh good,' said Julie. 'Of course if they do give out I can always crawl on hands and knees to the Ritz.'

Claire did not smile. It obscurely annoyed her that her sister, so poor, should look and talk like somebody as well off as herself. But she enjoyed exclaiming over Julie's shoes of such thin leather that they would fall to pieces on the flint-strewn paths leading to the Downs. She insisted on lending Julie some stout but battered brogues.

Leaving the house the girls climbed steadily, the Downs rising up ahead. The wind blew in their faces and Julie said she could smell rain.

'I used to be good at that when we were at Woodlands. Ma said I inherited it from her mother. A pity we never knew our Quaker grandpas and grandmas.'

'They seemed to die young.'

'And left Ma rolling. Aren't you lucky to be still rolling, dear twin?'

'Luck has nothing to do with it.'

Claire's little air of complacency was stuck all over her like fish scales.

'Swank away.'

Glancing at her from under her eyelashes, Julie saw Claire was annoyed.

'You do swank, you know. About all the cash you've been smart enough to make while the rest of us are on the dole.'

'None of you is on the dole. Viv is fine –'

'Much you know. When did you see her recently?'

'Last month.'

'Wonderful. Popped in on your way to a dinner with Stuart at the Law Courts and stayed five minutes.'

'How do you know?' exclaimed Claire.

Julie giggled and said she hadn't seen much of Viv either but Isobel had telephoned.

'For somebody who calls herself an artist and is supposed to live in a world of her own, Isobel's always blabbing.'

Claire was nettled.

Julie made one of her grimaces, plucked a stem of grass left over from the vanished autumn and chewed it. It tasted of nothing. The wind was getting cold.

'Brrh. My coat's silk and the wind goes right through it. I'm freezing. Shall we go back?'

'If you like.'

Julie swivelled round. The wind blowing at her back, penetrating though it was, did not have quite the same flaying effect. She plunged her hands into her pockets. Claire had already set off with swinging strides towards home and Julie caught her up.

'Wait a minute. I've something to say.'

'More jeering about money, I suppose.'

'Why shouldn't I tease you? Where's your sense of humour? Brother, you're not much fun any more, are you?'

Claire's pale cheek went an angry red.

'If you're going to be rude –' she said, swerving away. But Julie caught her arm and forced her to stop still.

'Listen to me. What are you going to do about Stu?'

It was totally unexpected, and before Claire could refuse to understand Julie went straight on.

'It's awful how he's changed. What have you done to him, for God's sake? He even looks smaller. You keep shutting him up, and don't let him get a word in edgeways. Do you want a henpecked fellow with no gumption for the rest of your snobby friends to be sorry for? Do you want them to be sorry for you too? I bet –' added Julie, reading her sister's face, 'I bet he isn't much good in bed now either.'

No reply.

'Go on. Is he?'

'We – we don't ...'

'Oh Christ, don't tell me he doesn't make love at all now? It's worse than I thought.'

Humiliated beyond belief, Claire began to cry.

Julie returned to London and telephoned, complaining that the horrible country walk had given her a horrible cold.

But from that afternoon, Claire at last saw what she had done. She hadn't known until now. Enchanted at the opportunity to show off, she had been a child in a tinsel dress twirling in the centre of the room while the adults watched until they couldn't stand the sight of her. Stuart had stopped loving her. It took Claire many weeks of tact and care before he returned to being the man she had married and who loved her so dearly.

But he did return. And made love again. And Claire's beauty glowed when it was given the offerings which confirmed its power.

She did not give Julie credit for what she herself had achieved. Treading carefully, beckoning back the man she'd almost lost, she soon forgot she had behaved in any other way. Her new grace became habitual to her. She began to defer to him, not crudely but with interest. She no longer took the lead at their dinner parties. Some of her county friends noticed and smiled with their husbands when driving home.

'Did you notice Claire tonight? We didn't get a single word about her money.'

'High time. She's a damned sight more attractive when she holds her tongue.'

'What a dreadful thing to say. I suppose you prefer women who happen to be dumb.'

'Not *you*, darling.'

Like the irrepressible Toad, Claire could not entirely give up boasting but she indulged her weakness when out of range of her husband and the family. On occasional lunches in London with her broker he encouraged her; and there were one or two indulgent women friends in Sussex who did not seem to mind. But country life, running on smooth wheels, seemed slow. She compared it enviously to that of her sisters, forced to work, to take buses, to eat in tea shops and to save the entire winter to buy a new coat, as Isobel had told her she was doing.

She decided to see more of the girls, and calling on Viv at Gladys Road, questioned her about finances.

'I'm sure there's something I could do.'

But Viv only smiled and was evasive. Claire felt snubbed.

256

Dissatisfied at not being allowed to help, although she had not spelled out to herself what form the help would have taken, Claire decided to see Isobel. She hadn't visited the shop before, and took a taxi down the King's Road.

Isobel, blushing with surprise and pleasure, introduced her to the owner. Delford Draycott was the soul of gallantry, called Claire 'Dear lady', and showed her round, describing the maps in his colourful way. Knowing she lived near Lewes, he produced an early nineteenth century map of the district and told her fascinating details about the city and the mapmaker. Claire bought it as a present for her husband. Isobel was proud of her mink-enhanced sister sitting in a cloud of Worth scent and saying 'How interesting' and 'Really?'.

When she left, graciously giving her hand to Draycott and presenting a cheek to Isobel, who for the millionth time wondered why her sister never actually kissed, Draycott said, 'Charming. Just a trace of family likeness, although of course the fair hair ... Now, Miss B, you must have your commission.'

Isobel gaped.

'But Mr Draycott, I never asked her to come here.'

He looked at her, narrowing his eyes from the eternal cigarette smoke and giving a grin.

'Miss B. This is going to be the first and only time in your entire life when you will protest at being paid. It is a historic moment and we must treasure it.'

He put his hand in his trouser pocket and pulled out some silver which was still warm.

Leaving the map shop, Claire took a taxi to Conduit Street. Madame Hawthorne came down the red carpeted stairs to receive her.

'I would like Julie Bryant to model some clothes,' said Claire.

'Of course. Mrs ...?'

'Lockton,' said Claire.

The lady now knew who Claire was, having learned from the indiscreet Julie about her wealthy sister. She settled Claire in a very grand room, full of roses and gilt chairs, and after a short wait in

257

came Julie. She wore a dark blue satin dress into which she must have been sewn, it was so tight across flat stomach, so smooth across narrow hips. Claire had never seen her sister at work before. Her first reaction was shock, for Julie had dyed her blonde hair a glossy oiled black. She advanced towards Claire with long threatening steps, raised her head, turned and sailed away to show the naked back of the fish-tailed dress. She moved, hips forward, shoulders back, like a dancer. Before leaving she gave Claire a look, as if to say, and *this* bit of satin costs hundreds of pounds.

The outfits Madame had chosen illustrated the Michou genius. Simple morning dresses, trailing afternoon gowns, lingerie, ball dresses. How could Julie be so quick, changing from spangled evening net to golfing clothes complete with clubs slung over her shoulder, then into a clinging nightgown, and finally a wedding dress with veil, bouquet and a page to carry her train?

Claire found the entire show fascinating and when it was over told Madame, all respectful attention, that the dark blue evening dress interested her. 'Maître calls that gown "Romance"' said Madame. Claire, unimpressed, nodded and said she would think about it. Madame accompanied her to the doors.

No sooner was Claire out in Conduit Street than her sister popped up from the basement like a jack-in-the-box. She was wrapped in her huge coat against the cold, her black hair in kiss-curls peeping from the brim of a tiny black hat. She ran up the steps.

'How did you like the rags and tatters?'

'Very much. Shall we lunch?'

'Suits me, but not the Ritz. I had a row with the head waiter and I'm sulking.'

Claire had no idea where to go. She had long forgotten her days of eggs on toast in tea shops off Harley Street. Seeing her hesitate, Julie hailed a taxi.

'The Hispano Suiza club, please.'

'Where's that?' Claire seemed to have lost the initiative.

'Round the corner. I always go there.'

One of many such places, the club had come into being during the Twenties in an old mews cottage; in the romantic days of carriages, grooms and stable lads had lived there. The entrance was up a flight of uncarpeted stairs, the club low-windowed, shabby and comfortable. A handsome black pianist was wandering musically over the keys. When he saw Julie, he began to play and sing:

'Stay as sweet as you are ...'

She laughed and waved to him.

The people sitting about, the atmosphere too, had a raffish charm. Julie went to the bar and bought two sidecars. Claire, who drank almost nothing, nearly choked over hers, it was so strong. Julie had a second and helped herself to some olives. She pulled off her hat and patted her liquorice-coloured hair.

'I'm thinking of changing my name to Carmencita.'

'I don't like it at all.'

'I never thought you would. Michou's idea. He says now I'm black he'll design things specially for me. He says fair hair hasn't what he calls the elemental. The attack.'

Claire wanted to know what the famous designer was like and Julie said, 'Oh you know, given to the dumps and then so excited about work he nearly kills himself *and* all his sewing girls.' She'd been to Paris twice to model for him.

'I stayed in a hotel which is so old it's falling down while you watch. The floors slope. When you put your suitcase down it slithers against the wall. And the pillowcases were filthy.'

She regarded Claire with a grin.

'You look okay, I must say. I bet you took my advice.'

Claire bridled.

'Come on, twin, don't pretend you don't know what I'm talking about. Stu. You got him back to –'

'I do wish you'd shut up.'

Julie relented. She hadn't the heart to tease after all. This sister was so reactive now. As a child, and then as a schoolgirl, Claire had given as good as she got. But this respectable young matron with the tinny voice (it hadn't been like that when she was younger) stirred in Julie a feeling not unlike pity.

259

Relieved at not being questioned on a mortifying subject, Claire asked Julie about her life. Julie's narrative was elliptic. She truly thought everybody knew the world which to her was nothing out of the ordinary. It was in what was called the fast set – the men were racing drivers or flyers or belonged to the Household Cavalry. They were heirs – perhaps – to great fortunes. The girls needed only to be beautiful. She talked carelessly of the parties, the clubs, even about cocaine.

'I mean, when I talked to Babs I could see what was going on from her eyes. The pupils had utterly vanished!'

Claire, horrified, had the good sense not to ask her talkative sister if she had taken drugs. During the meal Claire toyed with an omelette and Julie had black coffee and brandy.

'You'll ruin what's left of your looks.'

Julie looked pleased. Bored by flattery, she remained Frank Bryant's girl.

'I just like alcohol.'

'Stop liking it.'

'Claire. I love you. Are you serious about the blue satin? Hell,' consulting a tiny diamond watch Claire had not seen before, 'I must get back. Look, why not spend tonight in London? Give Stu a call and come and stay with me. I've borrowed the most thrilling apartment.'

After Julie had left, exclaiming, 'How lucky you are not having to toil and moil. Why haven't you got a conscience, knowing how we suffer?' Claire remained, drinking weak tea. The pianist went on with his music. There was something sad about his touch, and when Claire after some thought went over and gave him a pound note he raised his eyebrows, gave her a broad smile and said 'Swell'.

She returned to the cooling tea. She was thinking about the Michou dress. She decided against it, knowing she only wanted it because of the way Julie had worn it. She had fallen under Julie's spell again, had wanted the dress so as to *be* Julie; she used to feel like that at school. The dress would cost hundreds of pounds which she could well afford but when to wear it? It was too showy for Stuart's hunt balls. And so was Julie.

She took a taxi to Conduit Street and called in at Michou's to say she would not have the dress after all. Madame looked understanding, and Claire felt she would certainly buy something there in the future.

The 'thrilling' apartment just off Sloane Street belonged to one of Julie's many wealthy friends, and had been decorated in virginal white by Syrie Maugham. When Claire rang the doorbell on the first floor it was answered by a willowy young man who murmured, 'Sorry. You must take off your shoes.'

'I must do what?'

Julie appeared.

'There you are. Where did you get to? I absolutely rushed home to welcome you. I'm afraid Eric's right, we do have to pull off our shoes. It was a promise I had to make before Winifred lent me the place. Not a speck on her bloody carpets,' said Julie, in silk-stockinged feet.

In a long high-ceilinged room so white that it dazzled, Claire found some of Julie's old friends and a good many strangers. There was George Silver, fatter and more worldly than before, and Harold who looked more vacuous than Claire remembered, and one or two of the girls from the Dysart days, but more who were obviously mannequins, thin as racehorses, wonderfully dressed and with Cockney accents. The noise of voices mingled with the music from the gramophone, repeatedly rewound so that the thumping tunes and singing never stopped. A small tin of gramophone needles by the records was marked 'Very loud'.

Julie took her arm.

'I forgot to ask where you put your case?'

'I left it in the hall,' said Claire, deafened by the noise and wishing she had never accepted her sister's invitation.

'Didn't Eric show you to your room? Of course he didn't. My fault. No, his. Eric's the limit sitting glued by the front door. He just enjoys telling people to take off their shoes. He's a dancer and gets pushed around by the ballet masters, so he likes his bit of power.'

Claire was scarcely listening. She stared round at the pictureless white walls, the vast looking glasses, the Madonna lilies in great white vases, the piano from a Noel Coward play.

'Julie, whose flat *is* this?'

261

'Winifred's. She owed me a favour,' said Julie, with a daring look. Claire decided not to ask what she meant because her sister was longing to tell. They wandered into the crowd of chattering people. Julie, smoking from a long shagreen holder, fended off the men who came over to speak to her. She reminded Claire of a tennis player coping with attacking backhands.

'You know, I think we might try old Les,' she remarked obscurely, and dragged Claire over to the gramophone table where a man was busy rewinding once again. He was tall but stooped slightly, his shoulders broad, his figure good but spoilt by a cheap grey suit. His hair was far too long for the present fashion and heavy with brilliantine. He looked, thought Claire, like a bank clerk. But his smile was infectious.

'Les Bacon,' said Julie. 'This is my sister Claire. Bless you, my children.'

She vanished back into the crowd.

Les Bacon gave another of his smiles and shook Claire's hand. 'I've heard a lot about you.'

The cliché was a relief in a roomful of strangers; Claire was pleased that at least somebody knew who she was. He relinquished his charge of the gramophone to a young man with the face of a ferret who picked up three or four records, exclaimed 'Cripes', and chose a military march. It thumped away encouragingly.

'Let me find you somewhere to sit,' said Les Bacon. He steered her to the far end of the room where a very large over-cushioned white sofa was set between windows curtained with white velvet, then captured some cocktails from a passing waiter.

How strong Julie's drinks are, thought Claire, accustomed to a single before-dinner sherry. Les Bacon started to talk in an over-friendly way as if he had known her for months.

To her surprise Claire began to enjoy herself. Her mental criticisms of him faded. He was so easy and clearly so admiring. He asked her about country life.

'I don't know much of Sussex, I'm afraid, except the West Pier at Brighton.'

Claire said she lived in Lewes, but knew Brighton well. As

262

children, she and her sisters had always swum near the West Pier during the summer.

'Not the beach with that old wrecked boat at the top and one breakwater beginning to rot?'

'Why, yes!'

They exchanged the looks of immigrants in a foreign country who have found they come from the same village.

They talked about Brighton and when Les Bacon remarked that he must take her there sometime to look at the beach Claire did not say 'Oh!', her usual reaction to something she thought impertinent. In the company of a man who grew more attractive as the hours went by, Claire felt relaxed, happy and only slightly drunk. People began to dance, shoeless, on the white carpet. A new man had taken charge of the gramophone, the music was romantic. More visitors arrived, to take off their shoes, to greet each other with screams of recognition, to gather in knots or sit on each other's laps. Sometime during the evening Eric, the dancer, circulated with a big silver tray of food and Claire and Les shared a plate, eating from their laps. After the meal they, too, began to dance. He pressed his cheek against hers: his was very thin, she could feel his cheekbone.

'They dance like this in the States,' he said.

Returning to the sofa, they sat closer than before, drinking strong black coffee.

'I wish you'd tell me more about yourself.' Claire's voice was softer than the tone she used to her husband, children, sisters, friends. She looked softer too, and both beautiful and tired. Les Bacon said he worked in advertising. He wrote some of the words she saw in advertisements.

'Slogans, you mean?'

'That sort of thing. Guinness is good for you. Bovril prevents that sinking feeling.'

'Did you write those?'

'Not exactly,' said Les, indicating he'd had a hand in them somewhere. 'I've just done the words for a new ad to be broadcast on commercial radio.'

Snuggling close to her, taking her hand and holding it out to admire her rings, he began to recite:

'H can just spell happiness if you will take the test,
I is to invite you, our wireless is your guest ...'

There was a good deal more of the stuff, which spelled out the name of a particular wireless featured in the advertisement.

'It's good,' said Claire and asked him to recite it all over again.

The crowd at the party was growing, the noise drowned the gramophone, the laughter was deafening and Les leaned over and whispered in her ear.

'Let me take you to the Gargoyle. If I don't look out Julie's going to drag you off and introduce you to somebody else.'

It was two in the morning and freezing, the pavements scintillating under the street lights, when Les took her in a taxi to the club.

It was as crowded and smoke-filled as Julie's Syrie Maugham drawing room, but here the voices were low, the music alluring. Claire wanted to dance again because it meant being in Les's arms. They drifted on to the tiny floor and stared at each other. She scarcely knew where she was. She felt, not drunk, but bewitched. The sensation pushed away every thought but one. She did not remember the solid figure of her husband, the children safely asleep in Sussex, she did not think of marriage vows, safety, even about herself. She was in this man's arms. And that was all that mattered.

Les Bacon felt the same. He loved women and they never resisted him. Work ate up his days hungrily but his evenings were spent on women whom he could effortlessly take to bed. He could not count the girls who had said 'Yes'. He never seduced virgins, they did not interest him. He went to bed with married women, and they must always make the first move. Their beseeching eyes flattered his vanity and stirred his quickly roused sexuality. In exchange for the tribute to his male power he made love with skill and, in a way, with passion. So everybody, thought Les, was happy – he was a great optimist.

Julie's sister intrigued him. Conscious of class as people on the escalator of success must be, he judged Claire Lockton to be a real lady in the old-fashioned sense, which Julie Bryant was certainly not. He liked Julie, but had not been to bed with her; apart from being unmarried, Julie never hunted men, they hunted her. Les Bacon didn't admit that Julie's lack of beckoning offended his pride; he told himself she was not his type. She was too unpredictable and at times too damned silly.

But Claire in her dark expensive dress, her pale hair like cornstalks, her faint flowery scent, was his cup of tea. He wanted her, as they moved to the sad music played in the small hours before the dawn.

It was five in the morning when he took her back to the Sloane Street flat and at the door took the spare key from her cold hand to fit it into the lock. The flat was ghostly. The curtains were pulled close and the great white room showed only as dim acres of gloom. The guests had vanished like ghosts. There were no dirty glasses. No bottles. Nothing but the smell of smoke and the scent of the lilies, filling the room as if it were a funeral.

They lay down on the carpet and made love.

Claire returned to Sussex the next day in a state of bliss and terror. She fell asleep on the train and woke in the broad winter day knowing that she looked awful. She spent some time at Lewes Station in the ladies room, making up her face and arranging her hair and her hat. A blissful feeling kept coming over her, a sensation starting somewhere near her heart and fizzing down her body to end in her weakened legs. She could still remember Les's lovemaking, still recall the texture of his greasy hair and the taste of his kisses. He had whispered obscene things to her while they were making love. Lying in Les's arms had been the strangest thing that had ever happened to her. And her fear was nothing to do with guilt or the thought that Stuart could find out. It was quite simply that she might never see Les again.

Julie had been asleep when Claire left the flat. Nobody had been about and, so exhausted that she felt sick, Claire had one loyal thought: shouldn't Julie be woken so that she could go to work?

She gently tapped at the bedroom door. There was no sound.

And when she had slowly opened the door she saw two naked bodies, scarcely covered by a blanket, immobile in the half dark. Filled with something like horror at herself and her twin, she tremblingly closed the door. Out in the passage she had to lean against the wall.

When he returned home that evening Stuart did not appear to notice the dark rings under Claire's eyes. She told him about Julie's party and the flat. He chuckled, remarking that he was glad *he* hadn't been there, it sounded a shambles.

Claire went to bed early. Coming to bed an hour later after he had sat reading by the dying fire, Stuart crept quietly into the room and saw she was deeply asleep. He often wondered at the way Claire slept. Like a leaf. She never stirred, never made a sound; just lay there, rending his heart.

A day went by. Claire thought, dreamed, planned and finally drove into Lewes where she could telephone without being overheard by Nanny, her housemaid or the listening house itself.

Julie sounded bright.

'Come and stay any time. You've only got to ring first and if I'm not around Eric will let you in. Any time.'

'If you're sure.'

'Don't be an idiot, Claire. It was fun the other night, wasn't it?'

A pause.

'I like your friend, Les,' managed Claire.

The answering laugh jeered.

'He likes you too. He just said so. Les?'

Claire heard the sound of voices.

Julie said, 'He won't speak to you now. He says he won't give me the satisfaction, what *does* he mean? He says why don't you come up today? He's only here to lunch but informs me he could be back around eight. What do you say?'

Claire telephoned Stuart and left a message with his secretary. She spoke to Nanny Macallister who was Scots, efficient, a miracle with children and an ogre to weak-minded mothers; and too wise to show that she was pleased Claire was going to be out of the way again. When Claire kissed the children goodbye, they clung and became noisy until quelled by Nanny. The moment their mother left the room, they forgot all about her.

Nobody, it seemed, cared that Claire was leaving Lewes this afternoon. Nobody but herself, thirsting for Les and asking in desperation why he would not speak to her. She knew nothing about men. She knew about being adored and proposed to; she knew about Stuart whom she had mishandled until Julie diagnosed the trouble. Following another woman's advice and not her own vanity, Claire had won him back. Those worries were in the past.

She had fallen in love. She hadn't chosen the man because he was suitable, affected by her beauty; she had not complacently accepted the courtship of yet another besotted male. She was no longer the neat, collected, poised and matter-of-fact girl she had been. She resembled a boxer, punch drunk and tottering on his feet. She was dazed.

She had committed a mortal sin: she had slept with Les. For half an hour, lying on the floor, he had made her forget everything but sensual bliss. For that brief and now lost sensation, she had put herself outside the law. If Stuart found out he could divorce her and she would lose husband, children, home, position; all the real things which had made Claire's life what it was, until Les sat down beside her.

She brooded on her train journey to London. Men who had fallen in love with her had been grateful for whatever favours she gave them. One of her past admirers, a young doctor whom she had almost married, had embraced her after a dance, and when she had allowed him to touch her breasts through her thin silver lamé dress, had gasped, 'I shall never forget tonight.'

Claire believed that was how things were. Men never forgot when you let them kiss you. They begged, and sometimes you gave. It had not been like that with Les, she had almost felt that *she* had done the begging. And now they were lovers, he had not even tried to telephone her.

She did not go to the Sloane Street flat until she calculated that Julie would be back from work; she disliked the idea of Eric, the dancer, opening the door to her. But she need not have worried, there was no sign of him standing guard. When she rang the bell, it was her sister who opened the door, grinned and did not bother to remind her to take off her shoes. Claire kicked them off out of respect for the absent owner, on whose stainless carpets she had lost her virtue less than a day ago.

'Look who's here. And actually left work early, can you imagine that?' said Julie, pulling Claire into the long white room where Les was sprawling on a sofa. He did not stand up when the two girls came in, but stretched out one hand.

'Oh,' said Claire. 'Hello.'

'You look nice,' said Les. 'I've come to take you out to dinner.'

'Bless you, my children,' said Julie, her phrase of the week. She made the sign of the cross over them.

Claire said nervously, 'I wish you wouldn't.'

'Claire's a much better Catholic than me, Les. You look out.'

'I like convent girls. They're sexier than the others.'

Julie yawned. 'I must leave you. I'm doing a show at the Café de Paris tonight for charity. The tickets are twenty-give quid each. What does FRF call twenty-five quid ...? I remember. A pony.'

'Julie's told me about that priest of yours,' said Les to Claire. 'Come and sit by me and tell me more.'

She did sit. She felt shy.

Julie went to change, going in and out of her room, raising her voice and still chatting as she brushed her sleek hair and buttoned the jacket of her suit. She gave a running commentary on charity evenings, the cramped quarters where if you weren't careful you could put an elbow into another mannequin's eyes, the lechery of aged men who had dumped their wives and were set on catching one of the girls for the evening and the martyrdom all mannequins suffered because men thought they were 'game for a bit of hanky panky'. She finally said good night and threw the key into Claire's lap, pausing at the door to give her sister a look of mockery.

She slammed the front door.

There was a lull.

'I want you,' said Les. He bent over, pushing Claire against the cushions and gave her a kiss which lasted five minutes.

CHAPTER FOURTEEN

Isobel settled into her new job as if she had never whispered 'This way, please', to customers stumbling into the dark to enjoy another Hollywood fairytale. She rarely went to a cinema now, preferring to go with Larry to galleries and afterwards to share bacon and eggs in his digs. They were happy; they made love; they were companionable. Sometimes in Gladys Road when they were laughing together, Viv thought they were like two friendly children at play. Isobel was painting hard which meant that sometimes, but not always, she was in a good mood. By the end of February the miserly daylight was a little more generous. She began another series of studies of Viv, whose intense gaze during the sittings seemed to stare across Isobel's shoulder at her own secrets.

Delford Draycott – 'please call me DD, everybody does' – was a pleasure to work for except when he returned drunk from Fleet Street. Then Isobel had to bundle him into the cramped back office and shove him into the swivel chair. Elbow on desk, he would snore off the worst of the drink.

With the inevitability of traffic lights all turning red when you are late for an appointment, Draycott was invariably the worse for drink on the afternoons when knowledgeable customers called into the shop. She managed as best she could, but Isobel was tensed with nerves when this happened, certain that at any moment DD would reel in, breathing dragon fumes. She never felt safe when her employer was hidden away in the back office.

In the mornings DD was fresh, helpful, informative, and he

taught her about maps. He described the huge fires of the past which had decimated map supplies. During the Great Fire of London the centre of the map, book and print trade had gone up in a roar of flames; almost nothing had been saved. In consequence maps from before that date were rare indeed. Isobel became particularly interested in map decoration and was soon quite an expert on the subject. She enjoyed showing customers how the styles reflected the artistic fashions of the times: the pageantry of the Tudors, the harmony of the Baroque, the eighteenth century cartouches – delicate wreaths of flowers and leaves surrounding a church, a country dance, a cottage. In the early nineteenth century there were classical ruins and dark romantic-looking trees.

But when her boss was hidden away in the back office during a working afternoon, Isobel was very anxious. She kept expecting him to stagger in when she was talking to a customer, mumbling, 'W's th't the sh'pbell?' What should she do? Was she poised enough to laugh off poor DD's state? One afternoon this did happen and the customer, a little blonde woman in furs, looked at him, exchanged a glance with Isobel, and laughed. She bought a map, too. Isobel could not believe such luck would happen a second time.

She enjoyed her job, apart from worrying over DD's drunkenness. But when she was alone it was not decorated maps, those voices of the past, which swam into her head. It was her painting. And then it was Larry. She was growing so fond of him. She felt rather possessive, and one evening when they were at Markham Square, just before he had to leave for the Essoldo, Isobel looked up from sitting on the bed and said fondly, 'How is your mother? You haven't mentioned her lately.'

'She's fine. Isobel, did you sell that Cumberland map you were telling me about?'

'No, and don't change the subject.'

'What subject?' He bent to the mirror to tie his black tie.

'Your mother. You know *my* family. You're friends with Viv and Kit, you've met Claire, you even saw Julie. You also know my father isn't my father but that grocer in the country. I confide in you.'

'Why do you do that?' he said without emphasis.

She looked at him, liking him, loving him with her body which had known him a short while ago.

'Why do you suppose? I love you.'

She said it, not with passion, which had cooled, but as she might say 'it's Wednesday'.

He did not answer.

She pressed the point.

'I know you help to keep your mother, I know your father's dead and you're doing those blessed exams. But why can't I meet her the way you meet Viv? Wouldn't she like me?'

'I'm sure she would.' The casual tone did not deceive her.

'Well, then?'

He had finished the complex fixing of his tie. He paused as if unsure what he was about to say.

'Mum lives miles away. Beyond the Docks. It's nearly two hours to get there. I have to change twice and walk the rest of the way. That's where I grew up. It's tough. I don't want to take you there. Sorry.'

'But –'

'Don't argue, Isobel. Let's forget it, shall we? Mum is all right, there's no mystery about her. She's a bit too fond of me but mothers are like that. Look at Viv with Kit. I just – I just don't want to mix my worlds. Don't ask me to.'

So she made no progress with Larry and was not exactly sure why she had wanted to. It was not that she thought of him as a husband; the idea of marriage was a distant one for Isobel. It was more a sense of symmetry. He was accepted by her family. She was a stranger to his.

Other problems soon occupied her. On a morning when March was glimmering across the Royal Hospital Gardens, DD arrived, merry and bright as he called it and rather earlier than usual. Over their morning coffee he remarked, 'You told me the other day you like to paint.'

'Yes. Yes, I do.'

'Did you go to art school, Miss B?'

271

She was surprised at the question. DD had moments of taking her unawares.

'I did, as a matter of fact. The St Helier.'

'I know, my child. Which is why I asked. I have one or two acquaintances in the world of the arts, including Colin Cleves, remember him? A teacher at St Helier. *Your* teacher, I gather.'

Isobel remembered Cleves very well. Square in body and sharp in manner. Never a word to say that you were doing anything faintly worth looking at.

'Mr Cleves didn't like my work. Or anybody else's,' she said defensively.

'Well, that's funny because I met him for a jar at El Vino's a couple of nights ago – he's begun writing an art column for *The Dispatch* – and I happened to mention the treasure now working for me. He spoke warmly of your talent, Miss B. So why haven't I been shown any of your work?'

Incredulous at the idea of snappish Mr Cleves praising her, Isobel was touched. She liked her boss, and his interest was encouraging.

'Let me see one or two things,' he said.

The following morning she arrived with a portfolio and Draycott, already installed at his desk, said at once, 'Do I see some work under your arm? Excellent. Let's have a dekko.'

When her boss was in this mood, thought Isobel, there was nobody more kind. He was expansive and humorous and fatherly. He lit a cigarette and looked at her through the smoke, his eyes twinkling. He was the picture of benevolence, a latter day Brother Cheeryble.

He went over to the big map table, and waited while she arranged her work for him. She had brought only drawings and pastels – the oils at home were rather unwieldly to take on a bus.

Draycott turned over sheet after sheet, and by some of the comments he made, Isobel realized that he knew far more about drawing and painting than she had ever guessed. She was ashamed at her own idea of him, as simply a salesman who owned a map shop, possessed some erudite knowledge about his own subject, and came back on some afternoons the worse for booze.

He paused at the series of studies of Viv.

'Aha. The elder sister. I remember she came here to fetch you one evening, when you'd just started work. She brought the child with her. Yes. Charming.' A pause. 'What a lot you have found to say about that young woman. In the eyes, for example ...'

He finished looking at her work, tidied up the sheets and placed them carefully back in the folder.

He reflected for a moment or two.

'Ever heard of Allan Josephs?' he said. 'I think you ought to meet him.'

'*The* Allan Josephs?' She spoke in such horror that he burst out laughing. 'But I'm not ready, DD!'

'A maiden dragged to the marriage bed. Tosh. If you are not ready now, when will you be? Yes, we must see Josephs together. I'll get in touch.'

Isobel stood, wishing she had never set eyes on her kindly boss. It would be better, she wildly thought, to be dragged by a rope to Tyburn than meet Allan Josephs whose very name scared her. He would look at her drawings and say 'very nice'. Isobel feared rejection in her work as shiveringly as some people feared it in sex. If Draycott's celebrated friend thought she was no good, she would *be* no good, not only now but in the future. She hid her work from people who might criticize it. She knew it was weak of her, but she couldn't show it to Julie, who teased, or Claire, who always missed the point. She did allow Viv and Larry to see it. Their interest warmed her like the gas fire in her bedroom. Allan Josephs loomed ahead like an ice floe.

'I'll ring him this afternoon. Remind me,' said Draycott, looking about for his packet of Woodbines.

The lives of Isobel and Viv were inclined to run in tandem. Physically unalike, they were akin, singing the same songs, catching the same colds. Although Viv had not told Isobel about her own good fortune, extra money was now enriching both their thin purses. Carlos's new allowance went regularly into Viv's bank. And

273

Isobel had been awarded five shillings a week extra from Draycott. 'You deserve it, Miss B.'

While Isobel was chilled with nerves at the threat of Allan Josephs, Viv was also trembling. Carlos had telephoned.

'Hola!' called a voice from hundreds of miles away. 'Vivien, it is Carlos.'

She wished she didn't tremble so.

'I am on my way. Already in Paris. Are you well? How is Christopher?'

There followed a meaningless exchange. As it happened, Kit had been ill with a feverish cold which had only just gone, but Viv knew better than to tell Carlos about it. His reaction to news of illness, however slight, was always exaggerated.

'I am telephoning to say I will be with you tomorrow,' said Carlos. 'I know he –' there was no other 'he' in Carlos's vocabulary to his wife – 'is at school, but I would like him to be at home when I come. Can you arrange it?'

'He will miss his singing class.'

'He misses his father also.'

Viv knew that was true, but was not going to admit it. Carlos told her the time he would be at Gladys Road. An expensive pause followed.

'I am asking something else, Vivien.'

She could hear that he was.

'May I have my son to spend one night with me at the hotel?'

Viv did not know why she shivered or why it was something she'd always dreaded. It would not be civilized to refuse. She said yes, that was all right and would he take Kit to school next morning and then return the little boy's suitcase? The very words were unbearable. She had never spent a night away from Kit before. Her eyes brimmed. Carlos sounded so grateful. It was good of her, he said, and went into a garrulous explanation as to why he wanted the child to stay with him for a night. He promised he would not tire Kit – they would both only stay up 'a little late' and go to bed at the same time. Poignant and unbidden was the image of her husband putting the boy to bed and creeping about a darkened room – like

274

many big men he was graceful and quiet – so as not to disturb him. She thought of Carlos lying awake, his eyes black as the night round him, listening to Kit's breathing.

'Thank you, Vivien. I will see you tomorrow. *Adios.*'

The telephone call had interrupted a piano lesson. Viv's pupil, Mavis, was easily the most unmusical of the children she taught. The moment Viv returned from the telephone Mavis began to play again, putting a dance-slippered toe on the loud pedal. After leaving Viv she was due in Knightsbridge for a dancing lesson with Madame Vacani.

As well as having no ear for music, Mavis was also Viv's richest pupil. Viv knew very well that the only reason her mother put up with Viv's dingy little house was because an Honourable Mrs Somebody had recommended her.

Sitting down by the child, Viv tried to calm her nerves. Mavis banged at wrong notes loudly.

It was a spring evening. A smell of earth and green things came in through the open French windows of the small room which opened on to a patch of garden. When Isobel returned home Viv wondered if she should confide in her. But Isobel scarcely muttered a greeting before escaping to her bedroom studio. She did not want to tell her sister that Draycott had arranged for her to meet the alarming Allan Josephs next day. She fled to her room to go through every sheet of work and see if any of it would not disgrace her.

Viv was half relieved not to break her own news. She put Kit to bed, taking longer than usual to read to him. He looked up to her placidly when she kissed him good night.

'Can I have Horsey in bed with me?'

'Darling, you have got the rabbit and the bear.'

'And Horsey,' said Kit, squashing himself against the wall while the stuffed toys luxuriously spread themselves. As she left the room she heard him say, 'Come on, Horsey. No talking.'

She knew his habit of falling instantly asleep. Kit went out like a light as soon as Viv went downstairs. The house was quiet. Upstairs Kit slept. Two rooms away, Isobel, she supposed, was painting. Viv stared out at the dusk which each moment took away more colour from the hedge and the grass. Why am I afraid of Carlos? What can he do to hurt me? He only wants Kit for one night. And he's helped us so much with that money.

'That money' was how she described to herself the generous sum now paid monthly into her bank. Isobel still painstakingly paid a good slice of her salary to Viv, who felt guilty about taking it. Nevertheless, she didn't want to talk about Carlos to her sister. She didn't want to talk about him to any of her family. To salve her conscience she paid Isobel's money into a post office account which she planned to give her 'when I have time to explain'.

Restless, unsettled, Viv went into the drawing room. The fire, unfed, had turned as grey as the dying day. She leaned her chin on her hands and thought about Carlos. She remembered the last time he had been here. And the time before that. All the times since she had run away from him. She was drawn to him still and something in him made her afraid. She felt that if she made the slightest move, she would be lost. But how would she be lost by returning to him, whose joy at having her back would be so passionate and so extreme? She wished someone could advise her. But who? She felt too shy to go to FRF, whom she had not seen for so long. As for her own father, he and she had never been alone together since the day he left Woodlands. In a way, thought Viv, Pa resembles Carlos. Such a masculine man. A central core, a kind of thrust, a domination. They must decide, rule. Frank had been like that when he had been their father and the head of the house; perhaps Grace had preferred the role of stately humility. As for FRF, he was too mocking for Viv's taste and besides, he had been responsible for introducing her to Carlos; he was Carlos's friend. She knew that worried him, she had seen it when they talked. Poor FRF, thought Viv, he wouldn't dare advise me again.

It was odd, but the man she wanted to talk to was Stuart Lockton. She felt at home with her brother-in-law. For a moment she tried to imagine what it would have been like to have Stuart as a husband. She could imagine them getting on well, laughing at the same jokes. But Stuart could never have fallen in love with her – she was a mouse compared to Claire. She remembered the look on Stuart's face when he stood at the altar and Claire came towards him: he looked as if he could not believe she was his. And then Viv remembered something else, so sharply that for a moment she caught her breath: the way she'd felt going up the aisle towards Carlos.

Swerving away from pain, she fixed her thoughts on Stuart. Would Claire think it odd if I rang him, she wondered. But why should she? It's a compliment to her if I need her husband's advice.

She rang the Lewes number. Stuart answered.

'It's Viv. I'm so sorry to bother you. Are you and Claire right in the middle of dinner?'

'No, no, Claire's in town with Julie.'

'Is she? I didn't know.'

'Some party or other. My wife has taken to parties,' said the voice with its familiar chuckle. 'I'm sure Julie didn't invite you because she knows you wouldn't go.'

Only Stuart would have said that.

Viv agreed that she didn't enjoy parties any more and the words struck him, for he said thoughtfully, 'Any more?'

'Well – perhaps I never did.'

'Nor me, Viv. Nor me. If you want Claire, I can give you a number.'

'Actually,' said Viv, with a slight laugh, 'it's you I want.'

'Good. What can I do for you?'

She explained what had happened, punctuating her sentence twice with 'you'll think me stupid'. The second time he interrupted. 'I never think that. Go on.'

When she finished, she half hoped for one of his hearty laughs, the rumbling assurance that she was fussing. She waited like a child alarmed by a small cut in his finger, holding it out to have it bandaged. She wanted Stuart to tell her that her worries were absurd.

All he said was, 'How does Carlos strike you when you see him?'

'Fatherly. Wanting more of Kit.'

'And of you?'

She pretended to laugh again.

'No, not any more. He's accepted that it's over between him and me.'

'I'm not sure if that's good news or bad. But we won't talk about it just now. What about Kit? You're giving Carlos a good deal by allowing Kit to spend a night with him. He'll be grateful.'

'Oh, he is!'

'Then it seems to me you can set your own terms. What exactly are you afraid of, Viv?'

'Kit being upset. A strangeness. And –'

'And?'

'And its effect on *him*. On Carlos. To have Kit his own for a whole day and a night.'

'You mean you are allowing him to hope.'

'Yes. But I'm not sure what he will hope for.'

'Only you can know that, Viv. When you see him tomorrow, be kind. He is more hurt by what has happened than he'll show. We men are like that. Some of us.'

Carlos arrived at the house the next day with unusual punctuality. He wore clothes which were foreign to Viv's eyes, accustomed to the sombre tones of Londoners. His suit was pale and exaggerated in cut to show his strong shoulders. His tie of blue satin exaggerated his olive skin and black eyes. He had no luggage and explained, after giving Viv his customary bend of the head, a kind of salutation, that he'd already been to the hotel and had seen his room.

'It is comfortable, and there is space for Kit to play with his trains.'

With a strange tenderness which changed him and which she did not recall ever seeing when he was in love with her, he said he knew how Kit liked his trains.

'We can fit the rails on the floor in our room. And take care not to lose any of the points,' he said seriously. 'I had to change our room, the first one had a lumpy carpet.'

I wish you'd stop, she thought. She tried to harden her heart.

The suitcase was packed with the little boy's night things; she had already explained to Kit that he was to stay the night with his father. Kit had been impressed.

'Shall I be in this hotel for always and always?'

'Of course not. Home tomorrow.'

'How can I have my bath?'

'Papa will give it to you.'

'He doesn't know how to.'

'Then you can show him, can't you?'

Going up to the nursery she found the child, who had heard his father's voice, collecting at least ten stuffed toys. They filled his arms and the larger ones kept dropping to the ground.

'Shall I tell you something?' he said. 'I don't like hotels.' He stood clasping his unmanageable burden, his eyes full of tears. Viv had expected this and managed to remove the larger toys just as he began to howl. With her back to the door, she did not see Carlos come in. Crossing the room he scooped the child into his arms and laughed.

'Are you *crying*? Because we are to stay in a hotel where we can make the trains go round and round on the floor? And here I have brought you a new *ferrocarril* station from Spain with a porter on the platform, and a vanful of vegetables.'

'Where is it?' demanded Kit, angry and curious.

Standing at the door, watching the man and boy leave the house, Kit sniffing and comforted, she forgot – in the small dramas of a small child – any advice she should have given her husband.

CHAPTER FIFTEEN

Frivolous, easily led and easily bored, Julie was above all sociable and social. She detested, she scarcely ever had to suffer, her own company. Her thoughts did not interest her much; Julie was for laughter and sensation. Growing up with a somewhat humour-ic and conventional mother, Julie had developed from childhood a kind of automatic reflex, a gainsaying to Grace's rules. She had to swallow a desire to contradict every word her mother said.

But Claire had been comfortable living under her mother's sway: she had never truly wanted to be a rebel, and as she grew older Grace's ideas became very much her own. She thought like Grace, developed many of her traits, deplored the slapdash or the out-of-the-ordinary; her way of serving meals was uncannily like her mother's. Everything had to be just so. It was this comforming which began a separation between the sisters who had called themselves the twins. When they were children, Julie managed to lead Claire into mischief, to share helpless gales of laughter with her, to whisper in corners. By the time the two girls reached their late teens, Julie's power over Claire was gone.

It amused Julie when her sister, fresh from the mists of respectable Sussex, agreed to stay with her in the flat. It tickled Julie even more when through another mist – of thick cigarette smoke – she saw Claire flirting with Les Bacon. Julie liked Les well enough – he was always good at a party. He wasn't bad looking, although he always reminded her of the errand boy who had delivered the groceries to Woodlands. But Les was such a liar. Julie found it quite hard not to show him that she didn't believe a word he said.

At the party when Julie had introduced Claire to Les, and the couple had sat down, staying together on the sofa for what seemed hours, absorbed in each other's company, Julie had now and again watched them thoughtfully. It had been obvious from the start that they were attracted. A good many women took to Les – his manner with them was flattering, even ingratiating, but Julie judged that it was more than that with Claire. He seemed genuinely fascinated by her sister. Julie had been rather pleased about that.

In the way of people who drink too much and resent their friends sticking to lemonade, of drug-takers who will go to much trouble to praise and offer drugs to their friends – 'one sniff won't hurt you, wait and see how you'll love it!' – Julie preferred her friends to go in for sex. Amoral and casual, regarding lovemaking as the best way to round off an evening, she had been irked by her twin's married chastity. Knowing it was wrong, she wanted Claire to behave as she did. Everything to Julie was either fun or no fun, and seeing Claire's expression as she sat close to old Les Bacon was distinctly in the first category.

There was another cruder reason for Julie to be pleased Claire was staying in the flat and had taken up with Les Bacon. Julie was advancing steadily into debt. Mannequins were badly paid; they were expected to be grateful for the honour of working for a famous designer, with the chance to buy model dresses second hand for a pound or two. Julie's salary went nowhere, and she was forced to borrow money whenever possible. George Silver had been a great help until that source dried up – on her third request, he simply laughed.

'I'm not a fool three times, darling. I thought you said the money I gave you was a loan.'

'Oh George.'

'Yes, yes, there's no need to pout, we know how desperately sexy you are. Apparently my cash has all been swallowed up. Now you want some more. Stupid of me to ask. What do I get in return?'

'Me?'

He laughed again. 'That's not enough security in the bank. And anyway I've already spent that, haven't I?'

Not offended, Julie made a horrible grimace at him and left his office empty-handed.

Claire, by happy chance, had turned up at just the right time when Julie's bills, stuffed into her suitcase among her knickers and bras, were growing alarmingly fast. Winifred, who'd lent her the apartment, had made two stipulations. Nobody must wear shoes in the white drawing room. And Julie must pay the gas, electricity and telephone bills during her stay. Generous but not stupid, Winifred fixed for the bills to be sent in every four weeks. They had begun to arrive with upsetting regularity. While her sister was still deeply asleep after a party and a night out with Les, Julie sat up in bed, eyes narrowed, considering ways and means. The conclusion she came to was simple enough. The time to attack was when Claire first woke up.

Sex, exciting, exhausting, thrilling, unimagined sex, made Claire sleep as deeply as if she had swum to the bottom of the ocean. She had been so happy with Les last night: girlish and funny and reactive and admiring, as melting as a beautiful ice cream under the rays of a Mediterranean sun. Claire fell in love and so did he. They laughed as people do who find delight in each other. They sat, wrapped round, looking with curiosity at each other's exhausted faces.

'You don't know your own power,' he said, rocking her to and fro in his arms: they spent hours in his flat, in a disordered room filled with books and threadbare furniture and cushions.

After what seemed to her an entire night of lovemaking, Claire slept like the dead.

The pale London sun was shining through the edges of the curtains when she woke to feel somebody gently tapping her arm. She opened her eyes to see Julie in a blue and gold kimono standing by her. Julie went over and drew the curtains. At the sudden entrance of light, Claire had to cover her eyes.

Julie perched on the bed and handed her a cup of black coffee.

'What's the time?'

282

'Quarter past one.'

Claire sat up as if Julie had stuck a knife in her leg.

'I haven't rung Stuart!'

'Calm down. He rang earlier. I said we'd had a big party and you were still out for the count.'

Feeling there wasn't a word of the sentence she should be glad to hear, feeling she was in collusion, feeling she didn't know where she was, Claire muttered thank you.

Julie studied her sister, who really did look a wreck. Had there ever been such rings under anybody's eyes? Old Les must be better value than I imagined, thought Julie. Claire's pale hair straggled, her eyeshadow was smudged, she had a lump on her lip. Somebody has been biting you, my girl. Well, well.

'How was your evening?'

Claire visibly pulled herself together. She had the sensation that every bone in her body was broken.

'Nice.'

'I didn't know what to tell Stu about when you're going home.' She read Claire's face easily.

'Do you think I could ...'

'Get away with another night? I don't see why not.'

A smile, touching in its absurdity, radiant in its joy, full of hope and self deception, beautiful and crazy, spread across Claire's love-scarred face.

'Julie. How can I thank you?'

It was what Julie was waiting for.

While Claire spent the rest of the day recovering – she arranged to meet Les that night – Julie left for Michou's with a usually empty crocodile handbag stuffed with money. Fifty pounds.

She was full of good resolves as she travelled to Conduit Street. She would pay the cash into her bank. No, she couldn't do that, the overdraft would swallow it. She would pay the gas and the damned electricity. No. Perhaps it was better to pay the telephone bill. She'd have to pay cash, how did one do that? Criminally undomesticated, Julie skated through life without once looking down to test the ice.

The fifty pounds took a comfortable amount of space in her

handbag and when she paid her bus fare and saw the wedge of banknotes, she gave them a wink.

Peter. The money meant lots and lots of Peter. Her spirits soared.

She had never meant to have anything to do with Peter Southey. He was not the kind of man Julie went in for – not at all. He'd come to Michou's one morning accompanying a hardfaced socialite, the Honourable Mrs Reggie somebody. He'd sat, as such escorts did during dress shows, courteous and bored. And then, as Julie swayed towards them in an oyster-coloured satin evening dress, he gave her a look of strangely sweet fellowship.

The afternoon was very cold and when Julie emerged up the basement steps of the showrooms huddled in her huge coat, there he was. She was very surprised.

'Name's Southey. Peter Southey. I suppose you wouldn't have some tea with me? Joan had to go on somewhere,' he said vaguely.

Lanky and silent, he walked with Julie into the golden rooms of the Carlton Hotel, ordered tea with the expertise of a man who practically lived in the place, and turned his grey eyes on her.

'I'm so glad.'

'Because I'm here?'

'Oh yes.'

She did like him. She liked his round face and thin Ronald Colman moustache, his quiet drawling upper-class voice, his worn tweeds, the red carnation in his buttonhole. She did not understand why she liked him so much and so soon.

Peter Southey told her then and there over the tea cups that he was 'awfully afraid I've fallen in love with you'. It had happened this afternoon. It had happened the moment she came into the room and walked across the stage in that 'silk thing you were wearing'. She was the loveliest girl in the entire world and the way he felt about her was not a joke. Not a joke at all.

'I am,' he said with his beautiful politeness, 'your slave.'

'It isn't every day that a grandee like you becomes the slave of a clothes horse like me.'

'A clothes horse,' repeated Peter Southey with an adoring sigh.

He told her a little about himself, pleased when Julie asked questions. His father was a baron. But that was only the second least important title, wasn't it?

'Is it? I didn't know.'

Peter Southey murmured about marquises and earls. Much Julie cared. To the outrage of a woman at a nearby table, she leaned forward and kissed his cheek.

Julie's sudden feelings for him, the unfamiliar sensation that a day without him was a day of being dead, had come just about the time that she was lent the white flat. Since then they had met on every possible occasion, although now and again he was forced to go down to the country to see relations.

'You know how it is ...'

One bereft week, he had to go to Ireland, to Leopardstown to help with the horses, whatever that meant.

Lying in her arms, meeting her for meals, walking with her in Hyde Park, telephoning her daily, Peter told her about his family and his life. His father had been a lieutenant in the Blues – all the Southeys for generations had been Army people – but had left the service after gambling away most of his inherited money. He and Peter's mother now lived in hotels.

'Mother doesn't like having to do things for herself,' Peter said tenderly. He was devoted to his parents, and took Julie to meet them in their present home, an opulent Kensington hotel. Julie was disappointed in his mother whom she thought distinctly stupid, with a vacuous laugh, too much make-up and hair dyed a brassy yellow. I suppose, thought Julie with youthful pity, she was once a blonde. And her taste in clothes was too young and too fussy. Peter was so charming to her that it hurt Julie's heart. His father was stocky, quiet, wrapped up in himself. Julie thought his wife bored him. He gave Julie a kindly incurious look. When he did speak, the tones of his voice were so like Peter's that Julie's heart hurt more than ever.

As a lover, Peter was irresistible. He was passionate and funny and cosy and adoring – her slave. And he was as poor as she.

To Julie this was distinctly not fun. All her lovers had money and one or two, like George Silver, a great deal. There was always enough for cocktails, night clubs, enough to lend – which meant to give – her five pound notes for taxis and flowers. She collected, and pawned, gold bracelets; at times she had half a dozen. When given an unexpected present, Julie was wonderful value. Nobody accepted with more generosity. She exclaimed, kissed, she rayed with delight. There was no getting away from the fact that money meant a good time.

It was a dirty trick of fate that she'd fallen in love with a man who was so broke. Peter, in the Regular Army, had been posted for three years to India, which explained a faint alluring tan still on his face and arms. On returning to England his Colonel bluntly informed him that he must leave the regiment. When Peter gasped, 'But why, sir?' the colonel silently held up a fistful of unpaid bar bills. The total amounted to more than Peter's pay for a year.

His father had been angry when his son told him the news, and said nothing. His mother laughed.

'After all, darling, you've still got your grandmother's allowance.'

The allowance was very small indeed and just about kept Peter going for the time being. He was living at his club and knew his grandmother would pay *that* bill later, from pride. He had been drifting round Mayfair, invited out by friends, wearing a carnation and without a plan in his head when Julie, in an oyster satin dress, had walked towards him.

'We're the Babes in the Wood,' he whispered as they lay in bed in the apartment. Julie sighed and hugged him. He was hopeless. That was how it was. Hopelessly in love, hopelessly without a job or money. Hopeless. And despite floating across pale carpets at Michou's, she was nearly as hopeless as Peter.

In the early evening of the day she had magicked money out of her rich sister, Julie met him for a glass of champagne. She paid.

'Darling,' he said, kissing her wrist, 'you're wonderful.'

Julie thought so too. She beckoned the waiter for two more glasses.

She gave Peter a vivid delighted smile. Her twin was the answer to everything. The beastly bills would be paid; Claire would write cheques which wouldn't even make a dent in all her money. Claire would also help 'here and there' when Julie needed some ready cash.

Ignorant of the new role being prepared for her, Claire bathed, dressed slowly, had some more black coffee and finally telephoned Stuart. She explained – 'Silly me' – that she had a bad headache after the party, and would he mind if she didn't come home until tomorrow? Her voice was genuinely exhausted and Stuart, concerned, agreed at once. He would look forward to seeing her tomorrow he said, 'and do get some rest.'

When she dutifully asked after the children, he gave his short laugh.

'They're still here. Still bursting with rude health and making a racket.'

'And Nanny?'

'The Scottish dragon we know and love.'

Satisfied that life at the other end of the railway was shipshape and Bristol fashion, Claire had more rest, went to the hairdresser, and was dressed in clinging coffee-coloured marocain, looking tired but pretty, when the front door bell rang. Oh, he's early! she thought, and ran to answer the door.

The figure standing there was not the tall, easy, rather stooping man with a sexy smile whom she expected. He was shorter and broader, grey hair thickly curling on top of his head and a ruddy face.

Frank Bryant.

'Hello, my daughter. You're a stranger. I was expecting your sister.'

Claire gave a tinkling laugh and said 'Hello Pa' and how was he? Her spirits fell to the ground.

'I've come to see Julie. She said I'd find her in,' said Frank, stepping into the hall. He saw, through open double doors, a vista of pure white.

'God bless my soul! Has your sister come into money again?'

'The flat belongs to one of her friends. She lent it to Julie when she went to New York. Shall I give her a message, Pa? She may not be back for ages. I mean, not until very late.'

It was the nearest, it really was far too near, Claire dared go to rudeness. But she was desperate. He looked grave but merely said wasn't she going to ask him in?

Claire was forced to take him into the snow-white room. Leaving footmarks across the carpet, he sat heavily down in a cushioned chair and put his hands on his knees.

'Julie's a flighty one but she'll turn up. So, daughter, are you going to pour us a sherry?'

Claire escaped to the kitchen and opened every cupboard. She found champagne and brandy, liqueurs and whisky. She returned with whisky, a siphon and a cut glass tumbler, apologizing for the dearth of sherry.

'Whisky will do very well. Good health.'

He lifted his glass to her and drank thirstily. It was a long way from Hornsey to Knightsbridge. The bus had been ahead of time and had deliberately hung about at more than one stop for minutes on end.

He turned his steady gaze on his second daughter. He had never been close to Claire. She looked like poor Grace but to her father's mind she would never be a tenth as interesting. When she'd been young, Grace had been quite an enigma. This girl looked a real lady, with a good figure. Nothing unexpected there. A father to four daughters, he still thought of them as they'd been when he left Woodlands. Their characters appeared to him unchanged, all except Julie's, the daughter he actually knew as an adult. He was ashamed of how little he knew of the other three, how much he'd given up his responsibility towards them. And all for Connie and a bit of bed. But there it was; you did such things and only dolts were sorry afterwards. Frank wasted no time in thinking 'if only'. He had a bad conscience just the same.

Claire was more nervous than she showed. Her poise stood her in good stead – she looked cool enough.

Frank drank up his whisky and then said, as if in appeal, 'I was sorry I couldn't come to the baptism of your little son.'

'Pa. I have two children. We asked you to both their baptisms.'

Frank Bryant looked very uncomfortable. The inconsiderate

288

habit children had of growing up, the difficulty of grasping the fact of being a grandfather, came to mind.

'That makes it worse. I'm sorry, Claire. What are their names, your lass and lad?'

The Northern words reached Claire through a sex-clouded haze. She said 'Anthony and Clarissa', and Frank, who thought the names pretentious, fished out a notebook and scribbled down dates of birth. He put the book back in his breast pocket.

'What about a post office account for each of them? Just a small nest egg, but regular.'

'That's very kind of you, Pa.'

'No, it's not. It would have been right and proper for me to remember when they were born. You must forgive me. I'm no father to you.'

He said it without contrition, as if he did not suppose she had noticed. She couldn't help smiling, and at the moment when she had the grace to forget herself the bell rang again. At least she didn't run to the door.

When Les Bacon came into the room Frank stood up and Claire introduced them. Les accepted a drink and chatted amiably with Frank Bryant in the manner he used for clients in business, a dash of respect, a touch of particular interest. Frank Bryant liked him immediately. The two were getting on like a house on fire, while Claire sat sipping lemonade and intent on her own performance, when Julie rocketed in.

'Pa! I clean forgot.'

'No harm done.'

He went to her with an alacrity he had not shown to Claire, and gave Julie's thin painted cheek a smacking kiss, then held her at arm's length, meeting her laughing glance and telling her she looked a proper scarecrow. Claire smiled in a strained way, wondering how long she had to remain imprisoned by daughterly politeness. It was Les who rescued her. He finally said he was afraid they must go.

'Or we'll be late for the theatre.'

'That's nice,' said Frank Bryant who never went inside a theatre and revered anybody who did. 'What are you going to see?'

'*Cavalcade*. The Noel Coward musical at Drury Lane.'

By the promptness of the reply Julie knew he'd said the same thing many times before.

When the two had gone, Julie refilled her father's glass and made a fuss of him. She gave him a hug. She sat her weightless self, all seven stone, on his knee and pulled his grey curls.

'Why have you come to see me, making 'orrible dusty marks on Winifred's white carpets?'

'I want a favour,' he said, lifting her off his knee as if she were a small child and setting her on her feet. Julie promptly collapsed on to the floor and leaned against him. She loved him. She never saw him, or almost never, and she loved him. Apart from Peter he was the only masculine reality in her unreal life.

'A favour. What in the name of Hades, Pa, can *I* do for *you*?'

'Why, I count on you sometimes, my girl. Yes, you're the one I can count on. We know where we stand, don't we?'

For an absurd moment Julie wondered if he was going to ask her for money. Afterwards she put the crazy thought down to a saying of her old teacher's at school: 'Everybody's mad for five minutes in a day.' Julie's mad attack passed. Pa asking her for money! He was the Northern epitome of that old-fashioned virtue: honesty. 'I always pay my bills, I can say that for myself.' However bitter her mother had been towards him she had never denied his honourable way in their finances.

'Yes. We do know where we stand,' she said, thinking, we stand upon love, I suppose.

'It's about Con.'

Oh God, thought Julie.

He gave a wheezing sigh, drank deeply and put the glass carefully down on a marble-topped table.

'It's my Con's birthday next week, she's fifty – but you mustn't breathe that to a soul. I want to give her something, you know. Something that'll set her up a bit in her own estimation. She doesn't much like being fifty.'

'You mean clothes.'

'Yes. Clothes,' said Frank as if speaking of Folies Bergère feather head-dresses or gold embroidered camisoles. 'I'm blamed if I know what. I thought you'd help me. I measured a favourite dress she wears,' he added, and out came his notebook again.

Julie's heart swelled as she looked at the neat line of figures.

'What would Connie say to a model dress by Michou? One of his customers is a South American; she's just about Connie's height and size. She was over recently and Michou designed an entire wardrobe of clothes for her – lovely, they are. But she didn't buy a thing because a relative suddenly died in Ecuador, and now she's in deepest black. Michou's landed with the stuff. Every time he sees that line of dresses he bursts into tears.'

Frank looked embarrassed at the picture of a weeping man; a sissy, no doubt. Women's clothes, women themselves were a mystery to Frank. It was a sour joke of heaven's to have given him four daughters. He found the opposite sex perplexing, never followed their reasoning, never expected or understood either their moods or their joys. But he did know that his daughter worked somewhere damned expensive.

'Would a dress meant for that South American lady cost a fortune?'

'Of course not, I could get one for a quarter of the price. Less. Poor Michou would be glad to see one disappear from the rail. He loathes failure. Now, let's see. Connie's favourite colours are beige and white, aren't they? There's a dress that might be perfect for her.'

Frank Bryant looked at Julie in silence for a moment, then said, 'You're a dear girl. I don't care who says different.'

They arranged that she would bring the dress to Hornsey at a time when Connie would be out. It had to be a surprise. He'd have the money waiting, he said. Hanging on his arm like a schoolgirl, Julie saw him out.

True to her word, she picked out the dress, simple but a beauty, at Michou's the following day. Madame Hawthorne, who was in charge of unsold model gowns, told her graciously that she need not pay for it. 'Maître dislikes that one for some reason.' But it

291

would be sensible for Julie to hide it when she took it home from the showrooms. Maître was quite capable of deciding, because Julie wanted it, that it was a masterpiece.

Julie telephoned her old friend Harold to drive her to Hornsey.

'Quite like old times' said poor Harold, who never gave up hope. He was embarrassingly glad to see her and Julie was kind to him on the long journey to her father's house and back. Frank had been overwhelmed, almost speechless, when Julie appeared with a magnificent silver box across which 'Michou' was scrawled in black. And when she told him she had been given it for nothing, he could scarcely believe it.

Pleased with herself, pleased with her father, Julie sang dance tunes with Harold all the way back to Sloane Street. She let him kiss her quite passionately when they said goodbye.

For the next two months, the twins saw a great deal of each other. Claire became practised at deceptions as old as marriage itself. After wifely days in Sussex, she travelled to London and Les drove her to his ramshackle flat to make love. They dined in little restaurants in Hampstead. They stayed together until the small hours, when Claire always insisted on returning home to Julie's.

Then suddenly Les became very busy at his advertising agency. Once or twice when Claire arrived in London in her usual state of excited longing, she had to wait at the Sloane Street flat for more than an hour. Les never telephoned to say he would be late and she grew crazy with frustration. When he appeared at last, grinning and easy, he was amused at her desperate welcome.

The affair was as violent as ever. He had only to be in an empty flat alone with her to take off his clothes. She was satisfied by his thin pale body and hungry for his impossible-to-grasp heart. She did not understand him.

Julie did, but said nothing. She had taken old Les Bacon's measure the first time she had met him at one of her own parties. She guessed that he was a man to whom sex wasn't only important because it was enjoyable but also because it fed his vanity. His lies sprang from the same source. Les told lies to impress. He wished to

292

prove, over and over again, how irresistible he was and how clever too. If you agreed, as Claire helplessly did, nobody could be more devoted or more fascinating. It was curious, thought Julie, how Claire and old Les resembled each other. They were both dyed-in-the-wool swanks. Sometimes when Julie was with them, Les would boast about his success at work in a way that would have made Julie's other friends stare. Claire smiled proudly, as if at the prizegiving for one of her children who'd been first in class. Did she really believe Les's claims to fame?

And where, Julie asked herself, was Stuart in all this? A voice on the telephone, to whom Julie was always friendly and casual. It's starting to be a mess, thought Julie. She forgot how it had amused her to begin with.

She had little time at present to think much about Stuart or even about Claire. Lack of money was gnawing again. It arrived like a rat with bared and poisoned teeth. She'd spent her fifty pounds on Peter and herself; they had enjoyed every penny of it. But the four-weekly bills kept arriving, printed in red. The most worrying was the telephone which the Post Office threatened to cut off. Peter paid it by pawning the gold half-hunter his grandfather had left him. Julie knew he loved it, and when he told her what he'd done, she cried.

Then the worst happened. One morning when she was having a cup of coffee in the kitchen, an official in a cap arrived at the door. 'Sorry, miss. Come to cut off the gas.'

'*What?*'

Accustomed to the wails of the indignant, the man from the gas company patiently explained. He showed her two bills, both in warning scarlet. Julie was getting angry when Claire appeared, modest in a dark satin dressing gown. She frowned at the sight of her sister, whose kimono was gaping, raising her voice to a man in a cap.

'What is the trouble?' said Claire.

The man knew a lady when he saw one. He also knew, with a glance at the wearer of the kimono, one who was not. He explained.

Claire quelled him with a cold stare, said her sister must have

293

overlooked it – 'She has been extremely busy recently' – went to her room and returned with her handbag. She paid him in pound notes. Very politely, he thanked her.

'And where is the receipt?' asked Claire freezingly. 'Kindly give me a receipt at once. And don't forget in future that it is most necessary if you are paid in cash.'

The man obeyed in subdued silence.

The front door shut on him. Julie burst into giggles, saw Claire's expression, stuffed her hands into her mouth and tottered into the drawing room. She fell across one of the sofas.

'Oh, oh, what a hoot. You were marvellous. He actually saluted you!'

Claire did not smile. She no longer felt beholden to Julie. If she wanted to, she could stay in Les's flat on the nights she could get away from Sussex. She asked, still as icy as she had been with the man from the gas company, why Julie hadn't paid the bill. Julie straightened her face. Bills paid by friends and allies always had an intoxicating effect on her for a while. She explained that she was broke. Smiling up at Claire, it occurred to her that the moment was ripe. Claire had just seen how difficult things were. And after all her twin was rich and it was she, Julie, who'd introduced her to old Les who was giving Claire such a good time.

'The subject's as boring as hell, but to tell you the truth I'm stony,' sighed Julie. 'It isn't my fault, honestly, I do try. But the fact is – not a bean to be seen.'

'There's your pay.'

Julie shrugged.

'Mortgaged. Promised. Spent in advance.'

Claire was already annoyed. Les had telephoned to cancel their date. He knew very well that she was finding it more and more difficult to get away from home, yet he'd been perfectly cheerful about letting her down. 'Sorry, sorry!' was all he said. She was very offended. It hurt too much to admit it to herself, but somewhere in her thoughts she knew he wasn't as keen as he used to be.

'What am *I* expected to do about you?' she said sharply.

Julie raised butterfly eyebrows.

'Have a heart. You're rolling and I'm the church mouse. You've got money to burn.'

'It isn't meant for burning and you burn it all the time.'

'We're not going to have a lecture, are we?'

'Yes, Julie, we are.' Claire fastened the top button of her dressing gown. For a moment she forgot Les. She was the queen of Lewes who had saved her husband from bankruptcy, the woman who with a clever broker and an eye for land now owned acres and farms and enjoyed studying her investments.

'You've always been a fool with money, even when we were children. I know you're the generous one of the family,' quoted Claire with a rare hint of savagery. 'Everybody used to call you that. You borrowed off me when we were fifteen and sixteen so you could give Ma an expensive birthday present. You never paid me back.'

Old grudges, ludicrous, pitiful, like scabs which bleed if you pick at them, began to show. Claire thrust out an arm covered with them.

'If you're asking me to lend you more money, the answer is no. I lent you fifty pounds last month.'

'So you've been counting,' said Julie, with a jeer.

It was Claire's turn to raise her eyebrows to her hair-line. She gave a metallic laugh.

'Counting. Of course I have been counting. What else does one do with money, pray, but count it. Put it in the bank. Invest it. Or does one throw it into the gutter as you apparently do? I lent you fifty pounds last month, twenty pounds a week ago, and I have just paid your electricity bill.'

'And you've used no electricity, I suppose?' said Julie, loathing herself for using filthy and feeble weapons, but very angry. 'You've been going to bed in the dark, I suppose, when you and Les heaved away in *my* bedroom in *my* flat.'

'Don't be disgusting.'

'Why not? You are. We just have different ways of being disgusting.'

'I have done nothing to deserve such a description.' Claire was white in the face.

'Haven't you? You're as bad as I am. Don't smile in that beastly way; you're going to see the similarity if it kills you. You say I sponge off you. You're self-righteous and pious about it. I must "see the light". Manage on my pathetic salary. Accept that I'm broke. Well, *I* say you're as mean as hell with that money you got from Ma and were clever enough, yes I give you that, to make into much more. I say you take and take and what do you give back? I introduced you to the man you're so crazy about. I let you sleep with him here in this flat when you want to. Don't look as if you're going to burst, you can have your turn in a minute. I say you're mean. Mean. And I pity you for it. But I'm not sitting here to be read a sermon. You've deceived Stuart. You've lied. You and old Les are both liars in different ways. But when you give something to someone, Claire, you should mean it. You let me thank you for the measly cash. You accepted my thanks and hugs and all the time you were noting it down in some bloody bank book. Were you going to charge me interest? That would be like you. Three per cent on presents. Do you charge interest to Viv and Isobel when you give them anything - which is probably never?'

Claire sat like a stone. She was as furious as Julie, but not given to insults. In any case, she was not good at them. She walked straight out of the room to her bedroom and began to pack. Without another word she left the flat.

Julie let her go. She wished she'd slapped her face.

But Claire had not been as unaffected by the row as her stony face seemed to show. She had packed, stripped the bed, even opened a window. But when Julie flung herself into the bedroom after Claire had gone, still furious, still obscurely ashamed, still feeding the anger so that the fire would not go out and leave her shivering, she saw a curious thing.

Claire had a habit, she'd had it as a girl, of sleeping with her jewel case under her pillow. At twelve years old, when all she had possessed was a gold chain, a holy medal and a bracelet, she used to wrap them in a handkerchief and sleep with them tucked under her sleeping head.

As Julie pulled the pillows across the bed to shake them, she saw the jewel case.

296

It was a slim roll of pink leather into which you could put bracelets or rings in small separate compartments; the whole thing folded neatly and was fastened with a pink leather strap. Squatting on the bed, Julie opened it.

The case was crammed.

Julie knew her sister liked jewellery and had often teased her about 'Claire's rocks', borrowing the word from gangster films. Now all Claire's rocks were exposed to her astonished eyes as she emptied the contents on to the bed.

Like a magpie which pecks up glittering objects only to drop them into its nest, Claire collected jewels. She did not wear many of them, she merely bought them. There were dark emeralds which would have cost two years of Julie's pay, slender snaky diamond bracelets shining with red and yellow fire, strings of creamy pearls. Julie had never seen her sister in any of the treasures spread out on the bed. Earrings were out of fashion but there were half a dozen pairs, the opals FRF had given her, diamond earrings hanging on chains, ruby earrings surrounded by pearls. How strange Claire is, thought Julie. She sleeps with these things under her pillow just like Viv's Kit takes his rabbit to bed.

She let the jewels fall through her fingers, yellow and green and dark blue and glowing pearl. She felt like the Count of Monte Cristo on a lost island when he found the abbé's treasure.

Winding a long pearl necklace round her wrist, she smiled.

CHAPTER SIXTEEN

The Berkeley Hotel faced the Ritz in Piccadilly but did not compete with that French-designed establishment. It had no air of 1900 Paris-in-London. The Berkeley was modern and to Julie and many other young habitués it was more fashionable. Julie liked the ballroom, the band and the style. She liked the absence of foreign ambassadors, the light-hearted atmosphere, the very Thirties feeling which suited her mood and that of her friends. The staff at the Berkeley, the tall ex-sergeant major who was head porter, the short expansive maître d'hôtel, the fat Portuguese lady who looked after the coats, all knew Julie. They had known her in her affluent days and were not aware that she was now comparatively poor. She simply appeared quite often, dressed in glorious clothes and apparently as wealthy as ever.

Julie had always superstitiously believed in her own luck, and after Claire slammed out of the flat, a cable arrived from New York. It was from Winifred who was returning to London far sooner than she had expected.

For once, thought Julie with satisfaction, I shan't need to dump myself on my friends in that dilapidated house in Ealing or sleep on Viv's sofa at World's End.

She did some telephoning, went on a short shopping expedition and took a taxi. She swept into the reception hall at the Berkeley and signed her name.

'Mr Southey has already arrived, Miss Bryant. You will find him in the lounge.'

298

She walked through intersecting golden-coloured rooms; the walls were decorated with great modern looking glasses reflecting, over and over again, her thin figure, her clinging suit, her dark shiny hair.

There was Peter, long legs outstretched, reading the racing pages of the evening newspaper. Seeing her he stood up, put both hands on her shoulders and stooped to give her a gentle kiss. They might have been a young society couple engaged to be married. Julie smiled and sat down beside him.

'What an extravagant creature you are, darling Julie. Are you quite sure you can really afford all this?'

'I certainly can. For us both. Winifred's due back in a few days and I don't want to hang around polishing the glasses. You and I can stay here at the lovely Berkeley until I get fixed up somewhere else. There are sure to be other chums who will go abroad and lend me somewhere.'

She gave an expressive wave. A waiter came up, believing she was ordering a drink. Julie agreed she would like one, please.

Sitting comfortably together, the sound of traffic muffled by thick velvet curtains, Peter and Julie exchanged looks. Nothing suited them more than spending money. They were good at it; they understood how to enjoy it; they were very connoisseurs of luxury. It was a trait they had in common, as two people might have an ear for music. They were sunflowers turning to face the sun.

Julie did not tell Peter where her money had suddenly come from; he was – well, he had been – an officer and a gentleman. It was one of the things about him which made her smile and feel very tender, an unfamiliar sensation in Julie's heart. Peter believed she'd had an unexpected windfall. Preferring not to lie, she had said it was 'something to do with Ma's money'.

After all, that was not exactly untrue.

They had a leisurely lunch, went to Bond Street to buy Julie some shoes and to Savile Row to choose Peter a cravat. Later they returned to the Berkeley for tea, then went up to Julie's room to make love. Lying in bed with Peter, sharing the pleasures of love – he was so passionate and so simple – Julie's conscience did not give

299

her a qualm. She had only taken four pieces from Claire's jewel case. She'd deliberately picked out rings which Claire couldn't possibly wear, every one of them hideous. Her sister must have bought them because of the stones they contained; perhaps she would eventually decide to have the rings redesigned and reset – but that would be years away.

Julie had been perfectly cool when she made up her mind to appropriate her sister's property. There was a sort of poetic justice about it. She was still angry with Claire, outraged by her meanness and, in a schoolmistressy way, disappointed in her. There was no cruelty in taking old but valuable stuff which Claire had bought simply as an investment. Julie had extracted the four rings, refastened the case and put it back under the pillow. Then she set off, walking with a spring, to a jeweller's shop opposite the Brompton Oratory. It was small but classy, its window filled with black velvet trays of antique, expensive rings; Julie had noticed the place when in a rare fit of piety or conscience she'd been to Sunday Mass.

The jeweller, small and thin, said a respectful good afternoon. She explained, 'I've some odd bits I don't much like. I wonder if you might be interested in buying them?'

He examined the rings closely. There was a ruby half hoop whose stones reminded Julie of raspberry jelly, and an emerald ring in which the emeralds resembled small sickly dollops of crème de menthe. Two more rings were just as ugly. The old man studied them, then took them into a back office for a few minutes. There was a pause and two of his clocks chimed. When he finally returned he offered her, ring by ring, an enormous amount of money. Golly, thought Julie, Claire's full of surprises. She asked the man, using a good deal of charm, for cash. Undisturbed by the request, he paid her in clean fifty pound notes. Once again, but with what a difference, Julie's handbag was bursting.

In a taxi on her way to meet Peter she invented an alibi. There had been a party at the flat that day. Lots of guests were almost strangers. Somebody, goodness knows who, must have discovered the case and nabbed the rings. I shan't need the alibi for months, if at all, she thought. But I've got it by me.

She and Peter settled down to the delight of being rich. Julie telephoned Madame Hawthorne and truthfully said she was not feeling herself. Madame gave a little shriek. 'Suppose you are sickening for something. Maître might catch the infection. Do not think of showing your face in the showrooms, please.'

So Julie and Peter were alone together, and happy.

She told nobody where she was. She covered her tracks, not from intent but from carelessness. It did not occur to Julie to ring Viv and Isobel and she certainly wasn't going to speak to Claire now – or ever. As for her father, she had kept her promise and delivered Connie's present and probably would not see him again for months.

Staying in style in one of Mayfair's richest hotels, dancing every night, seen only by one or two wealthy acquaintances who waved gaily from the dance floor, Julie had all but vanished.

Claire returned to Sussex thoroughly upset, her mind full – not of her recalcitrant sister – but of Les. She couldn't think what to do next. She was helpless and miserable. She had an unbreakable rule – that the man should telephone the woman. She had often remarked on this to her sisters, saying with a smile that as far as she was concerned she'd never telephoned a man in her life. Even now that she was married, she expected Stuart to do most of the telephoning; it had always been Stuart who rang Julie's flat every time Claire spent the night there.

Attempting to settle to a beautiful Sussex spring, watching Nanny and the children in the garden while she sat on the terrace, Claire fought a long battle with pride. She thought with heat and longing of Les. At last she capitulated, went into Lewes and telephoned from the post office.

'Hello!' said Les, sounding pleased.

She did not suspect that his rule was her own: Les never telephoned women.

In shame she heard herself say, 'Can we meet?'

'Tonight? Are you at Julie's?'

'I'm in Sussex.'

'Why don't you pop on to one of those trains you tell me are so

301

comfortable?' He knew the effect he was having. And he did want to see her. That too.

Claire said she would.

She did not risk telephoning Stuart at the office. Suppose he raised some objection, suppose her usual excuse sounded hollow. She scribbled a note to him. It said merrily that she was mad and had completely forgotten she'd promised to go and see Viv and little Kit tonight; she was taking the fast afternoon train. 'Back tomorrow by lunchtime. Promise!!'

London was looking its best, thought Claire, who was early and decided to walk from Victoria to Sloane Street. She enjoyed walking and set off with a loping stride through streets she now knew pretty well, squares where the hedges of privet were freshly green and the trees too. In eighteenth- and early nineteenth-century crescents, window-boxes were sprouting blue hyacinths. She was on her way to see her sister but was no longer angry with her. Julie was irresponsible and always had been; one must simply not give in to her, thought Claire. She was good at forgetting Julie's insults, and in any case, thinking of Les and knowing she would be in his arms tonight, she felt kind. The sun shone down on her elegant figure and pale pretty face; one or two men glanced at her approvingly. She noticed and pretended that she hadn't.

It was late in the afternoon, about the time Julie returned from Michou's, when Claire fitted her key into the heavy street door of the flats, thinking how lucky it was she'd forgotten to return her keys during the quarrel. Claire never lost her temper; it seemed incredible that she had been so angry yesterday. She might actually have pitched the keys into her sister's jeering face. How very peculiar of me, thought Claire. Well, it's all over now. She could never be cross with Julie for long and had quite forgiven her for wanting to borrow more money.

Yes, she thought, we will make it up and forget it ever happened. She climbed the stairs to the first floor and let herself into the flat.

There is a human instinct which can tell when somebody else is in a dark room even if they make no sound. The same instinct in reverse told Claire the place was empty – and more. She had a strong feeling, a certainty, that her sister was gone. She went straight into Julie's room. It was stripped bare. The long sliding doors of the wardrobe were pulled back; every dress and jacket, every pair of shoes, had disappeared. There was a note in Julie's scrawly handwriting on the dressing table.

Winifred,

Thanks a million for the marvellous time! I've arranged with your Mrs Pratt to come and clean Fri. before you get back. We practically NEVER walked on your carpets.

Love and all that,

J.

Claire wandered through the deserted rooms. She was intensely, absurdly disappointed. She knew her sister's flighty ways, her sister's unexpected unheralded moves. Yet she felt so let down that she could have wept. I suppose I could ring her at Michou's, but we couldn't make it up on the telephone, she thought.

She had imagined she would be spending the night here with Les, not going to his smelly Hampstead flat where the ashtrays were never emptied. Passion overcame such things, but only just. Although she still had a prickle of pleasure at lovemaking to come, she felt upset. She missed Julie so badly. Standing irresolute in the hall, she remembered that she had always kept a spare pair of shoes in the wardrobe of what had been her room. She was sure she had forgotten them when she packed in a fury yesterday.

Going into the bedroom made her shiver. It was exactly as she had left it, the bed stripped, the window open. It brought back a rush of angry emotion and the hatefulness of the quarrel. Only the pillows remained on the bed and wondering if, in her haste, she had also forgotten her nightdress, she lifted them up.

Shock hit her like a blow in the stomach.

How *could* she have forgotten her jewel case? Any of Julie's questionable friends could have stolen it – its contents were worth thousands! Her own lunatic carelessness came to her in its enormity. It was unbelievable. And all Julie's fault for upsetting her. She no longer missed her sister, no longer regretted her; she was simply appalled rather than grateful at finding her property, and still icy with the shock of realizing how easily it could have been stolen. Almost without thinking, she unfastened it and spread the jewels and necklaces upon the bed.

The detective inspector at Elizabeth Street police station was a dignified man who resembled a middle-aged doctor. He treated the owner of the stolen property with concern, as if listening to her describing her symptoms. He took addresses and telephone numbers, and with a sergeant accompanying him, walked back with Claire to the flat. Together the two men searched the empty rooms; they even took fingerprints, of which there were scores. Claire in a moment of insight thought that was probably for her benefit.

Returning to the station Claire was asked to sign some papers. The inspector explained that a description of the stolen property would be circulated at once.

'Of course there are hundreds of jewellers and pawnshops in London, madam. As you'll understand, we may not have news for you for some time. Weeks, even. One good thing: you have given us a most exact description of your property.' It was unusual for anybody, particularly a lady as young as Mrs Lockton, to sit at a desk and describe the missing jewellery in professional terms.

'Gold ring. A quarter of an inch thick, set with six dark rubies in a straight row, and small star-shaped inlays of Brazilian diamonds.'

Promising to keep her informed he showed her politely to the station door.

Claire's night of illicit love lost some of its flavour after two hours with the police and the realization that if the rings were not traced she would have to make a claim for them through Stuart. He had arranged all her insurances. She foresaw a good many lies ahead. Would the quarrel with Julie convince Stuart of his wife's utterly uncharacteristic action in forgetting her jewel case? The fact that it was true was neither here nor there. Supposing Stuart did not believe her.

Until two days ago life had been exciting and thrilling, sexy and dangerous. Now it descended over Clare like a suffocating cloak. Lovemaking with Les was not the same. He laughed when she told him of the theft. For the first time since she had met him she was aware of his total selfishness. And after they made love he had a bath which she thought insulting.

She returned to Lewes by the earliest train, having telephoned Stuart but been put through to his secretary. She was tired and miserable during the journey. Why did she still feel it was essential to see Julie? Was it because Julie could tell her who had been in the flat after Claire had left? Would Julie, who'd teased her about her acquisitiveness from childhood, be the one to understand how upset she was?

Her bitter quarrel with her twin, not Les's lovemaking, lay heavy on her heart.

When she stepped out of the train the last person she expected to see was waiting on the platform. Stuart, the collar of his old tweed coat turned up against a sharp east wind, saw her and raised his hat. She almost ran.

'Oh Stuart. How kind of you.'

'Yes. Well.'

He did not kiss her but she was fussing with her overnight suitcase and didn't notice. He took it from her and they went out of the station to his car. He opened the door for her and put the case in the back.

'I'm taking you for a drive.'

Then she did notice.

'I want a word.' he said.

Stuart got into the car, slammed the door and drove off in the direction of the Downs, turning at the crossroads. And Claire knew. She saw his profile, the aquiline nose, thrust-forward chin. She felt slightly faint with fear – he will divorce me, my life will be destroyed. Then her mind began to work. She told herself he couldn't possibly have evidence, could he? But how could she be certain of that? Perhaps he had had her watched.

She was silent as he turned the car again on to a rough road, almost a track which rose steeply. He finally drew the car to a stop on a flat stretch of turf above which a great bluff of the Downs curved up into the clouded sky. He switched off the engine.

'Well, Claire?'

It was useless to dissemble, but she did so just the same.

'What do you mean, Stuart?'

'Spare us both the performance. You know what I am talking about. You have been having an affair with some chap in London. It's been going on for weeks.'

He wound down the window without asking her and the wind from the Downs was cold. It made a hissing noise through a few stunted thorn bushes. It smelled of the spring. She stared down at her hands. At the fashionable wedding ring, thin as a piece of grass, and above it the eternity ring, as it was called, shining with the largest diamonds Stuart had been able to afford.

He did not look at her.

'What are you going to do?' she said in a whisper.

'I have not decided. What do you say for yourself?'

'You won't listen if I say I'm sorry.'

'I don't suppose I will.'

'You would never understand.'

That was a mistake. He gave a smile like a sneer.

'Understand that you went to bed with another man? No, I don't understand. And don't tell me why.'

In those five words, Claire saw that she had not lost him. He hated her. He was a calm man whose violence lay buried alive. He could have killed her. Men did things like that, thought Claire for the first time in her life. But she knew he still wanted her, and what had happened was a savage blow both to his sexuality and his vision of herself. She must be careful. She was walking on the edge of a cliff from which they could both fall. To their deaths.

'Could you forgive me?' She said, and shivered and closed her eyes.

Stuart turned and looked at her for the first time. She was very pale and drawn. She was not the radiant girl he had scarcely believed was his. Nor was she the conceited mother or the woman who boasted when her money had saved his career. She was a creature at his mercy as a deer might be, or a wounded bird.

'I suppose I could. That depends on you.'

'On my promises.' Her voice was scarcely audible.

'No. Actions.'

'I will never see him again.'

'Of course you won't,' he said, not accepting the vow, and unnerving her again. He sounded contemptuous. 'I forbid you to go alone to London. If you want to see your sisters, I will take you.'

She swallowed. She had lost her magic power over him. The spell was broken into bits. Although he was not going to abandon her she wondered if she would ever get him back. The first time it had been easy – by holding her tongue she had set things right. Now it was both different and terrible. She had lost his admiration, his adoring belief in her, the things which had kept her, so to speak, alive.

He switched on the car engine.

'So we understand each other,' he said. Then he drove her back to the house and returned to his office.

Anthony and Clarissa, done up to the nines by Nanny, with pristine white socks and gleaming faces, had tea with their mother. Anthony snuggled up and said he loved her. Clarissa concentrated on cake. When Nanny removed them to take them to bed, Claire with a semblance of naturalness called out that she would come and say goodnight.

The telephone rang later. An unfamiliar voice said, 'Mrs Lockton? Detective Inspector Cole here.' He told her, not without satisfaction, that the rings had been traced.

Stuart said nothing during dinner until she told him about the theft. He gave her a dark steady look when she confessed to having forgotten the jewel-case. Trying to raise the icy temperature, Claire said 'I suppose I shall have to go up –'

He interrupted.

'I will take you tomorrow night.'

'Oh, but I couldn't bother you –' she began. Then, seeing his face, she went scarlet. It was awful to know how many of her subterfuges he had not believed. She had become a liar to him, and a poor one at that. She blushed to her ears, her whole neck burned.

307

After the meal they had coffee in the drawing room, still in silence. Stuart began to read and Claire sewed. An owl flew across the dark Downs, hooting like a lost soul. She went to bed early, her head aching, undressed and climbed into the double bed. She was sure he would sleep in his dressing room: it was the gesture she'd read about in novels, the sexual abnegation, the way of saying he could not bear her near him. She knew he cared for her enough to allow her to stay here. But that was all.

Claire lay open eyed. This was her home and in her way she loved it. She loved, perhaps with self-reflecting fondness, the pretty children she did not look after, bath, read to and scold. And she loved with strange unfamiliarity the stony-faced man who had frightened her. Les evaporated in her mind and body as if he had never possessed either. She lay straining to hear Stuart's footsteps, longing for him and knowing he would keep away.

He came into the bedroom quietly. She had already put out the light and now pretended to be asleep. She heard him move round the room, undressing, making as little sound as possible. His thoughtfulness told on her nerves: he was taking care not to wake her from the kind of politeness he'd use with anybody. It was part of Stuart and had no value at all.

She waited to hear his footsteps crossing the carpet with a dull soft sound and the door open which led to the dressing room. There was the smallest pause. Then she heard him approach the bed. He carefully pulled back the covers so as not to disturb her, and climbed in. The bed gave under his weight. She lay a little longer, frozen into stillness, keeping the pretence of sleep. But she could not do it any more, and crept towards him. With a sigh, he put an arm round her and they began to make love.

As they approached the Elizabeth Street police station Stuart said as if in the middle of a thought, 'Leave this to me.'

'Of course. But –'

'I would prefer it,' he said with his new authority. Thinking with trembling relief that she was safe again, loved again but changed, she said did he know everything there was to know about the

308

matter? Yes, he said. He recalled the rings, he had been with her in Brighton when she had bought all four at once. Stuart had a visual eye and even remembered how many emeralds there were in the heaviest of the quartet of jewels.

The sergeant greeted Claire like an old acquaintance, 'Good morning, Mrs Lockton.' She nervously introduced Stuart and they were told the detective inspector was ready for them.

'It's very good news,' said the sergeant, a big hearty thirty year old, as he took them through to the office.

The detective inspector, sitting in an office almost devoid of documents, greeted Claire with doctorish politeness but seemed relieved that she was accompanied by a member of his own sex. He addressed his remarks to Stuart, describing the circulation of the list of 'stolen valuables' and the complications of getting useful information across an area the size of London. It was a preamble to his success story; Stuart was interested but Claire fidgeted. She was going to get her rings back, so why didn't they get on with it? The inspector spoke a good deal about the problem of discovering the culprit.

'We have been informed by the porter at the flats that a great many people visit the place, sir. People of all kinds,' said the inspector with a certain understatement. 'Of course that makes the job harder. They'll all have to be traced and interviewed. The first thing we need from Mrs Lockton is her sister's home address. Apparently Miss Bryant is not at her place of work at present. She will be able to give us the addresses of her friends and so on.'

Claire was suddenly so tired that she could have fallen asleep leaning back against the hard wooden chair. The strain of the last forty-eight hours came over her. The cruel quarrel with Julie, discovering the theft, the night with Les, the ordeal with Stuart, her fear and her return to his arms; all these things had left her drained. Despite the reconciliation she had been awake for hours while Stuart slept beside her.

She could no longer concentrate on the talk between the two men and was only grateful that Stuart had taken charge. Her attention was fixed on trying to keep awake. She could not hear what they were saying.

309

Stuart, looking over at her, suddenly said, 'My wife's a bit under the weather, Detective Inspector. I think I'll take her out for a breath of air.'

When Stuart took her by the arm and led her out of the police station, she swayed a little. In the cold morning air she revived. But her eyes were heavy.

'Sorry. I do feel a bit muzzy.'

'I know.'

He paused.

'That's not why I brought you out here, Claire.'

He kept hold of her arm and walked her round a corner into a narrow street of narrow houses lined with high black railings. There was nobody about except a ginger cat who looked at them fixedly, then padded away tail erect. Exhausted, Claire leaned against the railings.

'Claire,' he said in a low voice but with emphasis. 'I know you're tired, but you must listen. Julie was in the flat when you left after the quarrel, wasn't she?'

'Yes. I told you.'

'Had she given any of those shindigs of hers lately?'

Claire tried to pull herself together. 'No. Oh Stuart, I know I kept saying there had been parties, but *please*.'

'Listen,' he said for the second time and raised his hand as if to brush away what she'd just said. 'Wake up and pay attention. When you were in the station just now, you didn't hear a word the inspector said, did you?'

'I did at first.'

'But not just now? Thank God for that. His sergeant called to see the jeweller who bought your property yesterday and got a description of the woman who sold him the rings. Don't interrupt. It was your sister.'

'I don't believe you!'

'I don't give a – I don't care if you do or you don't. It is the truth. He showed me the description.'

Stuart looked straight at her.

'Black-haired, young, about twenty-three –'

310

Again Claire tried to interrupt but he stopped her and said impatiently, 'Will you listen? She wore a suit with fringes all along the arms and round the hem of the jacket. Very high heels. And a bracelet shaped like a snake.' That bracelet; how often Julie had made jokes about it. It had been a gift from George Silver who had told her she reminded him of the serpent of the Nile.

Stuart waited. He expected Caire to burst out, angry and disgusted. He waited for her to rant.

All she said in a trembling voice was, 'What – what will happen?'

'When they find out who she is? They already have, Claire. They have got the evidence they need, a complete description of your sister from the porter at the flats. What do you expect will happen? Julie will go to prison.'

'Of course she won't, we won't accuse her or –'

'Press charges?' he quoted. 'That's not how it goes with the law. They have evidence, you see. You could go in and tell them you want the matter closed. You could stand up in court and talk until you're blue in the face, saying you've forgiven her, she's your sister, and naturally you want her to be let off. They wouldn't take a blind bit of notice. She's committed a felony and when they catch her she'll go to gaol.'

'Then they mustn't.'

'Indeed,' he said dryly, 'they mustn't. What would become of Julie if such a thing happened? What damage would it do, God help her?' He plunged his hands into his pockets and stared at the stone slabs of the pavement.

'There's only one thing to be done. You must tell them you gave her the things.'

'They'd never believe me!'

'They will. Under certain circumstances.'

The awfulness of what had happened was strongly in Claire's mind. She saw her sister, filled with spleen, finding the jewel case, saw her immoral triumph when she set off to sell what she had stolen. No wonder Julie was not at work, now her pockets were stuffed with money from Claire's rubies and emeralds.

'But what must I do? What can I do?'

311

'Well,' said Stuart, rubbing his chin, 'you'll have to act out of character.'

'I don't understand you.'

'You'll have to tell them you were drunk.'

He watched to see the effect.

Last night his wife had been beaten down, a veritable penitent, a Mary Magdalen. But there had been a difference – she had not been ravaged with grief over her adultery, but because he had found it out. Stuart had caught her, not by the dingy use of a private detective, but by instinct. He had known what Claire was doing by every tone of her voice and every beat of his own heart. He had watched in pain, thinking it must soon be over. Then he had known he could watch no longer and that to do nothing was cowardice. His heart had begun to harden, listening to her glib silly lies. He had detested her. Not any more.

Poor Claire, he thought. Her sister is in danger, yet she's simply shocked at an insult to her own self-esteem. She is going to be forced to present herself to respectable policemen as a drunkard.

'Come here.' He took both her hands and pulled her to him. 'We're talking about your sister, Claire. Your favourite sister. Do you want her to spend a year in Holloway? Do you want her coming out in twelve months looking like a skivvy, pathetic, changed, possibly for ever? She's an empty-headed girl with a generous heart and no more idea of morality than that cat over there. To know she was nearly caught will frighten the life out of her. You love her, don't you, for God's sake? Then what you've got to do is to go into the station with me and tell lies and do it well. I'll back you up. We'll confess that now and again you go on a binge. You remember nothing of what happened afterwards, you simply blank out. We'll own up to your partiality to gin. Yes, I know you detest the stuff, and won't that be part of the joke to you and me? Now, let's go. We'll get Julie off the hook and *you* will take the blame. Perhaps,' he added, 'it's as it should be.'

With a feeling that everything for her was spoilt, Claire said goodbye to Stuart and took the train home. She couldn't bear to

312

remember Inspector Cole's expression when she and Stuart told him, with apologies and in Stuart's case shamefaced laughter, about her drunken bouts, her habit of giving away her property and totally forgetting she had done so. The inspector listened and said nothing. He was a man whose job was to deal with all kinds of human behaviour and he was used to the worst. During the interview he did not once look at Claire.

Having put his wife into a taxi, Stuart walked down the Brompton Road and found the small rather exclusive jeweller's shop. He introduced himself. The man, who had a number of bad debts and, for all his shopkeeper's politeness, a low opinion of human nature not unlike that of the inspector, was suspicious. He had already talked to the police and realized that, since the property was stolen, he stood to lose a great deal of money. He was gloomily waiting on events. When the gentleman told him abruptly that he would pay whatever the rings had cost him, he was staggered. Stuart wrote out a cheque, said it was 'a family matter. If you want more details, you can ask at the police station. Still. Not much point, is there? Since you've lost nothing by the transaction.'

Still astounded, the jeweller managed some thanks.

Stuart then took a taxi to Conduit Street and went into the gilded doors of Michou's. For the next two hours he hunted for his sister-in-law. He telephoned Viv, who knew the name of some of Julie's haunts merely from sisterly interest – she had never been to any of them. He also had the names of a couple of Julie's clubs from Claire. He went to the Hispano Suiza and the Gargoyle. He enquired at the Embassy and had a talk with the head porter at the Carlton Hotel. He drew a blank.

How easily people can disappear into the great whirlpool of a big city, he thought, standing on the pavement in Bond Street by Asprey's. He was looking idly across the street when he saw them. Julie and Peter Southey were walking slowly down the opposite pavement deep in talk.

Stuart did not hail them. There was a bulldog in him, or more accurately a bloodhound. He followed at a distance until they turned into the Berkeley Hotel, and went through the entrance

313

after them, pausing just long enough for him to see the couple cross the foyer and go to the reception desk to ask for a key. Julie and Peter Southey disappeared into a gilded lift.

Stuart ordered a drink and an evening paper and sat down in the lounge with a view of the lift. He knew why they had gone upstairs. Stuart was a patient man, it was why he made a good solicitor. He did not care how long he had to stay with his paper, a cigarette and a dry sherry. At last, a good hour or more later and for the umpteenth time, the lift opened on to the ground floor. Julie and her tall companion emerged in evening dress.

There was a timed moment Stuart had foreseen, when the young man went to the reception desk again to hand in the key. Julie lingered slightly at a distance, rearranging the heavy folds of a long shimmering evening dress. Stuart strode over. He stopped her first exclamations with a bald: 'You're in trouble. Get rid of your friend.'

Unlike Claire, Julie did not blush or react. She merely said casually, 'Okay'.

Without hurry, she wandered over to Peter Southey. He looked surprised, glanced across at Stuart, nodded and pointed to the bar, indicating that he would see her there later. When he'd gone, Julie came back.

'Come over to my table,' said Stuart. 'And you'd best sit down.'

My God, he thought, these Bryants. Two in twenty-four hours, both so different and both so pretty.

'What's the mystery, Stu?' enquired Julie, bright as a button.

'Let's say that the panic's over. It was grim while it lasted. You stole four of Claire's rings and sold them to a jeweller in the Brompton Road yesterday. Which is why you're staying here spending the ill-gotten cash. You committed a felony. In my experience I should judge twelve months. What do you say to that?'

'What am I supposed to say?'

He admired her just then. But he knew *she* knew there were no men with handcuffs waiting by the swing doors.

'Your sister got you off. You can hear later how, but it was nicely done and you're in the clear, no thanks to you. You are an idiot. More of an idiot than I would have thought. What's more, a recognizeable one. How many criminals wear Michou get-ups covered in fringe?'

'Oh God,' said Julie, grimacing.

'As you say. Are you paying for that presentable young man to stay here with you? Or is he paying for you?'

'Some hopes. Poor darling, he's broke to the wide.'

'So you're footing the bill. I thought as much. Well, Julie, the money you have at present belongs to Claire and I'll thank you to give me what's left after you've settled your bill. Now. We'll have a drink and do some sums. And you can stay one final night in this cage of gold and then you'll have to get back to real life.' He looked at her quizzically and repeated, 'What do you say to that?'

'Not much,' said Julie.

CHAPTER SEVENTEEN

Allan Josephs was celebrated, wealthy, and constantly photographed for the society columns, a glass in his hand and a pretty woman on his arm. Gossip writers kept their eye on him; he was in the centre of fashion. Nobody knew exactly where his money had come from. He had arrived in England as a very young man already comfortably off; he seemed to have a good many connections in the City. He now owned a small and classy publishers, and a smaller and just as classy gallery. He was knowledgeable and sympathetic to the arts, and knew writers, painters, poets, dramatists, even dress designers. He was a friend of the temperamental Michou.

By nature, he was the busiest and most bustling of men. Handsome, he had a long sad-looking, olive-skinned face, and eyes which outdid those of Carlos Santander in a melting melancholy. Looking tragic, life amused him. People too. He had been entertained when his Fleet Street friend DD boomed across the Garrick Club, 'I have found you a new protégée, dear fellow. A little girl who works for me. She can paint –' DD kissed the tips of nicotine-stained fingers.

Two or three days after this, Josephs appeared at the shop. Draycott welcomed him effusively and pretended that his rich friend had come to buy a map.

'What can I show you, my dear chap? Military maps are all the rage just now.'

'Later, DD, later.'

The visitor walked over to Isobel who was busy retouching picture frames.

'Josephs,' he said, and stretched out a hand on which a great ring dully shone, 'and you must be Isobel Bryant.'

Draycott had only mentioned her name once to Allan Josephs: he had a positively American gift for remembering.

Isobel shook hands, looking embarrassed and then picked up the tube of gold paint again. But she was not allowed to escape the visitor's attention.

'So where are these paintings DD has been telling me about?'

He smiled at the girl's expression. He liked to attack at once and when she stammered that her work was all at home he said,

'I'd very much like to see one or two of your things, Miss Bryant. Would it be possible for you to bring them along to my house sometime? Good, good,' he added when she did not reply. 'What about tomorrow, the day of rest? How would that suit? Here is my card.'

With artists, old or young, Allan Josephs preferred to call at their studios, wander round, have a chat surrounded by the paintings, in the right atmosphere. But Draycott had mentioned that the girl was poor; she probably wouldn't like that at all. Isobel thanked him and said yes, she could come.

His business completed, Josephs then refused a nineteenth-century military map which Draycott had impulsively produced and was spreading out for examination.

'Not my style, DD. So sorry.'

He said goodbye.

When he had gone, Draycott looked mischeviously across at Isobel.

'Like him?'

'Of course, Mr Draycott.'

'No you didn't. He scared you out of your wits.'

'He did sort of jump, and I wasn't ready.'

'That's how he catches talent. Never takes no for an answer either. Go along to his house tomorrow. It won't be a waste of your time.'

317

Draycott smiled, screwing up his eyes to avoid the smoke of his cigarette.

Nothing had been further from Isobel's thoughts than the idea of showing her work to a professional. Other students she'd known in her St Helier days had told her they were 'trying for the RA. After all, why not? It's free and they can only say "No"' One or two had indeed succeeded. Larry, who deeply admired her talent, had even gone to the trouble of finding two galleries where young unknowns could show their wares, the New English Art Club, and the London Group. But he saw even as he encouragingly talked that Isobel had no intention of going to either.

She thanked him and muttered that she'd remember and would try later. He gave her a kiss, thinking to himself that he need not have bothered to try and help.

Thanks to Delford Draycott, Isobel was trapped into the very thing she feared: the moment when somebody connected with the arts would tell her, directly or indirectly, that she was no good. Wailing to Viv (who was not sympathetic), Isobel packed three oil paintings, interleaved with cartridge paper, encased in brown paper and tied with string. She filled her portfolio with water colours and pastels. Feeling as if she were on her way to the gallows, she took a bus and walked to the address off Belgrave Square.

Allan Josephs' house was tall, lofty, pillared and of considerable size, built in the pompous 1850's. It could well have been an embassy. When the butler showed her up to a double drawing room, she stood with her parcel and her portfolio and stared at the walls. They were hung with magnificent paintings, some of which she recognized. She felt sick.

Allan Josephs came into the room and gave her a brisk handshake.

'Shall we put them on the table?'

Poor Isobel undid the string round her oils and placed them, sheets of paper still protecting them, together with the portfolio, on the huge inlaid marble table. It was drawn up to face French windows overlooking a back roof terrace set about with flower pots.

Josephs began with the oils. He looked at each in silence,

scratching his chin. Then he leaned them, facing the wall nearby and undid the tapes of the portfolio. He slowly turned over the sheets. Isobel stood like a prisoner in the dock; images of docks and executions had been in her head all morning.

The portfolio began with a series of studies of Viv and Kit. She had used her favourite sanguine, the dark chalk coloured red with iron oxide much favoured by artists in the Renaissance. The drawings had been carefully fixed, for the slightest touch would have smudged them. She had started the studies when Kit was a few weeks old – there must have been twenty or more, right up to the present with a drawing of him, solemn, large-eyed, standing as if to attention.

'Yes,' said Allan Josephs.

He examined water colours of Chelsea, of her view from the World's End window, a chalk drawing of Larry, a half finished water colour of Julie. He looked at that for some time and remarked, 'I believe I know this girl.'

Then he went through the whole sheaf again, putting one or two on an easel which he pulled out from a corner of the room.

He stood arms folded.

'Good.'

Then, 'Not so good', discarding Isobel's favourite oil painting of Larry.

At last he turned to where she stood at a distance, looking into space.

'I think, yes, I believe we may have got an exhibition. Have you any more for me to see?'

'Yes, but –'

'But you've shown me the pick of the bunch? I might disagree with you, Miss Bryant. An artist isn't necessarily the best judge of his own work. I remember once rummaging in a studio paper-basket ... So, shall we say a total of thirty-five or thirty-six? Some oils, watercolours, your sanguine drawings and so on, nice little show. How much have you at home?'

'Quite a lot,' was the faint reply.

He gave her a quizzical look.

319

'Then we must see it all. Of course we may well need more, supposing you and I agree on quality. Could you manage to come here again? The light in this room is very true, I always find. Come in a taxi, I know how cumbersome it is for artists to hump their work about. Chargeable to me since I'm to handle your work. That is, if you would like me to do so?'

Isobel stuttered almost incomprehensible thanks. She found it hard to speak because of her pounding heart. Just then the telephone obligingly interrupted and Josephs picked up the receiver, at the same time pressing a bell in the wall with his left hand. The butler reappeared. Her host, with a gesture both kindly and peremptory, indicated that his guest was leaving. He mouthed 'see you very soon' and then began to talk, brisk but wooing, to his caller.

The weeks that followed turned Isobel, always inclined to overdo things, into a fanatic. The good weather held, the dawn came early and she was up, bathed, dressed and working while the world was asleep. She looked dazed from concentration when Viv called her to breakfast. Draycott liked to congratulate himself daily on the introduction to Allan Josephs, 'I have these inspirations sometimes,' he would say.

Discussing the exhibition which Isobel could still scarcely bear to mention, Draycott told her she might take a morning off for her painting now and again. He would not, he said, offer an afternoon.

'I do sometimes return from Fleet Street just a fraction pixillated, Miss B.'

When Isobel finished her work in the afternoons, she hurried to the bus as if to a lover. Arriving at the corner of Gladys Road, she literally ran home and rushed upstairs.

Larry was as delighted as Viv at the news, and saved up for champagne which the trio shared one evening, sitting in the back garden. Before the bottle was finished, Isobel had excused herself and left them. It was a measure of her sister's love, and Larry's too, that they did not exchange a single glance.

Isobel wasn't sure why she was desperate to produce her best work to satisfy Allan Josephs. What exactly was she hoping for? She painted the way a horse ploughed a field – it never occurred to her to resist. She had sold only two paintings in her life, one to FRF and the other to Stuart; in both cases she'd told them they paid her too much. Alone in her studio, she realized at last that what she longed for was for her paintings to be seen. The old days of hiding them from criticism and curious eyes were gone for ever. She didn't yet connect them with money; but she did need people to look at them – her work was her form of talk, of telling what she had perceived both in the world and in the hidden places of her soul.

She needed her two eyes for every moment of her artist's life. But her nature had become as one-eyed as the Cyclops. She now had little interest in her sister and Kit, and something between herself and Larry had paled and faded, a kind of content. But how could she find time to stop and revive it, running as she did down the King's Road towards what was left of the day?

Allan Josephs called in at the map shop to arrange for the taxi ride, which meant Isobel would deliver more of her work for his inspection. When she arrived at his house and spread her paintings out on the Italian table, he chose quite a number she was not particularly pleased with. She did not argue but meekly accepted his verdict.

When he said good night, Josephs assured her, 'No desperate hurry, Miss Bryant. We've got until the autumn.'

But Isobel did not slow down. Looking from her window, she saw that high summer was gone. The best days, the fresh days, were over. And the daylight had begun to wane.

Viv, too, noticed the dying of the green. When she walked Kit home from his dancing class, great flat plane leaves floated down in front of them on to the pavement. Kit kicked them, raising a dust. Watching the little boy as he jogged ahead she thought how long it was since Claire or Julie had seen him. Weeks. Claire telephoned sometimes, but there wasn't a word from Julie. Viv did not feel that she could ring Michou. The only time she'd nerved herself to do so her sister had not been there and Madame Hawthorne had been very cold. Viv was too cowardly to ask if she knew where Julie was living.

There were other heavier thoughts. Momentous things had been happening in the country to which Viv had once belonged. Nearly two years ago King Alfonso had abdicated, news which alarmed Viv very much. She still felt related to Spain, it never left her imagination and sometimes she still dreamed in Spanish. She thought often about Carlos and wondered fearfully what the abdication was going to mean to him. The newspapers reported that the king had said he was giving up the throne 'because I no longer enjoy the love of my people. I am determined to have nothing to do with setting one of my countrymen against another in a fratricidal civil war.' It was announced that a republic had been set up in Spain.

Carlos had not visited London to see Kit for some months and when he did arrive Viv timidly asked him what was happening. He looked tired and grim and at her tentative question, made a gesture of disgust.

'The new government is weak. Weak.'

'But isn't that because it is new and has to get to grips with difficulties? Things are sure to change for the better.' She fixed anxious blue eyes on him.

'Everybody is discontented, nobody is satisfied; and the new government is corrupt.'

He changed the subject.

That had been two years ago. Viv had taken to reading the newspapers, trying to understand the politics of her husband's world. They were difficult and she could see they were dangerous. Journalists wrote of the anarchists in Barcelona who wanted 'to destroy the state and strangle the priests' and poor ignorant Viv trembled. She spoke of it to nobody. Isobel scarcely mentioned Carlos, and her two other sisters seemed to have disappeared from her life.

One evening Viv and Kit arrived home after school; the weather was sultry and airless and Kit was in a fidgety mood, precariously balancing on the line of diagonal tiles placed point upwards to edge the tiny front lawn. As Viv held his hand and he jumped frog-like from one tile point to the next, the telephone rang in the locked house. She ran in hurriedly, expecting a pupil's mother.

322

'Vivien?'

It was Carlos.

Since the experiment, as Viv called it to herself, of allowing her husband to take Kit away to spend a night with him at his hotel, Carlos had twice reappeared to ask for the same favour. Kit was now accustomed to the treat and went off, child and man hand-in-hand, talking nineteen to the dozen. Viv's nervous fears had proved groundless. The child returned, bursting with news, quoting his father and in excellent spirits. But new interests came every day and Kit soon forgot Carlos – until the next time.

'Viven. I am in London. Is it called the bad penny?'

She gave the expected laugh.

'It is good of you to let me have him.'

She gave the required answer.

'Might I come at once?'

How could she say anything but 'of course'?

She packed an overnight suitcase, and Kit was changed, smartened and ready when Viv heard the sound of a taxi drawing up. Nobody came to Gladys Road in taxis except her wealthiest pupils with their mothers – and on rare occasions, her other sisters. Viv was waiting at the front door.

The sight of Carlos's back as he stood asking the taxi driver to wait, gave her a pang. How moving were people's backs: her son's, her sisters'. Carlos's back was heavy shouldered, his clothes pale and foreign, his black thick hair curled at the nape of his neck. The sight hurt her. She gave a bright calm smile as he walked up the path. She had no chance to say more than good evening before Kit rushed past like a rocket and hurled himself into his father's arms.

Carlos caught him and kissed him, closing his eyes. Viv's pain increased. Carlos looked almost in pain himself, eyes shut, clasping the child so tightly that Kit squealed.

Still holding him in his arms, Carlos said, 'I am sorry not to have given you more notice. But some financial matter brought me to London; it was necessary for me to be here. It seemed such a good chance for me to see Kit, I could not miss asking. It is all right, is it? He will be back tomorrow.'

323

She said 'of course', her voice taut and not natural. She talked for a moment or two about Kit's clothes. If it happened to rain, and there was always the chance of a storm with this heavy weather, would Carlos be sure not to get Kit's feet wet? She had packed a change of shoes, Kit caught cold so easily. Carlos agreed, looking very serious.

The taxi was still at the gate; the driver had not switched off the engine which purred as if to hurry them. Carlos looked down at his wife who stood, small and fair and quiet, at the door of the ramshackle house. He settled his son more comfortably in his arms.

'Have you thought about what I asked you?'

Viv had no idea what he was talking about. Seeing her expression he gave a smile which was not a smile.

'I ask you to come to Spain with him.'

He always had difficulty with the English 'h', and he did now. His accent was more pronounced than usual.

'Oh. Yes, I remember. But I thought I said –'

'That you would tell me the answer the next time I was in London.'

Kit thought his parents very boring when they paid no attention to him and said could he get down, please. He was sure Mama had forgotten his jigsaw puzzle. She answered automatically and Carlos set the child on his feet. Kit scampered back into the house.

His absence heightened the tension. Carlos merely stood, his eyes on his wife.

She said in a thin voice, 'I'm sorry. I – I can't.'

'You need not stay at the Casa Nueva.'

'But –'

'Is my country so repulsive to you now?' he said. His whole face and body changed. She felt threatened and indignant. He had implied in all their dealings that he had accepted the separation. People made mistakes, terrible mistakes, and that was what she had done when she consented to marry him. What had they in common? What tied them together?

'Carlos,' she said.

She never called him by his name and immediately his face lost

324

its brooding cloud. But she did not see that.

'Carlos, I thought you and I had agreed.'

'I agreed to nothing. I know you love your own country,' he said without sarcasm, looking at the mean little house and the grass sprouting between the red and black tiled path. 'I knew you had a *postración nerviosa* when you ran from Barcelona. Yes, I know –' he held up his hand as if to stop some kind of traffic roaring towards him – 'I know you were sometimes a little unhappy.'

'A little!'

'Yes, a little,' he doggedly repeated, 'But we will not talk of that now. Kit will be here in a moment. We must not quarrel.'

'No. We must never.'

'Good. We understand that at any rate. Ah, here he comes,' as the child, in conversation with his rabbit and carrying a large jigsaw puzzle in a box, reappeared. 'Vivien. I ask you again. I ask for the last time. Will you come for a short while to my country? Will you let me have my wife and son together even if I must visit them in a hotel?'

The awful reasonableness of his request frightened her. With a sudden brimming of tears that she dared not wipe away in case Kit noticed, she said in a low voice, 'No, I can't. It is cruel of you to ask me.'

She said a bright watery goodbye to Kit, who, picked up again in strong arms, waved as he was carried off to the waiting taxi.

Viv's cramped drawing room at night carried a faint illusion of the country. The French windows opened on to the patch of back garden. Walls divided one villa from the other, they were scarcely five foot high, but the English passion for privacy had erected wooden lattices, weathered and cracked by rain and sun yet stout enough to support rambling roses and honeysuckle. The shrubs thickened as the years went by and branches grew down on Viv's side of the fence to scent the night air.

She roamed round her limited domain, from kitchen to dining room, into the drawing room again and out into the garden. She sniffed at a piece of late honeysuckle and picked off a dead rose.

She looked at her watch and continued to wander. A day had gone by since Carlos had taken Kit to stay; now they were due back in half an hour.

Isobel had upset her the previous evening. Returning from an annoyingly busy day at the map shop, she was tired and scratchy when Viv, usually tactful with the artist, blurted out her news. Carlos had appeared unexpectedly and taken Kit to spend the night with him.

'*Again?*'

'I realize it is a bit soon.'

'Much too soon. You'll have to put your foot down. He can't march in and appropriate Kit whenever he feels like it.'

Viv had the human desire to contradict somebody speaking her own thoughts aloud. She murmured, 'After all, Kit is his son.'

There was no further exclaiming from Isobel; she already had her foot on the stair.

Somehow Viv had wanted to tell her sister about Carlos's invitation, and her own refusal. But Isobel was shamelessly absorbed in her own affairs and in any case whenever Viv mentioned Carlos – goodness knows she did it rarely enough – her sister's reaction was always the same. An automatic antagonism. It was as if Isobel, having taken on the job of champion, did what was expected of her and that settled that. It was not what Viv wanted – perhaps it never had been. Viv scarcely understood her own feelings about her broken marriage. Her sisters certainly didn't. It seemed twenty years since Viv had left Barcelona and returned to Grace ... and when she had come home, how often she had tried to explain fully. It had been useless. She had seen in their eyes that she was speaking a language incomprehensible to them.

Looking at her watch, she saw it was at last half past five. She no longer wandered restlessly about the house but went into the drawing room and sat down by the open window. She would see the taxi arrive from here. She sat quietly, imagining Kit's bright face and high little voice. The street was very quiet.

An hour later she was still there.

At first she waited confidently. Then, growing uncomfortable, began to invent reasons why they were late. Was Kit ill? She told herself not to be a fussy fool. In the end she could bear the waiting no longer and telephoned the hotel.

'Is Señor Santander in?' she asked, trying to sound calm.

'He left before luncheon, madam.'

'You must be mistaken,' said Viv quickly. 'I mean Señor Carlos Santander. He has a little boy with him.'

'Yes, madam. Master Christopher,' said the porter. 'We've had the pleasure of seeing the little fellow here once or twice before. Very excited he was when I helped them into the taxi. They were catching the boat train from Victoria. Do you wish for the gentleman's address in Spain? I'm sure I could get it for you at Reception.'

Stammering a refusal she put down the telephone. For a moment she sat frozen. She was like a woman who answers the door to be confronted by a policeman with terrible news. She could scarcely take it in. Carlos had taken Kit. Last night when he'd asked her to bring Kit to Spain he had been giving her a last chance. Now he had kidnapped her son.

She began to cry. She kept saying aloud 'Oh God, oh God', but it was not a prayer; it was a moan of anguish. She sat repeating the words and helplessly weeping when the telephone rang. It was Isobel.

'I may be a bit late, I thought I'd –'

'Isobel.' Viv was sobbing.

Her sister unconsciously used the same words.

'Oh God. Oh God, Viv, what's happened?'

'He's taken Kit.'

The story poured out. Isobel gabbled that she'd come home at once and that Viv must ring Claire.

Directly she spoke to her, Claire said, 'Stuart and I will come up right away. Don't do anything until we get to you. Does Isobel know? Good. We must ring Julie.'

'I don't know where –'

'Stuart does. This needs us all. Sit tight till we're with you.'

The family arrived at intervals. Isobel came first, catapulting into the house to take Viv in her arms and, all emotion, all sympathy, made her feel worse. Julie, summoned like a pale white-clad apparition, was more comforting. She swore.

'Of all the bastards! What in Christ's name does he think he's doing? I could kill him. Kit's *yours*.'

'And his,' said Viv, walking round and round like an animal in a cage.

'You had the baby, didn't you?' said Julie savagely. 'What did *he* have to do with it except in bed – sorry, but he makes me sick. How dare he kidnap your boy? We'll get the international police on him.'

She wore a white ball dress. She had been staying with a fellow mannequin and the girls were about to go out when Claire telephoned. Julie walked straight out of the flat, taking the taxi they had ordered. Her girl friend hung out of the window, shouting crossly, 'When will you be back?'

'How do I know?' yelled Julie.

'Could we really get the police?' asked Isobel, extinguished by Julie's ferocity and feeling useless.

Viv stopped her in her tracks.

'Of course not. Carlos will be in Spain by tomorrow morning. In Spanish law the father has all the rights. The mother none.'

Julie folded her arms across her satin bosom.

'Viv, if you don't stop crying you'll break my bloody heart. Did you have no idea Carlos was planning this? I can't believe you didn't guess something and if so why did you let him have Kit at all?'

Viv rubbed her swollen eyes.

'When he came to get Kit yesterday evening he asked me if we'd go and stay in Barcelona.'

Julie's large eyes grew larger.

'You mean go back to him?'

'N-not exactly,' said Viv, sniffing and crumpling up a wet handkerchief. 'He said Kit and I could stay in a hotel if that's what I wanted.'

There was a moment's noticeable silence. Neither Julie nor Isobel looked at each other but they both had the same thought –

what had happened was simple, after all. In their different ways, Julie coarsely, Isobel sentimentally, they had been aghast at the brutality of what Carlos had done to Viv. It was such a sudden and uncharacteristic gesture of cruelty. Utterly unlike him. Now they understood.

'I suppose taking Kit is his way of getting *you* to come to him,' Isobel said timidly.

Julie shook her head.

'That's too obvious. There's another reason why he did it – apart from badly wanting Kit. What happened, Viv?'

'Nothing happened,' said Viv in an almost inaudible voice, 'except that he asked and I said no.'

But Viv knew Julie's instinct was right. In some poignant way Carlos's offer had put him at her mercy and in return she had mortally wounded his pride. Pride; it was the very centre of Carlos, the great crimson vein branching out into his limbs and pumping through his heart.

Giving her sister a look of sympathy, almost of pity, Julie went to the window.

'I do wish Claire and Stu would hurry.'

Her war with Claire, like the earlier separation from Isobel, was healed. She had seen her twin two or three times since the day Stuart appeared at the Berkeley to tell her of her fate. But what was difficult, still difficult for two sisters once united, was that Julie wasn't sorry.

The girls had been pleasant enough to each other, perhaps because Stuart was at the meetings, which he arranged. The trouble was that Julie didn't consider selling a few of her sister's rocks anything to make a drama about. What she'd done to Isobel had made her ashamed. She'd slept with Isobel's man and had deliberately wounded her a second time by blurting out about her sister's illegitimate birth. Even now Julie remembered that with disgust.

But Claire! It was only Stuart's benevolent taciturn presence which had restored a kind of peace. Stuart's behaving just like the solicitor he is, thought Julie with irony.

She knew *he* knew she wasn't sorry. Perhaps Claire doesn't like me any more, she thought. Well, it's her fault, she shouldn't be so rich. It wasn't Claire and her stupid jewels which were making Julie's heart ache so much, which woke her in the night, and stole away her laughter. It was Peter; he was leaving England.

Unselfishly trying to forget her own misery, Julie went to the kitchen and made tea which Viv found it difficult to drink. The three sat in silence as if nothing could be done until Claire arrived.

Finally Isobel said, 'Ought we to ring FRF?'

Viv shook her head.

Julie added, 'What about Pa?'

Viv did not want to see him either. At last there was the sound of a taxi. When Viv went to the door, Stuart was waiting to put his arms round her and press her very close. This time she didn't want to cry. Claire, too, kissed her. For once she didn't offer a cheek in an imitation embrace.

The four Bryants had not been together for a long time – not since they'd gathered to see Claire in her presentation dress before she went to Buckingham Palace.

The greetings were subdued. Everybody sat down.

Stuart said calmly, 'Now, Viv. What exactly happened?'

Viv answered briefly. When she'd finished, Julie exclaimed, 'But you haven't told him what Carlos wanted. Stu, he asked her to go and stay with Kit in Barcelona. In a hotel if she didn't want to go to the house.'

'I see,' said Stuart. Then to Viv, 'And you refused?'

'I said I couldn't.'

'How did he take that?'

'He wasn't angry. He didn't say anything. Just left with Kit.'

Stuart took his pipe from his pocket, looked at it, and put it away again.

Isobel, lured by drama, said, 'Julie thinks we could go to the international police.'

'I told her that's impossible,' said Viv flatly. Stuart, who knew something of international law, agreed. Viv sat staring at the carpet; there was a stain where Kit had spilled his milk yesterday. She'd meant to scrub it clean. She felt like a woman in a thick fog groping to find a street name and wandering further into oblivion. Part of the suffocating miasma was the thought, 'Kit will forget me'.

'Viv, do you think Carlos will go straight home to Barcelona with the child?' asked Stuart, breaking the pause. 'Surely he must realize that's the first place you'll look.'

'I don't know where he'll take him.'

Claire, who had said nothing until now, looked up sharply. She was disturbed by the listless voice. Claire was a fighter. She did not turn like Cleopatra and flee back to harbour. Stuart, too, had heard the tone and seen the way Viv was lying back in her chair. He said quietly, 'Sorry to keep nagging at you, Viv, but who will look after Kit when your husband gets the little chap back to Spain? Your mother-in-law, from what I gather, is a bit old for the job. What about Carlos himself?'

Forced to reply, Viv said that Spanish men did not look after their children. And even if she were well and strong, the Señora would not do so. She had not brought up her own son; she had had a nurse.

Something in the conversation, some hint of the life Viv had led and the family into which she had married, came to Claire just then. She had always had the best memory of the four sisters. She sometimes remarked that she could remember the past as clearly as if she were running a film. When she wanted to see them, there in her thoughts were all the things that had happened, and the people and the places. She said suddenly, 'Viv. Didn't you tell me there was a girl in the Barcelona house when you lived there? A cousin or something.'

Viv stared. And then whispered, 'Asunción.'

It was not Claire, reliable and wealthy, who was to travel with Viv to Spain; it was Julie. Isobel could not leave London: her exhibition was due to open in a few days' time, and Stuart – only too glad to accompany Viv – decided that his presence might offend Carlos far more than that of one of her sisters. Viv agreed.

Claire wanted very much to go, but although she could not say so, she was nervous of leaving Stuart so soon after the trouble between them. She felt she must re-establish herself in his eyes and it would not be easy.

So Julie, to her surprise, found herself elected.

Quietly, without a word of showing off, Claire paid for everything: tickets, sleeping compartments on the train, any necessary hotels. The girls were given thick books of travellers' cheques. The hardest part for Claire was giving her twin a great deal of money.

When the three-day journey started, and Julie was with Viv, first crossing the Channel and then in the train from Calais to Paris and on towards the south, she decided that what they were going to need in the ordeal to come was determination. She must try to instil some gumption into her sister. For many hours Viv said almost nothing. When Julie stole a look at her, Viv was staring out of the window, her face set. But time went by, and they took another train after they had crossed the frontier; they began to advance steadily into Spain. And it was then that Julie noticed her sister beginning to revive.

It grew warm, then hotter. Outside the windows stretched a huge landscape baking in the sun. When the train drew up at a noisy crowded station, Viv leaned out of the window and shouted in Spanish to a woman with a trolley. She bought Julie a fan.

Julie waved it to and fro, amused at first. But all she raised was a hot breeze which lifted her dyed black hair from her sweating forehead.

The stifling heat, the arid land, the dark bluish-grey mountains on the horizon, affected Viv favourably. So did the dark-skinned people trooping into the dining car. She began to talk more to Julie. Once, speaking to the waiter in her English-accented near perfect Spanish, she actually laughed.

During the day the sisters were alone in their compartment. The beds folded into a banquette whose patterned velvet scraped against their silk-stockinged legs. At midday and in the evening – as late as ten o'clock – they made their unsteady way to the dining car. Here they were served interminable meals: salads swimming with oil and shining with black olives, mounds of rice from which peered overlarge prawns which reminded Julie of small and malevolent crocodiles. Neither girl ate much and the waiter, who thought them foreign and beautiful, looked sad. At night they slept in the airless sleeping compartment, deafened by the noise of the train, forced to keep the window open and soon blackened with smuts.

After dinner on the train Julie said, lighting a cigarette, 'Do you really think he'll take Kit to Asunción?'

'It's very possible. Asunción's family live by the sea. Carlos used to say he preferred to summer by the sea.'

'To summer?'

'Sorry. It's the Spanish verb for to holiday.'

'Will Carlos be there too?' asked Julie. Her cigarette, bought with the fan on the platform, was as fat as the cigarettes smoked by the factory girls in *Carmen*.

Viv thought for a moment or two.

'I've been trying to put myself into his mind. I think he will not be there. He will expect us, you and me, or Claire and me and possibly Stuart, to come to Barcelona. He'll be ready for us. With a lawyer, I suppose.'

'If we *do* find Kit at the cousin's we'll have to grab,' said Julie. She looked fixedly at her sister, adding, 'Strong enough, are you?'

'Yes.'

'Feeling brave?'

'Feeling more hopeful.'

'Suppose Kit isn't –'

'Oh Julie. Oh Julie. Don't say that!'

The journey was over at last. They descended on an evening so hot that it lay like a dead weight upon them, to the platform of a small station. In the distance was a land of wavering horizons. Julie had never known such heat. As they crossed the road, followed by a stout porter strung round with their suitcases, dust rose in silken eddies, completely covering their shoes.

In the shade of a line of palm trees were two waiting fiacres. The porter called to the first and piled in the luggage. The poor patient horse wore a straw hat, its ear sticking out from carefully-cut holes. When the girls climbed into the carriage the driver did not touch the horse with his whip: he made a clucking noise and it began to walk, very slowly, down the blazing street.

So this is the village where Asunción lives, thought Viv. She looked at the white houses, the glittering sea. When she and the young Spanish girl had said goodbye, Viv had asked for her address. Asunción, giving it to her, had looked pleased and surprised. And when Viv left Spain she'd written to her. She had dreaded the reply, knowing Asunción's strict religious principles. But although the letter was reserved, it at least wished her 'happiness in your English life'. Since then they had exchanged Christmas cards.

'You seem certain she'll be here,' remarked Julie, as they climbed from the fiacre and a porter emerged from the small building calling itself a hotel.

'People don't move in Spain.'

'She may be married.'

'No. She told me she wants to take the veil.'

'*Be a nun!*'

'Why yes,' said Viv, picking up a small hat box. 'But she hasn't entered yet. I know she'll tell me when she does.'

'A nun,' repeated Julie. 'I say, Ma would be pleased.' And she gave Viv a wink, more to keep up her own spirits than her sister's.

The main feature of their enormous bedroom was a vast double bed. Viv suddenly remembered the *cama de matrimono* she'd shared with Carlos. It, too, had been decorated with a good deal of brass. This bed was also draped with mosquito netting like the veils of a bride. Julie surveyed it.

'Crumbs, we'll have to share. I've never slept with one of my sisters before.'

'We could sleep head to toe,' suggested Viv.

'Not necessary. There's acres of room. Oh Viv, what a hoot.'

Now that she was here, in the village which had only been a name on the map of Spain, Viv was as calm as Claire. She unpacked her few clothes and put them in the marble-topped chest of

334

drawers. She washed her face in the flower-decked china basin, and wondered aloud if there was a bathroom somewhere.

Julie was looking through the Venetian blinds. The hotel faced the bay, an inlet of the sea. In the dazzling sun the water had turned a blinding silver; there was no horizon, it simply vanished into the sky. The beach was white, deserted except for some strangely-shaped fishing boats drawn up on the sand. The sea was flat and calm; Julie couldn't hear a sound of waves. A rider on a horse went by, clip-clopping in the silky dust.

Julie pushed aside the mosquito net to sit on the bed and Viv exclaimed, 'Be careful! Don't tear it or we'll be bitten to death.'

'Okay. Well, Viv. What next?'

'We'll find out where Asunción lives.'

'And spy out the land.'

Viv did not know what to reply. Julie frowned.

'What's wrong? When we've discovered where the house is, we must work out how we do it. Grab Kit, I mean.'

Silence.

'That's the plan, isn't it?' persisted Julie.

Viv said slowly. 'But it's so –'

Viv relapsed into silence. Julie waited. Waited some more. Threw her eyes up to the ceiling. Even in the suffocating heat at the other end of nowhere, she wanted to be up and doing. Her Anglo-Saxon energy had not yet been strangled by the pitiless sun and replaced with lassitude. She couldn't believe her ears when Viv finally said,

'Grabbing Kit back is so –' another pause – 'so un-Spanish.'

Julie felt as if Viv had socked her on the jaw. So far, the prospect had been promising – righting her sister's wrongs, restoring child to mother; Claire's generosity with money. Stuart's approval and Isobel's admiring eyes had added even more flavour to the adventure. But now ...

'Viv, what are you talking about?'

'They're such people for honour.'

'Oh really? He *kidnapped* Kit.'

'Not exactly.'

Julie was annoyed. She undid her suspenders and peeled off the

335

stockings which had been glued to her legs. She hitched up her skirt, lay back and waved her bare legs in the air – they were no cooler. Still with legs in the air, she said, 'What have we come all this way for? To let Carlos keep him?'

Viv sat down carefully. The long folds of netting hung between them in dingy yellow.

'Oh Julie, I want Kit so much. It feels like dying.'

Another pause. Julie was out of practice at keeping quiet but she managed it.

'But I can't go against Spain', were Viv's final desperate words.

Julie allowed an interval.

'Then go round it,' she finally offered.

Viv fidgeted. She played with the net, resisting the desire to put her finger in a small hole. She finally said, 'I'll try.'

Tactless Julie, careless Julie, the only one of the quartet who said what she thought and relished startling her audience, was unwillingly struck. She peered through the net at her sister. But it was too dark to make out her expression.

They dined in a lofty-ceiling whitewashed room whose high windows faced the sea. The windows were open and mosquitoes came in now and then, whining. It was eleven at night before the meal was over. They neither of them said a word about Kit. They talked about Isobel's paintings and Viv's pupils. Julie described Michou's new collection.

'He's getting soppy. Sucking up to the Royal family and the Ascot lot. All they like are frills.'

After coffee, the two girls went out into the paved hallways where Viv spoke to the porter at the desk by the front door. Her Spanish sounded remarkable to Julie – how did one get one's tongue round that lisp? Viv was fluent and fast. The man took her respectfully to the open doors and gestured down the road which led away from the sea.

Viv thanked him and returned to Julie.

'He says the Casa de los Flores is ten minutes' walk away.'

'Fine. Shall we go?'

They walked out in silence. The moon was enormous, making a

336

path across the water. Everywhere was hot. Everywhere was still. But not quiet, for the night whirred with cicadas which thrummed and buzzed. Then all the little insects suddenly stopped as if at the wave of a conductor's baton. Julie could smell the exquisite heavy scent of flowers.

'What's the betting there'll be broken glass all along the top of the wall? And it'll be too high for us to climb,' she remarked. She did not expect Viv to reply and of course she didn't.

They finally came to the villa which stood in large gardens but was visible from the road. It was spacious and peeling, with signs of past elegance in an elaborate balustrade along the top of the roof and rusting wrought-iron gates of the kind seen sometimes at the entrance to rich vineyards. The girls stood and looked through the gates. The garden was full of palms, and cactuses whose flowers had sprung up and died, leaving withered knobs. The gravel path was weedy.

Julie stared at the house.

'I wonder if Kit's really there.'

Viv, too, was staring. She could see two windows alight on the first floor. Nothing else.

'What do you think, Viv?'

'I don't know. I don't know.'

'Are you going to ask for Asunción?'

'Tomorrow. Yes, I'll ask for her. If Kit's here she'll tell me. Let me see him.'

'Maybe Carlos is here too.'

'I don't think so. He told me he has to stay in Barcelona. Because of the political situation.'

'He manages to come to London to pinch –'

'Julie, do shut up.'

Viv was wondering, desperately wondering why her mother's instinct did not work. Shouldn't a woman whose body had borne a child *know* if he was a few yards away? Her womb as well as her heart told her nothing.

Julie shook her arm.

'I think we ought to go back and get some sleep; and try in the

337

morning. If we draw a blank, we'll just pack our cases and go and look in Barcelona.'

'Would you? Would you really come with me?'

'What do you think? We'll go on until we find him.'

Viv scarcely slept, it was too hot. But that was not why. She lay in the double bed trying not to move, while her sister lay in the effortless slumber of someone young and tired. A church clock chimed the half hours and Viv listened while the short night and the long half-dawn passed, counting the chimes until it was six and broad day. Then she climbed out of bed, tucking the net into her vacated side, and with her bathing costume on under a thin summer coat went out of the hotel and down to the beach.

It was the hour when everything is new-made, absolved, which makes a man or woman believe in paradise. Fishermen sat by the water's edge as they had sat by the sea of Galilee, mending their nets. Viv left her coat on the sand and walked into the sea. The water was cool after the night gone by, but as still as a lake. Shoals of tiny transparent fish darted away as she swam out of her depth. Worn out from lack of sleep she tried to make her mind as blank as the cloudless sky. Whatever today holds I won't shed a tear, not a single one; to keep calm is the way to be strong, she told herself. Emerging from the water she dried her face and arms in the already warm sunshine, pulled on her coat, not caring that her wet body made the coat wet too and went barefoot across the lonely road which lay waiting for pitiless day.

The swim had strengthened Viv's resolve. Today is the beginning, she thought. If Kit is not here, Julie and I will go and find him in Barcelona.

She and Julie breakfasted on the balcony of their room. Julie, who usually reeled with sleep, was wide awake and envious that Viv had been in the sea. They drank their coffee and watched the fishermen. But as Julie stretched out a hand to refill her coffee cup, Viv said, 'We ought to go.'

'At once? Do you think –'

'Julie, I think nothing. Only that when Carlos and I got back from our honeymoon it was just like this. Hot, hot, hot. And people

338

got up so early. They did everything before ten.'

'Okay. Here we go,' said Julie, and pulled a dress over her naked self, dropping her kimono on the floor.

Out in the morning without a breath, the sea had once more turned a silver which hurt the eyes. It was impossible to hurry, but the girls walked as fast as they could manage, turning into the road which skirted the villa. As they went towards the house they saw that the rusty gates which had been padlocked last night were open and a mule cart drawn up at the entrance. The driver, a fat dark man, was talking with an elderly servant, clearly from the house, who stood answering him and smiling.

'We'd better wait until they finish their chat,' murmured Julie.

'They won't finish. They'll go on for an hour. We must walk in. I'll say we are calling on the family,' said Viv.

As they came level with the cart she called out politely, 'Holà.'

The couple stopped talking and simply stared. Julie found it so strange. It was as if the man and the woman had suddenly seen two animals they had never set eyes on before in their lives. They stood in silence and gaped. They were not rude, simply fixed in wonder.

Sedate as a girl at a garden party, Viv murmured something and passed them. Julie was slightly behind her. As they walked further away from the gate, the couple began to talk again, but in low voices.

Julie's thoughts whirled. She was sure that at any moment Carlos was going to appear. She tried to be ready for the fray – but it was difficult in this heat. They came nearer the house, and the weeds which had burst through the gravel path and died, made a curious rasping noise under their feet.

At the steps, Viv paused.

The door was open. In front of it a faded sunblind hung motionless, concealing the interior of the house. Motioning Julie to follow, Viv ascended the steps. She pulled a bell.

Not a sound.

'Try again,' breathed Julie.

Viv tugged, but still the bell, long rusted, did not speak.

Somewhere behind the sunblind were the faint sounds of voices. And then – something else.

The high unmistakable voice of a child.

Viv spun round, reaching for Julie.

'*It's Kit!*'

'Kit!' gasped Julie, clutching back. 'We must go in!'

'No. No.'

'*Viv, we must.*'

'No!' cried Viv, as pale as death. 'It would be an insult. Believe me. Julie, come back!'

She dragged at her sister and for a crazy moment Julie struggled to free herself. Then she saw Viv's face. And gave a sigh which came from the bottom of her soul.

'Oh Christ. You Spaniards.'

Viv lifted the curtain slightly and knocked on the door, calling out the word she'd used at the gate.

'Holà? Holà?'

There was a nearer sound of exclamations, a scurry of feet and the curtain was pulled aside.

A young girl, lint-fair, with a long face and a high nose stood in the doorway.

When she saw Viv she stretched out both arms, her face radiant.

'La Señora.'

It was Asunción.

Shakily laughing, they embraced. Viv introduced Julie and the girl shook her hand and bowed. There was no chance to talk, for with a sound of scampering and sliding feet somebody came rushing out of the house. Kit saw his mother and gave a shout.

'Mama! Mama!'

She fell on her knees and caught him as he charged towards her. He laughed as she embraced him.

'Asunción *said* you wouldn't come, but I just knew you would! I can speak Spanish now, can't I, Asunción?'

The child was already tanned and his hair bleached by the sun was as blonde as his mother's. Beaming at Viv, Kit jigged up and down tugging at her hand and saying she must come and see his toys.

340

Asunción said gently in Spanish, 'We will go into the garden and talk with Mama.'

'And Aunt Julie too,' said Kit. 'Aunt Julie,' he began, taking her hand, 'shall I tell you something?'

He led the way through a dim half-shining house.

The garden at the back of the house was far larger than could be seen from the road. It was spreading and dry, with stretches of grass burned yellow in the heat and many, to Julie, unfamiliar trees. There were almost no flowers except those which had survived from being in the trees' shade, patches of long-stalked daisies.

Asunción drew up heavy chairs for the visitors. She said quietly, 'I must speak to my mother. I will come back very soon.'

She returned to the house.

Kit climbed on Viv's knee and talked and talked. He looked healthy, happy, handsome. Julie, who knew nothing of the very young, marvelled that children were so heartless. It was clear he had been perfectly content to be whisked away from London and dumped in a foreign land. As for Viv all she did was listen and stroke the sun-bleached hair.

Carrying a tray, Asunción returned. Julie heard the welcome sound of clinking ice. Drinks were poured: a lime cordial, cloyingly sweet, carefully passed to Viv and Julie, a smaller glass for Kit. Julie said casually, 'Hey, Kit, isn't that a toy train over there under that tree?'

'I've got three.'

'Come and show me.'

He climbed from his mother's knee and took Julie off towards the trees.

When they were alone, Asunción said, 'You are staying in the hotel, yes?'

'I have not come on a visit, Asunción.'

The girl looked puzzled. Viv began to understand.

'What did my husband tell you, Asunción? What reason did he give you why Kit is here in Spain and not with me?'

Asunción, silent by nature, not clever but with much intuition, looked deeply at Viv and did not reply. Viv said in a pained voice,

341

'Did he tell you I had given up my own child? Did he say I had agreed he must be reared as a Spanish boy? Yes, I see that is what he said. Asunción, it is not true. Carlos came to visit us in London, and I gave permission for Kit to stay with him for one night. I have allowed that before. This time Carlos did not bring him back to me. He stole him away.'

Still the girl did not speak. She looked and looked.

Forcing a reaction, Viv asked, 'Why did Carlos bring Kit to stay with you?'

Asunción had to answer that.

'Because of new troubles in the city. There was a riot and two men were killed. Carlos had not expected it. He says he will come often to see Christopher. But he dare not keep him at the Nueva Casa at present. His mother will not go away, nor will Carlos. But the child is safe with us.'

'I see.'

'You guessed he would be with me, then, Señora Santander.'

'Oh, Asunción. I do wish you would call me by my name.'

Across the burned grass, Kit was lecturing Julie, who squatted beside him under the tree.

Asunción looked at the little boy.

'You want to take him away.'

'It will mean great trouble for you.'

'I do not think', Asunción weighed each word, 'my cousin will be angry with me.'

'But very very angry with me,' said Viv.

She leaned forward, her arms on the rough wooden table in front of her. Only later she found that a splinter like a long thorn had pressed into the soft part of her upper arm. She leaned forward while Asunción looked away across the grass at the child.

Viv knew she was being judged. Asunción, grave and naive, unworldly as any of the novices she would soon join in the religious life, was her judge. She was also a symbol of Spain and of Viv's anxious conscience. Viv explained hesitatingly and unhappily, how she had found it impossible to stay with Carlos in the Nueva Casa.

'Asunción, do you know, you were my only lifeline.'

342

'He is your husband.'

'He became a stranger to me. Out in the city day and night. Away so often. A stranger.'

The girl did not say, 'Do you not love him?' She was incapable of asking such a question. It would be ignoble; in a way it would be a sin. Viv told her how Carlos had asked her to come to Spain and that she had said no; then Asunción did stop looking at the little boy and turned her eyes towards Viv. The girl gave a shuddering kind of sigh.

'Asunción,' Viv said. She did not know how strange the request was. 'You must let me have my son.'

'That is true.'

'Do you think Carlos –' she couldn't finish the sentence.

'Yes,' said Asunción, 'it will greatly hurt him. He has been very happy.'

But Viv knew, her body knew, that Carlos was never truly happy and perhaps was suffering even now. She was too absorbed in her own dilemma, too absorbed in the child, too forgetful of herself, to know that he might be suffering over her.

'I will tell my mother that Christopher's mother has come for him.'

Asunción stood up. Her long eyes filled.

'You wish my sister and me to meet her, of course,' murmured Viv.

'Please. Yes.'

Asunción looked towards the little boy. A big tear rolled down her cheek.

Viv had sworn she would not cry and she didn't now. She also stood up, stretched out her hand and took Asunción's. The girl tightly held it.

'My mother will understand that he has to leave. He is yours and you are an English lady. She has never met an English lady and will ask you no questions. To my mother, all people but her own family are strangers.'

Later the sisters were greeted by a small plump woman, shyer than her daughter. Julie, subdued by the sombre house and the

343

dignity of their companions, had her hand graciously taken, herself gravely studied. Asunción vanished up a shadowed staircase and returned with Kit's luggage and a basketful of new toys.

It was only after the Bryants had left, long after the long day was over, when they were on a train crossing the dark landscape and Julie and Kit were asleep, that Viv began to cry.

She cried because she loved this sad and noble country whose language ran in her head like a great river. She cried because she loved Spain and had wounded Carlos to the heart by stealing back his son. And she wept bitterly because she knew at last how much she loved Carlos who had given her when they made love some part of this country of his. It lay embedded in her body, like the splinter which reddened the inside of her arm.

CHAPTER EIGHTEEN

A telegram arrived at the house in Gladys Road when Isobel was having a bath. Dripping and draped in towels she went to the door to be greeted by a telegraph boy, pillar-box hat on the side of his head, who gave a loud whistle.

'Phew. A stunner!'

He presented her with the telegram.

'You are My Heart's Delight.' He burst into song and fell on one knee, hand on his heart.

'Don't be a *fool*,' snapped Isobel, snatching the envelope and speaking as if she were his own age, sixteen behaving like twelve.

'Any answer?' enquired the boy. He jumped up, dusted his uniform trousers and fixed her with a look of admiration. He did hope the towel would fall off.

Clutching it in one hand she tore open the telegram with difficulty.

'GOT KIT SAFELY. ON OUR WAY BACK. HOME FRIDAY. LOVE JULIE.'

'No answer,' snapped Isobel.

'And where you are, I long to be!' carolled the boy, dodging Isobel who lunged at him and only remembered her towel just in time.

The invitations for Isobel's first show had gone out. 'Allan Josephs has great pleasure in inviting you ... work of a new young artist ...' Isobel's name, dismayingly large, was slap in the centre of the invitation card.

The telegram had said Viv and Julie would not be back for a

345

week. They are taking their time on the return, thought Isobel. She guessed that Viv did not want an exhausted crotchety child back in London. Alas, they would miss her show.

She was much on her own during the week before the opening. Feeling jumpy, she insisted on working at the map shop every day, although Draycott said that of course she could have the time off. With the necessary amount of pictures completed, with work delivered to the gallery, the last thing that Isobel wanted was time to think. She tried to do a new drawing of Larry when she returned from the shop.

They had only made love once during the past few weeks. They had been in his room, and it had happened unexpectedly – a hurried, far from blissful quarter of an hour.

'Your heart wasn't in it,' he said, looking down at her.

'My heart is with you.'

'Sometimes.'

He did not make love to her again and she missed that. But intense work had swamped her, and she put it out of her thoughts.

Now the evening of the show had come at last. Allan Josephs told her to be at the gallery 'well beforehand'.

'Why?'

'For a glass of champagne. DD wants to toast our success. And there may be a couple of my close friends to meet.'

Josephs looked at her without sympathy, noticing not for the first time her childish habit of biting her bottom lip.

'Come along, young woman, you're delightful when you don't scowl. People are going to like the work.'

'How do you know?'

'Because I do.'

Alone in Viv's little house, Isobel carefully put on the only dress left from her days of riches. It was of black taffeta with small cut glass buttons of turquoise blue down the front. She reddened her lips, something she often forgot, and brushed her dark hair, so unlike Viv's and Claire's, and never as sleek as Julie's dyed locks. Allan Josephs had ordered a taxi, which arrived too soon. Isobel kept it waiting.

346

The first person she saw when she arrived in the quiet street – the gallery doors were wide open – was Claire who had just that moment descended from another taxi.

'I'm afraid I'm early,' said Claire, smiling. 'I hoped you wouldn't mind if I came straight here from the station. Stuart wanted to come with me, but he won't be along until later. There's an important meeting at his office.'

The new Claire tried to put her husband's affairs before her own.

'Isn't it wonderful about Kit?' she went on. 'You've heard, have you?'

'I got a telegram this morning.'

'Mine came last night. What do you think happened? One supposes that Carlos just gave in.'

Claire looked as if she was going to remain on the pavement chatting about the family. She seemed to have no idea that she was standing at the entrance of the gallery, that a poster bore her sister's name in large letters, and that the sister in question was white with nerves. Josephs bustled out.

'Isobel, what are you doing out in the street? Advance and be recognized. And this must be the lovely sister from Sussex.' He knew all about the Bryants. He extended his hand and clasped Claire's gloved one. His powerful sexy presence shone straight at her like sunlight and Claire reacted. She became even more the lovely sister and produced clichés with aplomb, as Josephs escorted them both into the gallery. He handed Claire over to a good-looking young man in worn tweeds with a red carnation in his buttonhole. It was Peter Southey.

Faced with Peter, Claire gave a strained little laugh. She had seen him the moment she came into the gallery, with a thrill of alarm. He had always been at Julie's parties where she'd met him a number of times. She tried not to remember that it had been Peter lying naked beside Julie that morning in the darkened bedroom. And he was the lover with Julie at the Berkeley when they had been spending her money.

But it was not Peter's past with her sister which frightened Claire and made her use so false and bright a voice: she was afraid

347

he would talk about Les Bacon. Worse, that Les was coming to the show. It did not happen. Pleasant and casual, Peter only spoke about Isobel's paintings and together they went to admire a series of her chalk drawings. Thank heaven there was no sign of Les. When she calmed down, Claire realized that this simply was not Les's world, and he would not be the sort of man whom Allan Josephs would invite here.

She was vaguely aware that her companion did not look as handsome as he used to do, was perhaps a little pinched. She noticed that he did not mention Julie once. She had no idea it was because Peter could not bear even to ask where she was.

Josephs put an arm round Isobel's shoulders, escorted her round and introduced her to his friends – the gallery was filled with them. A tough abrupt looking man with an attractive smile – Josephs told her he owned racehorses and collected pictures – bought two of Isobel's studies of Viv. She blushed with pleasure when Josephs glued red circles on the frames. She was feeling shy and excited.

Installed at a desk by the door was another of Josephs' friends, a tall self-possessed young woman of the kind Julie would call classy. Her name was Milly Standish and according to DD she was 'a jewel'. Milly had the task of writing out orders for the sales, and taking addresses.

A waiter circulated with glasses of champagne. The room grew hot, smelling of French scent, alcohol and the heady odour of paint and varnish. The show had been on for an hour when Stuart appeared, kissed Isobel, and said to Allan Josephs, 'I hope the one I've had my eye on hasn't gone yet.'

Stuart's practice had been looking up, and a picture by Isobel was the first treat he had decided to allow himself.

'Which one is that?' Isobel's patron was interested at once.

It was the largest, and thus the most expensive oil of Viv and Kit. Josephs had called it the star of the show. He commended Stuart's taste. Isobel noticed that he seemed to have his arm round her rather heavily when he was talking about the picture to Stuart. She smiled, saying nothing, knowing perfectly well that he was afraid she was going to reduce the price. She didn't dare.

The talk was loud and vivacious, the atmosphere cheerful; there was a good deal of laughter. Allan Josephs smiled to himself. People who were not enjoying things weren't as noisy as this. Tonight there was a relaxed partyish air about. Ah, he thought, I was right.

Isobel's nerves had disappeared and she actually began to enjoy herself, with Josephs beside her and DD booming facetious compliments and just drunk enough to be fun. Across the room was Claire, looking poised and elegant, and dear Stuart who had bought the painting. She wished Viv and Julie could have been there. It was only then that she realized she hadn't spoken to Larry. She threaded her way through the crowd, receiving congratulations like a bride at her wedding. The gallery was not large – it only took Isobel a minute to realize that Larry was not there.

The party finally ended and the efficient Milly, collecting her papers together, said she would telephone Allan Josephs in the morning. He was with Draycott, the owner of the horses, and a pretty middle-aged women with red hair. He invited Isobel to come with them to the Savoy for a celebration supper.

'It is kind of you, Mr Josephs. *Everything* is kind of you. I don't know how to say how grateful I am.'

'Nonsense. You're telling me you won't come. I don't blame you. First shows usually give painters a headache. See you tomorrow. I must talk to you seriously,' he said, having never done anything else.

Peter Southey had gone. Claire and Stuart left the gallery with kind goodbyes. Isobel slipped away.

She was so disappointed about Larry that she felt absurdly near to tears. She couldn't believe he had missed this evening – it wasn't possible for him to have mistaken the date; they had spoken about it only yesterday. She had asked him to come early, 'I know I'll need your moral support.'

Head throbbing, she walked away from Belgravia, into the King's Road and towards Markham Square. The show faded from her thoughts, the voices evaporated and she thought about the last time Larry had made love to her. How quickly it had been over and how unlinked to him she'd been during their short embrace.

It was later than she realized when she went through the square to his digs. She stood in the road and looked up to see if there was a light in his window. There was.

The front door was never locked. There were five flats in the tall narrow house and the occupants came and went at all hours. In the way of Londoners, they scarcely knew each other. Climbing the eighty-two stairs, Isobel saw doors of flats propped open in the Indian summer night, and heard wirelesses playing dance music. When she reached the top floor, Larry's door was also open; wedged with a wooden door-stop shaped like an elephant, which she had given him. Hurrying into the room, she almost fell over it.

Larry was sitting at his desk. He turned round, half stood up and sat down again.

'I should have thought at least the Ritz.'

'What does that mean?'

Her angry reply had no effect. He looked her up and down, taking in the silk dress she rarely wore, turquoise buttons winking in the electric light.

'Didn't Josephs ask the famous artist out to celebrate?'

Isobel kicked the elephant out of the way and slammed the door shut. She leaned against it.

'Why didn't you come?' she said.

'I'm surprised you noticed.'

'Larry!'

'Why should it matter if I came to the do or not?'

Hearing the voice, which was vicious, she was appalled.

'You stayed away on purpose to hurt me.'

'I stayed away, Isobel, because I am perfectly aware my presence wouldn't make a blind bit of difference one way or the other.'

'But it did! It did!'

'Come off it. Tell me something else. Did you sell some pictures?'

The voice was unkind.

'A few.'

'How many?'

'I – I don't know.'

He gave something like a laugh. 'There isn't an artist living who

350

wouldn't know how many pictures he sold on the first day of a first show. Well? How many?'

'Eighteen, I think.'

'Eighteen. Out of thirty-six. My God, your friend Josephs must be crowing. Congratulations.'

'You don't mean that,' she said angrily.

'Yes I do. You're clever.'

'Larry. What's happened? Why are you looking at me like that? Are you angry because we made love and I wasn't any good? I knew I wasn't; it was all messed up by work. I am sorry. And you've sometimes tried to make ...'

She stopped, about to speak the only true insult to a man. She was terrified at what she hadn't said.

But Isobel's luck, which waxed and waned, was with her this time for Larry wasn't listening. He fidgeted with the papers on his desk, looked at the fountain pen and then began to tidy up a pile of manuscripts and books, reminding her of Claire with the cruet set. He arranged them symmetrically.

Isobel relinquished her position of condemned man against a wall awaiting execution. She went to the attic window. Over the roofs the moon was rising. It was a curious orange colour. Even in great cities people called that a harvest moon. Larry saw her profile against the dark sky. She was like a child. She could hurt excruciatingly, he thought. And didn't know. Didn't ever know.

She turned round, blurting out, 'I suppose what it comes down to is that you can't love me very much since you kept away on the most important night of my life. Go on, say it. Say you don't love me.'

'Why?'

'Then I'll know where I am.'

'Don't you know where you are, Isobel? That surprises me. I thought one knew in one's guts when one had a success. Here you are, the new young painter with the mint-new talent. Quite a little star.'

His gibes fell like dud fireworks across the carpet.

The emotions which had filled him, wounded love and

351

indignation and a flash of hatred, were calming down as the sea calms at last after a strong wind has dropped. The water still heaves and the swell can make you seasick but the dangerous waves crash no longer. Isobel remained at the window and the romantic moon sailed above her head. He said after a while, 'I wish you'd sit down.'

She went over to a hard-backed chair and sat, looking at him steadily in the way one of the drawing masters at St Helier had demanded of his students. If they so much as glanced towards a window he stopped talking. Her dark eyes, so unlike her sisters', remained on Larry. I hope to God she isn't going to cry, he thought. Her stillness was ominous.

'Isobel. Let's forget our differences. I apologize for not coming to your exhibition, and yes, I did it on purpose to hurt you which I admit was pretty despicable. I'm sorry. Now, there's something else I have to say.'

At the apology, and the final sentence, she was so solemn that for a moment he could have laughed. If only Isobel didn't keep looking twelve years old.

'You haven't asked me about my examinations recently, have you?' he said mildly.

She did not know what self-control it took him to moderate his tone. In her work-crazy selfish way, she had utterly forgotten his work, his hopes and anxieties. She had literally come here to his room and they had made love and all his books and papers had been piled on the desk and she hadn't noticed a thing.

'That's true.' Her voice lifted, her face changed, she was sure they were going to be happy again. 'I'm sorr –'

'Oh Isobel,' he interrupted.

The tone was unmistakable. She felt misjudged and her expression changed back to gloom.

'Some weeks ago, I sat for the Civil Service examination. Yesterday I had the news that I'd passed.'

'But that's wonderful!'

'Isn't it?' he said sarcastically.

Back she went again to looking twelve years old.

He began to speak carefully. The sarcasm had drained away. He used a voice she could not mistake. Oh, he'd rehearsed this speech made to the beautiful tormenting girl he'd known for over three years, the mistress who was no mistress, the painter who forgot him to run to a canvas. He loved her and she drove him mad.

'Isobel. This is important. To me and I hope to you. I have been offered a post as a junior Civil Servant. A very junior one, of course, but it isn't bad and nor is the salary and it has a real future. I've accepted.'

'But that's —'

'Wait a bit before you overwhelm me with congratulations. It is in Malaya.'

'Malaya!'

'Yes. The Malay States. Shall I show you on a map?'

'Larry — what are you saying?'

'I'm saying that all this stuff,' indicating his books and papers, 'is over at last. I'm leaving the Essoldo and selling that damned dinner jacket. Until I get to Singapore, that is, where I have no doubt I shall need new evening togs. One probably wears them every night. Isobel, I pulled it off. I passed every one of those bloody exams and I can earn enough to have a decent life. I've told my mother. She's sad that I'm going abroad, but very proud, bless her. I can send her some of my salary, too. She'll be more comfortable than she is now. And what is most important of all —' he paused. She continued to fix him with schoolgirl intensity. 'At last I can ask you to marry me.'

It was the first proposal of marriage Isobel had ever had.

'But — but —'

With the instinct of love, he had foreseen her reaction. He began to explain patiently. He told her his salary and his prospects. He talked of the Far East — some books from the public library were on his desk and he had a map ready. He produced the official letter confirming his job.

She listened and nodded. She studied an exquisite sepia photograph of palm trees bending over deserted sands.

Closing the atlas and half smiling, he said, 'Well, child? Are you going to be Mrs Daniels?'

'I can't.'

'Of course you can. You're supposed to love me, aren't you?'

'Oh, I do, I do. But I can't go out to Malaya, it's so far, I couldn't leave England. I've only just started to paint. I couldn't, I couldn't.'

There was a moment's awful silence.

'I don't understand. Why couldn't you paint there? The place is beautiful. Orchids. Great trees. Jungles. The strangest country. You could be another Marianne North, that painter you told me about. You could paint the tropics.'

'*Larry, I can't.*'

The voice was the wail of somebody in fear of drowning. It had in it an extraordinary sound on the verge of despair. Standing up – she was already on her feet – he came to her and put his arms round her waist and rocked her to and fro.

'Oh. Poor Isobel. Poor Isobel.'

CHAPTER NINETEEN

October came and the plane leaves floated down, flat as pancakes or curled like boats, from every tree in Chelsea. In the Hospital Gardens Kit went through them knee-deep. Returning to his friends and the dancing school, the little nursery in Gladys Road and the London life, he had not yet forgotten Spain. Once when Viv was saying goodnight he said accusingly, 'Asunción read me *two* books.'

He often spoke of his father, 'Papa liked this', 'Papa did laugh when I told him that.' He would look at Viv from under his eyelashes, knowing it upset her and hoping for a reaction.

Viv smiled and replied calmly, although it was a stab to her heart. After a while, failing to annoy and busy with his own affairs, Kit forgot that particular game.

The day she returned home Viv telephoned FRF. He listened in silence and when she finished, asked, 'So you have just arrived?'

'Yes, FRF.'

'And you've sent the two telegrams?'

'You mean Asunción and –'

'And Carlos. Then you must write and tell him that you're sorry. You are, aren't you?'

Viv said that she was. It was true in a way. What she did not dare to say was 'but *he* took Kit first', as if snatching the child had been an awful kind of contest.

'Good. Come to Brighton with Kit soon and see me. I'd like that very much.'

Obeying the priest whom Julie had once called Reverend Francis Conscience, Viv sent the telegrams and wrote the two letters. The one to Asunción made her cry. She took a great deal of trouble with the letter to her husband, writing it two or three times before she was satisfied with it. 'I'm truly sorry for giving you such a shock,' she wrote finally. 'Of course you must see Kit in London. But you must promise never to do what you did again.' Her pen wanted to write more.

Viv settled down to the early winter, her pupils, and the enjoyment of her sister's success. Isobel had not stopped working at the map shop, although Allan Josephs complained.

'I can sell your work, Isobel. Not all of it and not right away, but people like your paintings and this is an important time for you. What are you doing, still hanging about with DD? I'm well aware that part of your duty is to shovel him into the back office to sleep away the Fleet Street fumes. I know my old friend.'

She bit her lip. Here we go, thought Josephs. It was the sign she was not going to agree.

'I need a regular salary.'

He did not reply, but twisted his eyebrows. They both knew how much her paintings had fetched at the show.

'The idea of painting all the time gives me the habdabs, Mr Josephs.'

They were in his drawing room one cold evening, after she had finished work at the shop. He stared into his sherry glass, then up at her with the face of a poker player.

'Very well. I submit. For the time being.'

On the last day of the show, he telephoned and asked if she would like to visit the gallery. 'And we'll both say goodbye to the pictures that have been sold.'

She laughed and agreed. She left the shop early, and walked in the chill half dark. At the gallery, the efficient Milly was on duty and full of apologies.

'Mr Josephs just rang. He really is so sorry, but the two directors of Josephs & Macklin Publishing have arrived unexpectedly from Switzerland,' said Milly. Isobel had no idea whom she was talking about.

So Isobel, who would never have come to see her own work again if Josephs had not invited her, stood for a moment or two, looking round. Apart from Milly, who had returned to her books and papers, there was not a soul about. The emotions of the past were all round Isobel just then. She went to a portrait of Larry, sitting at his familiar paper-strewn desk. Behind him was the window with its shabby green curtain and view of the rooftops. He had a pen in his hand and had just turned as if to welcome her.

'We're not having *another* sitting, are we, child?'

She was looking miserably at the painted face, noticing for the hundredth time a freckle at the end of his nose, when a voice said,

'Well, lass?'

A hand touched her.

'Pa!'

'What a bit of luck,' he said, smiling all over his face. 'I read in the paper, well, Con did, that this show of yours would be over today. I came to take a look before it's too late. Thought I'd pay a call on you and Viv later and see the little lad as well.'

Isobel was touched and shy.

'It was kind of you, Pa. Did you have to wait ages for a bus?' The Londoner's question.

'It was not so bad, not so bad. Worth it. Now, are you going to tell me all about your pictures? You're a one for a surprise. I never knew you'd turn professional. But before we start let's take a look at you.'

He grasped her hands and held her at arm's length, like a partner in an old-fashioned dance. He studied her critically.

'You're turning into quite a beauty. Now show me all you've done.' He put on his glasses and began to read the catalogue.

Isobel took him from picture to picture: she had never done such a thing before. Her sisters looked at her paintings and said nice things. They rarely criticized, even Julie. Larry had done more, he'd heaped her with praise. As for Allan Josephs, all he said was 'Yes' or 'No' or 'We might improve that one, don't you think?'

Frank Bryant wanted to know who and when and how and how long. The only portraits he did not comment on were those of Larry although he studied them for quite a while. When the tour was over he thanked Milly who looked at him over her horn-rimmed glasses until Isobel introduced them, and then gave a social smile.

Isobel and her father left the studio.

'We'll get a bus home to Gladys Road,' she said.

'In a bit. I'd like a cup of tea first. Do you know anywhere round here?' Frank looked without hope at the long street of Victorian elegance, pillared houses, high railings and not a shop in sight. Isobel took him by bus to the old ABC shop. Going through the door gave her a pang.

They sat at a table in the window and Frank ordered a pot of strong tea which he drank thirstily; Isobel had a teacake of the kind she'd always liked the best.

'You know what,' Frank said, setting down his cup, 'you and I are strangers. The only one of my girls I've never spent time with. You were too young at the time of the divorce.'

'Nine and a half.'

'The age to forget your old dad easily, I daresay.'

Isobel had a pause. She balanced a teaspoon on her forefinger.

'Pa. I know you're not my dad.'

He rubbed his nose.

'Julie told me all about that. Very upset at what she'd done. Mended between you now, is it?'

She did not know whether to be glad or sorry that her dramatic announcement had fallen flat.

'Yes, we're fine. Not a cross word. But Pa –' her voice was slightly hoarse – 'I went to see him. You know. The other father.'

That did take him aback.

'You never did!'

Isobel told him about the journey which seemed so long ago and the man in the grocer's shop. She finished with pride, 'When I saw him I didn't feel a thing.' She had forgotten the fantasy that her natural father had been Augustus John. When the story was over Frank Bryant gave a kind of chuckle.

'You're a bran tub of surprises. Paintings. Long-lost parents.'

'*He* isn't a parent. I didn't even like him.'

358

Frank Bryant said nothing. He was astounded at the tale. He thought of the girl across the table as his own child, he always had done. He was impressed by her talent; where on earth had that come from? He was proud of her and glad to see her, and couldn't help being pleased that she dismissed Grace's one-time lover so briefly. But he didn't expect her to declare that she thought of him as her father. He poured some now cooling bright red tea.

'Am I allowed to ask something?'

'Anything, Pa.'

'That painting you were staring at when I came into the gallery. Chap at a desk. Is he your chap?'

'He used to be.'

'Is that why you were looking so blue?'

'Oh lord,' said Isobel.

She began to talk about Larry. He listened, now and again rubbing his hand over his cheeks as if to decide whether he needed another shave. When she finished he said, 'And so you're feeling bad about him.'

'Horribly.'

'Why?'

'He asked me to marry him and I practically rushed out of the room. I was so selfish. Such a coward. Stupid, stupid, stupid.'

'Sorry you didn't accept him?'

'I'm not ready for marriage. Probably never will be. But I'll never find anyone like Larry again.'

'I don't expect you will,' he said annoyingly. 'Why should you? You had a choice and you made it. No good wringing your hands about it. In a way, you'll think it far-fetched, but your choice wasn't unlike mine. I chose Con. I gave up poor Grace and, as for being a parent, what kind of fist did I make of that? No job at all. It was Con I wanted and Con I got. You want to paint and you feel marrying that chap and going to – where is it?'

'Malaya.'

'That's the place. Going there would stop you painting or change it or something.'

'I don't know why I feel like that. I wish I didn't.'

'No, you don't. You chose right. And I know I did. We feel guilty, the both of us, that's the price for having our own way. We must pay up and shut up.'

They walked home to World's End. She linked her arm in his and after a while, with a snort at his own thoughts, he said,

'So you saw Clanfield, did you? And never breathed a word to him who you were?'

'Oh no!'

'Grace once said, I wasn't sure I believed her, he was like a Greek god.'

'He's still very handsome.'

'Like his daughter.'

Isobel tightened her grasp on his arm.

'I'm not his. I'm yours.'

'That's nice.'

They walked on. It was almost dark and they talked about Viv and Kit. He'd only seen his grandson once before and was looking forward to it. As they turned into Gladys Road he said, 'Good for you, all that with your chap. They say it's good for an artist, a bit of pain.'

Isobel did see Larry again. He was very good to her – for a while. Later he was angry. And at last accepted that he'd never win her. She was too much of a coward to see him off; their goodbyes were said on the telephone.

His absence, her heartache, did not stop her painting.

Julie's autumn and winter exhausted her. When Claire came to London, given permission by Stuart who could see very well that she now spoke nothing but the truth, she took Julie out to expensive lunches. In the position of saint who had pardoned a sinner, of wealthy married sister generous to a broke and unreliable sibling, Claire was at her best. She always was when she behaved well.

Julie's appearance worried her.

Lunching at the Ritz one cold day – Julie drank too much – Claire remarked charitably, 'You know, you do look pretty awful. Do you eat at all?'

'Of course. Huge stews and things.'

'Liar. You're so thin.'

'Michou quite likes us to look at death's door.'

'Julie!' A pause. Claire picked at a delicate fragment of sole meunière, then looked up.

'What *have* you been doing to look like that?'

Julie managed a grin.

'Not pinching anything else, darling.'

It was the first time the unmentionable had been spoken about and Claire, at Julie's mercy, began to arrange the salts and peppers. Julie leaned her chin on her hand.

'Poor Claire, I am a bitch. I never said I was sorry, did I?'

Deeply embarrassed, Claire said, 'You did to Stuart.'

Julie, who had done no such thing, admired her brother-in-law's wisdom. She kept a serious face.

'So I did.'

'He told me how you felt, Julie. And ... and I do understand about you being in love with Peter Southey and all that. Do you still see him? He was at Isobel's show, did I tell you? So nice.'

Julie, the fastest changer of clothes at Michou's, was pretty good at other kinds of change. She said gaily, 'Didn't you know? Peter's gone. I mean, for good.'

Claire, looking blank, asked where and when.

Julie shrugged. 'Poor Peter, he was hoping to fix up something in Ireland. He seems to have a load of cousins there and he wanted to work with the horses, whatever that means. It all fell through. Then some blasted relative, he has scads of them, who owns property in Sydney offered him a job there. On the wireless! I couldn't believe it, that upper-class voice of Peter's. Won't the Australians loathe it? Anyway, I daresay the job's been got through influence. The relative, the uncle, is filthy rich. And it is a job. He couldn't stay in London any more and his parents wouldn't – wouldn't lend him another bean. So he had to go. I saw him off at Tilbury,' finished Julie brightly.

She had trailed down on a freezingly cold morning, taking a dirty train to Tilbury with Peter. They'd gone on board ship together, and down to his cabin. But the clergyman with whom he was sharing had already arrived and was unpacking. Peter couldn't even kiss her.

They went back on deck and stood holding hands. Julie thought she would scream aloud with agony. Whenever she heard seagulls over the Thames she remembered that moment.

'Yes, of course he had to go, as there was a good job,' said Claire, relinquishing the salts and peppers.

Julie was sorry for her sister and patted her hand.

'I'm glad you've forgiven your ghastly twin. Hey, I've had a brainwave. Why don't we give a party for your birthday? We haven't had one for you since Woodlands. Do you remember how FRF polished off all Ma's whisky and she was so annoyed?'

'A party,' echoed Claire, pleased as a child.

She beckoned to the waiter, who arrived with respect and a large bill. Her good mood surrounding her, Claire paid and added an unusually generous tip.

'We could give the party at Viv's,' said Julie. 'All the Bryants together for a celebration. Plus one or two of Viv's local friends, and the man who put on Isobel's exhibition, Allan. He seems to have turned into a Svengali. And we might have –'

'Stuart and I will give the party,' said Claire, taking breath. She had never given a big party since her marriage. She felt proud and quite excited.

'Claire, it'll only be a bother,' said the habitual party-giver, 'I can help Viv and she won't mind.'

'But I'd *like* to give one. So will Stuart. Don't tell the others until Stuart and I have everything planned. Yes, a party is just what we need. Viv and Kit must come and stay. And you and Belle, of course. Kit's little cousins simply love him,' concluded Claire in a maternal voice. She had once happened to see her children playing with Kit without the usual battles over ownership. Julie, later on the same occasion, had separated the tots, purple in the face as they struggled over cars and doll's prams. Now she amiably agreed.

Before coffee arrived, Claire asked a porter to order a taxi for Julie. She could not be late back at Michou's. Wonder of wonders, when the taxi arrived, Claire paid for it in advance.

The birthday party became her idea. In the next few weeks there were a good many telephone calls, and various obstacles to be overcome: from a working Viv, a painting Isobel and a difficult-to-track-down Julie. But all the sisters said how much they were looking forward to it.

Viv was busy as winter set in and nervous only when the telephone rang. She was invariably sure it was her husband. And it was invariably one of her pupils' mothers. Isobel, rather withdrawn since Larry had left for Malaya, finally agreed to give up working at the map shop. Allan Josephs' efficient Milly said she'd take on the job temporarily until Draycott found a replacement. She had a soft spot for him. As for DD, he was somewhat in awe of Milly and Isobel wondered if he would come back from Fleet Street in the afternoons marginally more sober.

Josephs decided to let Isobel have the use of his gallery as a studio. It was centrally heated and the light was excellent, and he had no plans as yet for another show. Other projects engaged his interest.

'The gallery will give you room to move,' he said.

Every morning, Isobel left Gladys Road, disappearing into the winter mists with her painting materials strapped on her back. She was imitating an old photograph of the painter Cézanne, setting off up the Mont St Victoire. Burdened as she was, with paint-box, palette, sometimes canvases which weighed a great deal, she looked most odd. But when Viv suggested it, Isobel refused to leave her things at the gallery overnight. She was full of superstitions.

She confided in Viv one evening when she came home and the work had gone well, how much she still missed Larry.

'There's a sort of hole in my life where he used to be. I suppose I'll get over him in the end.'

'Of course you will,' agreed Viv, looking at her sister who sat on the floor, her face lit by the fire to an olive-tinted gold.

'What about Patrick? I thought he'd turned up again.'

It was a name from the past, but Viv had seen him when he had appeared asking for Isobel, one late afternoon.

'I said I'd go out to supper with him next week. I like Patrick. He's changed, you know, since I lived at Dysart.'

Viv thought he had done nothing of the kind. What she'd noticed had been that his attitude to Isobel had changed. He was impressed with her. She suspected that Patrick, like many journalists, was a fame snob.

Isobel brooded, warming her paint-splashed hands – her nails were disgraceful – by the fire.

'Have you got over Carlos?'

'I'm not sure. I do rather dread the day when he turns up again. After what happened.'

'But how do you feel about him?'

'Oh, you know,' said Viv, shrugging.

Isobel was deceived by the casual don't-much-care voice and nodded sagely, one woman who'd suffered over love to another.

'I suppose you ought to get a divorce,' she said.

'Of course I shouldn't. I'm not going to be excommunicated and nor is Carlos.'

Claire's party glimmered like a ring of candles at the end of a particularly raw November. All the sisters felt it, the giver of the celebration, most of all. She looked forward to her own party with delight. Claire's new personality suited her. She hadn't become, overnight, tender like Viv, imaginative like Isobel, gallant like Julie. But she was less pleased with herself and now and then more of a mother to her children. As for her way with Stuart, she usually relied on him, liked to defer to him, and was positively wifely. In a way she was at his mercy, having discovered he was not the slavish adorer after all. The vanished Les Bacon had not been worth a farthing compared to Stuart.

'I must order the champagne for the night you hit the ripe old age of twenty-six,' said Stuart during breakfast, when they were talking over details of the party. 'Are you baking a cake?'

'Viv is the best cook. She said she'll bring it with her.'

'Did you tell the girls you don't want any presents?'

Stuart had a vision of three penniless sisters-in-law forced to buy rich gifts for the only member of the family with money. He wondered, with the realistic love which flooded through him when he looked at Claire, if she would get the point. Perversely, he was not going to spell it out. Claire sat presiding – it was the only word – behind the silver coffee pot.

'Oh,' said Claire, quite her old self, 'they wouldn't take any notice if I did tell them. We're such present-givers in our family.'

It was time for him to leave for work and she followed him into the hall to help him on with his overcoat and brush the shoulders. He enjoyed the little service.

As it happened, Julie's thoughts about the coming birthday and the problem of presents ran on roughly the same lines as her brother-in-law's. He had underestimated the pragmatism of the Bryants.

She telephoned Viv.

'This birthday lark. I trust you are not going to give her anything, are you? She's got too much already.'

Viv laughed.

'I thought I'd make the cake as my present. What do you think?'

'An inspiration.'

'What about you, Julie?'

'I shall wheedle old Madame Hawthorne. You'd be surprised what one can find at Michou's in drawers and cupboards. Will you talk to Isobel and tell her what we've decided?'

When Viv spoke to her, Isobel had the answer at once. She was going to give Claire a little pencil drawing of Claire's two children which Isobel had done from memory after visiting Sussex one day some months back. Claire had never seen it.

'I'll get it mounted and framed. No, on second thoughts,' said Isobel, 'Claire wouldn't like my kind of frame. She'd better have it done herself in Lewes. It'll be *sure* to be gold with wiggly bits. Do you think I'm being mean?'

'I think you're being sensible.'

The day of the party dawned with November's usual ill temper; it was bitterly cold. A glaze of frost made the pavements slippery, the dead leaves in the gutters were enamelled with diamonds like

365

ostentatious jewels in a Bond Street window. Julie, who had told Madame she would not be working for the next two days, counted her money – it was less than she'd hoped – packed, took Claire's present in its Michou box and left the flat in Marylebone Road while both her mannequin friends were still dead to the world.

She shivered as she took a taxi to Victoria. She wore a black silk coat which was the height of fashion, edged with narrow bands of white mink. It had been designed as a coat to be worn between seasons, not for freezing London winters. Julie had pawned the voluminous coat which used to be such a comfort against the cold. The money was in her wallet. In no mood to travel third class, Julie sat in the Brighton Belle in lonely splendour. The train, almost empty, slipped away into the misty suburbs as if journeying into a dream.

Now and again, in spite of her daring-young-girl-on-the-flying-trapeze attitudes, Julie wished it was yesterday. Her father's nature was in her somewhere, a reverence for the past which in Julie's case became a longing to look at the sea. The good old sea which she hadn't set eyes on since her mother died. She felt unsettled, uprooted. Peter was lost to her; she would never see him again. She thought of his lounging figure, drawling voice, the fresh red carnation, the ease of making him laugh, the bliss of making love. A decision which she'd been dodging ever since Peter had left her entered the compartment and sat down on the first class seat opposite her. 'Well?' it said, 'What's the answer?'

Julie needed the sea.

Brighton was as misty as London, but cleaner. It was almost colder, and she pulled the fur collar closer to her neck and tugged her hat down to cover her tingling ears. Dogged and shivering, she set off down the steep street leading to the front.

There was the sea. Grey, not calm; a storm of two days ago had created long waves topped with yellowish foam which surged forward, crashing on the shingle, sucking back with an indescribable sound, part hiss, part rattle, a thunder she had known since childhood. Stiffened uselessly against the wind, she made her way to the West Pier and what the family had called 'our beach'. It shelved

366

sharply down, edged by a breakwater so worn by storms that it resembled in places a row of rotten teeth. There was the exact spot under the lee of a rowing boat now vanished where her mother used to sit week after week all summer long. Her daughters played on the shingle and, as the tide retreated, on the hard ribbed sand. Down the shelving pebbles, the soles of their feet hardened, they ran like skimming birds. Oblivious of the silk coat, Julie sat down on the stones and stared at the sea.

Half an hour later she was walking toward St Gregory's which looked, thought Julie, worse than usual. FRF had admitted his church was more like a gaol than a house of God. Today it reared up out of the mist, so grim and gaunt that Julie could not imagine anyone consenting to be baptized or married there; even buried. As she was about to cross the road, a hand gripped her elbow.

'What are you doing, woman, coming to bother me? And shock my innocent parishioners? No respectable woman would wear heels as high as that.'

Francis Freeman kissed her, Julie tweaked his ear, and they went into the presbytery which stank as always of cabbage. That's quite a talent of Mrs Duffy's, thought Julie. How does she do it? FRF, who had not noticed the smell for years, took Julie up to his study. That had not changed either, except that the four Bryant photographs were draped with four brand new rosaries.

'Well, I'll be – where did you get those from?'

'We opened a holy shop. Statues and holy pictures and such. We do a brisk trade on Sundays.'

'Mine's the worst. What a revolting colour. Poison green.'

'Rubbish, it's good old Irish green. It only needs a sprig of shamrock. Sit down and warm yourself.' He patted the visitor's chair by the fire. 'I must say, Julie, you're a darned sight too thin.'

'Have to be, in my job.'

'Wriggling up and down in fancy get-ups. You still don't need to have all those bones sticking out.'

He was heartier than usual because her appearance shocked him. He poured her a Scotch. Her sisters would have laughed at the idea of whisky at eleven in the morning or any other time. Julie

367

accepted it, lit a cigarette and crossed her legs. Then she pushed off her shoes.

'How much of our news do you know, FRF?'

'Some of it. The kidnap, of course. What was Carlos thinking of? Poor man.'

'Did you disapprove of what Viv did?'

'I'm only referee in this one. I told Viv so.'

Julie screwed up her eyes against the smoke.

'How we do rush to you in our troubles.'

'Not enough. My fault. I don't come to London to see you all. Parish work gets more, not less. And it's no good my saying I'm always here if you need me. That never does with the young.'

'I went down to our beach,' she said, apropos of nothing.

He took it the way she meant it. He used to meet the Bryants there on summer afternoons. He remembered Grace's calm greetings. But that was before Frank left her. Who was calm, thought the priest, at the death of love?

'Claire's birthday party tonight,' he said. 'I shall be seeing all you girls together for a change.'

'Claire said you were coming.'

'I can't wait,' he said, and laughed.

But that was what he was doing. Julie knew he would never question her directly and it came to her that there were things FRF did not – perhaps must not – know.

Those bloody rings for instance. In FRF's book, which was that great heavy Bible on the pulpit, theft was a sin. Was it a mortal one? Julie was hazy about that. Then there was Claire sleeping with old Les. Another sin, probably blacker, since the Church came down like a ton of bricks on the sins of the flesh. So there had to be bits missing from the priest's affectionate knowledge of his four friends. Did that make a difference to his judgement?

'I know we're meeting tonight, but I came now because I wanted you to myself,' she said.

'Another drink?'

'Yes, if you'll have one.'

'I shall force myself,' he said, busying himself with the bottle and

368

the siphon. A sort of harmony fell between them. A hoarse voice from somewhere below stairs shouted that it was going, Father, and dinner was in the oven and don't forget to turn off the gas this time. The priest went to the door and shouted some mutual joke or other and there was a guffaw. The front door slammed.

He returned to his chair and sat down again.

Julie studied her stockinged feet.

'I fell in love a few months ago. For the first time, actually.'

'And?'

'And he's gone. To Australia of all places. Couldn't be further, could it?'

'Did *he* love *you*, Julie?'

'A lot. As much as I did.'

'Couldn't you have gone with him?'

'Oh FRF. You didn't meet him. He's hopeless.'

She lit another cigarette, then said coolly, 'Somebody else has asked me to marry him.'

'Well. That sounds good, if you are fond of him.'

'I am. Not like Peter, but I am. It isn't good, though. He's divorced.'

'I see. You're right. Not good at all.'

Julie wrenched off her hat, some kind of dark felt, crushed it between her hands and rolled it up very small, the way mannequins did who needed to travel with many hats. She smoothed her smooth hair which was as shiny as a blackbird's feather.

'FRF ... he's rather *old*. Sixty.'

'Good grief.'

'You think that sounds awful.'

'I'm not exactly overjoyed. Divorced and sixty. You don't need to tell me why you are considering this magnificent offer.'

'Yeah. Sure,' said Julie with an American twang, 'he's filthy rich.'

He gave her a look of curiosity. He was not pleased at what he'd just heard. The Bryants had different claims on his affection, no particular girl was his favourite, he loved them all. But Julie was the girl who amused him, the one who fell off trees. It was boring, it was desolate, that she should decide to do anything so obvious. But

369

where was he in all this? Would the girl, so worn and so lovely, with dark marks under her eyes from God knows what, listen if he were unwise enough to preach? Where did his duty lie?

'I believe you think I don't even like him, FRF!' She had been watching his expression. 'How cynical you're getting. I like him a lot. He's fat and kind and funny and American, and I love being with him. We get on so well. He was married to a woman who was hard as nails and wouldn't let him see his kids. He was soft as butter with her, but he loves his children – he has three, grown up now, older than me. He is very very nice.'

'Worth giving up your religion for?'

He had said it.

Julie gave a smile filled with mischief. She looked like a boy caught with a penknife edging coins out of somebody else's money-box.

'I'm not giving it up. There's my clever way round.'

'Getting married in a registry office.'

She looked deflated.

'I thought I'd surprise you.'

Freeman didn't say that in a life of religion nothing surprised him.

'So you've decided to marry your rich old man. Is that what you've come to tell me?'

'I thought you'd rant and rage.'

'No, you didn't. You hoped I would.'

'That's true. It would have been a relief. I could have raged back.'

'My poor child.'

The tone of pity reached her and the tired eyes shone as if with tears. Then she was back to the girl he knew. She laughed.

'Here's how it is, FRF. I didn't know until I went down to our beach what I'd decided. Suddenly I saw that I really do care for Buck, that's his name, and that he might, he just might make such a difference. Wouldn't it be funny if he turned out to be my salvation?'

'Very amusing indeed.'

'Oh, FRF, at least be on my side about something! I'm as

370

hopeless as my poor Peter, you know. I'm not steady like Viv or sensible like Claire or gifted like Belle. I'm me. I don't much know what the me is, but Buck does. He values me. If I marry him in a registry office I shall only be living in sin, won't I? I mean,' she gaily added, 'when he dies I can repent.'

The priest gave a sudden snort into his whisky, which went straight down his nose.

Viv and Isobel arrived at Lewes in the dark, with Kit muffled in a thick coat, woolly hat, long scarf and mitts. His cheeks were scarlet with cold and excitement. Every journey to Kit was around the world in eighty days and during the time on the train he had suddenly come out with information about going to Spain. 'I was sick on the boat and Papa had to mop it up.'

Stuart met the travellers at the station and when they arrived Claire was the soul of hospitality; wood fires burned in what seemed to Viv half a dozen drawing rooms and in the bedrooms too. Kit was scooped up by Nanny with her own two charges and taken, interested and unprotestingly, to the nursery.

Isobel and Viv were shown their rooms; both of them had a hot bath.

'How smart everything is,' said Isobel coming into her sister's room wearing the black taffeta and turquoise buttons. Viv was in a pale brown velvet which Carlos had bought for her in Spain. She was sitting at the dressing table doing her hair and could see her sister's reflection in the mirror.

'You look lovely, Isobel. I do think it's nice, don't you? Seeing Claire happy.'

'She is, isn't she? But Julie looks as if she's miles away.'

Viv said wistfully, 'I never know what Julie's thinking.'

Downstairs, the Locktons' friends had begun to arrive. Viv's birthday cake, beautifully iced and decorated, had been placed on a silver cake stand and the county wives, none of whom could have achieved such a masterpiece, paid Viv a good many compliments. Stuart opened champagne and somebody put on the gramophone.

It was unlike any party Julie had ever been to, and to her

371

surprise she enjoyed it. The food was delicious, and the guests exchanged every cliché in the book. The atmosphere was full of goodwill; not a soul was even fractionally drunk. Even the music was unfamiliar to Julie. Richard Tauber kept singing his heart out. Stuart liked the tune and put it on over and over again.

Julie enjoyed herself: the county friends were nice to her and the husbands laughed at her bad jokes. Her Michou dress, cut to enhance every bone in her body and with her back naked to the waist, was the only astonishing dress in the room. And today she had made up her mind.

Viv and Isobel never went to parties, and had a very good time. Isobel was asked to dance by young men who, in the Woodlands days, Claire would have called suitable. Everybody seemed to know about her show, and she was treated with smiling interest. One of the young men sweeping her into a quickstep remarked, 'I say, I've never met a painter before.'

FRF did not dance, although Julie said she was sure he was good at it. He stood, a tall figure in priestly black, talking to Stuart and Claire and making them laugh.

Sussex parties were no all-night affairs; by midnight all the guests had kissed Claire goodbye. Nobody was left in the firelit rooms but Richard Tauber, the sisters in a group on the floor, Stuart at the gramophone, and FRF who had been persuaded to stay the night.

Richard Tauber stopped at last and Stuart put on a record of Layton and Johnstone. It was the one he'd bought for Claire when they were engaged to be married. There was a sad sweet lilt about it:

Here in your arms I can't remain,
So let me kiss you once again,
Goodbye, sweetheart, *auf Wiedersehen*,
Auf Wiedersehen, my dear.

Claire sang the words and leaned against her husband's knees, forgetting that she was crushing her dress.

Viv went quietly out of the room to go and see if Kit was asleep.

She found him tucked up, his rabbit in his arms, looking more angelic than was possible. Leaving his room she descended the long staircase. She could hear the music, which came from the drawing room through the closed doors. She thought she heard something else like a soft tapping. Claire's maids had gone to bed hours ago and Viv thought perhaps one of the visitors' cars had broken down. Such things used to happen when she'd lived at Woodlands.

She hesitated and then crossed the hall to the front door.

Standing in the porch, seeming to fill it with his broad figure, strangely pale, was Carlos.

For a moment the shock made her dizzy.

'I am sorry. I am sorry. Did I frighten you?'

He looked half frozen. He had no luggage.

'I don't understand – how are you here?'

'I came from London. Mr Josephs – is that right? – told me where you and Isobel had gone. I visited his house.'

'But how did you find us?'

'I took a train. There were no taxis. I walked from the station, I was afraid you might stay here for many days. I had to see you.'

'Oh Carlos.'

He took off his overcoat and put it down carefully on a chair.

'Do I give you much embarrassment, Vivien?'

'Of course not.'

She was trembling. His southern face looked so cold and when she took his arm she could feel the cold through the thin jacket. She led him like an old friend into the drawing room.

The scene round the fire was of unison and music and – when everybody saw who had arrived – welcome. Stuart and FRF sprang up to greet him. They went over to him, thought the watching Julie, like a phalanx, a male defence against the women in the room. Carlos gave explanations and apologies. He still looked very chilled and pale and Stuart, exclaiming about the walk from station, poured him a brandy. Claire hurried off to arrange a room.

'We have lots of space, thank goodness.'

She was soon back again, saying she had lit the fire. There was talk of journeys, of how Carlos had found them through Isobel's patron. He had known about her show because Claire had sent him a newspaper cutting. Somehow the evening trailed to a stop after the appearance of the wanderer. Soon everybody stood up, yawning and saying goodnight.

Stuart turned out lights and put a guard round the remains of the fire, saying to Viv who still lingered, 'You go up, Viv. I'm sure you're tired. I'll look after Carlos.'

When the two men were alone, Carlos gave Stuart no further explanations. He accepted what Stuart called a nightcap. They talked pleasantly for a short while and Stuart took him up the stairs and down a passage to the room Claire had quickly prepared. The gas fire glowed. To the Spaniard the air was blessedly warm.

Stuart disappeared, returning with pyjamas and a dressing gown.

'How can I thank you?'

'My dear fellow. Glad to have you.'

When he was alone, Carlos sat down on the bed and slowly took off his shoes. He stared into the reddening clays of the fire, seeing nothing, deaf to its comfortable roar. But when the door quietly opened, he heard that.

Viv came in, wearing an old camelhair dressing gown she had had as a schoolgirl. He stood up and faced her as a man might brace himself against a heavy wave. Viv saw the resemblance; she had often watched strong swimmers in the rough seas of her childhood.

She went to a chair by the fire and sat down.

'Have you – have you come for Kit again?'

'For Kit? Good God, is that what you thought?'

'I didn't think anything. Only you are here so suddenly.'

'To see you. To see you.'

He did not go near her. He did not touch her. He sat looking at her, seeming to Viv to be the very soul of his country at its most tragic and dark.

'My mother is dead, Vivien.'

'Oh Carlos!'

'Yes. It was a shock. It was sad. Not for her – she died in a day and –'

He could not go on for a moment or two. She longed to burst out in sympathy and sorrow, but he kept the distance between them. She said. 'You must grieve so much. I will pray for her. Do you –' she hesitated – 'do you wish me to come back for the funeral?'

'No. No. Vivien. The funeral was last week. I came to tell that – that I have left Spain. Do not start up like that, hear me out. I have never told you properly how bad things are. I, and my friends, have known it for a long time. Barcelona is full of anarchist sympathizers. The Church is hated. On the other side, the workers are hated in return. I should never have asked you to come there. I do not know what will happen but it will be bad. I had begged my mother,' he said in a tired voice, 'for weeks, I had implored her to come with me. She would not. She said that whatever happened she would live and die in her home. That is what she has done. Perhaps from choice, I do not know. But I knew I could not, cannot stay. I have come to England where – where my heart is. I shall not be a burden to your country. I have money,' he said with his pride.

'It is so strange. I never imagined you could –'

'Give up Spain? Nor did I.'

It was no time to say it, but she had to.

'If you thought things were so bad, why did you –'

'Take Christopher? I was crazy. But you said you would never come to me, and I had him with me that night and he was so precious. I could not stop myself. You must not think,' he added, still with the solemn look, 'that I would have taken you and him to danger, if you had consented to stay with me a little. At that time, even now, it was – it is – safe for a while. Later it will be terrible. But I should never have taken him from you. It was very cruel.'

'Were you angry when Julie and I took him back?'

'I don't know. I do not remember.'

The silence was filled with the noisy fire.

To Viv, looking at the man still braced against her as if she were the wave which could knock him down and drown him, the very sight broke her heart. Where was the enemy who had imprisoned her in the Nuevo Casa? Where was the man who had left her so alone? She ran over and knelt beside him and put her face on his

375

knees. For a moment he did not move. Then he began to stroke the bent blonde head. There they stayed, while Carlos stroked her hair and Viv buried her face in his lap. When she looked up, she met his dark glance bravely.

'I love you. I love you,' was all she said.

'I know, *querida*. I have always known. You never truly meant to leave me. You have always longed to come back.'

Oh Carlos, she thought, as he took her in his arms and they pressed close, you believe that because of pride. And why shouldn't you? Why shouldn't you?

Little, Brown now offers an exciting range of quality titles by both established and new authors. All of the books in this series are available by faxing, or posting your order to:

Little, Brown Books,
Cash Sales Department,
P.O. Box 11,
Falmouth,
Cornwall,
TR1O 9EN
Fax: 0326-376423

Payments can be made as follows: Cheque, postal order (payable to Little, Brown Cash Sales) or by credit cards, Visa/Access/Mastercard. Do not send cash or currency. U.K. customers and B.F.P.O.; Allow £1.00 for postage and packing for the first book, plus 50p for the second book, plus 30p for each additional book up to a maximum charge of £3.00 (7 books plus). U.K. orders over £75 free postage and packing.

Overseas customers including Ireland, please allow £2.00 for postage and packing for the first book, plus £1.00 for the second book, plus 50p for each additional book.

NAME (Block Letters) ....

ADDRESS ....

....

....

☐ I enclose my remittance for ....

☐ I wish to pay by Visa/Access/Mastercard

Number ☐☐☐☐☐☐☐☐☐☐☐☐☐☐☐☐☐☐

Card Expiry Date ☐☐☐☐